I0544452

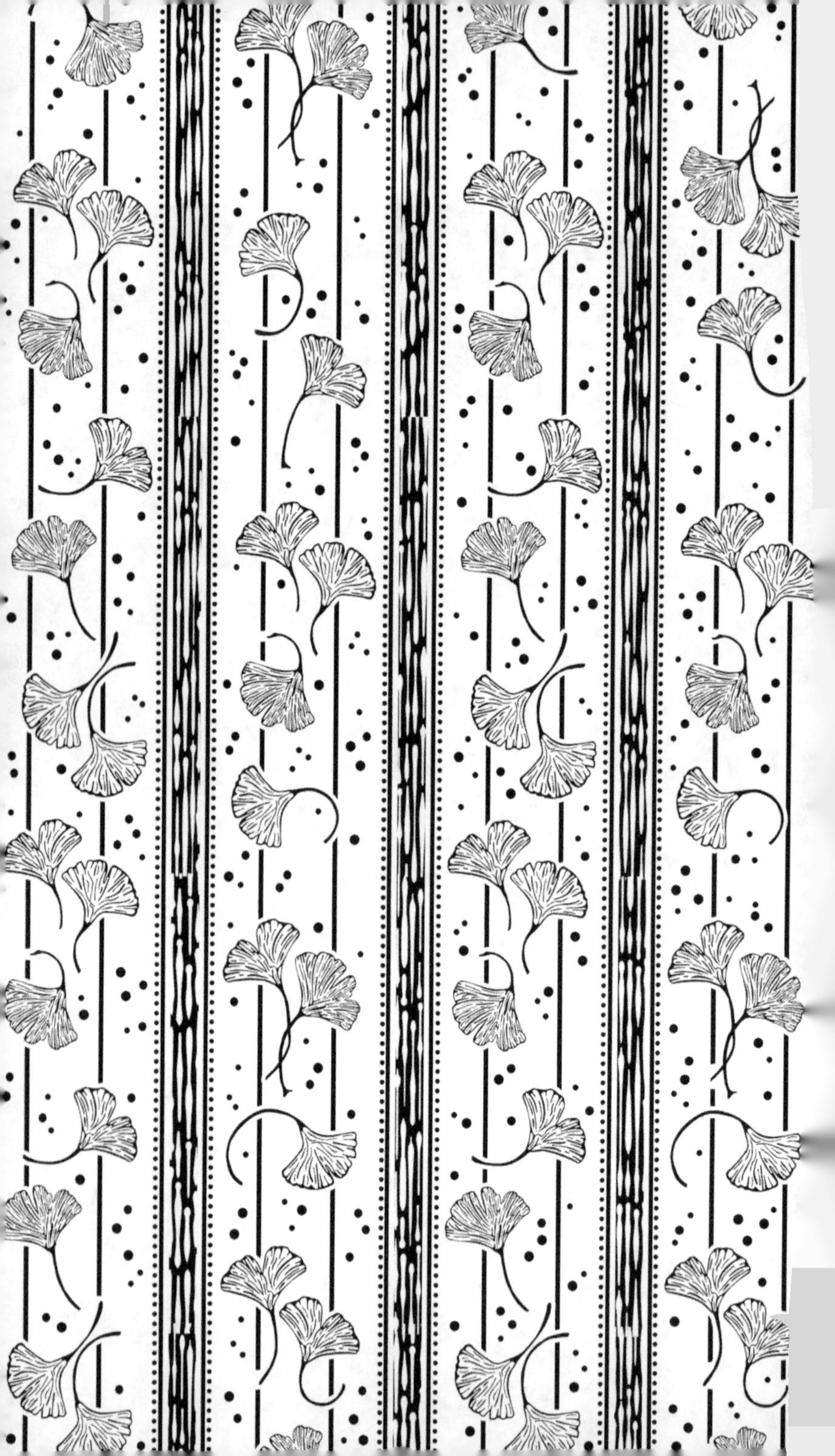

BY FORTHRIGHT

FORTHWRITES.COM

Amaranthine Interludes 1 & 2
Lord Mettlebright's Man
Suuzu and the Nine Nippets of Legend

Copyright © 2023 by FORTHRIGHT
ISBN: 978-1-63123-087-5

Cover Art & Jacket Design: Elza Kinde | bumblebess.com
Audio Book | narrated by Travis Baldree

TWINKLE PRESS

because trust is beautiful

A MESSAGE FROM FORTHRIGHT

AMARANTHINE INTERLUDES

Over the course of their writing, the books in the **Amaranthine Saga** *and the short stories in the* **Songs of the Amaranthine** *collection have been overlapping in interesting ways. Each informs the others, and new details are always coming to light. The same can be said of the new* **Amaranthine Interludes** *collection, in which* Lord Mettlebright's Man *takes the lead. Jacques has the years since his serialization began in 2018. LMM runs behind the scenes of the first four books in the Amaranthine Saga, starting immediately after the events of Book 1,* Tsumiko and the Enslaved Fox.

The format of Lord Mettlebright's Man *is unique. The story unfolded in 100-word snippets posted to the blog at ForthWrites.com. Little by little, bit by bit, readers gained new appreciation for Jacques Smythe of the Uppington Smythes. If you're intrigued, you're also in luck. Another Amaranthine Interlude is just beginning. Drop by to begin my newest serial,* Coop and the Elderbough Trackers *(Amaranthine Interludes, #4).*

And if you haven't yet explored the option, reading (and rereading) is truly a pleasure with the audio editions, narrated by Travis Baldree.

TABLE OF CONTENTS

CALENDARS AND CHRONOLOGIES
PR. AND N.S.

During the writing of Lord Mettlebright's Man, *I introduced timeline terminology developed by the Amaranthine Council. It's become the international standard for relative dates (similar to the usage of A.D. and B.C. by human historians) with the Emergence as its pivot. Both calendar systems are in use, with the Integrated Dateline having secondary importance. It's primarily used whenever people want to reckon time in direct relation to the Emergence.*

Prelude *– before the Emergence, noted as PR. (eg. Dragged through Hedgerows is set in PR. 5.)*

New Saga *– after the Emergence, noted as N.S. (eg. Tamiko and the Two Janitors is set in 5 N.S.)*

To help anchor Lord Mettlebright's Man *in the new timeline, let's run through a few events.*

0 N.S. *– The Emergence (February, in conjunction with the Lunar New Year. Because wolves.)*

- *The Five step onto the world stage, representing the Amaranthine clans, who wish to make peace with the international community.*
- *From their home in America, the Cooper family put two and two together. (see* Dragged through Hedgerows, *Songs of the Amaranthine, #3)*
- *American reporters coin the term "Riven," a label that catches on and persists (eg.* The Riven Report *is the popular weeknight news show that Grandpa Reaverson never misses in Bk3 / 5 N.S.).*
- *Hisoka Twineshaft is inundated by reports from criminal investigators and cooperates fully, appointing Kith handlers, directing Amaranthine trackers, and forming a special taskforce.*
- *Ever Starmark is born in November, and the world is immediately won over by the "first" human-Amaranthine hybrid.*
- *Harmonious places Ever into Eloquence's hands as a fosterling.*

- *"Heart of a Dog," a documentary about the two loves of Harmonious Starmark, first airs on Christmas Eve*
- *Lilya Ward is born to Michael and Sansa at Stately House. Hours later, Kyrie Hajime-Mettlebright is born on the Smythe Estate in Uppington, England.*
- *Argent Mettlebright becomes a member of The Five, replacing Nona Hightip as the spokesperson for the fox clans.*

1 N.S. – *The anniversary of the Emergence becomes a week-long international holiday.*
- *Jacques Smythe of the Uppington Smythes (age 23) invites himself to Stately House (with no intention of ever leaving again).*
- *Stately House opens its doors to crossers, becoming an orphanage and boarding school.*
- *Jacques founds the Fundoshi Swim Club.*
- *Akira Hajime (age 14) visits Stately House for the first time, along with his best friend Suuzu Farroost.*

3 N.S. – Lord Mettlebright's Man *resumes in December 3 N.S., shortly before the events of* Kimiko and the Accidental Proposal.
- *New Saga High School will open its doors to students on January first.*
- *Keishi's Star Festival preparations take place in January, a few weeks before the Fourth Anniversary of the Emergence.*
- *The Rogue kidnaps a young woman from the public sector. In order to divert attention, Hisoka asks Kimiko Miyabe to court Eloquence Starmark in front of the whole world. Pagentry ensues.*
- Kimiko and the Cycle of Moons *begins where Book 2 leaves off.*

5 N.S. – *The events of* Tamiko and the Two Janitors *take place in August thru December 5 N.S.*
- *The Five has expanded to seven members and the group is now officially referred to as the Amaranthine Council.*
- *Thanks to lingering resistance and superstition in America, the Elderbough Initiative encourages reavers to locate and support*

unregistered family members. Melissa Armstrong answers the call.

- *An attempt on the Orchid Saddle, one of four weapons known collectively as the Junzi, brings a thief known only as the Gentleman Bandit to the attention of the Amaranthine Council.*
- *American actress Pim Moonprowl makes history as the first openly Amaranthine actress on prime time with the debut of* Pure Instict.
- *After news of their engagement breaks, Crossing America, starring Ash Sunfletch, begins turning the tide of American opinion as Amaranthine enclaves in each U.S. state "step out" of hiding.*

11 N.S. – Lord Mettlebright's Man *resumes in early spring the year before Kyrie and Lilya will attend*

- *Timur Michaelson calls home, alerting his family ot the fact that he's stranded in the north of England while awaiting the birth of his twenty-fifth child.*

12 N.S. – *The events of Books 4, 5, and 6 take place this year.*

- *The Amaranthine Council now boasts fifteen members.*
- *In the U.S., governmental restructuring has resulted in Amaranthine representation in congress. Cyril Sunfletch announces his candidacy in the next presidential election.*
- *Lilya and Kyrie will spend the summer as campers at Wardenclave.*
- *Eloquence and Kimiko welcome the birth of their first child.*
- *Boonmar-fen Elderbough, who has been tracking the Rogue, follows a scanty trail across oceans and runs up against a barrier. He calls in a favor.*
- *In October, Akira accompanies Juuyu Farroost to America, where Argent has set a trap for the Gentleman Bandit.*
- *Meanwhile in Keishi, the Chrysanthemum Blaze is stolen from the treasure room at Kikusawa Shrine.*
- *Jacques Smythe arrives in California, as ready as anyone can be for the events of Book 6,* Pimiko and the Uncharted Island.
- *Suuzu and the Nine Nippets of Legend details several pivotal events happening at Stately House while Jacques and Akira are away.*

LORD METTLEBRIGHT'S MAN

Lord Mettlebright's Man

"Michael explained that you're taking on a new job—lofty world leader—which leaves Stately House without a butler. So I applied for the position." A playful smile eradicated any trace of subservience. "You're a tough act to follow."

Argent wearily shook his head. "Go home, Jacques."

His smile faded. "I can't."

"Can't, or won't?"

Jacques caught the corner of Argent's sleeve in a wordless plea, also of Amaranthine origin. Someone had *definitely* been coaching him. He would have words with Michael later.

Taking a shallow, shaky breath, Jacques whispered, "I'm willing to beg."

"You know how?"

For an answer, he bowed at the waist and touched his lips to the inside of Argent's wrist. Argent growled in annoyance, and Jacques flinched. But the fool clung desperately to his hand, properly pressing his forehead to the spot. Would he grovel next?

But a hot tear splashed onto Argent's palm, and then another, and his heart sank. Of all his tormentors, why was this insufferable brat the only one to come back, to bother to learn how, to give what no one else ever did? Apologies.

Tsumiko and the Enslaved Fox

PART ONE

Summer of 1 N.S., four months after the first anniversary of the Emergence, following close on the heels of the end of *Tsumiko and the Enslaved Fox*. Jacques Smythe has brazened his way into Stately House and shows no sign of leaving.

1
SELF STYLED

Jacques Smythe struck a pose in front of the hall mirror, admiring the cut of his coat over striped trousers. Tails had been the right choice. The ascot was a trifle pretentious, but bowties were more Argent's thing—stiff, snooty.

Non. If Jacques was doing this, he'd do it his own way. He preferred some tousle in his turn-out and flop in his foppery.

"Playing lord of the manor?"

"*Au contraire!*" In the past week, Argent Mettlebright's manner had moderated from poisonous to acid. Enough improved to push his luck. "*You're* the lord. I'm your butler."

"*Tsk.* Go home, Jackie."

2
CHANGE IN CIRCUMSTANCES

Of Jacques' earliest memories, the most vivid centered around Argent, a magical creature that his aunt and uncle had somehow tamed. Silvery pale and flawless, with the eyes of an animal and the manners of a prince, Argent was fae and fantastic and little Jackie's first love.

"You expect to *serve* this household?" Argent's brow arched.

"Faithfully!"

"Are you aware that service implies *work*?"

"Yes, my lord."

"Stop that."

"Stop *what*, my lord?"

A low growl reverberated between them, but Jacques adopted a tranquil expression.

"So be it." A tight, wintery smile. "I wonder how long you will last ... *Smythe.*"

3

FAMILY STYLE

As dinnertime neared, Jacques took a post behind Argent's chair.

"What is this? You are doing … what?" asked Sansa, sliding bowls of roasted vegetables onto the table.

He tried a winsome smile on the reaver woman. "I'm serving at table."

She drew herself up imposingly. "Stately House has no servants."

Michael, her husband, said, "You don't need to wait on us. You're our guest."

"An *uninvited* guest," Argent reminded.

Sansa ignored that. "Your place is here. Sit."

Jacques insisted, "I'm taking Argent's old place."

"Foolish boy, I would not wish my former place on anyone," said Argent. "Not even you."

4

WIZARD

On bad days, when nightmares and dread came creeping, Jacques would bring tea to Michael's office. The reaver always welcomed him with a smile and nattered on about sigilcraft and wards, a modern-day wizard surrounded by spell books and crystals.

Rapping, Jacques breezed in and set out tea things.

Michael addressed his laptop. "Did you like the aquamarines?"

"So-so." The accent was American. "Better capacity, finicky as pheasants. Hey, who's that?"

Michael leaned back. "Smythe is our new butler."

"Fancy!" The young man grinned. "You stoked for the first drop?"

"*Moi*? I've dropped nothing."

Michael said, "He means the orphans."

5
HOME MAKER

Jacques' hand wavered over the sugar bowl. One of the worst things about living here was that day-to-day conversations took place in Japanese. These people could be plotting death or deportation, and he'd potter along in ignorance. "Orphans?"

"We've been converting rooms." Michael seemed confused by his confusion. "You didn't know?"

Jacques simply repeated, "Orphans?"

"Tsumiko has opened Stately House to children of mixed heritage …."

Michael went into greater detail while Jacques tried not to be devastated. Argent would accept children simply because they were part-chicken or part-goat yet shun someone who wanted a place just as much. *Non* … more.

6
HEY YOU

Ginkgo represented too many uncomfortable truths, so Jacques labeled him Tsumiko's *beastie bestie* and pretended the gardener didn't exist.

"Hey, you … Smith."

"*Smythe.*"

The half-fox, who cradled a drooling baby, seemed amused. "You really want me to call you *Smythe*? Dad's only doing that to annoy you."

He drew himself up. "It's my name."

"I thought your name was Zzzhahk," he said, giving the 'j' a playful buzz.

"Are you mocking me?"

"Depends." Peaked silver ears twitched. "Are you mocking Dad in that get-up?"

"Wait." Jacques blinked. "You speak English?"

Ginkgo snorted. "Surprise. Guess you can call me *beastie bestie-sensei*."

7

ISSUES

To Jacques' extreme dismay, Ginkgo foisted the baby on him. "I can't! Take it back."

"Little bro isn't an *it*. He's a crosser. Like me." The half-fox stepped closer. "Nothing to be afraid of, Jacques."

"But ...!" He was shaking now.

Ginkgo's hands came up under his. "Dad said you're dragon-skittish, so we're starting with a half dose."

That was only part of the problem. "I'm *terrible* with kids."

"That's not what Tsumiko says."

Jacques grumbled, "You wouldn't understand."

"You'd be surprised." The animation faded from Ginkgo's face, leaving him looking exhausted. "My story's not much different than this little guy's."

8

JUMPING TO CONCLUSIONS

Ginkgo snorted. "Your *face*."

Jacques schooled his expression. "I wouldn't have though Argent capable of ... ungentlemanly behavior."

"Dad didn't want what happened. For a star's age, I thought he didn't want me."

Jacques looked away. "He *doesn't* want me."

"No?"

Ginkgo's sly tone made Jacques suspicious. "No. To him, I'm *Smythe*."

"Behind your back, you're 'idiot boy.'"

"Lord. And that's better?"

"Tons better. Dad's a fox. Listen less, look more."

Oh, Jacques had looked plenty. "At what?"

"How about the company you're keeping." Ginkgo offered his finger to the baby. "Dad wouldn't have sent his sons if he didn't care."

9

SPECIAL SCHOLARSHIP

Take him back." Jacques didn't want to be near the source of so much dread, pain, and fear. He tried to push the baby away, but Ginkgo didn't waver.

Warm hands steadied his shaking ones. "About school. Dad says you should be at university."

"I dropped out." He risked a glance at the baby—scales, spots, claws—and quailed.

"Michael's starting a school here. We're enrolling you."

"What *kind* of school."

"Non-traditional."

"For crossers," accused Jacques.

"And butlers."

"You expect me to mingle with Argent's precious orphans?"

Ginkgo frowned. "They won't be orphans anymore. Once they're here, they'll be ours."

10

THIS SAME DREAD

I *know* how Kyrie came to us," said Ginkgo.

Jacques didn't want to discuss his nightmares.

"And I can understand why you're scared. This little guy's related to the monster who hurt your family. But Kyrie's not a monster any more than you are."

"*Pardonnez-moi?*"

"This ... your revulsion. It's probably really similar to how Dad felt about you and the other Uppington Smythes, his tyrants and tormentors."

Jacques whispered, "Argent thinks I'm a monster?"

Ginkgo's ears drooped. "I just said you're *not*."

But all of Jacques' bravado flowed away, leaving clarity and despair. He was the dragon in Argent's nightmares.

11
FOCAL POINT

Back up a few steps," Ginkgo ordered gruffly.

Jacques obeyed and all but fell into the depths of a leather chair, baby and all. It occurred to him that the half-fox looked enough like his father to be … interesting.

Ginkgo huffed. "Don't go there."

Jacques went there anyhow.

"You really *are* an idiot boy. Focus."

"Focused."

"Think of it this way. The cruel beast who sired Kyrie might want him back."

Jacques peeked down into solemn ruby eyes.

"Nobody in Stately House would ever let that happen."

"How lovely for him."

Ginkgo's expression softened. "*And* for the one holding him."

12
IN THE WINTER GARDEN

Kidnapping's a crime, you know." Ginkgo joined Jacques on the kitchen sofa, cramming close so Kyrie could see him wiggle his ears. "Thought you didn't like kids."

He didn't. Far from it. But keeping Kyrie close led to moments like this—touching, talking. "I'm more related to him than you are."

"How do you figure?"

"Birth mother's husband's first cousin."

Ginkgo put a plushie into Kyrie's clawed hands. "Humanly speaking, I'm his birth mother's distant cousin's stepson. But by Amaranthine reckoning, I'm his brother. I'm closer."

"Not if I'm his favorite."

"Challenge accepted." Ginkgo added, "Kyrie'll need kin who care."

13
FELINE OF FEW WORDS

Jacques hadn't climbed a tree since his tomboy days, but the half-forgotten skill came through. He was intact, which was more than he could say for his pants. Seams had ripped, and bark was chafing. Small matters compared to the lurid gaze of Sansa's red-eyed beast.

"A little help here!"

Stately House's security guard stepped through the undergrowth. He wasn't really Jacques' type, but brawny, brooding, and bashful had never looked better.

"Mr. Deece, I could kiss you. That feline attacked me!"

"She was only teasing."

"*Of course* you'd take her side." Then Jacques squawked in outrage. "You. Speak. English!"

14
LIKE A KITTEN IN A TREE

Deece sent Minx off, then rose through the air as if gravity didn't apply. Jacques clung stubbornly to his branch, feeling uncooperative. How dare these people exclude him when they were perfectly capable of courtesies and conversation?

"Come here." Clawed hands were reaching, orange eyes pleading. "I will not hurt you."

"I *am* hurt!" Jacques glared at Deece through tears, angry enough to lash out. "Am I so hateful? Am I to be driven out?"

The Amaranthine lowered his hands. "No?"

"Why have you never talked to me?"

Deece looked up, looked away, and finally looked back. "I am … shy?"

15

A QUIET EVENING AT HOME

Weak and wilting, Jacques became something the cat dragged in. He failed to struggle against the indignity. Probably because the brawny, brooding, bashful idiot was petting his hair.

Deece carried him into Michael's office. "Tonight. He needs tending."

"You've always preferred privacy," Michael countered.

"I hurt him."

"*Are* you hurt?" Michael hurried forward.

Deece mumbled, "Not injury. Neglect."

"Ah." Michael nodded. "Jacques, will you join us tonight?"

"Going somewhere?"

"No, we stay in—bathing, grooming, tending, and sleep."

Jacques' gaze darted between them. "You sleep together?"

"Every other week or so, according to Deece's needs."

"Lord. Does your wife know?"

16

LEARN AS YOU GO

Jacques knew worse ways to be caught with his pants down. "I've heard this is traditional. You've gone native?"

Michael chuckled. "This has always been my home, and the onsen has been here for centuries. But felines *are* responsible for my occasional forays into grooming."

"Cats." Jacques slowly unbuttoned his shirt. "Like Deece?"

"Only recently." Michael's expression turned nostalgic. "You see, my mentor at academy was a cat."

"Hisoka," supplied Deece. "My uncle."

Jacques did a double-take, and not simply to admire Deece's angular collarbones. "Hisoka ... as in *Twineshaft*?"

Michael's pants hit the floor. "Sensei was both attentive and fastidious."

17
WALLOWING IN IGNORANCE

A ll right, there?" asked Michael. "You're very quiet."

"I'm brilliant," Jacques lied. "Why wouldn't I be?"

"Deece is clearly concerned, and I trust his senses over my own."

"I don't understand."

"Ask me anything."

Jacques bit his lip so hard, it would be swollen. "I don't even know what to ask."

After a lengthy pause, Michael sighed. "Forgive me. I've been remiss in my role as reaver."

This was getting old. "I don't know what that *means*."

"One role is hospitality. It's our duty and delight." Michael came and hugged Jacques from behind. "Tonight, I'm extending that hospitality to you."

18
TOO MUCH INFORMATION

N othing in Jacques' experience prepared him for Michael's matter-of-fact lecture on feline grooming customs. He was clearly knowledgeable. A trifle longwinded. And hands-on. Lots of bare skin and bath oil, kneading and purring.

Though the man used words like reciprocity, sensuality, and hedonism, the evening never strayed into kinky territory.

"... feline males who haven't been chosen rely on one another for ..."

Class was in session, albeit in the nude.

"... reminiscent of dragon culture—allowing for gender reversal— but based on feminine whim rather than the worship of ..."

Jacques was just dozing off when Argent strolled into the room carrying Kyrie.

19

FLOUNDER

Jacques slipped under, but Deece hauled him up and steadied him while he spluttered.

"Argent!" Michael's tone held an unaccustomed edge. "It's intensely rude to interrupt a grooming session!"

"I need a word with Smythe."

Michael stood unwavering, arms folded, tone stern. "Really. Couldn't it have waited until morning?"

"Tomorrow will be too late."

Jacques shook back sodden curls, cheeks scorching and paling by turns.

"Argent is concerned," murmured Deece. The cat clansman hadn't let go. Jacques rather hoped he wouldn't.

"Something happened?" asked Michael.

Argent waited until Jacques lifted his gaze to say, "Lord Mossberne is on his way."

20

NAMED FOR SHRUBBERY

Jacques tried to place the name. Every Amaranthine clan seemed to be named for shrubbery or constellations or random bits of topography.

"Aren't they early?" asked Michael. "The Five weren't due for a fortnight."

"Mossberne is arriving ahead of the rest."

Jacques might not be up on all the tiresome politics and particulars, but everyone knew about the five clan leaders responsible for the Emergence—cat, dog, wolf, fox, and … *mon dieu.* Surely not!

His fragile heart cracked further. Jacques wanted, *needed* to run, but he feared he might faint first.

Amidst shouts and much splashing, he succumbed to fear.

21
CHASTISEMENT

When Jacques revived, he wasn't in his own bed—mattress too soft, sheets too rough. And musky with a scent that hadn't come from a bottle.

"*Swooning*, Smythe?" Argent perched near the foot of the bed, burping the half-dragon baby he counted as a son. "You really are too fond of drama. A butler must not swoon."

"Yes, my lord." Jacques clutched covers. "But … dragons are coming."

"*Tsk.* What color are Kyrie's eyes?"

"A fine merlot. Or perhaps a syrah."

Argent's lips twitched. "If you meet a dragon with eyes of the same vintage, you have my permission to swoon."

22
IN TRUE FORM

All right, there?" asked Michael, who wore pajama pants and was toweling his hair.

Jacques' eyes widened at the sight of an enormous feline hunched down behind the reaver. For a moment, he thought Sansa's beast had tracked him down, but this cat was larger, brindled, and had eyes like expensive cognac. Jacques whispered, "*Behind* you."

Argent huffed.

Michael stepped aside with a showman's flourish. "Deece Evernhold. This is his room. Will you continue with us? The lesson's not over."

"A proper butler cannot take refuge in ignorance." Rising to leave, Argent quietly added, "Go gently. He still has nightmares."

23

GREEN EYES

Jacques was sulking. "Is Argent trying to distract me by throwing other men in my path? I won't be distracted!"

Michael smiled. "Did you come to Stately House hoping for romance?"

"I love Argent," he declared staunchly.

"So do I."

"I loved him first," snapped Jacques.

Michael plumped pillows. "Ginkgo actually has that advantage."

Jealousy clawed at a soul already raw. "You really love him?"

"Not in the same way I love my wife or my children, but yes. We share a bond."

In those few words, Jacques recognized his desperate need and blurted it out. "*I* want a bond."

24

CONSENSUAL ARRANGEMENTS

Admirable. And possible, provided you're patient." Michael gestured between them. "If you were Amaranthine, manners would dictate that I ask permission."

"For what?" Jacques asked warily.

The man smiled. "May I touch you, Jacques?"

"Why? Where?"

"I'll hold you while we sleep. Or you could hold me, if that's more to your liking."

Jacques gave in to disbelief. "What are you after?"

"Trust." Michael indicated the oversized pussycat huddled in the corner. "Deece wants to offer comfort as cats do, with closeness."

Jacques did a double-take. "He's licking his chops."

"Hiding yawns," Michael corrected. "He's knackered."

"Then ... come to bed."

25
ONLY HUMAN

Jacques didn't grasp much of Michael's lecture on the history and etiquette of tending. Long story short, it felt good, as evidenced by Deece's nonstop purring.

With a rumbling wall of fur at his back, Jacques relaxed against Michael, who embodied fraternity and fidelity and what Jacques assumed was fathering. He had little firsthand experience with doting.

But envy made him prickly. Only reavers could tend. Only reavers held an Amaranthine's interest. And he was only human.

Deece rumbled contentment, and Michael encouraged closeness.

Something inside Jacques eased under their attentions. Maybe tending was also good for a lonesome soul.

26
HOLDING PATTERN

Jacques dreamed, and fear found him in the darkness—cruel teeth, slashing claws, and the imminent threat of messy dismemberment.

He woke mid-thrash, and the voice that roused him came again. "You are safe. We are here."

"Deece?"

The cat yawned.

Michael stirred in his arms. Jacques couldn't remember making the switch from held to holding.

"Bad dream?"

Jacques hummed.

Deece's arm stretched around, pulling them closer. Jacques was almost positive the bump against his bare shoulder was a kiss.

"Want to talk about it?" asked Michael.

"*Non.*"

"Tell me anyhow?"

Jacques spoke, and courage found him in the darkness.

27

FAILS TO MEET EXPECTATIONS

Jacques would have skipped breakfast if Tsumiko hadn't found his hideaway and taken him by the hand. When she asked a question in Japanese—presumably about his presence in an upper-story linen cupboard—he picked through his scant vocabulary for a word of explanation.

"Scary."

She smiled and offered a slightly different word.

Had he bungled the pronunciation? Jacques tried again.

Tsumiko replied, "Not scary. Cute."

In the kitchen, they found a beautiful person babbling and trilling over Kyrie. Hardly the thundering portent of death Jacques had been dreading.

Was it possible to fear dragons who indulged in baby talk?

28

BUSINESS AS USUAL

Jacques went about his self-proscribed duties as if Stately House were dragon-free. Either he was wildly successful in avoiding their guest, or Lord Mossberne was making himself scarce. Therefore, dragons were far from mind when Jacques strolled into Michael's office.

The usual pot of tea would have hit the floor if not for Argent's intervention.

"Thank you, Smythe," Argent murmured, hands supporting his shaky ones. "You may go."

"Nonsense. He should stay," countered Lapis—brown-skinned and blue-haired, with a gaze like sapphires. "Why foster unwarranted fears when you can teach your man to treasure the glorious gift of my friendship?"

29
FULL MEASURE

J acques stood there, stranded between opposing desires—to be allowed to flee the dragon or to be asked to stay by Argent.

Incomprehensible words were traded—sharp, shrewd—and the dragon seemed to be enjoying a victory until the fox took his revenge by taking back the baby.

Pushing Jacques into a wingback chair, Argent settled Kyrie in his arms.

"What happened?" Jacques hugged his shield.

"A difference of opinion. Lapis thinks me overprotective."

"Of me?" That was a pleasant thought.

Argent brows lifted. "You have only dealt with his kind by halves. Are you ready to double the measure?"

30
SPROUT

L apis came early at Tsumiko's request."

Jacques stole a peek at the dragon lord.

Argent continued, "I have no prior experience with dragons."

Trilling softly, Lapis interjected, "And so in his *infinite* wisdom, Lord Mettlebright called upon a bachelor from the heights, even though my experience with hatchlings is limited to having been one."

"*Tsk.* You confirmed what we could only guess at."

Jacques studied the baby in his arms. "Is Kyrie sick?"

"The dragon crosser equivalent to teething."

That gave him a jolt. "He's spouting fangs?"

Argent guided his hand to a spot hidden by Kyrie's downy fringe. "Horns."

31

CONCERNING DRAGONS

Lapis Mossberne remained at Michael's desk, daintily sipping tea and turning delicate pages in an antiquated book, all calligraphy and gilt-edged illumination. "Do fangs *concern* you, Mr. Smythe?"

"Perhaps."

"Universally?" he pressed.

"I never minded Argent's." Catching himself, Jacques mumbled, "His lordship's."

"Give him a taste."

Jacques' lashes fluttered, and his gaze sliced toward Argent.

Lapis trilled, and Kyrie—clever thing—echoed. "I meant the little one. Offer him a finger and be thoroughly gummed."

"Kyrie knows your scent, your sound," said Argent. "Taste is more intimate."

"Become dragon-kin," urged Lapis. "And the fangs still forming will become your defense."

32

DEVILISHLY UNFAIR

Quite sure he was playing with fire, Jacques dared to question Lord Mossberne. "Are you dangerous?"

"No."

Heady relief washed over Jacques, for it must be true. This was wonderful! He should be grateful. He should be glad.

"He *is* dangerous," countered Argent.

Jacques fidgeted under a critical gaze. Should he believe the monster who was telling him what he wanted to hear? Or the master who was raising a terrible possibility that Jacques didn't want to believe? This was devilishly unfair.

The dragon lord drawled, "*Argent!* I am no more dangerous than you are."

Argent pointed at Lapis. "Precisely."

33
PAINFULLY HONEST

Oh, very well." Lapis set aside his tea. "Dragons have a way with words. We can be very persuasive."

Argent bluntly said, "He lies beautifully."

"I could," countered the dragon lord. "I generally refrain."

"*Tsk.* You overwhelmed Smythe with one word."

Lapis hummed. "Is he as susceptible to your lies?"

"His lordship would never lie to me!" Jacques exclaimed. Then quailed before their pitying looks.

"Words are only one form of deception," said the dragon.

"I trust him." Jacques' chin lifted. "I love him."

Lapis' tone gentled. "I didn't ask for your secrets, dear boy."

"It's no secret," he muttered.

34
HAVE IT OUT

Jacques stormed out, but Argent quickly found and cornered him. "I cannot give you what you want."

"You don't *know* what I want."

"I do." He cocked a brow. "I always have."

Jacques colored. "That was before."

Argent sniffed lightly, which was mortifying. Jacques tried to will himself calm.

"W-with you, I'm safe from the monsters."

"What if *I* am a monster?"

"Not you."

"I *have* lied to you. Repeatedly."

"Not anymore," Jacques staunchly declared.

"You are caught in a lie right now."

Suddenly, the world tilted and shifted, and Jacques was standing on the seam between sand and sea.

35

FACE YOUR MONSTERS

This is what Lapis meant. Dragons lie with words. Foxes use illusions."

Jacques had been inside, yet suddenly, he was ankle-deep in waves. "This is a lie?"

"This is real enough," said Argent. "Though you may think it a nightmare."

He tugged at soggy pantlegs. "Because you've *ruined* my favorite shoes."

"Because this is the truth."

Jacques turned and immediately shied away from the sight of a basking dragon. "Show me a lie instead. You lie *beautifully*."

"Most would consider Lapis beautiful. Especially up close."

"I don't *want* to get closer."

"I know." Argent offered his hand. "Neither do I."

36

WHEREWITHAL

Jacques dug in his heels almost as hard as he gripped Argent's hand. "I *can't*."

"Focus on me."

It was a relief to turn from the glittering sprawl that was Lapis in all his glory. "*Really* can't."

"Even if I were to reward your courage?"

"How?"

"In a manner commensurate to the challenge." Argent held his gaze. "You will ... enjoy yourself."

Jacques found the wherewithal to mutter, "I won't hurt Tsumiko."

Slow in coming. Gone too soon. If a lie, it had certainly been beautiful. But Jacques thought it sly enough and wry enough to be true enough, that smile.

37
NO SAINT

Jacques was entirely unprepared to face a dragon. No armor. No sword. No sainthood in the offing. "Commensurate," he checked. "Something I'll enjoy."

"Vastly more than I will."

"Because that's a real dragon."

Argent inclined his head. "That is Lapis in truest form."

"Lord." Jacques wasn't quite ready to face this. "Does he breathe fire?"

"No fire. He is a river dragon." Argent's brows arched. "You are probably also safe from splashing, since Lapis does not care for saltwater."

"He's rather large."

"Compared to you." Argent sighed. "You may be defenseless, but that does not mean you are without defense."

38
FIGHT OR FLIGHT

Jacques squared his shoulders, turned around, and fought the urge to flee.

"Can we further define terms?" Jacques lacked the nerve for this. Even if he were to admit that sunlight on dragon scales created a prettyish shine, he preferred to admire it from a safe distance. "Perhaps a hint to my prize?"

Argent didn't answer.

"As incentive?" Jacques wheedled.

Not so much as a *tsk*.

Miffed, he aimed a pout over his shoulder, only to encounter the muzzle of another monster. Or a blessing in disguise. Because scrambling away pushed him closer to the dragon.

Wouldn't Argent be pleased?

39
LORDING IT OVER

J acques backed into a wall and tried to climb it, only to realize that it was Deece.

Ginkgo arrived. "Really, Dad? You needed to do this *now*?"

Pale eyes narrowed familiarly, and Jacques swayed. *Mon dieu.* He'd *known* about Amaranthine taking animal form, but he'd never imagined *this*.

On went Ginkgo. "The plan was allaying his fears, not multiplying them."

The fox managed to look both haughty and unrepentant.

In other words, like himself.

And recognizing his master in the monster, Jacques mastered himself enough to ask, "Argent ... *you*'re serving as my defense?"

Ginkgo snorted. "Not that you need it."

40
COMFORTING TRUTHS

R eady for this?"

"Do I *look* ready?" Jacques muttered.

Ginkgo eyed him critically. "You look nervous."

"Petrified."

"What if I told you Lapis is vegetarian?"

"I wouldn't believe you." Still, Jacques allowed Ginkgo to tug him along.

"But would you feel better?"

"A little," he admitted. "Tell me something true instead."

"He's blue."

Jacques sighed. "Something *comforting*."

Ginkgo lowered his voice. "He's embarrassed."

That was unexpected. And surely unfounded. "I cannot imagine why."

He whispered, "Tsumiko is curious as three kittens in a basket, so any minute now, she's going to ask–"

Jacques interrupted, "What's wrong with his wings?"

41
SPEAKING AS A FRIEND

That." Ginkgo's ears lay crooked against his hair, like they were cringing. "Word of advice. Like foxes and their tails, never question dragons about their wings."

Jacques lowered his voice. "Rude?"

"Extremely personal." Ginkgo's eyebrows lifted. "The same goes for an Amaranthine's blaze."

"Which is …?"

"Looks like a tattoo. More of a birthmark, really." He cleared his throat. "A blaze is private."

Jacques was uncomfortably aware of Deece's proximity. How many times had Jacques traced the indigo pattern uncovered during last night's grooming? "Really? Because there was lots of purring."

Ginkgo nodded thoughtfully. "That's probably fine then. But that's cats."

42
I.LL NOT GO EASY

Jacques had long cultivated a careless nature. Not with appearances—*heaven forbid*—but with relationships. Easy come, easy go. But last night had been compelling. Unequal to anything previous. Unique. And Jacques wanted Deece and Michael to include him again.

Possibly even always.

And that little wake-up call scared Jacques, because he was used to losing the things he wanted most. Like Argent.

Coming here had been far from easy. And whether devastation or humiliation awaited, Jacques wouldn't easily let go.

Possibly even never.

So Jacques turned his back on the fox and the dragon and reached out to Deece.

५३
THERE WAS PURRING

Deece reached back and soothed, "Take your time."

As if this was still about dragons. As if Jacques wasn't in the middle of the mother of all meltdowns. "I need a private word."

Drawing him aside, Deece asked, "What do you want?"

"Forgiveness, I think." Jacques stiffly added, "I won't make excuses. I imposed on you in the manner of rakes and cads."

"Me?"

"Your blaze. You didn't say anything."

"Oh." Deece offered a small shrug. "Your pleasure was innocent."

Jacques supposed that summed up everything about the previous night.

"And … we felines enjoy attention. Almost as much as dragons."

५५
THE SEDUCTION OF DRAGONS

Deece usherer Jacques to where Sansa now waited.

She briskly asked, "You are familiar with grooming, yes?"

How should he answer? Did she know about last night? What did she think of her husband consorting with a person of his inclinations? "It was very nice, marm."

"Dragons are wily, not easily contained." She presented him with a green plastic pail. "But they can be seduced."

Oil—warm and scented.

Sansa ordered, "Beguile him."

Argent was suddenly there, rolling up his sleeves. Dipping his hand into the oil, the fox approached Lapis's hindquarters. "Come, Smythe. We will subdue this dragon together."

45
STEADY ON

Jacques' fingertips lightly grazed the dragon's scales.

Beside him, Argent showed no such delicacy. "Put your back into it, Smythe. He is far from fragile."

Jacques cautiously pressed against their azure iridescence.

"Both hands," urged Argent.

Jacques reluctantly mirrored his motions.

When the dragon warbled, Jacques leapt back. But Argent chuckled and kneaded harder. However, they soon reached one of the wings that dragged limply in the sand.

"No cutting corners." Argent gently pulled and straightened.

Something was wrong with them, but Jacques knew better than to ask.

Argent answered anyhow. "They have become too heavy for Lapis to lift."

46
HARMLESS

Jacques warmed somewhat to his task, but it was a large one. "Why are the others not helping?"

Sansa had retreated to a bonfire, where more oil warmed. Michael, Tsumiko, and the rest waited there, at safer distances.

"Lapis is sensitive to potent souls."

"And mine is impotent?"

Argent actually looked amused. "Quiescent."

Jacques smoothed oil into wingfolds. "Not a reaver?"

"He abstains from tending." His tone softened. "He has no excuse to withhold himself from your touch."

"You're shy of reavers?" Jacques prodded a vast rib. "Are you allergic or something?"

Argent's lips twitched. "Ask him later. Over tea."

47
TRUE BLUE

Hands busy, the grip of Jacques' fears loosened enough for him to twist and tug at them, seeking their root. Argent had never dismissed his fear of dragons. Never denied its rightness. Only pushed him to refine it. To define the danger.

Lapis didn't feel dangerous. Jacques could see him clearly in his mind, sipping tea, turning pages. Mannerly and manicured. Genteel and generous. "Pretty is as pretty does."

"Wise as serpents, harmless as doves." Argent straightened to survey their progress, idly wiping his hands on his thighs. "If you like, I understand that Lapis is equally susceptible to pedicures."

48
SPEAKING FROM EXPERIENCE

The next time Lapis warbled, Jacques didn't jump away. However, he made sure to keep Argent between him and the business end of the dragon. And searched for signs of danger.

No unsightly jut of teeth. No ominous jet of steam.

No hissing or flicking or gaping about the maw.

Only a luminous pair of sapphire eyes set into a shapely head, crowned by horns that looked more like pale coral than the antlers of a forest animal.

"Make peace, or you will be sorry," said Argent. "Train with Lapis or spend your years dancing attendance upon Kyrie's every whim."

49

UNDER THE INFLUENCE

What have you there?" Lapis asked in mellow tones.

Jacques blinked. He couldn't remember picking up the pen, yet there was a sort of rune-thingie on the paper before him. "I drew this?"

"With my guidance."

"Does it do anything?"

"Certainly." Lapis fluttered his fingers at it. "If imbued, it should function."

Ginkgo snorted. "Lapis, shouldn't you prompt him to do things he'll *want* to resist?"

Lapis hummed. "Not at this juncture."

A blue-tipped claw drew across the sigil, which sparkled, lifted, and spun away with a twinkling like chimes.

Jacques reached for it and whispered, "Can we do another?"

50

THE DEVIL YOU KNOW

Did you forget me?"

"What if I said *yes*?" Argent sighed and said, "You shall have your prize, Smythe."

"If it pleases my lord."

"It does not."

Jacques' step faltered. "I don't?"

"Not *you*, idiot boy. This … thing. I am being compelled." Argent pulled him along. By the time they reached the stairs, he'd mastered himself. "It would *seem* I have an image to maintain. Twineshaft is threatening to appoint an avian attendant."

One thing was clear. "You don't want one."

Argent grimly contemplated the floor. "Am I right in assuming you would *enjoy* being in charge of my closet?"

51

IN THE CLOSET

We will amend your job description. In addition to whatever other ridiculous duties you have invented for yourself, you will attend to my wardrobe."

Jacques gasped. "I get to dress you?"

"What *are* you thinking?" Argent rolled his eyes. "Rest assured, I can dress myself. However, you will choose attire appropriate to the occasion."

So saying, Argent threw open the doors to a room *catastrophique*.

"This is your domain. Assemble, organize, and maintain a wardrobe suitable for public appearances. And when absolutely necessary, you will attend me during my travels."

Surveying the wreckage of finery, Jacques whispered, "You ... *need* me."

52

EVE OF DESCENT

Ginkgo hauled Jacques through the newly renovated rooms above the kitchen. "Nice, right?"

Nursery. Naproom. Dormitory. Classroom.

The tour continued through a suite of rooms with its own staircase. Ginkgo guided him down and out into a walled garden. "For the mares."

"The what now?"

"Healers from the horse clans. They'll help Tsumiko with the little ones."

"This is all so sudden," Jacques protested.

Ginkgo took him by the shoulders. Jacques found a *soupcon* of comfort in the connection, but none in his words.

"*You* were sudden. *This* has been the plan for months." Ginkgo warned, "First drop arrives tomorrow."

53
FIRST COME. FIRST SERVED

When Jacques opened the door to Adoona-soh Elderbough, he was unprepared on three levels. For her size, because the spokesperson for the wolves towered. For her growl, since she rumbled like a volcano on the verge of disaster. And for her first deed, which was to thrust a gangly child into his arms.

"Take this one. Least likely to bite. Argent!"

Jacques gaped at Adoona-soh, then risked a peek at the closer threat. Blue eyes blinked fearfully from under a thatch of dun hair. Surprise silenced him, if only for a moment.

"Lord. Are you aware that you have horns?"

54
PRAT

The child mumbled, "Yessir. And these." With fatalistic resolve, the boy lifted his leg, displaying a cloven hoof. As if expecting screams or censure.

Jacques was too good a butler to succumb to either.

Still. Hooves. "You've brought us a faun?"

"Don't be ridiculous," scoffed Adoona-soh. "Goat clan, not deer clan. He's a kid."

He bowed to her superior knowledge. "Very good, marm."

She eyed him with ill-concealed amusement. "His name's Nonny."

Jacques drawled, "Hey, nonny, nonny."

The kid called him a rude name.

And quicker than you could say *hey, diddle, diddle*, Jacques realized something vital.

Nonny spoke English.

55

DONE A RUNNER

Argent appeared suddenly, as if he'd been leaning against the door this whole time. He relieved Adoona-soh of a tawny-tailed toddler who hissed and bared tiny fangs. "Desist," he chided.

Like *that* would help.

She went limp.

Touché.

Whatever Argent had done, it had the opposite effect on Nonny.

"Lemme go." The boy strained away. "I'm stronger'n you."

Jacques had no trouble grasping the underlying threat, and he didn't fancy a hoof to the vitals. But the kid was quaking. So Jacques started walking. Away.

"Smythe?"

Lengthening his stride, Jacques made the corner of the house and kept on running.

56

KIDNAPPER

Why?" puffed Jacques, once they'd gained the garden. "Why're you scared?"

Nonny wriggled and pushed. "*Fox* is why."

That was a bother.

Firstly, because it would have been in poor taste for someone with an unreasonable fear of dragons to frown upon an unreasonable fear of foxes.

And secondly, because nothing could counter the fact that Argent *was* a fox—sharp and blunt and cunning. Things people only overlooked if they didn't have to deal with him regularly. Or if they loved him devotedly.

"Right. Here's the thing."

Nonny stilled expectantly.

"Ignore what he says and see what he does."

57
LOFTY PERSONAGE

Jacques smuggled Nonny into Michael's affable oversight via the kitchen door.

On his way back through the house, Jacques inclined his head toward the newcomers ascending the stairs. Two ladies—presumably the mares—chatted in Japanese. Tsumiko now cuddled the cat-tailed girl, and Sansa had secured a sullen boy in need of a stylist.

In the foyer's brighter light, Jacques paused to neaten. Lord. Not simply children. Children who shed.

A thunderous knock startled him into action. Opening the door, Jacques looked up and further up. And wondered where Argent had gotten to as another Amaranthine bent close. And sniffed.

58
GIFTS FOR THE HOSTESS

So *you're* the one." Harmonious Starmark, large as life. "I've been wanting to meet Stately House's new butler."

Jacques' attention flicked briefly to a second specimen of strapping masculinity who looked on with famously copper eyes. Two older children—perhaps ten or twelve—clung to his hands. As if crossers were in vogue as hostess gifts when visiting Lady Mettlebright.

"Everyone's curious." The spokesperson for the dog clans oozed *bonhomie*. "You're Argent's kin …?"

"He is Smythe." Argent stalked forward, inserting himself between Jacques and their guests. "He belongs to Stately House."

"Oh, be frank." Harmonious beamed. "It's the same thing."

59
DISCERNING PALATE

I ntroductions went overlong, and Jacques managed to avoid the welcoming feast, having no appetite for such delicacies as *finger of chicken*. So absurd.

He was still sulking in his linen cupboard when the younger Starmark tapped lightly and proffered a dainty crystal goblet. "My father sends his compliments and would like your opinion of his gift."

"Why?"

"Argent spoke highly of your palate."

"*Naturellement.*" Jacques lifted, tilted, swirled, and sniffed with patent hauteur. Luminously pale, bedizened by tiny galaxies. Holding the first sip in his mouth, he closed his eyes and knew bliss.

"What *is* this?" he whispered.

"Star wine."

60
GENEROSITY ITSELF

J acques savored another mouthful, which mixed and mingled with his senses, mellowing his mood. He lifted the glass and blinked slowly. Was it... glowing? "I didn't know you could bottle starlight."

His companion chuckled. "It's not made *of* stars. It's made *by* stars."

Important distinction. Heartening, even. Jacques sipped and swayed peacefully within the wine's thrall. "Who were you, again?"

"Valor."

"Seriously?"

"You would not be the first to find humor in our traditions."

"Could be worse." Another swallow. Lovely stuff, star wine. "Stodgy or Manky or Pudge."

"More?"

Jacques nodded happily. "Very generous."

Valor winked. "Generous is my aunt."

61
LOWERING INHIBITIONS

I s there another bottle?"

Valor circled both arms. "A cask."

Sufficient inducement to descend. Perhaps he could make canapes. And it was never too late for chocolate. "Tell me another name in doggish."

"I have a sister named Rampant."

Jacques struck a pose like the rampant lion of heraldry. "*Raaawr.*"

Valor's smile broadened. "My younger brother is Eloquence."

"Poor sod. Want me to call you something more sensible?"

"I would be honored." Valor offered his palms. "Give me a nickname as a sign of our friendship, and I will both take it to my heart and answer to your call."

62
TO THE CASK

R ather high-flown, but if Jacques had a name like Valorous or Vigorous or Vainglorious, he might've waxed equally poetic.

Valor's gaze was bright. "What would you consider sensible?"

"Mark."

Laughter rumbled pleasantly. "Mark Starmark?"

Jacques poked the dog's chest. "Like Jean Valjean, but shinier. Or Bond, James Bond. There's a debonair ring to it."

"I see the sense."

The ceiling seemed to be moving. Jacques tipped his head back to watch. "Mark, are you carrying me?"

"You finally noticed."

Jacques thought perhaps his tastes could run to dogs, even if their names were culled from a thesaurus. "To the cask!"

63

LANGUOR

Jacques relaxed everything—languid, but far from mindless. For instance, after close contemplation of the embroidery on Mark's collar, Jacques concluded that the crest Argent shared with his sons was superior in every way.

"Better cellars, though." Which made him wonder. "Stars have cellars?"

"Perhaps we should rethink that second glass." Mark sounded like he was teasing.

Jacques lifted his empty goblet and his eyebrow. "We should toast your new name."

"And I will match your generosity."

"You want to toast me?" Wait. That sounded a trifle culinary. Although, if wine was involved, wouldn't that be poaching?

"I'll nickname you."

64

COME INTO MY PARLOR

Downstairs was warmed by candlelight. Various parlors overflowed with strangers with tails. And *not* the sort Jacques flaunted.

"What ho?" he objected. The competition would be fierce.

"Adoona-soh's pack is encamped in the woods." Mark lowered him to a settee, radiating concern. "What's upset you?"

Jacques pouted. "They'll drink all the wine."

"Shall I secure your next taste?" he offered, droll in his generosity.

Holding his gaze, Jacques solemnly urged, "Make me proud."

Only after his new friend strayed from view did Jacques realize that he wasn't alone on the settee. Star wine was both lovely stuff ... and potent stuff.

65
SURELY NOT

Jacques needed a moment to unfreeze, then scuttled into the settee's corner.

"You must be Jacques Smythe." The newcomer pitched his voice to soothe. Perhaps for the sake of the wee creature asleep in his arms. "I'm Deece's uncle."

Deece? Jacques wavered between relief and disbelief. "For a moment, I thought you were *him*."

"Whom?"

"That Twineshaft fellow. The one with the Japanese name."

"Hisoka."

Lord. It *was* him. Wait. Had it come up before? Jacques promised, "I won't tell."

With the very same smile he used to great effect during television interviews, Spokesperson Twineshaft said, "Hold out your arms."

66
RUBBISH

Surely not. My duties don't ...!"

"Your arms," repeated Hisoka Twineshaft, already shifting his hold, making the transfer.

Unable to escape, Jacques bore up under the solid weight of a boy with stripes patterning his cheeks. "Sir, I'm rubbish with children."

"You know enough. Indeed, you made Gilen's placement possible."

Jacques could only shake his head.

"He needs you."

Doubts building, Jacques shook his head more quickly.

"He has been inconsolable." Hisoka held a finger to his lips, touched the boy's shoulder, and something came undone.

Gilen startled awake. Large eyes filled with tears, and he began to prattle. In French.

67

MOTHER TONGUE

As the young crosser's onslaught grew increasingly articulate, Jacques reassessed his impressions. Seven, perhaps eight. Small, but husky. Sad, yet frustrated. With his father. At this foreign place. And by the cat who'd carried him off.

"Is he a terrible brute?" asked Jacques, eyeing Hisoka Twineshaft suspiciously.

The rant ceased as quickly as it had begun. Jacques noted that Gilen's pupils were round, lending them a reassuring touch of humanity.

"*Français*," the boy whispered.

"Half," Jacques conceded. "On my mother's side. Are you in need of assistance? Because if Monsieur Twineshaft has been a terrible brute, I'll report him immediately."

68

VERY GOOD

Gilen whispered, "*Non.*"

"*Tres bien.* Or you and I and the whole world might be lost." Jacques poked the boy's round cheek. "I'd never met anyone with stripes before."

A clawed hand delivered a return poke.

"I could call you Stripe." Jacques scanned the room. "I'm to receive a nickname myself. And another glass of wine."

Gilen petted his cheek, as if enchanted by the rasp of stubble.

At his questioning glance, Hisoka supplied, "Facial hair. A quirk of humanity."

"Tell that to your eyebrows."

Hisoka's lifted, and his smile lost its air of diplomacy.

And it was *tres bien.*

69
QUIRKS OF HERITAGE

A handkerchief appeared, and Jacques immediately recognized the *faux pas* that was Michael's only fashion statement. Magic or no, his gaudy bracelet looked like a dowager's baubles.

"Sensei!" The man exuded boyish delight. "*Always* a pleasure."

Jacques indicated the weepy boy. "You. Take him. Please?"

But where Nonny had gone easily to Michael, Gilen nearly strangled Jacques with desperate clinging.

"Ah." Michael shook his head regretfully. "Instincts rebel."

"*No* reavers," explained Hisoka. "Gilen is also uneasy with females."

Jacques could relate. Still. "Why?"

"A quirk of the feline clans." The cat paused. "And an understandable consequence of his mother's ... disfavor."

70
MAKE MY APOLOGIES

M ind the ascot," grumbled Jacques. "I cannot fend off Monsieur Ward if I am creased or rumpled."

Gilen's hold gentled, though he roughly butted Jacques' chin.

"Apology," interpreted Michael. "Or appeal."

"Shoo." Jacques flicked his fingers. "I'll make your apologies to Stripe."

Michael banished himself from the immediate vicinity, and Gilen gave Jacques' neckwear an apologetic pat. "Not Stripe," he mumbled.

Jacques hummed. "You're right. Too trite. We'll sort out something better."

Just then, Mark appeared bearing a tray with matching goblets—one of star wine, one milk. And topped the evening by uttering three magical words. "Argent wants you."

71

ARGENT WANTS YOU

Buoyed by those words, Jacques attempted to stand, but Gilen was a substantial little critter. Tiger heritage, judging by his patterning. "Off you get."

"*Non.*" The boy butted his chin again. "Stay."

"As if I'd leave," scoffed Jacques. "Even *you* cannot chase me away."

The boy retreated long enough to let him up, only to reaffix himself most ardently. Jacques offered the goblet of milk to Gilen, clinking it with his own. "Cheers."

Gilen drank greedily. Still, the grapple-hold did not loosen.

Nothing else for it.

"Canapes. Now." Jacques savored another mouthful of starlight, which proved entirely inspirational. "And Deece."

72

AMUSE BOUCHE

Jacques set Deece and his uncle to slicing, mixing, and spreading. Their compliance was a pleasant surprise. "Do cats do like dogs do?"

Mark topped off his glass. "In what sense?"

"Nicknames."

"If befriended by the packs." Mark indicated Hisoka. "For instance, he's Posy."

How amusing. Jacques adored gossip, and these tidbits were tasty. "Why?"

"His cloak."

Jacques scrutinized the illustrious cat. "*What* cloak?"

"I don't wear it in summer."

"Maybe Michael can magic you some snow."

"While my former apprentice is capable of much, weathercraft belongs to the wind." Hisoka was suddenly very close indeed. "Are we exchanging names?"

73
INTENDED USE

Trade names?" asked Jacques.

Mark helpfully explained, "An exchange of names—like the giving of a nickname—signifies the beginning of a bond. Posy is a good friend to have."

Jacques turned to Gilen. "Should we befriend the brute, since he isn't *so* terrible?"

The boy paused in licking his fingers, having finished all the canapes within reach. But his attention was nowhere near Hisoka.

An amused drawl came from behind. "Is star wine safe for human consumption?"

Jacques staggered forward, pressing a finger to Lapis's lips. "Do *not* say it isn't," he commanded fiercely. "I won't believe such heresy."

74
HUSH YOUR MOUTH

Jacques was distracted by the smoothness of the dragon's skin. Rich brown, without any trace of ash or stubble. Under his fingertips, Lapis's mouth curved into a smile.

"I'll not bar you from any wholesome pleasure." Turning Jacques hand, Lapis leaned his cheek into it and observed, "You're happy."

That reminded Jacques why. Lowering his voice, he confided, "Argent wants me."

Lapis whispered, "What holds you back?"

Jacques petted and pondered. Ah, yes. "Chocolate."

"Yeah? I know where Sansa stashes the good stuff." Ginkgo stood in the doorway, arms folded across his chest. "Which one of you got him drunk?"

75
THREE MORE WORDS

Jacques contemplated the breadcrusts and kipper brine on Sansa's counter. The overgrown battler would undoubtedly track the wreckage to him, but that was a problem for tomorrow's Jacques.

Tonight's Jacques was loading his pockets.

"Sure you wanna do that?" asked Ginkgo.

He lifted the tin of caviar without hesitation but hesitated over the chocolates.

Ginkgo reached past him, snagging a few bars with hand-painted wrappers. He gave one to Jacques and one to Gilen, keeping the third for himself. "I have a further message from Dad."

While not as magical as the first, these were equally compelling.

"*Now*, idiot boy."

76
IN THE GREAT GREEN ROOM

Jacques arrived in the naproom with his cortege. They escorted him toward a rocking chair where Tsumiko rocked Kyrie. Finding the floor absurdly squishy, Jacques sank to his knees. Maybe it came off courtly?

From his perch on a tuffet beside her, Argent received them with a warning look and an upraised finger.

But then Ginkgo started handing out squares of chocolate to the children. As did Gilen, all shy smiles despite the language barrier and lady beacon.

Jacques glanced about and murmured to Deece, "Where's your uncle?"

"Tidying up."

Hisoka Twineshaft, legendary orchestrater of the Emergence, turned scullery maid.

77
FORWARD

Shuffling forward on his knees, Jacques went to Tsumiko, intending to warn her about Gilen's apprehensions, forgetting that her grasp of English was as solid as his on Japanese. Even so, Tsumiko was an understanding sort of person. Soft and warm.

"Do you like chocolate? It seems the posh sort."

And suddenly, everyone was quiet.

Mark looked wary. Lapis bit his lip. Deece fidgeted. Ginkgo gestured wildly, then simply rolled his eyes.

Tsumiko smiled and touched his hand, murmuring something, and Jacques looked to Argent for translation.

Argent's expression was unreadable. "My bondmate kindly suggests that you release my tails."

78
GETTING HANDSY

Jacques snatched back his hands, reached pleadingly, and quickly recoiled. Nobody would believe a protestation of innocence. His *tendre* for Argent was well established. Though his best chance of survival was an immediate appeal to Tsumiko, Jacques couldn't look away from Argent's cool gaze.

Claws reached for him, and Jacques squeezed his eyes shut. *Don't hurt me. Don't hate me. Don't send me away.*

Argent applied pressure, bowing Jacques forward until his forehead touched Argent's knee. An ornamental posture that opened the way for mercy.

"This is Lady's favorite uncle. He is kin, so you may call him Uncle Jackie."

79
NO GO

Tsumiko lifted Jacques' head, her dainty hands framing his face as she spoke.

"She calls you 'highly favored one.'" Argent's lips quirked. "Her sense of humor tends to the biblical."

Jacques smiled wanly.

"She wants you to stay," Argent translated. "I expect you to stay."

He swallowed hard. "Please, my lord. I meant no disrespect."

Argent's brow arched. "How much wine have you had?"

Jacques recognized the out. Also, that someone had stolen his glass. And further, that his misfit yearnings could damn him. Even so, he blurted, "Not *nearly* enough!"

Huffing softly, Argent murmured, "There will be other opportunities."

80
JAPANESE TO ENGLISH TO FRENCH

Staying was more involved than Jacques expected. And more immediate. Wedged between Ginkgo and Gilen, he helped relay Argent's bedtime story to a homesick little boy.

Ginkgo's translation had all the ambiance of a fable, but the tale being spun was more new than old.

A fox and his lady.

A den and its protection.

A home and its blessings.

Argent was handing down family history to its newest members. And he'd waited for Jacques before beginning. His breath caught.

Ginkgo's ears pricked his way.

"Am I dreaming?" Jacques whispered.

Slinging an arm around his shoulders, Ginkgo said, "Maybe later."

81
TREAD LIGHTLY

Was she ... like Kyoko?" whispered Jacques.

Argent's brows knit.

"Gilen's mother rejected him?" He glanced Kyrie's way. "Like Kyoko."

"Their situations are quite different." Argent drew him aside, drew a sigil on his palm. "Gilen's *father* is human, a cosset in the cortege of Gilen's mother. Feline traditions make their situation ... delicate."

"He's not an orphan?"

Argent hesitated. "That term does not technically apply to *any* of these children."

Jacques caught on. "Their Amaranthine parent doesn't want them."

"Or does not know about them. Or cannot publicly own them." Argent nodded. "Reaver Dulcet is trusting his son's future to us."

82
OVERCROWDED

Jacques couldn't possibly fall asleep, not with a room full of people who didn't seem to treasure privacy half as much as he. Tsumiko had excused herself, but Jacques was pillowless and pajamaless and put to bed early.

Like a child.

He wasn't accustomed to sleeping on the floor, to doing without silk and solitude. True, Deece's closeness was reassuring. In case of nightmares. But Jacques was restless and rumpled and really very confused.

Because he suddenly stood on the edge of a sunswept garden. And his hands and his height were all wrong. Like another self.

Like a child.

83
ROLL CALL

Flowerbeds encircled a tidy lawn where children played. Jacques recognized them. Hard not to.

Gilen with his banded tail.

Tawny, the little feline with a big hiss.

Raife of the unfortunate hair.

Mori, whose eyes were far too old.

Mei, who clung to Mori and called him brother.

But where had Nonny gone?

Jacques stuck to the fringes, checking behind shrubs, waving when he spied the kid. Nonny skulked out of hiding and trotted over on nimble hoofs. They were the same height.

"Uncle Jackie?"

"Well spotted." Jacques whispered, "What *happened*?"

Nonny's face was ghost-pale. "This is a fox dream."

84
NOT HALF BAD

Jacques grabbed Nonny's hand, which was cold, and asked, "Why do foxes scare you?"

"I'd be interested to know that myself," interrupted a voice. Ginkgo eased carefully to the grass a short distance away, Kyrie cradled against his shoulder. "Wanna tell me about it?"

Nonny shook his head.

"How about I ask questions?" Ginkgo wiggled his ears for Kyrie's benefit. "Ever met a fox before?"

The kid nodded.

"Young like me, or ancient like Dad?"

Nonny shrugged.

"Silver? Red? A vixen, maybe?"

Jacques winced when Nonny's grip tightened.

"We're not all bad." Ginkgo smiled crookedly. "Or half-bad, in my case."

85
NOT MY JOB

Jacques marveled at the dizzying speed with which Ginkgo gained Nonny's trust. Then again, Ginkgo was something Jacques never would be. Fond of children.

He should be *glad* of the transfer of Nonny's affections. Relieved, even.

Jacques shuffled backward.

Babysitting wasn't in his job description. Never would be.

"Hey. Runt." Ginkgo gave a casual jerk of his chin. "He wants you."

"Argent?" he squeaked. Jacques *hated* how young he sounded.

Ginkgo chuckled. "This is better than baby pictures."

He scowled.

"Go on, little Jackie Smythe." He nodded encouragement. "It's not often you get a second chance at a first impression."

86
DRAGGING FEET

Jacques cherished—even hallowed—his first impression of Argent. He didn't *want* to redefine something that had defined him. But the Argent who awaited wasn't the formidably formal creature with an icy hauteur who'd served tasty tidbits and subtle insults at teatime.

The fox sat among the flowers, surrounded by swaying tails and a flock of... *not* butterflies. Jacques tried to track one's flight path. Were those wings or fins?

"Jackie." Argent crooked his fingers. "They are quite tame."

Jacques stalled. But then he registered Argent's silken, silver-trimmed finery.

"*Argent!*" Outrage warbled through his boyish falsetto. "*Mon dieu.* Your pants!"

87

SOILED AND SPOILED

Jacques stomped forward, pointed down. "You are sitting in *soil*."

Argent placidly took note of his setting.

Reaching out to test the fabric, Jacques' pique redoubled. "This is silk, isn't it? Oh, for shame!"

"With all you see before you, *that* has priority?" Argent huffed. "You have changed."

Had that been a compliment? Jacques would not be distracted. "*You* are the one who needs to change. This cloth may already be spoiled!"

Argent silenced him with an upraised finger. "My wardrobe is truly your greatest concern?"

"It's the only part you gave me." Jacques' face heated. "It's all I have."

88

BAD MEMORIES

Little Jackie Smythe." Argent's fingers brushed a flushed cheek. "This is how I remember you."

Jacques turned his face. "Don't treat me like a child."

"My treatment of that child plagues me." Argent sighed. "I was … unkind."

Suddenly, it occurred to Jacques that the one wanting to make a fresh impression was Argent. He rolled his eyes. "If you want to be kind to me, be kinder to your clothes."

"That is all you want?"

"*Non*." Little Jackie Smythe stuck his nose in the air and coated his words in sarcasm. "If you want to *spoil* me, I've a list."

89
CREATURE COMFORTS

Enlighten me," challenged Argent. "What sets the man before me apart from the spoiled boy who haunts my memories?"

Jacques breezily summed up. "*Adult* interests."

"Too vague." Argent waved a hand. "You promised a list."

"I want … an espresso machine and a French chef to make breakfast pastries. Fine cheeses and a cellar filled with star wine. Access to an excellent tailor." After a moment's thought, he added, "And a place to hide."

"Your linen cupboard no longer suffices?"

Jacques hadn't realized Argent knew. He indicated the queue for Ginkgo's piggyback rides. "They'll *follow* me."

"Much as you followed me."

90
SIMPLE PLEASURES

Jacques impulsively added, "*And* I want Bon-Bon to be jealous."

"That one may be difficult." Argent's gaze drifted out of focus. "Your brother rarely looks any farther than the reflection in his mirror. Your triumphs will likely languish beneath his notice."

Giggling softly, Jacques confided, "He can *always* tell when I'm happy."

Something in Argent's expression shifted. "Happiness is your ambition?"

"*Oui.*"

"A vague goal."

"But easily reached."

Argent's head tilted. "You believe you can be happy here?"

With an injured look, Jacques declared, "I've been happy *several* times this evening. And having your undivided attention hasn't dampened my mood."

91
WHAT.S YOURS IS MINE

appiness," Argent repeated thoughtfully. "You have always been the sort who finds it easily."

Once again, Jacques suspected a compliment. Perhaps even a touch of envy. "Add it to my job description."

The fox's lips quirked. "I hardly think it necessary to formalize a self-indulgent pursuit."

Jacques didn't like being so thoroughly misunderstood. But maybe it was understandable. What little information he'd gleaned about Argent pointed to enough *un*happiness to span hundreds of lifetimes.

"You have it backward, my lord." Catching Argent's hand, Jacques pressed his forehead to his inside wrist. "The happiness I most want to find is *yours*."

92
UNDESERVING

o not pledge yourself so flippantly, Jackie." Argent pulled away. "I cannot give you what you want."

So frustrating! Hadn't they covered this? "I'm trying to tell you that you already *have*!"

Argent tugged. Jacques tumbled. He found himself gathered close, tucked up under the fox's chin.

"Is that so?" asked Argent. "That is ... gratifying."

Jacques slowly relaxed. "I wish this was real."

"While not precisely real, fox dreams can be true."

"Tell me something true," whispered Jacques.

Argent hummed and huffed. "As this *is* a dream, I do not deserve scolding for the state of my pants. This time."

93
ALWAYS THE QUIET ONES

Jacques woke in rumpled clothes, with a tin of caviar stuck to his cheek and a purring Deece warming his back.

At the pitter-patter of approach, Jacques resignedly peeled open an eye. "Right. Who were you again?"

No reply.

"Raife does not speak," murmured Deece.

"*You're* one to talk." Jacques eyed the boy's ridiculous hair. "Well, what language do you *think* in?"

The child reached out to rub Jacques' cheek.

"Lord. What *is* it about stubble?"

"The tin made an impression. Cyrillic letters. Like your caviar, Raife is Russian."

"But he understood my question." Jacques hummed. "Raife, let's discuss conditioner."

94
FELINE COURTESIES

Pushing unsteadily onto his knees, Jacques was knocked back by Gilen's arrival. The half-tiger was happy and vaguely sticky. Jam? Syrup? What had he—and his dearly beloved suit—ever done to deserve this? Jacques tried not to make a face, but he may have whimpered.

Deece appeared at his side. "Invite him."

Jacques obliged by switching to French. "You are invited."

"Me?" Gilen's cheeks went pink.

Extending a bouquet of something herbaceous—mint, perhaps—Deece said, "We must uphold feline tradition."

"*We?*" Jacques echoed. "I'm no cat."

"But you want to bathe." Deece quietly urged, "Let us groom you."

95
UNCLES AND NEPHEWS

Jacques supposed he was there to translate. Or because of the arrangement with Gilen's human father. An honorary uncle. Yes. Quite.

"... try it with Deece." After a lengthy pause, Hisoka's hands stilled. "Jacques?"

"S-sir?"

"*Sensei* will do. Are you all right?"

Jacques gripped his knees. "This is highly irregular."

"Gilen needs to learn this part of his heritage." Hisoka smiled charmingly. "Nephews emulating uncles. What could be more natural?"

Jacques shot a pleading look at Deece, who'd submitted to Gilen's tentative kneading with purring patience.

And so the grooming lesson continued apace, with Hisoka slipping effortlessly into French. The beast.

96
IN NEED OF BREAKFAST

Jacques woke alone in Deece's bed, stomach growling. Pilfering a clean tunic, he crept to his own room, startled to find it still morning—barely. A quarter of an hour found him presentably coiffed and hastening toward the kitchen in hopes of a hearty elevenses.

Ginkgo slouched on the battered sofa under his winter garden and greeted him with a knowing smile. "You reek of catnip."

"Do I?" Jacques tugged at his vest. "Is it offensive?"

His gaze lingered. "Not if they're treating you good."

Just then, Michael strolled through the door, arms full. "Ah, Jacques. *This* should please you!"

97
MORE IN STORE

You found it," remarked Ginkgo.

"Right where he said it would be." Michael slid a box onto the counter.

Jacques hardly believed his eyes. "We had an espresso machine?"

"In storage." Michael's smile deepened toward indulgence. "Argent said you *required* one."

Yes, he'd wanted espresso. And more wine. With an uneasy glance at Ginkgo, Jacques asked, "How drunk was I last night?"

"Not *that* drunk."

The edges had gone fuzzy. Boyhood and bargains and making Boniface jealous. "I *asked* for this?"

"Don't you remember?" Ginkgo took a tone that was all cloak and dagger and conspiracy. "There was a *list*."

98
ENTIRELY REASONABLE

It's not my place to make demands," Jacques muttered.

Ginkgo lightly pointed out, "Tsumiko's the one Dad's out to impress."

"When it comes to wives, hell hath no fury," joked Michael.

"Nor heaven such glory," smoothly interjected Argent, startling them all.

Jacques flinched. "My apologies, my lord. Last night is something of a blur."

"Am I then exempt from the remainder of your demands?"

"If they were unreasonable."

"Far from it. And most have already been arranged for. This way, Smythe."

Jacques was hungry. He wanted coffee. But Argent had taken him by the hand, and he wanted that more.

99
PAST WARDS

All the way upstairs, Jacques caught flashes of memory from the night before. Nothing too embarrassing. Nothing too compromising. "Was the dream real?"

Argent simply dragged his hand forward to touch a set of double doors Jacques couldn't remember, even though they were near the fox's closet.

"Where …?"

Opening the door, Argent pulled him through, saying, "I brought him," then something in Japanese.

Tsumiko hurried forward, and Jacques suddenly realized where he was. A private parlor within their suite. Their *room*. And upon the table lay an extravagance of itsy bitsy pastries that could rival the finest bakeries in Paris.

100
FINDING THE WORDS

Jacques' tension ebbed away as—for once—Argent fully embraced the role of translator, allowing him to converse with Tsumiko at greater length than usual. Nonsense and non sequiturs. Quips and questionnaires.

"*Non!* Him?" Jacques licked delicate flakes from fingertips. "But this is the work of a master pâtissier!"

Tsumiko answered in pleased tones, and Argent supplied, "He has *many* skills."

Jacques leaned in. "Teach me a word."

Argent hesitated. "What word?"

"Not *you*. Her." Jacques rolled his eyes. "I'm talking to Tsumiko."

With a barely-there *tsk*, Argent translated.

Tsumiko smiled. "Yes?"

Jacques quietly asked, "How do I say *happy*?"

101
SO FOXY

Jacques loitered long after the last crumb was consumed. "I could get used to this."

Argent raised a cautionary finger. "*This* will not be your sanctuary. It is one of mine."

"Where are the others?"

"Here and there." Argent's vagueness had a sly quality. "Sometimes nowhere."

No doubt he was alluding to foxish magic. Jacques asked, "Can you hide in dreams?"

"Not for long." Argent paused to include Tsumiko.

"Up," she said, pointing for emphasis. "Way up."

Jacques glanced at the ceiling. "Upstairs?"

"Beyond," corrected Argent. "Yonder."

"The roof?"

With a considering look, Argent asked, "Would you like to see?"

102
REACH BACK

Safe, safe," chanted Tsumiko, whose push was both persuasion and permission.

Very sweet, except that she was pushing Jacques toward a three-story drop.

"Your hand," ordered Argent from across the sill.

"Yes, my lord." Jacques tried not to look down as he threw a leg over. "Why are you doing this?"

Argent smirked. "It is my way."

Jacques forced himself to move, ignoring self-preservation, relying heavily on Tsumiko's goodness. Lord, why was Argent so good at feeding his frustration?

"Are you punishing me?"

"Idiot boy." With one tug, Argent took Jacques' life into his hands. "I am rewarding your trust."

103
LET.S NOT QUIBBLE

ord Mettlebright lofted them skyward in a swirl of silver fur. Jacques wasn't even a little bit tempted by those tails.

"Peace and trust walk hand in hand," intoned Argent.

"Two things are *very* wrong with that statement," Jacques snipped. "First, we're not holding hands."

"*You* are the one who let go."

Jacques' arms tightened around Argent's shoulders. "Second, we're not walking. *Mon dieu.* Have you always been able to do this?"

"Since boyhood, but not always."

Jacques sobered at this reminder of Argent's enslavement.

"And now that you are listening," said the fox. "There is more. Hear me out."

104
THE CATCH

ou are remarkably unremarkable."

Jacques dragged his attention from all the down. "Was that compliment or criticism?"

Argent shook his head. "An ordinary human—unendowed, uninitiated. Yet unconcerned by species."

"We're making lists? You left out *unrequited.*"

He tutted. "You flung yourself at us, heedless of consequences. Without invitation. Without encouragement. Without pay."

"Money is no object," Jacques grumbled.

"*I* was your object. Not that you had any hope of catching me."

Jacques snorted. "That's what unrequited *means.*"

"My lady calls your arrival a leap of faith. Which has led to a remarkable reversal." Argent's expression warmed. "We caught you."

105
EXCELLENT REFERENCES

Jacques was less concerned with who did the catching, so long as the outcome was mutually satisfactory. Relinquishing his death grip, he dared to rest his head against Argent's shoulder. "Never let go. *Especially* not now, but also never."

Argent hummed. "Speaking of claims, did you know the wolves have a nickname for you?"

"Mark said he'd give me one."

"Did you imagine that he forgot?"

"Nobody mentioned it."

"*I* am mentioning it."

"Why you?"

"Because your nickname is allusive. I will protest on your behalf if it offends you."

Intrigued, Jacques asked, "What does my nickname allude to?"

"Me."

106
ME IN A WORD

You are familiar with the dogs' unique naming sense?"

Jacques shrugged. "Theirs are easier to remember than wolf names."

"By design," acknowledged Argent. "Dogs embrace a word of personal meaning or significance. Words that embody a strong emotion or a future hope."

"You're making lists again."

"Cheek."

"Are you being cryptically longwinded because my new name will offend me... or because it offends you?"

That seemed to startle Argent. "No, Jacques. It's a good name. Even Tsumiko agrees."

Jacques' indignation flared. "Everyone else knows?"

"Word travels fast in a pack." Argent huffed and sighed. "They have begun calling you Devotion."

107

DRAMATIC EQUIVALENCE

My feelings for you are what define me?"

Argent huffed. "You sound surprised."

Jacques asked, "Given the circumstances, wouldn't they disapprove?"

"You left your kin and crossed land and sea, abandoning everything to join with me here."

Nearly everything. There had been eight suitcases to wrangle at the baggage claim.

Argent continued, "This is comparable to a wolf leaving their pack in order to join a dog clan. To turn away from the moon, to lose their tail, to take a new name. These departures require a special kind of courage, usually born of love ...."

"*Unrequited* love."

"... or mutual respect."

108

TO EACH THEIR OWN

Do you mean to say that you respect me?"

"Really, Smythe. If you are going to be my man, you should pay closer attention."

Jacques pouted. "*Nobody* pays closer attention to you than I do!"

Argent sighed. "I did not *mean to* say anything. I said it. Why doubt me?"

"You're not this nice."

"And yet I have your trust, your respect, and your devotion." Argent stiffly added, "Your utter refusal to be intimidated by me is ... rare."

"That makes us unique. Exclusive." Jacques proudly tapped his chest. "I'm your one and only man."

"A claim I intend to formalize."

109
LIFE CHOICES

Jacques wasn't a respected kind of chap. He wasn't even a respectable one. His life choices always triggered scandals. What would dear Maman say if she found out an Amaranthine intended to claim him?

"Will it hurt?" he asked a little breathlessly.

Argent frowned. "I do not even *want* to know what you are imagining."

A capricious laugh was out before Jacques could stop it. "Disappoint me gently."

"I wish to become pactmates."

Argent's gravity had a sobering effect. He expected Jacques to make a life choice. To choose him.

How queer. Jacques had never felt this way before—undeserving.

110
GENTLEMAN.S AGREEMENT

How does this work?" asked Jacques.

"I keep you close. You keep my secrets."

"You'll confide in me?"

"That is my intention," confirmed Argent.

"Like what?"

"Who can say? I am anticipating a future need." He returned to the original question. "Pactmates can formalize their commitment in any number of ways. As you are a gentleman, a handclasp would suffice."

Jacques immediately offered his. "My hand is yours."

Argent firmed his grip. "For now, we could exchange names."

"I already know ... oh!" Jacques was proud of himself for catching on. "My lord, have *you* earned a nickname among the packs?"

111
LAYERS OF MEANING

Argent's lips quirked. "Anyone who has regular dealings with canines may find themselves with a nickname."

Oooh, he was *deflecting*. Jacques rubbed his hands together. "Yourself included?"

"Yes."

"Don't you want to tell me?"

"I can hardly prevent you from learning something that is widely known."

He still wasn't saying. Jacques wondered why. "Is it embarrassing?"

"Not at all. Indeed, it is increasingly appropriate."

"Why are you being cryptic?"

The quirk deepened into a smirk. "All the wrong reasons."

"Is it polite to tease pactmates?"

"If they enjoy it."

Jacques … did. "Will you tell me?"

"Certainly. Harmonious dubbed me Flourish."

112
DECAMPMENT

The wolves left first, and Jacques was suffering from withdrawal. He loitered in the corner of the garden where Deece could be always found—morning and evening—performing some kind of martial arts battle dance.

"Ever do this without a shirt on?" he asked.

Deece halted the whirl of his quarterstaff thingie and ventured a tentative, "No?"

"You're right. Of course. Terrible idea." Wolvish fashion usually involved exposed skin. He'd been spoiled by having all those bronzed and brawny Elderboughs loitering about half-naked.

"Perhaps *I* can banish your ennui."

Jacques hadn't heard Lapis arrive.

"I have a proposition, Mr. Smythe."

113
CHOOSE WITH CARE

For me?" Jacques perked up. Lapis wasn't the propositioning sort, since he was careful about the sway of his words.

"I am seeking a place to sleep."

Right. Amaranthine sleep patterns. "You need to … hibernate?"

Lapis smiled. "Deep rest leaves us vulnerable, so few like retiring alone." He intentionally phrased every sentence in ways that left Jacques a choice. "Argent has allowed me to request your attendance."

"I can't stay awake that long."

"Neither can Hisoka remain closeted for the duration. You and he could *share* the burden I will become." Lapis studied his gem-studded manicure. "I have prepared enticements."

114
LOANER

Jacques couldn't believe it. "You don't mind?"

"The sequins? Of course I mind," grumbled Argent. "They are ridiculous."

"Sequins have their place. Trust me. It's a gala. You must be grand." Jacques adjusted Argent's lapel. "And I was *talking* about Lapis's invitation."

"Why would I mind?"

"I'm *your* man. Not his." Jacques would have liked to be guarded more jealously.

"Lapis is in similar circumstances to Gilen."

Jacques couldn't imagine what a half-tiger and a dragon lord might have in common.

Argent elucidated. "Neither is comfortable with reavers."

"Why not?"

"Perhaps for the same reason I am uncomfortable with sequins."

115

UPPER STORY

When Michael escorted Jacques to a dull doorway, everything *looked* normal enough. "Are there wards?"

"In overlapping layers. We all contributed—me, Sensei, Argent, and Lapis himself." Michael reached for Jacques' hand and winked.

The entire hallway bloomed into etched lightning.

"Lord. Is it dangerous?"

"Not at all. We're simply making certain Lapis won't be interrupted."

Inside, Hisoka Twineshaft propped against the headboard of a four-poster bed, calmly reading a paperback while Lapis Mossberne cuddled against his thigh. Jacques felt like a stranger, an intruder on Amaranthine intimacies.

But he also felt left out. "Here, now! You started without me?"

116

LAVISH PROVISIONS

Michael laughed. "I told you we should have roused him and tucked them in together."

"Did you?" inquired Hisoka, turning a page.

"I'm sure I did." Michael teased, gesturing toward provisions heaped on the bureau. "All the little loving touches are from Lapis."

Expensive chocolates. Tea things. Tinned biscuits. High-end bento boxes. And a sparkling decanter. "Is this …?"

"Star wine," Michael confirmed.

Jacques hid his pleasure by perusing a teetering stack of books. "Lord Mossberne reads romance novels?"

Hisoka said, "I speak for the cat clans, Mr. Smythe. Not for Lapis. Save questions of a personal nature until he wakes."

117
SAFE

Michael eased back a corner of the comforter. "Come, take Sensei's place."

"The chair will suffice, surely."

Hisoka patiently disentangled himself from Lapis. "Dragons like shared heat."

Lord. "Is he aware of my … preferences?"

Michael's gaze softened.

"Are you referring to your fear of dragons, your devotion to Argent, or your orientation toward males?" inquired Hisoka.

Jacques nodded.

Michael gently said, "You're here because you make Lapis feel safe."

"Most people treat me like a threat. Once they know."

Hisoka asked, "Are their fears justified?"

"*Non.*"

With a small smile, Hisoka warned, "*Yours* may be. Lapis talks in his sleep."

118
CHANGING OF THE GUARD

Taking Hisoka's place, Jacques watched with fascination as Lapis whiffled and grumbled and patted around. "He knows I'm here?" he whispered.

"Yes, certainly!" assured Michael. "Sleep comes in stages. Lapis is still nominally aware of his surroundings."

Knuckles bumped. Claws hooked. And in one sinuous slide, the dragon lord laid claim to his new bedmate.

Michael chuckled. "On some level, he's been waiting for you."

Arms locked around his waist, and Jacques kept his hands well away from temptation.

"It's all right, Jacques." Michael gestured encouragingly. "Your touch, like your presence, will reassure him that it's safe to go deep."

119
THE LAST COOKIE

Jacques lost his awe of Hisoka. They were just two chaps with questionable taste in literature and an appetite for chocolate-dipped biscuits.

"Why are you doing this?"

Hisoka glanced at the empty tin and apologized. "Did you want the last one?"

"I meant Lapis. Why are *you* overseeing his naptime?"

"I suppose I'm returning favors."

"He did you a favor?"

"Lapis let me convince him to join the Five."

Jacques considered. "Did you know you'd need a dragon?"

"I didn't realize how much."

"How'd you even know you might?"

His smile was secretive. "I heard a song among the stars."

120
DEMANDING BEDFELLOW

Lapis really *did* talk in his sleep. And without his usual inhibitions.

Jacques emerged from a pleasant haze to discover his shirt missing. Hisoka was back, reading in the chair.

"Did he …?" Jacques was almost afraid to ask. "Did we …?

"You obliged an entirely innocent request." Hisoka smiled. "He likes skin-to-skin contact."

Jacques rolled his eyes. "Dragons are demanding bedfellows."

"Yet you've accepted him with open arms." Hisoka closed his book and shed his tunic. "You may slip away and attend to your needs."

He tried to wriggle free, but Lapis murmured, "Silly boy, don't go."

So Jacques stayed. Happily.

121
THREE ABED

The ticklish trace of a finger woke Jacques. It wasn't Lapis. The dragon lord was asleep in his arms as usual. Why was Hisoka drawing on his forehead? "You're here, too?"

"So it would seem."

Jacques asked, "Did you mean to be?"

"I let my guard slip. Never wise among dragons."

"Too right." Jacques checked his forehead.

"That sigil should allow you to escape."

A fine idea. But he couldn't resist teasing. "You're susceptible to dragon demands?"

"So it would seem."

Since things couldn't get much more personal, Jacques dared to ask, "Where do *you* go when you need sleep?"

122
CALLED IT

Hisoka settled back on his pillow. "I used to go to Harmonious, but that's become less convenient since the Emergence."

"Clashing schedules."

"I do have nephews I trust."

Jacques brightened. "Deece."

"Here?" He smiled slyly. "Are you offering to become my safety?"

"I couldn't *protect* you, but I could hold you." Jacques awkwardly added, "If you wanted."

Without fanfare, Hisoka said, "I accept."

"Really?"

"Unless Argent objects. And if he can spare Deece."

Jacques innocently added, "And Michael?"

Hisoka hesitated too long.

"Hasn't anyone ever called you on it before?" Jacques prodded the cat's bare shoulder. "He's obviously your favorite."

123

DUTY CALLS

Instead of wearying of his isolation, Jacques dreaded its end. Seven days at most, that's what Michael said. And that was today. "Nothing wrong with a little lie in."

"Mmm," agreed the dragon lord in his arms.

Jacques couldn't sense Betweener magic, but waking up was an ordinary thing. Everyone did it, even Amaranthine. Still, Jacques hadn't noticed.

"Unhappy to see me?"

"Only to see you go."

"Ah. I must, you know."

"Duty calls," Jacques mournfully acknowledged.

"Silly boy." Lapis smiled. "I may not sleep as often as you do, but I need rest with similar regularity."

"You'd … come back?"

124

A GOOD NIGHT.S REST

If welcome. How long was I deep?"

Jacques held up seven fingers.

Sapphire eyes widened. "Did I really? You must be a good influence."

"Is a week overlong?"

"Usually, I catch three-day naps between appointments." With a sleepy smile, Lapis asked, "May I depend on you in the future?"

"I've never been dependable before."

"Me, neither. Not to look at me."

"Hisoka speaks highly of you. His dragon."

"*That* title belongs to another." Lapis sat and stretched. "It is Argent's great fortune to have you here."

"He'd argue the point."

"Nonsense," countered Lapis. "He speaks highly of you. His man."

125
UNMISSED

Jacques returned to his room, bathed, and dressed with care. It was back to buttling, even though he was still a trifle hazy on the job description. The halls seemed overlarge after his confinement. And unusually empty. Where was everyone?

Wandering from one room to the next, Jacques found no one to greet him. No one waiting on him. After the glow of being useful and wanted, it was a blow to realize how appallingly little he contributed to the running of Stately House.

A sudden clatter of hooves startled him, and he turned to meet a one-boy crosser stampede.

126
WORST OF THE WORST

Nonny collided and hid his face against Jacques' hip. It took a few moments to realize that the kid was swearing at him. In tears.

Jacques picked Nonny up. "*Mon dieu*. What's happened?"

"You *left*!"

"Not really."

"Everyone thought you were gone!"

"You missed me?"

Nonny punched his arm. "I hate you."

"Hey, Nonny, nonny. Forgive me ...?" Jacques coaxed. "I was a thoughtless beast not to take my leave properly."

"The worst. The worst of the worst."

"Is anyone else angry?"

"Everyone!" Nonny assured.

Lacking corroborating evidence, he asked, "Where *is* everyone?"

"Garden. There's a party for the real kids."

127
HOMECOMING

Real kids? Are you not real?"

"Not born-here real," Nonny muttered sulkily.

"Who was born here?"

Michael's children, as it happened. Jacques had known baby Lilya had older siblings, at least in a vague, disinterested way. Names mentioned in passing. "I have met Isla."

"Yeah, her. She's nosy and bossy." Nonny wrinkled his nose and further reported, "Annika's just little, and Darya's grumpy and bossy."

"I appreciate the warning." Jacques carried Nonny through the side door that opened onto the full-bloom garden that was Ginkgo's domain. "All girls, then?"

"Nah. Timur's pretty good," admitted Nonny. "Oh. And Lady's brother came."

128
NECESSITIES OF LIFE

Lady! Lady! Lady!" called Nonny, waving his whole arm. "I found Uncle Jackie!"

Tsumiko hurried over, resplendent in a red-flowered kimono. *Much more suitable than the nonsense she'd worn while in Uppington.*

"You look happy, Lady Mettlebright."

She was usually so much more reserved, but something had her aglow in a way that made Jacques wistful. Ah, to be more than tolerated. Ah, to be unreservedly loved.

Her English was little better than his Japanese, but he rattled on. "Nonny tells me your brother is here."

"My brother," she confirmed. "Akira."

"You should introduce me! Everyone needs a favorite uncle."

129
BEACH BOYS

The purportedly grumpy Darya was a spirited teen with her mother's looks and her father's poise. She coaxed Nonny away with cupcakes, leaving Jacques to escort Tsumiko.

Ginkgo met them at the garden's edge and lifted Tsumiko. "I'm not letting you totter down the stairs in this getup," he said in English before switching to Japanese to scold.

The brother had apparently abandoned the party in favor of the beach, where sun-speckled waves were crashing with enough enthusiasm to fill the air with shimmering droplets.

Pegging Akira was easy because the other boy wasn't Asian. Or human, for that matter.

130
GOING NATIVE

Jacques considered the two teens who sat far enough into the shallows that every wave washed around them. The tropically bronzed Amaranthine stole an arm around Akira's waist.

The boy turned, and his eyes went wide.

Jacques supposed he did look rather well in his new suit.

Bounding to his feet, Akira asked his sister something.

"Lord. You've gone native," exclaimed Jacques.

Following his gaze, Akira glanced down at himself. Unflustered, he reeled off something in cheerful Japanese.

Ginkgo chuckled. "Seems he left the packing to Suuzu. That's his friend's notion of a bathing suit. Ever heard of a fundoshi?"

131

SKINSHIP

Tsumiko was serene, so Jacques gathered that there was nothing scandalous about the baring of buttocks.

Ginkgo went on paraphrasing. "Sounds like Timur—he's twelve—went to ask Sansa for cloth. He also plans to—as you say—go native."

"Akira." Tsumiko beckoned her brother closer. "Jacques Smythe. Uncle Jackie."

It was the barest of introductions, in more ways than one. But Jacques offered his hand, and Akira jubilantly seized it.

"You're invited to swim," relayed Ginkgo.

"He expects me to strip down?"

"Yeah, pretty sure he does."

"Not without copious amounts of sunscreen."

Ginkgo said, "That can be arranged."

132

MEETING THE FAMILY

Will *you* be joining us?" Jacques challenged.

"Also arrangeable." Ginkgo's smile widened. "I'll bring stuff. Can you get along without a translator?"

Suuzu lifted a hand. "I am fluent."

"Then you're set."

Only after Ginkgo darted away did Jacques realize that he'd been cornered into accepting a buttocks-baring loincloth.

"Ojisan?" Akira stood with head cocked, eyes bright.

"He asks if you are his uncle," translated Suuzu, whose hands settled on Akira's shoulders, clearly anxious to maintain his monopoly.

"Yes. I am his sister's son's mother's husband's cousin." And because it only seemed polite, he asked, "May I touch your boy?"

133
PENT UP

I am Suuzu Farroost. Akira is my classmate."

Jacques tried to do the thing Argent always did with his eyebrow. It must have worked a little.

Suuzu's gaze dropped. "Touch is unavoidable. Akira can be … demonstrative."

"Ojisan!" The kid suddenly threw his arms around Jacques in a fierce hug.

"Quite."

Words flowed in Japanese, with Tsumiko sounding both pleased and pleading.

"Akira does not remember his father or mother," translated Suuzu. "They are orphans, and their closest relationship is apparently with a lawyer. She warns that you will undoubtedly be subjected to a lifetime of her brother's pent-up filial devotion."

134
ROYAL RECEPTION

Akira chattered at Suuzu, whose expression softened. Tsumiko laughed and kept correcting her brother's pronunciation. Or something.

At a loss over the language as a whole, let alone nuances, Jacques could only look to Suuzu for help.

"He says you look like a prince," said Suuzu. "Akira is calling you Oji—*Prince*—rather than uncle. A play on words. His intention is not mockery, but affection."

"Prince Jackie, is it?" Jacques smiled crookedly. "Sorry to disappoint. I'm nobody important."

"Not so. You are important to Akira." Suuzu extended a clawed hand and softly inquired, "May I also call you *uncle*?"

135

MAMA.S BOY

Awhoop from above alerted Jacques to Ginkgo's return. He appeared to be racing Minx. Or rather, the boy clinging to the panther's back.

Jacques gasped at Minx's clifftop leap.

The boy shouted with laughter.

Tumbling off Minx, he jogged across the sand, waving a length of teal cloth, exuding grit and gumption. He squared off before Akira, talking fast.

Pivoting, he offered Jacques his hand. "I'm Timur!"

Nearly as tall as Jacques, the lone boy in Michael's brood was all windblown curls, thick lashes, and summer tan, carrying himself with a confidence Jacques recognized.

This boy was already a warrior.

136

DO MY COLORS

Ginkgo cheerfully presented Jacques with lengths of cloth in several colors. "Pick your poison."

"What about you?"

"Clan colors for me." Ginkgo turned, revealing a wad of blue mostly crammed into his back pocket. "What? You worried we'll clash?"

"I have standards," Jacques grumbled, selecting a subtly patterned green.

"Know how to tie it?"

"Haven't the vaguest."

"Figured as much." Ginkgo offered his palms. "Comfortable with me doing the trussing?"

He was. But he had *other* issues. Rolling his eyes toward a point along the beach, Jacques muttered, "I would rather not disrobe in front of Lord and Lady Mettlebright."

137
VIRTUOUS WOMAN

Dad'll bring Mom home first. Modesty is one of her virtues."

"A moment, please," Jacques begged and hurried to Tsumiko. "Your brother is charming. A good boy."

She brightened and asked something.

Argent translated, "What do you think of Suuzu?"

"Seems a good sort."

But Argent didn't translate, even though Tsumiko looked between them.

Jacques asked, "What am I meant to say?"

Argent's gaze drifted to Akira's friend. "Watch them. Watch over them. I want your opinion."

"As a butler? As an uncle?" Another possibility made Jacques uneasy. Tsumiko was religious. "Is she worried Suuzu will ... be a bad influence?"

138
MORAL SUPPORT

Argent startled Jacques by taking his hand. "Quite the opposite."

He spoke to Tsumiko, who took his other hand. Which didn't answer everything, but her gentle smile was reassuring.

"Watch them. Watch over them," repeated Argent. "You and I can discuss the matter later, since you are no longer at Mossberne's beck and call."

"If I survive *this*." Jacques tried to hide the fundoshi behind his back.

Argent smirked but only asked, "Do you require anything else?"

"Like a proper bathing costume?"

Argent blandly suggested, "I could send Deece."

"Oh!" Jacques held up four fingers. "Would you be so good?"

139
ACCEPTING APPLICATIONS

The moment Argent carried off Tsumiko, Timur tore off clothes like it was a race.

"Want me to hold up a towel?" offered Ginkgo.

"*Non.*" Jacques removed his coat. "I'd rather have your hands on me."

Ginkgo snorted. "Don't get your hopes up."

"The sea is cold, and there are children present. That *should* have a quelling effect."

"Pretend I'm some fancy-schmancy tailor."

"Lord. I wish." Should Jacques ever meet a tailor half so handsome, he'd probably be in love. "All the best tailors are wizened things."

"Dad's been looking for one, you know." Ginkgo's brows waggled. "A fancy-schmancy tailor."

140
FRATERNITY

A tailor?" Jacques perked up in more ways than one.

Ginkgo was kind enough not to remark. "It was on your list of demands. Not sure why Dad's so determined to fulfill them all. Try to relax."

Jacques stared determinedly into the sky and slowed his breathing to match the rolling waves.

Sighing, Ginkgo muttered, "Unclench."

This wasn't so different from feline grooming. This was fellowship. This was fraternity.

There was more twisting, some tucking, and a light slap that only made matters worse.

"Arse." But Jacques didn't really mean it.

Ginkgo grinned and hollered, "Hey, Suuzu, come help me?"

141
THE RESERVED TYPE

H ey, think you can work around my tail?”

"Certainly." Suuzu took the length of blue cloth. "Will my touch offend?"

"Nah, we're good," Ginkgo said in reasonable tones. "You're practically family."

Jacques was almost sure this declaration flustered the teen. It was hard to tell, though. Suuzu was the reserved type. So earnest, it was kind of cute.

While Ginkgo shimmied out of his jeans and shorts, Jacques thought it prudent to avert his eyes. So he was the first to notice Deece on the stairs, escorting the four "items" Jacques had requested from Argent—Nonny, Gilen, Mori, and Raife.

142
PISH TOSH

T hey descended *en masse*, lively in the manner of children who've had too much cake. Except for Mori. Eyes on Suuzu, the boy hid behind Deece.

"What's wrong?"

"It may be instinct," suggested Deece. "Suuzu is a bird of prey."

Jacques studied Mori. "And you're prey?"

The boy wibbled. "Mouse clan."

"Pish tosh." Jacques couldn't help smiling. "Mori, me boyo, you don't have a predator complex. You're just shy."

"How do you know?"

"Because you're part mouse, and he's all cat."

Mori looked up at Deece and actually giggled. It was nice to see some sparkle in his too-old eyes.

143
TO BE ASKED

Gilen bounded toward the driftwood pile, footloose and fancy-free and shouting in French, but Nonny's hooves gave him trouble. He wallowed in the sand until Timur lent him an arm, leading him closer to the water, where he'd find firmer footing.

Raife of the unfortunate hair seemed wary about the dress code. Smart lad.

Jacques indicated the pile of fundoshi and urged, "Pick a color!"

While Ginkgo and Suuzu helped the boys change for swimming, Jacques turned to Deece. For once, Stately House's bodyguard spoke first.

"Argent said you asked for them." Deece was practically purring with approval. "Thank you."

144
FRIENDS STAY

Jacques tried not to overthink how happy he was seeing Deece again. The feline wasn't his type but had good qualities. Easy on the eyes. Willing to share his bed. Fluent in English.

"Did you miss me?" Jacques asked sweetly.

Deece's chin tucked. It was almost a nod. "I kept busy."

"But did you *miss* me?"

"You had Uncle."

"*Oui*, but he comes and goes. We stay."

Deece managed a meek smile, almost like he didn't believe Jacques. Unacceptable.

Jacques wouldn't let Deece imagine himself deposed. He understood cats better now. "Come. Friends help friends apply copious amounts of sunscreen."

145
IF I WERE AMARANTHINE...

Touch was a reassuring part of feline culture. Jacques decided it might also be an important part of Jacques culture. "Would I make a good cat?"

"No." There was a smile in Deece's voice. "You are too disobedient."

Jacques sniffed. "What do you think, Gilen?"

"*Paon?*"

Amused, Jacques translated. "A peacock?"

"You *do* preen," muttered Nonny.

"A mink?" suggested Timur.

"Butterflies are pretty," said Mori.

Jacques smirked. "You think I'm pretty?"

Nonny blobbed lotion on Jacques' nose. "*You* think you're pretty."

"Miss a spot, and he will burn," warned Deece.

Thus, the joint application of copious amounts of sunscreen continued.

146
CARRIED AWAY

Jacques couldn't fathom the workings of boyish affection that resulted in his being bodily flung into the sea. He was feeling rather Jonah-ish. But before giving *much* thought to lurking whales, strong arms caught and carried him to the surface.

Shaking dripping curls from his eyes, Jacques drawled, "Shouldn't a cat dislike the water?"

"I do not usually go swimming," Deece admitted.

"You okay?" asked Ginkgo, treading water nearby. "You stayed under long enough to worry them."

The boys hovered along the shoreline, barely knee-deep and nervous.

Jacques offered a jaunty salute and murmured, "We may have a problem, gentlemen."

147
EXTRACURRICULAR

W e cannot possibly continue like this."

Ginkgo snorted. "Is this about the fundoshi?"

Jacques sighed. "Can *any* of them swim?"

Ginkgo paused, swore, and sloshed ashore. "Form ranks!"

"He means line up," Timur said helpfully.

By the time Deece let Jacques down, Ginkgo was ready to lay the blame—or credit—at his feet. "Uncle Jackie wants to add extracurricular lessons to your summer schedule!"

"Whassat?" hissed Nonny.

"School clubs," offered Suuzu. "Usually of a recreational nature."

Nonny stamped a hoof. "Whassat?"

Timur grinned. "Lessons *for fun.*"

Raising his hand, Ginkgo asked, "Who wants to join Uncle Jackie's swimming club?"

148
INCENTIVIZED

G inkgo immediately inducted the lot of them. "Michael wards our beach against sea monsters and sharks, but everyone who lives at Stately House needs to be a strong swimmer."

"What if we don't *want* lessons?" challenged Nonny.

"You'll miss out on all the best games if you don't," returned Ginkgo.

There was a muddle of questions and translation, with Timur and Suuzu proving their multilingual prowess. Jacques kept Gilen in the loop, but he couldn't say what games Ginkgo meant.

With a sly smile, Ginkgo suggested, "Akira, show us the one you were telling me about earlier?"

Tsumiko's brother grinned.

149

PLAYFUL PARTNERSHIP

A large bird burst on the scene, seemingly out of nowhere. Jacques started forward when the thing grasped Akira in its talons and made to carry him off.

Deece held him back. "He is safe. This is their game."

"*Mon dieu.*" Jacques crowded closer to Deece's bulk, no better than Mori, who was all but wrapped around the feline's other leg.

The bird—with plumage straight out of legend—circled lazily, a slow-motion glide. Then warbling a melodious warning, dropped Akira, who whooped and did a cannon ball.

Jacques tugged Deece's arm. "What *is* that?"

"Suuzu. He is a phoenix."

150

LONGEST FLIGHT

As sunset neared, Michael and Sansa came down to the beach. Roughing hair.

Cupping cheeks.

Wrapping towels.

Listening ears.

Each gathered up a weary boy. Ginkgo and Suuzu, too. Carrying the blissfully limp crossers up the long flight of stairs home.

Jacques whispered, "Did they have homes before?"

"Probably," said Deece. "Probably not like this."

He chuckled at the sight of Timur manfully piggybacking Akira. Good lads, both of them.

Suddenly, Deece scooped him up.

"Here, now! *Non, non, non*! I'll manage."

"Let me."

Jacques wrinkled his nose, which felt burnt. "Why should I?"

Deece mumbled, "Because ... I missed you."

151

MORNING MEANDER

Jacques stole a croissant from the rack where absurdly excellent pastries always seemed to be waiting and carried his coffee into the garden.

He strolled toward a row of festive banners rippling on a line above the cliff wall. Jacques was really rather proud of the shameless display. His own green fundoshi hung among the rest. Lifting his coffee cup, he toasted the freshly-painted sign—FUNDOSHI SWIM CLUB.

A flicker of lighter green caught his eye, and he startled badly. How had he missed someone perched on the wall, not four feet away? Salvaging his dignity, he murmured, "Good morning."

152

UNINVITED

With a graceful wave, the stranger said, "These are not the droids you are looking for."

Jacques blinked. "*Pardonnez-moi?*"

"Ignore me."

But this Amaranthine was difficult to ignore. Youngish, slender, and pale, with long hair in hues that were louder than life—spring green, chartreuse, and the soft yellow of primroses.

Jacques sipped his coffee, then asked, "Are you allowed to be here?"

"*Nobody* gets into Stately House without an invitation."

"I did." Jacques wondered if that meant something. Foxes were frustratingly subtle. "Who are you, then?"

Gemlike green eyes narrowed, and the stranger swore. "Who warded you against dragons?"

153
FELINE FORESIGHT

What? Oh, right." Jacques touched his forehead. Apparently, whatever magic Hisoka had traced there was still in force, despite Jacques' rigorous skin care regimen. "You're a dragon, then?"

The stranger rolled his eyes.

A dragon.

Lord.

Jacques reminded himself that *nobody*—save himself—got into Stately House without an invitation. And this fellow's eyes weren't anything like the deadly vintage Argent had warned against. Absinthe, perhaps. Or an obnoxiously trendy cocktail.

"Lapis was sleep-talking, and I needed the loo," explained Jacques. "It was Hisoka."

"Yeah, yeah. I recognize his handiwork." Offering his palms, the stranger proudly declared, "I'm Twineshaft's dragon."

154
UNCONFINED TO QUARTERS

I'm not supposed to be seen."

Jacques wasn't impressed. "You're sitting in plain sight."

"*Hiding* in plain sight. It's surprisingly effective for someone like me. Say, what tipped you off?"

"Green." He gestured with his coffee cup. "Your hair."

"You like this color?"

"*Naturellement*. A sprightly green does good things for my complexion."

"That'll do it. I once got spotted because someone was a fan of the band on my T-shirt." The dragon's attention drifted. "I'm officially confined to quarters. *So* boring."

Jacques followed his gaze downward. Should he be worried that Hisoka's dragon was spying on Stately House's lord?

155

ARGENT. TSUMIKO. MICHAEL. SANSA

On the beach below, a picnic blanket and umbrella were arranged. Sansa and Isla paddled in the shallows, giving Annika and Mei a swimming lesson. How they'd pried Mei from Mori's side was a mystery. Tsumiko sat close enough to the water that waves swished around her and a skittish Tawny. Poor kitten.

But the girls weren't being left out. Nicely done.

"Those four," said the dragon. "Their alliance will outlast any storm."

"Allies? *Non*. That's too impersonal." Jacques eyed Michael and Argent, who'd traded babies. Proud papas, unabashedly doting. "They are this family's heart and soul and breath and strength."

156

DELICIOUS

Jacques turned his back on the scene of domestic harmony. "Are you going to tell me your name?"

"Sinder."

"And why are you lurking about?"

He cast a sulky glance at the house. "I'm just a tagalong, stranded here for the festival's duration."

"Festival?"

"Ever heard of Dichotomy Day?"

"*Non*."

"Amaranthine festival, twice a year, culminates during the solstices. Suuzu had his heart set on spending this one with Akira, and my partner's his own special brand of helicopter brother."

So he had a male pronoun kind of partner? But they were hiding it? "How delicious. You're a secret paramour?"

157

THE OLDER BROTHER

Sinder's eyes widened. "We're part of a team! The *team's* the secret! Juuyu's not … *mine*-mine."

Jacques tried to fathom his reaction. "But you want him to be?"

"What? NO! I'm … oh, hell."

"I *told* you to stay inside." The older brother.

While he scolded in accented undertones, Jacques cataloged cascading black curls, flame-colored eyes, and an exquisitely-tailored suit. Gorgeous.

Jacques stepped between them. "Sinder was correcting a minor misunderstanding. I thought you were lovers."

The brother blinked.

Sinder blushed. "Semantic difficulties. He has different uses for partners."

Jacques gestured demonstrably.

"*Business* partners," stated Juuyu.

"Of a covert nature," whispered Sinder.

158

LEFT HOLDING THE BABY

Jacques timed his arrival in the kitchen to coincide with the return of the beach party. They came squelching in, trailing damp towels and shedding sand. Mustering up a reasonable attempt at solicitude, Jacques politely murmured, "Welcome back, my lord."

Argent passed him Kyrie.

Not the honor he'd been hoping for. Jacques valiantly inquired, "Shall I help you dress?"

"Thank you, Smythe."

He was so surprised, he slipped out of character. "Was that … *yes*?"

With a twitch of his lips that may have been a smile, Argent took Tsumiko's arm. "The closet near our suite. I will meet you there."

159

DISCRETION

Do you approve of Sinder?"

"Not unreservedly." Argent chose a tunic. "Please consider every word he utters to be shared in confidence."

"Yes, my lord." Jacques relieved Argent of his unfortunate selection and assisted him into something silken and scrumptious.

"What is this?"

"Appropriate."

Argent sighed. "What was your opinion of Sinder?"

"Young. Beautiful. Repressed." Jacques tucked and smoothed. "Somewhat in awe of his partner. Moderately jealous of the younger brother. The type who can't resist hinting he has a secret."

"Jacques?"

"Yes, my lord?"

"Remind me to ask for your impressions more often. Better yet, assume I want them."

160

IDLE HANDS

One other thing, then," warned Jacques. "He is bored."

"You expect this to cause problems?"

"Boredom led directly to some of my *greatest* debacles," he assured. "Also, I suspect our guest secretly wants to be noticed."

Argent hummed. "Entertain him."

"*Moi*? How?"

"He is a dragon," Argent drawled, as if that made everything clear.

Ah, perhaps it did.

"Admire him. Accommodate his every whim." Based on his scanty experience with dragons, Jacques ventured, "Supply him with paperback romances?"

Argent turned before the mirror, a pained expression on his face. "Sinder is a very modern dragon. The wifi password should suffice."

161

ALL VERY HUSH.HUSH

Sinder scanned the slip of paper with Stately House's wifi password with far more interest than the tray Jacques had manfully hauled up three flights.

"Tea?"

"Sure." The dragon shoved the paper into his back pocket. "Nothing better to do."

Time to fish for information. "You're meant to be clever, *oui*?"

"Very."

"Then keep me from blundering." He poured and passed *petit fours*. "Who knows about you?"

"You. Argent. Juuyu." He shrugged. "Hisoka, of course."

Jacques frowned. "That's all?"

"Didn't I mention that my job's *covert* in nature?" With an eyeroll, he emulated Hisoka's usual inflection. "I'm sure I did."

162

EXPECTATIONS VARY

Jacques' list of enjoyable diversions that two could share was both short and inappropriate. A second opinion was required.

He found Suuzu and Akira first. They'd curled together on a sofa while Suuzu attempted to rearrange every wisp of Akira's hair.

"You two!" Jacques blurted. "What do you do for fun?"

Suuzu answered in English. "He is human. I am Amaranthine. Expectations vary."

"You then."

"I find *this* relaxing, so he permits it."

Scintillating. "Do you ever get restless?"

"I am avian, *monsieur*." Suuzu smiled faintly. "If I am caged for too long, all I want to do is fly."

163

PERMISSION TO ENGAGE

May I take Deece into our confidence with regards to Sinder's presence."

Argent's brows lifted. "What did you have in mind?"

Jacques innocently answered, "I don't have the stamina to satisfy Sinder's every need."

His lord huffed. "You do this on purpose."

"Every time."

Argent asked, "Why Deece?"

Honesty, then. "He's big and bulky and brave, and I really couldn't manage without him. I can't see in the dark."

"Very well."

Jacques breathed easier. "Make sure all the sneaks are abed."

"What are you going to do?"

"Only what *must* be done." Jacques smirked. "We're going to wear Sinder out."

164

CATCHING UP ON PAPERWORK

Jacques waited until full dark before knocking smartly.

"It's open." Sinder sat amidst scattered files, scanning something on his phone.

"What are you reading?"

"Reports."

"What for?" It was a lot of paperwork.

"So I'll know what they say." Sinder tempered his sass with a smile. "I do this every night."

"Sounds dull."

He shrugged. "It's my job. And after a few days of radio silence, I'm behind."

"Will it take long?" Jacques was nervous and excited about his plans. Maybe that carried through.

Tossing aside his phone, Sinder said, "Nah. What's up?"

Jacques crooked a finger. "Come and see."

165

DIPPING AND DANGLING

It was a wonderful thing to be correct, and a great trial to have it go unremarked. Jacques sighed.

"Hmm?" Deece, the amazing gravity-defying Amaranthine, was seated in midair above the slowly rolling sea, with Jacques perched on his lap, bare feet dangling. With each wave, cool water tickled his soles.

"I was right."

"About?"

Jacques pointed down. "Him."

In a sudden flash of inspiration, he'd realized that Sinder hadn't been watching Argent with great longing. That's what Jacques would have done under similar circumstances. No, this dragon's lure was the sea, and he cut through it like a blade.

166

SEA MONSTER

Sinder shifted and called, "Aren't you going to swim with me?"

"I haven't any swimwear."

"Neither do I."

"I see your point. Just a mo." Back on sand, Jacques stripped and stowed his clothes. "It's mad, swimming with sea monsters."

Deece held his hand.

Jacques ducked under and pushed wet curls out of his face. Sinder rose from the water, looking like a siren. Jacques felt like a drowned rodent by comparison. "Lord, you're pretty."

"And you're plucky." Sinder sloshed closer. "I heard you're afraid of dragons."

"Within reason."

"Let me help with that."

Embracing the madness, Jacques answered, "*Oui.*"

167
NEVER AGAIN

"Pompadour! Pompadour!" Jacques flailed in the water. "Pompadour!"

Hands caught and lifted, and he was back in Deece's lap—high, if not dry.

"What's wrong?" Sinder called, treading water below them. "Why are you shouting random words?"

"It's not *random*. It's my safe word."

After a lengthy pause, Sinder snickered. "Your safe word is *pompadour*?"

"I was experimenting." Jacques shuddered. "It was a brief phase!"

"I … do not understand," admitted Deece. Such an innocent.

Jacques patted his cheek and checked the texture of his hair. "Too fine. But it's just as well. I don't fancy you in a pompadour either."

168
YOUNG BUCKS

Jacques yelped, and Sinder surfaced. "Did I nick you?"

"I'm *ticklish* there?"

"Where?" He wriggled his fingers threateningly. "Show me."

"You utter brat!"

"That's rich, coming from you." Sinder indicated Deece. "*He's* the mature one. Though I'm not sure which of us has the years …?"

Deece murmured, "I reached my attainment."

"But *young*, I'll bet," said Sinder. "Like me."

"Young?" Jacques echoed. "*How* young, comparatively speaking."

"In human years? *You* have the advantage."

Him. Eldest. "Does seniority net me anything interesting?"

"You netted a dragon." Sinder's teeth flashed in a coy smile. "Come on, sempai. I'll give you a ride."

169
JUST THE TICKET

Jacques crept into the kitchen and hesitated. Why hadn't Deece followed?

"Smythe."

Right. *That* would be why. "Yes, my lord?"

"You are dripping."

"More than is polite. Yes."

"Why?"

"Following orders, my lord." He saluted, then dabbed at his nose. "Fancied some seawater. Just the ticket."

Argent huffed. "Deece!"

The cat entered.

"Throw him in the bath. Return him here. We need to talk."

Deece angled his head toward the door.

Argent huffed again. "Sinder!"

Stealing inside, the shivering dragon looked young and uncertain.

"Bathe with them. Return with them." In gentler tones, Argent added, "There will be hot drinks."

170
THE GOOD STUFF

Used to leisurely soaks, Jacques grumbled when Deece rousted him from the bath. Then again, he was poised to nod off in its embracing heat. And Argent wanted him.

Selecting a silk dressing gown, he offered Sinder a jar. "Moisturizer?" *Such* a necessity after sea bathing.

"Got any oil?"

"I should hope so." Delighted to have found another skin care aficionado, Jacques rummaged for the good stuff.

They wafted into the kitchen behind Deece, only to find it dark, hushed, and lacking in libations.

"Took you long enough."

They whirled.

Argent leaned against the wall beside double doors. "In here."

171
CURRENT AFFAIRS

Jacques didn't want to let on that he hadn't known about the conservatory, so he kept his eyes on the cup Argent set before him. It was a delectable concoction—creamy and steamy, with the slight burn of liquor.

Argent served seconds and thirds from a piping kettle, leaving Jacques increasingly drowsy while the others droned on—the disgusting deeds of dragons, the foolishness of Americans, the founding of a new school.

"Which reminds me. Smythe?"

Jacques stirred enough to answer. "My lord?"

"Hisoka plans to return. He says *you* invited him."

"*Oui.* He wants to take me to bed."

172
EXCEEDS EXPECTATIONS

Are you *actually* drunk?" Argent bent close and patted his cheek. "You say the most shocking things."

"*Non.* I surprise no one." Jacques smiled a trifle blearily. "Least of all you."

"You exceed expectations."

"You would be disappointed if I didn't." Jacques remembered to add, "My lord."

Argent turned to Deece. "Hisoka is *also* aware of Sinder's presence. *Do* try to prevent anyone *else* from noticing."

Jacques' attention strayed to Sinder, who kept wafting his hand over his head, as if shooing a mosquito. "Slippery little beasts. I'd heard you were a collector."

That's when something landed atop Jacques' head.

173
PERFECTLY HARMLESS

Deece was there in an instant. "Hold still? It is … tangled."

"Let me," said Sinder. "Wow. Tame much?"

Argent huffed. "This garden is filled with Ephemera."

"Bits and bobs of *what*, exactly?" Jacques asked.

Sinder asked, "Couldn't he be taught to see?"

"Smythe has no reaver bloodlines." Argent's gaze turned speculative. "Try, anyhow."

"Sure." Sinder turned to Jacques. "Skittish?"

Argent answered for him. "Not about small creatures. He used to go about rescuing them when he was a boy."

"It's a dune prism... a lizardy thing, okay? Perfectly harmless." Sinder held his gaze and coaxed, "Look closely. Try to see."

174
EYE TEST

Jacques shook his head.

"*Tsk.*" Argent took his hand and traced something onto his palm. "Can you see him now?"

"Who?"

"The Ephemera in Sinder's hands."

"*Non.*"

With a sweep, Argent banished the initial mark and traced another. "And now?"

Jacques was honestly more interested in having his hand held. "*Oui?*"

Argent huffed. "We *know* you can see me."

Chastened, Jacques checked Sinder's hand. "*Non.*"

Another sweep of skin across skin. Argent blandly inquired, "Are you even trying?"

Jacques was tempted to feign blindness, but any thought of ploys vanished when he glimpsed a fantastical lizard, seemingly armored in mother-of-pearl.

175

ENTRANCING

Jacques gaped at the six-winged creature rubbing its dainty snout against Sinder's knuckle and creaking like an orchestra of happy crickets.

Meanwhile, Argent explained, "Here—more than any other place—privacy is assured. Until I am able to make similar arrangements in a neutral location, we meet here."

"Prettiest outpost I've ever seen," said Sinder.

"This is *my* sanctuary." Without a trace of apology, he warned, "You cannot return unassisted."

Sinder said, "How foxy."

Argent's hand dropped onto Jacques' shoulder as he added, "You *may.*"

Jacques really needed to stop gaping.

No small feat in a world filled with wonders.

176

REHASH

Jacques would have followed Argent anywhere. All in the job description. Not that he needed the excuse. Still, he was barely coherent when Argent led him into his closet and indicated the chaise lounge.

"Sit. Tell me."

"Must we have every conversation twice?"

"Yes, we must."

"Why?" Jacques whined. "The most shocking thing that happened tonight was your pressing liquor on potentially underaged Amaranthine."

Argent wasn't dissuaded. "Did you learn anything interesting?"

"Skinny-dipping with sea monsters is best done *after* establishing a safe word."

"*Jackie.*" Argent reached for him, only to pull back his hand.

Jacques' good mood rocketed downward.

177
TRUST FOR TRUST

This again? Jacques stormed, "I *know* my place."

"Not well enough"

"You think I don't know who has your heart?" Jacques didn't begrudge Tsumiko her place. She was the light of Argent's life.

"You think I do not know who has yours?"

Jacques slouched disconsolately. "It's different now."

"It is."

"I *belong* to you, now."

"You do." Argent rested a hand atop Jacques' head. "You did well today."

"Too right."

"You will not misconstrue my touch?"

Jacques snorted. "Does Akira misconstrue Suuzu's?"

"Go to sleep, Jackie."

He disobeyed as best he could, the better to enjoy Argent mussing his hair.

178
ENVIABLE POSITION

Jacques had no idea why Tsumiko trusted him with her husband, let alone her child. In the same position, he would've been suspicious, jealous. Yet when he woke on the chaise lounge in Argent's closet, it was because Tsumiko was tucking him in. With Kyrie.

Argent sat on the floor, head propped on one hand. Jacques had his other trapped. When he tried to pull back, Argent held him.

"She does not misconstrue our bond."

Our bond.

"Learn your place, Smythe." With a soft look in Tsumiko's direction, Argent included her in his demand. "Trust us to return your devotion."

179
A DEUX

They left him alone with Kyrie, who didn't seem to mind Uncle Jackie's lack of experience in the child-rearing department. Peekaboo tournament. Schmaltzy ballads. Fashion advice. French conversation. It was a lovely lie-in, but needs must.

"Time to come out of the closet, little prince." Jacques was dizzy for want of coffee.

Michael caught him on the stairs. "Ah! You're just the man I need."

While there were circumstances under which those very words could be highly flattering, Jacques suspiciously eyed the corresponding baby propped on Michael's shoulder. "Are nappies involved?"

"If only." Michael pointed upward. "There's a security breach."

180
UNDERSTATEMENT

Several wards have vanished in the vicinity of the third floor." Michael's smile turned apologetic. "While I try not to notice *every* little thing, I have a certain affinity for sigilcraft."

"Understatement."

"So I couldn't help but notice that Argent's new coral array is tuned to accept you."

Jacques cautiously admitted, "There is a guest."

"And there is a boy. My son Timur has a certain knack for wards. And for trouble."

"Understatement?"

"Afraid so." Michael told tales all the way upstairs. Reavers certainly had strange priorities. His boy was a perfect terror, and the man couldn't have been prouder.

181
SIGIL AND STONE

The upstairs hallway was quiet. "You sure your boy's here?"

"May I?" Michael offered his hand.

Feeling unaccountably shy, Jacques let him take hold and wished—not for the first time—that he'd had a man like Michael for a father.

The hallway bloomed into dozens of gleaming patterns that wheeled sleepily. Except where they were broken.

"Why does this work? I'm no reaver."

"You have powerful sigils on your forehead and your palm. Using the stone in my ring, I... well, I'm improvising."

"Will it last?"

"Sensei's sigil is already degrading. Would you be open to something more permanent?"

182
FRIENDLY PERSUASION

In the guest suite, Timur sat on the floor with Sinder, who asked, "What'll you be when you grow up?"

"Big."

"What else?"

"Strong."

Juuyu murmured, "They have been at it for half an hour."

Michael looked impressed. Jacques couldn't imagine why.

"Will you train to be a chef?" asked Sinder.

"Nope. A battler!"

Sinder smirked. "How about a butler?"

"Battler!"

"Sure about that? I might change your mind."

Timur laughed. "You can try."

"Touch my nose."

The boy did.

"Touch your nose."

Same result, but slower.

"Next session, sign up for butler classes."

Timur grinned impudently at Sinder. "Battler!"

183
ASKING THE WRONG QUESTIONS

Jacques found Juuyu difficult to read ... until those strikingly orange eyes settled on Lilya. Brows lifting slightly, he held out his hands in a silent offer.

Michael beamed as if he'd done something supremely clever and passed along his daughter.

"Are all Amaranthine foolish about babies?" blurted Jacques.

Juuyu calmly countered, "Is love foolish?"

Which ripped at Jacques, because he'd often played the fool. But they weren't talking about affairs of the heart. Letting his chin fall to his chest, he watched Kyrie reaching for Lilya. Jacques changed his question. "Are all Amaranthine wise about love?"

"Does love require wisdom?"

184
ASKING THE WRONG PERSON

While Michael put on a dad face and escorted Timur from the room, Sinder nodded at his partner. "You're wasting your time, Jacques. He always resorts to cryptic questions when he doesn't have any answers."

Juuyu frowned. "Can any one Amaranthine answer for all Amaranthine?"

"See what I mean?"

Jacques thought he did. "You've never been in love?"

Ignoring his partner's dig, Juuyu moved closer so that Lilya's reaching hand could meet Kyrie's. "Must one be in love to recognize it?"

"*Non.*" Jacques almost felt sorry for the guy. "Usually, the one in love is the last to recognize it."

185
IMPERFECT ALLIANCE

Your turn." Jacques lowered Kyrie onto Sinder's lap. "He should know dragons come in more colors."

"Hey!" grumped Sinder.

Juuyu was instantly at his side. "I can take him."

Sinder eyed him warily. "I don't need rescuing. Neither does the kid."

"Kyrie," reminded Jacques, who was enjoying the unintended drama.

"You do not like children," said Juuyu.

Pointedly snubbing his buddy, Sinder explained, "I'm no good with kids. Wrong temperament. We're shockingly selfish, dragons."

Juuyu warbled an unhappy cadence.

Jacques waved a finger between them. "How long have you been partners?"

Sinder grimaced. "Not long."

Juuyu corrected. "Not long enough."

186
DING DONG

Lord.

Jacques already hated Dichotomy Day. Gritting his teeth, he tumbled off the cot he'd set up in the front hall. Clutching his dressing gown shut, he swung the door wide. "Which one?"

The herald blinked. "Sir?"

"Which of the superlative children in Michael Ward's budding dynasty is *that* addressed to?" Jacques squinted in the predawn light. "*Mon Dieu.* Three at once? *Someone's* optimistic."

With a soft laugh and an apologetic smile, the courier listed, "Darya, Timur, and … Lilya."

"I am refusing the last. Michael's orders." He couldn't hide his shudder. "A seething Sansa is not a safe Sansa."

187

CONVERSANT

B on jour!"

Delightful. His eight-year-old Japanese tutor.

In no mood to bash his head against a language barrier, Jacques demanded, "*Why* is this *such* a big deal?"

Isla clasped her hands and beamed. "I'm glad you asked!"

Sensing an oncoming lecture, Jacques opted to make it torturous for them both. "*Non*. In French."

Partway through, Jacques dragged Gilen into the discussion. Shortly thereafter, he flagged down Akira, since Suuzu had the good taste to be fluent. Music to his ears.

Then Isla ran off to find a board game, and Jacques helped Akira scrounge for snacks.

And it was … fun.

188

DRAGGED IN

O nce the festival ended, the sky darkened, and the sea churned, as if the weather held off for their sakes but was making up for lost time. Most of the household took shelter in the naproom, which Michael warded against the worst of the thunder.

Jacques liked a little crash and sizzle in his life, so he was loitering at the kitchen window when Ginkgo dragged in.

"All battened down. Guess we won't float away just yet." Pushing back his hood, Ginkgo flicked his ears and jerked a thumb. "Look who I found."

Hisoka Twineshaft stood dripping on the doormat.

189
SUPPORTIVE FRIEND

Jacques helped Hisoka out of his shoes.

Ginkgo reappeared with a blanket, his ears canted worriedly. "Pushing your limits, Sensei?"

"So it would seem."

"What do you need?" Ginkgo looked worried. "Dad? Deece?"

"That may be wise."

Hisoka wavered in place, and Jacques quickly lent a shoulder. Pivoting into him, the cat pressed his nose firmly against Jacques' neck.

"Lord. How long since you slept?"

Argent strode in, sighed, and scolded.

Deece summarily scooped and bundled his uncle away.

Knowing he could still hear, Jacques called after them in French. "They know what you need. I know what you want."

190
URGENT CARE

Hand in hand, Jacques led the way past barriers that didn't apply to him.

"Sensei asked for me?" Michael seemed surprised.

"Not specifically. Doesn't matter. You're the one he wants."

"Isn't he here to see *you*? That's what Argent said. Well, *implied*."

"I'll watch over Hisoka if he wants, but I can't do that thing. Tending."

His step faltered. "How do you know he needs tending?"

"Flagging focus. Ominous pallor. Reprehensible posture."

Michael took the remaining stairs two at a time, blowing past barriers that no longer applied to him.

Following at a more sensible pace, Jacques sighed. "You're welcome."

191

HOSPITALITY

Leaning against the door frame, Jacques basked in the satisfaction of a job well done.

Hisoka was a mess. They'd stolen his clothes and roughed up his hair. He sagged against Deece and clung to Michael's hand. How often were the people who cared about Hisoka allowed to care for him?

Argent murmured, "Wise choice."

"*Naturellement.*"

Hisoka crooked his fingers.

Argent snorted. "You are summoned."

"Lord. At *least* offer the bloke a dressing gown." Jacques crawled across the mattress. "He takes his tea with milk. And I hid the chocolate biscuits under that tuffet."

Hisoka chuckled. And began to purr.

PART TWO

Autumn of 3 N.S., mere weeks away from the opening of New Saga High School in Keishi, Japan, shortly before the events of second book in the Amaranthine Saga, *Kimiko and the Accidental Proposal*.

192

GOLDEN BOYS

This way?" Jacques had Ever Starmark by the hand. Or vice versa, since the boy was in the lead.

"Yeth."

Harmonious Starmark was currently showing off his new school to Argent, leaving Jacques at a monumental disadvantage. Three-year-old crossers were quick, curious, and elusive.

"Such a simple rule. *Stay with Uncle Jackie.*"

Ever leapt into his arms, a feat that might've impressed Jacques more if he hadn't been dealing with crossers for a few years now.

"Dun be mad, Unca Jacks. I wiff you!"

Lord, he was cute. "Help me find Kyrie before his dad finds me, and we're golden."

193

LITTLE TRACKER

New Saga High School wasn't ready for students, but neither was it a construction site. The only workers Jacques spotted in the building were gardeners tending to the veritable arboretum in the student center.

Ever's tail wagged higher. A promising sign that success was near.

"See him?" asked Jacques.

The boy's face scrunched up. "*Smell* him."

How very canine. Helpful, though. Jacques might be immune to most dragon wiles, but camouflage was another matter. "Where did you go?" he grumbled.

"Here," chirped a small voice just above.

Kyrie balanced upon a slender branch. Hidden in plain sight. And inexplicably naked.

194
A BOY OF FEW WORDS

A re you stuck?”
Kyrie shook his head and extended a flower—apology and explanation in one gesture.

Jacques beckoned, and the boy dropped trustingly into his arms.

“Aren’t you cold?”

Warbling, Kyrie nuzzled Jacques’ shoulder.

Wrapping the fullness of his new cloak—bless its velvet lining—around Kyrie’s body, Jacques asked, “Why are you capering about *au naturel*?”

The boy pointed.

“Use your words,” Jacques coaxed. “It’s safe with me.”

“Keep clean?” His voice was light and sweet, almost musical. Argent had coached him to speak sparingly.

Jacques beamed. “Would that your father were *half* so kind to his clothes.”

195
WARDROBE EMERGENCY

Y ou took these off so they wouldn’t get dirty?”
Kyrie mumbled, “I promised.”

“These *are* your good clothes, your father’s colors.” Jacques shook out the princely silks, admiring silver embroidery. “Keeping clean *is* important, but you must keep warm, young master.”

The boy cast a longing look at his friend, whose breeches were made for tree-climbing and games of chase. “I want to play with Ever.”

Swaying words.

Jacques heeded them, but only because he could sympathize. “*Naturellement*! A change is in order. Your brother *insisted* I pack jeans.”

Without a backward glance or second thought, Jacques carried them home.

196
THE MOST IMPORTANT THING

Jacques had been nagged, mocked, and scolded for everything from the length of his hair to his taste in shoes. That's why he was resolved that head to toe—or *hoof* in Nonny's case—he'd accept their crossers.

"Teach me, *s'il vous plait*." It had become one of his most-used phrases. "I need lessons in Kyrie."

"And Ever?"

"*Oui*. I need lessons in Ever, too."

Like most young crossers, Kyrie didn't have words for everything that was going on inside.

"One thing," Jacques urged. "Tell me one true thing."

Soft as a sigh, Kyrie answered, "Love you, Uncle Jackie."

197
SMALL DOSES

As usual, Ever took charge. "Dis way!"

The boys sprang ahead, racing each other.

"Manners!" Jacques sang out. "I'm only human."

It was sad, really, having to teach children differences they didn't see. But the inequity was there. Little crossers needed to learn their own strength so they could temper it.

Kyrie turned back, calling to Ever. "Wait for Uncle Jackie."

Swaying words.

Harmless ones.

Hoped for ones.

Argent and Harmonious weren't *only* putting their sons together because they were both crossers. Anna Starmark understood more than most what was at stake.

Kyrie was Ever's inoculation against a dragon's sway.

198
HUNTING PARTY

In retrospect, Jacques supposed he should have notified someone he was leaving.

The Starmark compound was adjacent to New Saga's campus, a pleasant walk through a private wood. But he'd parted two precious boys from two protective fathers.

Hardly wise.

Still, Jacques rather enjoyed stirring up the kind of trouble that left him surrounded by strapping males. Especially ones as handsome as Harmonious Starmark's kin.

Merit loomed.

Laud glared.

"Dear me," Jacques drawled. "Is anything the matter?"

Prospect covered a smile.

Eloquence didn't.

Valor rolled his eyes and winked.

Harmonious shouldered through and announced, "For the record, *I* wasn't worried."

199
LITTLE BOY BLUES

Later, Harmonious cleared his throat. "Before Hisoka lays claim to you, I have a question."

"Concerning...?

"Fashion."

Jacques took a step back and gave the spokesperson a considering look. "Ohhh?"

Harmonious grinned. "Not me. Ever wants those ... denim trousers."

"Jeans are practical, durable." More to the point, "And Kyrie wears them whenever they play together."

"*Breeches* are practical. And durable."

"You disapprove?"

"Jeans aren't very … doggish." Harmonious glanced apologetically in Argent's direction.

"You'll need a pair." Jacques knew the way packs worked. "That way you'll match your son."

"Me?"

"Stature needn't be prohibitive. Our tailor is excellent. Avian, you know."

200

UNDISCLOSED LOCATION

He has a house?" Jacques couldn't recall Hisoka ever mentioning a home, although Isla lived with him.

Argent hummed an affirmative. "He does not publicize the location of his residence."

"It's secret?"

"It is undisclosed." With a flick of a hand, he indicated a park. "Twineshaft is making a vast concession for you."

Jacques glanced around uneasily. "We can't just walk up. What if you've been followed?"

"Hoping to deflect the paparazzi?"

"Neither of you deserve the hassle."

Tails fanned in Jacques' periphery, and Argent offered a hand, its palm glittering with sigilcraft. "From here, our location is also undisclosed."

201
CLAN COLORS

A bamboo-lined path appeared, marked by stone lanterns. Jacques spied the telltale shine of crystals. "Barriers?"

"Old ones. This has always been his home."

"Both Harmonious and Hisoka are from Keishi?"

"Twineshaft is indigenous. Starmark is a fairly recent transplant."

Argent ushered him into a sprawling building that buzzed with activity. Office workers were everywhere, most in Dimityblest colors. But the predominant color scheme confused Jacques.

"Greens and creams?"

"Twineshaft's clan colors."

"Then why is he always draped in gray?"

"I have often wondered that myself." Argent frowned. "For feline clans, the color of ash is the color of mourning."

202
FOR A GOOD CAUSE

Isla lives here?"

"She has a room," replied Argent. "And adjoining library."

"I assumed they were a little more ... alone together," Jacques admitted.

"Twineshaft has always been careful with females." Argent touched a stone before steering Jacques through an archway. "There are three floors of staff between them. I would wager Isla has never seen his private quarters."

"But you have."

Argent nodded. "So shall you. Are you clear on the timeline?"

"Quite."

"I appreciate your sacrifice."

Jacques was missing Christmas at Stately House. "Pish tosh. I'm your gift to Hisoka."

"Make sure he sleeps."

"Long and deep."

"Good man."

203
CHARMED, I.M SURE

ow many barriers *are* there?"

"The last three were more for sentiment than security." Argent's tone gentled noticeably. "From Michael's student days."

"Michael was apprenticed to Hisoka."

"Officially." Argent lowered his voice. "Michael was mine, first. Unofficially."

"Did Hisoka notice?"

Argent hesitated. "Perhaps. Yes."

Green carpet gave way to gray stone in a room dominated by a fireplace. An Amaranthine awaited, elbow artistically propped against an ornate mantlepiece. "Argent," he greeted. "And this must be the inimitable Jacques? Charmed."

His tailored suit had Paris written all over it. His coiffure was mahogany. Orange eyes showed over lavender-tinted glasses.

"Canarian Evernhold."

204
READINESS

ncle isn't here, yet, but I'll ... ah." Canarian trailed off when he realized Argent had vanished. "Does he do that often?"

"Leave me in the hands of another gentleman? Not often enough." Jacques was getting good at deflection. In his own way. "How would you like me?"

Canarian's face registered surprise. Then a *soupcon* of interest.

"So ... Evernhold?" inquired Jacques. They touched palms. "I know a Deece Evernhold."

"My baby brother."

There *was* a resemblance. "Deece had a sexy older brother? Happy Christmas to me!"

Laughing and looping an arm around his waist, Canarian said, "Cat is going to *love* you."

205
LIMITED ACCESS

Canarian opened a room dominated by another fireplace, this one deep and well-banked. "Of all the hearths within Uncle's home, this is perhaps the truest. Few see it."

Jacques understood the compliment and adjusted his posture accordingly. "When's Hisoka due?"

"He'll be here as soon as *this* is where he's needed most."

"*Magnifique.*" Touching the valise at his side, Jacques said, "I'll create the necessity, and he shall appear."

Canarian's brows arched. "Will he, now?"

"Never fails." Jacques crossed to the bed and began unpacking paperbacks, chocolates, and a biscuit tin. "Is there hot water?"

"For tea?"

"*Non.* A bath."

206
PRIVY

You want a bath?" asked Canarian.

"*He* will want one."

Beckoning with the flick of fingers, Canarian entered a spacious bathing chamber. "I was surprised to learn that he's been... ah...."

"...sleeping with me?" Jacques slyly finished.

"*Exactement.*"

He supposed this person had the right to ask. "We have things in common. We get along."

Canarian waited, clearly expecting something more.

"I don't want anything from him, and I have nothing to offer. Hisoka needs to *not* be needed by someone." As the tub filled with hot water, Jacques perched on its edge, legs crossed. "And I like to cuddle."

207
WITH INTENT

Jacques had just closed the tap when Canarian murmured, "I'm impressed."

"By?"

"You were right. Uncle's back."

"*Naturellement*. It would be entirely rude to let bathwater go cold."

"*That's* the necessity you created?"

Jacques decided not to correct him.

Hisoka propped a shoulder against the doorframe. "Worried about his intentions?"

"He shouldn't be. I haven't any." Jacques snapped his fingers. "Strip or be stripped."

Wearily, Hisoka dragged off his tunic.

"Are *you* staying?" Jacques inquired sweetly.

Canarian's smile turned mischievous. "Do you have intentions for me?"

"*Oui*. I want you here in case he falls asleep in the bath. Again."

208
THE ART OF MASSAGE

Grooming with felines was delicious. Cats craved touch. Went limp and clingy and pliant in ways that were entirely flattering. Still, Jacques remained *blasé*, even while supporting a draped and groaning Hisoka.

"Deece does this for him, too," he remarked.

Canarian continued kneading. "He's barely conscious."

"When will you learn?" Jacques chided.

Hisoka only sighed.

"You're attracted to males?" Canarian suddenly asked.

"Yes."

"But not my uncle."

Jacques thought that should've been obvious by now. "I told you. I'm quite frivolous."

"You're *friends*, aren't you?"

"He doesn't confide in me. We don't keep in touch."

"Perhaps … pactmates?"

"Nothing so formal."

209

ALL ADMIRATION

Who devised this?"

"My lord is cleverer than I'll ever be." Which wasn't an answer, but it was true. Telling the truth was important with Amaranthine.

"On your feet, Uncle. Something tells me that falling asleep in the bath would be *entirely rude.*"

Hisoka swayed like a drunk and toppled into bed. Jacques scolded in French until the exhausted cat sprawled across his chest. Ruffling pewter hair as it dried, Jacques encouraged purring.

"I was wrong earlier," said Canarian. "Or half right."

"Oh?"

"Cat's going to love you. And I will, too."

"For your uncle's sake?"

"For your dressing gown."

210

CHRISTMAS MORNING

Jacques was used to the lock-down that accompanied long sleep. Hisoka was utterly vulnerable. Forced to trust someone. Usually someone strong. Jacques hardly qualified.

Cheap romances.

Quality chocolates.

Tea and biscuits by the tin.

Holding and being held.

Idly turning a page, Jacques rolled his eyes and tossed aside the tawdry book in favor of stroking pewter hair. With Amaranthine, little loving touches were both welcomed and understood.

Affection could be lavish.

Love could remain chaste.

But that didn't stop a sudden spike of *want* when a darkly handsome stranger strolled through the door, arms filled with gaily wrapped parcels.

211

GIFTS COME IN MANY FORMS

Jacques hugged Hisoka protectively as the stranger deposited his parcels.

"You, my fine monsieur, are on the gift list of an *elite* set—Mossberne, Starmark, Mettlebright."

His accent was Latin, as were his looks, and his smile was sultry.

Canarian arrived, wheeling a tray of covered dishes. "May I present Catalan Evernhold?"

Cat. Jacques relaxed into a smile. "I've been assured of your love more than once."

"Consider me smitten." He slunk nearer. "I'm another of Deece's sexy older brothers, yes …?"

"Don't tease the man," chided Canarian.

Cat's green-eyed gaze never wavered. "It's only teasing if what's offered is withheld."

212

SPILL THE TEA

Cat helped Jacques from the bed, guiding him to a chair while his brother ensured Hisoka was comfortable. Confusion set in when Canarian rejoined them, pausing to nuzzle Cat's hair. Who in turn, lifted his face to accept a kiss.

Catching Jacques' look, Canarian explained, "He's been away for weeks."

"You're … brothers?" Jacques imagined Boniface. Egads. Impossible.

"Not precisely."

Over breakfast, Jacques lapped up gossip about feline matriarchies and the convoluted bonds shared by their consorts.

So decadent. So *naughty*.

Clearly, Jacques had been living with outliers.

"Well, sir?" Canarian inquired casually. "Will you help me settle Cat for sleep?"

213
GOOD COMPANY

Hello, handsome."

Hisoka stopped mid-yawn to peruse Jacques' scent.

"It's wee hours, the thirty-first," Jacques reported. "Want a biscuit? I saved some."

"Many thanks." Hisoka's eyes drifted shut. "Did my nephews make a pet of you?"

Jacques wasn't sure how to answer. "A bit. I didn't mind."

A hum. A smile. He reached across Jacques to caress Catalan's hair. "If you gain many more adherents, you will spend all your days in bed."

"Hardly a chore when the company's good."

Hisoka opened an assessing eye. "Agreed."

Jacques whispered, "*Merci.*"

Rising to kiss Jacques' forehead, Hisoka ordered, "Show me your blaze."

214
EXPERIMENTATION

It wasn't a true blaze. Not in the Amaranthine sense.

Only a handful knew about Michael's experimental sigilcraft. After several *suggestive* suggestions, Jacques let Argent choose an appropriate place for the tattoo.

"You're the only one who does it this way."

Hisoka nuzzled past the hair at Jacques' nape. "Oh?"

Jacques' heartbeat quickened.

"Argent uses foxfire, or so they tell me."

"And Lapis?"

"Wh-whispers to it in Old Amaranthine." *They* were always terribly polite. "And Michael sets crystals."

"Ready?" warned Hisoka.

He never was, yet never minded. Perhaps he was a masochist?

Fangs pressed to the back of Jacques' neck.

215
TASTE FEAR

This side of Hisoka was terrifying, yet Jacques let it happen. Not because he was developing a new kink. Far from it.

Growls subsided into purring, and Jacques squirmed when the licking began. "Lord, you're a tease."

"Hardly. Saliva is one of just a few bodily fluids utilized by the clans …."

No wonder they called him *Sensei*. Jacques hoped the droning lecture would calm his trembling heart.

"Jacques, are you afraid of me?"

"You can taste fear, can't you?"

Hisoka hummed. "Why do you persist?"

"Why else?" Jacques flopped onto his back and peered around. "Your way works best."

216
EVER THE TEACHER

Describe any changes," urged Hisoka.

Jacques shuddered and wondered if he was going into shock … or subspace. "I don't like danger, you know. Not into pain. Not my scene."

Hisoka looked worried.

"Is there an ideal outcome here?" Jacques didn't want to disappoint any of them. "What are you even trying to do?"

"Teach your soul to take what it needs."

Almost a straight answer. Hisoka *was* worried.

"I can't imagine I'm very cooperative," he joked.

"Rarely."

Jacques stared at the hole in the ceiling, where starlight danced.

"Do not give up." Hisoka quietly added, "I have reason to hope."

217
GETTING IN

Describe any changes," Hisoka repeated. "Have I harmed you?"

"Never better. Let me enjoy the view while it lasts."

"Ah. Ephemera?"

Jacques pointed. "Argent keeps those. Are yours tame?"

"I had not realized they were getting in."

"Beneath notice. Or above, in their case." Jacques felt sorry for them.

"You have a fondness for midivar?"

"They're part of my training. The more I handle them, the more I notice them on my own."

"How do you feel?"

"Detached." Jacques frowned. "Relocated? And still alone."

Hisoka hummed. "Do *you* have an ideal outcome, Jacques?"

"Can you turn me into a reaver?"

218
CHEAT

Hisoka said, "That's really a very dangerous question."

"Does it have an answer?"

Tucking the blankets around Jacques, Hisoka calmly covered old ground. "Reavers are a naturally occurring phenomenon. Their existence cannot be replicated by transfusion or by transplant. Even artificial insemination is counterproductive."

Jacques knew this. And he knew better. "There are cheats."

"Are there?"

"There are rumors."

"Largely baseless." Hisoka's face had gone stiff and stubborn.

Euphoria made it hard to think straight, but easier to imagine. Jacques patted Hisoka's cheek. "What happened the last time someone asked?"

"They did not like the answer."

"And ...?"

"Many lives ended."

219
NOBLESSE OBLIGE

Mon *dieu*. Don't look like that. I retract the question with all apologies." Jacques murmured, "It wasn't even for me."

"No? Most humans want our years."

"It's not your *years* I want." He grudgingly admitted, "I'm not sure *what* I want. Except perhaps to win an award for Best Uncle."

Hisoka blinked.

He blinked again.

Propping himself up on an elbow, Hisoka searched Jacques' face. "Are you saying you submit to these many *inconveniences* for the sake of another?"

"When you put it that way, it almost sounds noble." Jacques rolled his eyes. "*Do* keep the focus where it belongs."

220
LOOK AT ME

And that focus would be ...? Ah." Hisoka lapsed into a genuine smile. "You?"

"*Oui.*"

"And what do *you* gain?"

"You have to ask? I *adore* being the center of attention."

"I had noticed." Hisoka's smile took on smirkish leanings. "You are evading the question."

"What can I say? You're an excellent example."

"You are too kind." A purr made itself felt. "Are you putting yourself through all of this for Akira?"

"*Non.*" Jacques turned his head. "My reasons are entirely selfish."

"And what do you hope to gain?"

"Relief."

Hisoka blinked. "From ...?"

"Have you ever watched Suuzu watch Akira?"

221
OVERBOOKED

anarian said to let him know when you wake.”

"He knows.” Hisoka paused partway through a languid stretch and murmured, “Ah. Right. Isla.”

Jacques knew that Amaranthine could communicate wordlessly with their kin. All well and good if your nephew doubled as your personal assistant. But imagine dear Bon-Bon’s reaction if he were privy to his brother’s every thought.

"Would you do me a favor?” asked Hisoka.

He perked up. "You need me?”

"I do.” With traces of chagrin that Jacques doubted many saw, Hisoka explained, "Tomorrow is Isla’s first day of school. Would you escort her to New Saga?”

222
TAKING A TURN

acques declined the offer of a cab, citing the desire for a walk after a week in bed. He knew his way around Keishi and could call on the Starmarks if he needed assistance.

Strolling through a shopping district reminded him that New Years was rather a big deal in Japan. Unfortunately, the sky was looking far from festive.

"It’s going to rain today.”

People were staring.

With a genteel smile, he remarked, "You’d think a city overrun by dogs would be used to tallish men.”

Jacques basked in the attention.

Until the brooding sky spattered upon his good mood.

223
DOWNPOUR

Fat, frigid drops sent pedestrians scurrying. As umbrellas popped like toadstools around Jacques, he found cover under a scanty awning along the front of a tiny shop that sold novelties and sweets.

He would have preferred a cozy café.

Jacques knew from past experience that even a seemingly insignificant alley could lead to a whole array of tiny restaurants, but without Argent's nose to guide him, he'd be aimlessly floundering. And probably catch his death.

As the rain took to pounding, Jacques swore. "Where's a Starmark when you need one?"

Suddenly, a wolf loomed over him, close enough to kiss.

224
LOVELY

English?" inquired the wolf, whose accent was entirely British.

"Half." Jacques went for unflappable. "Good day to you."

"Lovely weather we're having." A smile lurked behind the Amaranthine's civility.

"Quite."

"Are you lost?" His eyes were a whisky sort of pretty, and raindrops clung to his lashes.

"What happens if I am?" Jacques asked hopefully.

An innocent blink.

Ah, well. Jacques was used to wolves, who were into moon maidens and monogamy.

But this one's posture shifted subtly into something assertive, even possessive. "Then ... I have you. You're safe. Where were you going?"

Jacques struck a receptive pose. "With you."

225
BE SO BOLD

I f I may be so bold, you're rather important to someone." The wolf sniffed lightly.

Jacques angled his head invitingly.

"Oh! May I?"

"By all means." Which would have come off more *come hither* if Jacques' teeth hadn't chattered.

The wolf crooned and gathered him close.

Jacques shamelessly slid cold hands under a fur vest, pressing into hot skin.

"You're adorned in so many pretty sigils, I was *already* curious. I'm glad you called me over." The wolf nuzzled and huffed. "My! *Twineshaft*?"

"I didn't call you over."

"You did." He cupped Jacques' cheek. "My grandsire's Harmonious Starmark. I'm Sonnet."

226
VIVE LA DIFFERENCE

J acques trailed a finger over a long stretch of exposed skin any dog would consider a fashion *faux pas*. "But you're a wolf."

"Thank you for noticing. Not everybody does."

As far as Jacques knew, wolves became dogs, not the other way around. "Were you fostered by the Starmark clan?"

"Born to. That's why I don't have a wolvish name."

Jacques couldn't have been more delighted by this new twist. "You *identify* as a wolf."

Sonnet's posture grew more confident, and yet the tip of his tail tucked. "My father doesn't entirely approve of my choices."

"Lord. I can relate."

227
SKYBELLOW

Sonnet sniffed and asked, "You're connected to my grandsire?"

"*Acquainted.* I'm closer to Mark. Well, *I* call him Mark." Jacques had to think. "Valor."

"My uncle."

Jacques reached up to touch a gray streak in the wolf's brown hair. "You're the first sable Starmark I've met."

"It's Skybellow. My sire left the packs to bond with a daughter of Starmark."

"Did he really?" Jacques drawled, "I wonder what *his* sire thought of his choices."

Sonnet actually tittered.

Jacques sneezed and muttered, "Nobody mentioned it was going to rain today."

Tutting, Sonnet offered, "My kindred run a tearoom nearby. Shall we?"

228
BACK DOOR

Jacques was thoroughly wet by the time Sonnet hustled him through an obscure gate and onto someone's back porch. "Cousin?" Sonnet called through an open screen. "May I beg a favor?"

Bare feet made no sound upon tatami mats.

Built and bronzed, this male had silver eyes and black hair arranged in a topknot. The flowered kimono hung open, suggesting wolf.

"Paltry!" Sonnet kissed the cousin's cheek. "Help me warm this human?"

Jacques was past pride. "Have mercy on this poor wretch."

Palms met. Nostrils twitched. Brows arched. Paltry remarked, "It's raining cats and wolves today."

In English.

Bless him.

229
WARM THE HUMAN

I'll bring towels. Strip him." Paltry whisked away, but his voice carried. "Churlish! I need the foot bath."

"Your cousin, you say?"

"Same tree, different branch." Sonnet was already at work on Jacques' fastenings.

Paltry returned and helped steal the rest of his clothes, all the while explaining, "My sire was brother to this whelp's great-grandsire, Glint Starmark."

"Are you a wolf?"

"More or less." He had an easy smile. "Mostly less."

Canine toweling was vastly less gentle than what could be had in a feline grooming session, but Jacques found the experience … invigorating.

Paltry huffed. "I'll bring clothes. Churlish!"

230
LACKING NOTHING

What sort of name is *Paltry*?"

The more-or-less wolf returned in time to answer for himself. "My mother bequeathed a proper one, but I go by Paltry. It suits me."

Jacques couldn't see how. Paltry wasn't lacking in size or generosity.

Silk settled against Jacques' skin, and he sighed with pleasure. Belatedly, he recalled that he hadn't parted with his own name. "I'm Jacques Smythe, currently of Stately House."

"Valor confirms it," murmured Sonnet. "And calls him Devotion."

Jacques hadn't heard his pack name in a while. "Checking up on me?"

Suddenly, the door slapped open, and someone singular entered.

231
CHURLISH

Jacques had seen his fair share of unique people. Horns, hooves, stripes, scales—he found such novelties charming. But Churlish was luminous.

Literally.

Paltry swooped in to take the steaming basin from another silver-eyed Amaranthine, this one wearing pale gray hakama, an oversized white hoodie, and a fetching pout.

"Go on," urged Paltry. "Greet our guests."

"*Your* guests."

Porcelain skin. Straight white hair, bobbed. An iced confection with delicate features. But it was the bedhead and bad attitude that Jacques warmed to. "You *actually* call him Churlish?"

Paltry grinned. "An endearment, I assure you."

Sonnet helpfully supplied, "His name's Cherish."

232
TEA AND SYMPATHY

Churlish muttered, "Welcome to Moonglade Tearoom."

And walked out.

"He's shy of newcomers," Paltry said apologetically. "Especially those who come through the back door."

Jacques asked, "Why?"

"You saw his true face. Front door customers see something else. Though I'm not sure our little tricks would have altered *your* perception. Argent wants you to see clearly."

"I'm immune?" Since becoming Argent's confidante, Jacques had willingly become a sigilcraft test subject. "You may rely on my discretion."

In the tearoom, they turned heads. Jacques didn't mind that. But when Sonnet poured, his manner grew disturbingly familiar. "Lord. Are you mothering me?"

233
IN ESSENCE

Old habit." Sonnet fiddled with his teacup. "Are you an orphan? I have some experience raising orphans."

"I'm afraid it's far too late to bring me up properly." Jacques sipped. "I have a stalwart father and a silly mother and a priggish brother who is the pinnacle of perfection in our maman's eyes. But they're not my family. Not anymore."

Sonnet's shoulders squared. "I understand exactly."

"Tell me about your orphans."

What a story.

Jacques was utterly diverted. "So in essence … you're a clan-fluid, crossdressing virgin mother. And you cook."

Sonnet tittered. "Oh, go on."

"I might be in love."

234
ONCE A MOTHER

Sonnet blinked. "You don't mean that."

"I don't mean it in the way you need it meant," Jacques admitted. "But I love you in my way."

His gaze dropped to his tea, but his tail swayed. "You're too kind."

Jacques really wasn't. Well, hardly ever. "You miss it. Mothering, I mean."

Sonnet hummed. "I came back for a whelping feast. Clarion took to me right off."

"But…?"

"Mum thinks fatherhood would suit me."

"Driving you into the streets on a frigidly awful day, where you happened upon a butler in need of mothering?"

Sonnet really did have the sweetest smile.

235

COME TO THE POINT

Argent considered Jacques a good judge of people, and Jacques liked to think that Argent was entirely correct. Unless neckties were involved. Then Jacques' opinion was really the only one that mattered.

So he placed an immediate call. "Michael? Be a dear and put Argent on."

While he waited, Jacques enjoyed a hint of drama—Paltry breezing about the tearoom while Churlish's silver-soft gaze followed him.

"Miss me?" Sonnet couldn't overhear Argent's end of the exchange. Security measure.

"You could stand to show a *little* enthusiasm."

"Yes, I *am* coming to a point."

"Lord. Fine. May I hire a wolf?"

236

MUST LOVE ORPHANS

That's rather a long story."

Jacques glanced down. "No, I'm not currently in possession of my pants."

"Look here! He's really more of a *she*."

"Claims to cook. Definitely a good mother. Orphan specialist."

"Yes, right here."

He handed off the phone.

"Sonnet Cook, sir, lately of Merritt House."

"No, I'm not currently in possession of his pants. I hung them up to dry."

"Quite. Nearly caught his death."

He blushed. "Nothing of the sort."

"Yes. I raised two. How many...? Oh? Oh, my."

"Very good, sir."

Sonnet slowly lowered the phone.

Jacques asked, "Well?"

He whispered, "I love you."

237
CERTAIN

Paltry poured from silver pots into china teacups, and Jacques basked in the familiarity. He and Sonnet lingered over Western-style cakes and pastries—Churlish's specialty, according to Paltry—until Valor arrived with Ever in tow.

The boy slammed into Sonnet's leg. "I knows you!"

"Yes, love. You certainly do." Sonnet's tail swung high.

Jacques held out an arm to Valor and coyly asked, "Where's *my* greeting?"

Valor snorted.

"Don' be sad, Jacks!" Ever suddenly swarmed onto his lap and kissed his chin. "I knows you, too."

With a burgeoning sense of camaraderie, Jacques echoed Sonnet. "Yes, love. You certainly do."

238
WAY BACK WHEN

With a promise to meet on the morrow, Jacques—now in possession of his pants—left with Valor, but they didn't get far.

"Listen up, Ever. This is important. Mum *loves* these."

He pointed into a shop next door called The House of the Noble Chrysanthemum.

"Mum?" Ever sniffed at the air.

"Lady Starmark likes traditional Japanese sweets?" Jacques admitted, "I'm surprised."

"They're a sentimental favorite," explained Valor. "This shop's been around for a very long time, and Mum used to frequent it."

Jacques filed away that tidbit, then asked, "What say you, Ever? Will you treat your lady mother?"

239

COORDINATED EFFORT

While Valor and Ever secured an entire tray of pillowy white mochi, Jacques texted Isla.

What time should I pick you up?

> **Can you manage 7am?**

Lord, no

> **I'll pick *you* up**
>
> **Safest**

You know me so well
I'm in Starmark territory

> **Perfect**
> **So is New Saga**

Do I need to do anything?

> **You may stand about,**
> **looking important**

What color is your uniform?

> **Green. Why?**

Coordination
What variety of green?

> **Diplomatic**

That is *not* a shade of green

> **It IS**
> **reaver palette**

He consulted a search engine and sighed.

I shall endeavor not to clash

> **Love you, Uncle Jackie**

240
GRUMPY GOAT

J acques next texted Ginkgo. Predictably, Nonny answered with a glaring selfie. Jacques wasn't sure if the goat-crosser had been designated Ginkgo's secretary or if he'd simply picked the fox's pocket.

You missed Christmas!!!

I'm sure you managed without me

Idiot
I mean YOU missed Christmas
You *like* parties
Argent's a scrooge
for making you work

Jacques couldn't think of a single glib thing to say. So he told the truth.

Christmas is too depressing
I ran away

Are you stupid?

Yes

Get home
You have a gift and everything

Moi?
Hey, Nonny, nonny?

Wut

Is it from you?

Yes
Arse

241

DO TELL

Uncle Jackie!"

Jacques uncurled one hand from his coffee cup long enough to offer a limp wave. "*Bonne année.*"

"Happy New Year, to you!" Isla returned, all smiles. "You're looking well."

"I promised to make an effort."

And it had taken one.

An amused Rampant Starmark had loaned him two daughters and bid him take whatever he needed from their stores.

Finding a length of painted silk including *just* the right shade of green had taken hours. Plenty of time to coax Lyric and Lavish into telling tales about the best-loved big brother who'd recently returned for little Clarion's whelping feast.

242

SMILE PRETTY

At New Saga's entrance, a welcome sign framed in tissue paper carnations awaited those wanting commemorative photographs.

"Shall we?" Jacques suggested.

Isla agreed, and he tried to find an angle that would show his ensemble to best advantage.

Valor Starmark sauntered up. "Want me to take the photo?"

"Would you?" Isla exclaimed. "Thanks, ever so!"

He chucked her chin with all the fondness of family. "You'll surely be a tribute to your Sensei's school."

It was *exactly* the right sort of compliment to offer. Isla's smile was never brighter than when inspired by Hisoka.

Jacques captured it with a tap.

243
PRIDE AND JOY

While Valor stepped back to frame the photo, Jacques fixed the angle of Isla's beret. "Are you disappointed? That none of your family could come?"

Rolling her eyes, Isla said, "You underestimate your importance, Uncle Jackie."

He searched her face, afraid that her smile was the brave sort.

Isla asked, "How can you care so much … and not realize *why*?"

Valor called, "Look this way!"

Jacques had never wanted a girl, let alone to hold hands with one. Yet here he was, hoping the shutter-snap would catch more than his good looks. Because Isla was *his*. And he was proud.

244
SKIPPING FORMS

This is a high school."

Jacques countered, "Isla may have skipped a few forms, but this is where she belongs."

"If you'd simply check," urged Isla. "You'll see …!"

"That name isn't here."

Isla angled her head, pursed her lips. "That's the first-year roster. I'm a third-year."

She was holding her own, but the administrator's incredulity only increased.

"Isla Ward," Jacques repeated, smile tight. "Third year."

"Are you meant to be her father?

"I have neither the years nor the pedigree," Jacques cordially assured.

"Because *journalists* aren't permitted inside."

"Do check the *correct* list," begged Isla. "Or I shall be late!"

245

DEATH KNELL

Someone will be with you shortly."

They were shut into a small waiting area, where Isla fidgeted upon the edge of her chair. When bells chimed the start of school, Isla looked as if it were a death knell.

Jacques' impatient simmer rolled into full boil.

While it wasn't his style, he thought he could refashion himself for Isla's sake. Taking her hand, which was far too cold, he said. "I know you don't want to make trouble for Himself, but Argent won't mind. I'll have this fixed in a trice."

"How?"

Jacques pouted forlornly. "Try not to be embarrassed."

246

PRIMA DONNA

Patting Isla's shoulder Jacques said, "My inheritance is far less auspicious than the ones you received, but it might just do."

"What do you intend to do?"

"My mother is a prima donna, my father's a prig, and my brother's a prat." With a wry smile, he said, "I'm going to go out there and get my way. For you."

Isla stood.

Jacques waved her back. "Leave this to me."

"I want to see." She reasoned, "It may be instructional for a diplomat in training."

"Perhaps you're right." With an entirely human shift in posture, Jacques murmured, "Watch and learn."

247

SUPERIORITY COMPLEX

We are done waiting," Jacques announced. It was a very royal *we*. "Find Isla's classroom assignment."

"Ridiculous. You're no reaver."

"I'm *not* a lot of things. You should be more concerned with what I am." A superior smile. A subtle aggression.

"You're a journalist."

"Having trouble with them, are you?"

"Repeatedly."

"I do sympathize. The paparazzi have beastly manners." A pitying sneer. A patronizing tone. "Her classroom? I'd rather avoid further unpleasantries."

The administrator paled. "Are you threatening the school?"

"Lord, you *are* an alarmist." An exasperated insult. A casual order. "Call security, then. I'm curious to meet Sentinel, anyhow."

248

EQUIPPED

Jacques *could* have verbally dismantled the administrator, but to what end? These days, his authority had nothing to do with the lords in his ancestry ... and everything to do with the lord he served. Jacques cast aside weapons gone rusty with disuse in favor of fresher inheritances.

From Michael, an unwavering optimism.

From Hisoka, a priority for peace.

From Argent, the longest of long views.

This kerfuffle wouldn't be a waste of time if Isla learned something. So Jacques opened the nearest window and casually propped his hip against the sill. "I say! Where's a Skybellow when you need one?"

249
HEAD OF SECURITY

What are you …?" muttered the baffled administrator, whose gaze snapped to a point outside the window.

Jacques turned in time to see Sentinel Skybellow step lightly onto the sill. Crouching until they were eye-to-eye, the dog clansman radiated dominance.

"Aren't *you* accommodating?" Jacques pivoted to present his palms while shamelessly matching Sentinel's dominant stance. With a slow smile, he murmured, "And how comely! Sonnet has your eyes."

"Aren't you Smythe?" Sentinel's gaze flicked to the others in the room. "What has happened?"

"A small misunderstanding, barely a trifle, easily cleared up." Jacques practically purred, "If you'd be so good?"

250
SORTED

Sentinel stepped into the office, and Isla offered her palms. "Sensei placed me here for the year. I'm in your care."

"Very generous of Twineshaft," Sentinel gruffly replied. "Shouldn't you be in class, Miss Ward?"

There was a shuffle of papers, and the administrator weakly announced, "Isla Ward, Class 3-C."

Jacques pulled Isla into a hug and spoke against her hair. "You are brilliant. You belong here. Never doubt that."

"Nope, *nein, nyet,*" she promised, kissing his cheek.

"Off with you."

She raced away without a backward glance.

Probably for the best, since Sentinel chose that moment to reassert dominance.

251
LET US AWAY

Sentinel loomed magnificently, and there was a shivery hint of growl underlying his low question. "Are *you* the one my son is running away with?"

He knew!

That simplified matters.

"Absconding with Sonnet happens to be next on my agenda." Jacques indicated the window. "Shall we?"

The big fellow's brows knit adorably.

Jacques couldn't fault Rampant's taste.

"You can see us off." Jacques cozied up but coyly warned, "Don't snag the cashmere."

Sentinel huffed, scooped, leapt.

Jacques pointed the way, as if he were in charge, and Sentinel grimly followed his lead, as if he didn't know where Sonnet waited.

252
CARRYING OFF

Sentinel's long, smooth strides carried them far. Sonnet's dad seemed a responsible sort, if a bit ... distracted. Normally, Amaranthine didn't tote around their human acquaintances.

A stutter-step called Jacques' attention upward.

Sentinel's widened eyes held the beginnings of worry. "Why is my son in a dress?"

"I rather think it's part of the whole mothering aesthetic." Jacques had no trouble singling out the tall woman who'd stepped straight out of a historical drama. "Carries it off handily, too."

Sentinel did that adorably-confused thing again.

Jacques patted his arm and murmured, "Steady on. There's a brave lad. I'll hold your hand."

253

MANHANDLING

Sonnet started toward them with little mincing steps that quickly lengthened into a businesslike bustle. "Is something the matter with Jacques?" Leaning close and touching his face, Sonnet asked, "Are you hurt?"

"Not a bit. Is there an Amaranthine equivalent for the term *manhandling*? If so, I quite enjoy it."

"Da?" Sonnet whispered, clearly still concerned.

Eyes wide, Sentinel mumbled, "I forgot myself."

Sonnet frowned. "How did you come to be together?"

Sentinel grumbled, "I could ask the same of you."

Jacques rested his head against Sentinel's shoulder, luxuriating in their mutual concern. So alike, these two. Where it mattered.

254

TWO SIDES

They took the quickest route to Stately House, which wasn't entirely legal and did criminal things to Jacques' hair.

Ginkgo waved from the limb of a sprawling tree.

Nonny planted his hooves, sniffed, and scowled. "How come he looks like a lady, but smells like a wolf?"

From under Sonnet's hem, a tail flashed. "Why, *thank you*."

The kid blinked. "British?"

"Lovely! We have something in common."

Nonny warily asked, "Are you a girl or a boy?"

Ginkgo dropped to the ground and rapped Nonny's head. "Don't be rude. A crosser should understand better than anyone about betwixts and betweens."

255

CONSISTENTLY INCONSISTENT

Nonny lost his combative posture and went to Jacques. "You can be both a boy and a girl?"

"Personally? *Non.*"

The kid snorted. "Don't be stupid. I *know* about *you.* What about this one?"

Ginkgo warned, "Nonny's not the only one who'll be asking. How would you like to be introduced?"

"I'm Sonnet."

"Mister Sonnet?" asked Nonny. "Miss Sonnet?"

"Just … Sonnet."

Jacques hugged Nonny to his side. "I believe they're after your preferred pronouns."

Sonnet's tail swayed. "*She* when I'm wearing shoes. *He* when I'm barefoot."

"That's dead easy." Nonny beamed up at Jacques. "She'll be in *our* swim club!"

256

REPRISE

Nonny ran ahead, eager to spread the word.

With a soft oath, Ginkgo started after him. "Sorry! Better introductions later, I swear."

The wolf raised a hand in silent farewell.

"Untuck your tail." Jacques offered his elbow. "Ginkgo's as good as his word, and you'll have your pick of welcomes. Drinking party. Grooming session. Midnight cookies."

Sonnet walked with him, sedate and silent.

Stately House soon came into view, and Jacques felt Sonnet tremble. "Excited?" he asked.

"Oh. Well …?"

For the second time that day, Jacques spoke a simple truth. "You are brilliant, and you belong here. Never doubt that."

257

SKIP THE JITTERS

Argent bowed them through the door, though his usual elegance was somewhat diminished by the little boy wrapped around his leg.

"I'm home," Jacques sang out. "Did you miss me?"

Brows arched.

"Not *you*, my lord." Dropping to one knee, Jacques crooked a finger. "Come to Uncle Jackie."

An upward peek for permission.

A soft huff to grant it.

Kyrie scuttled into Jacques' arms. "Help me welcome Sonnet? She's feeling a little shy."

A snuggle for Jacques.

A wave for Sonnet.

Argent prompted, "Can you say her name?"

Kyrie reached out. "Sonnet."

"Oh, love," she crooned, jitters banished. "I'm home."

258

FOUR PARENTS

Still ignoring Argent, Jacques asked, "Where's Lilya?"

"With Mum."

"Is it naptime?"

"Yes." Kyrie leaned up to whisper in Jacques' ear. "I am not sleepy."

Argent mildly suggested, "Shall we show Sonnet the way to the naproom?"

The boy solemnly said, "This way, please."

Argent sauntered after his son, leaving Jacques to escort Sonnet.

Jacques explained, "We all take turns overseeing sleep."

"And Kyrie's mum is there?"

"Ah. No. There are four parents at Stately House. *Sansa* is 'Mum.' She manages the kitchen." A thought occurred. "My lord, did you tell Sansa about this?"

Argent glanced over his shoulder. "No."

259
PUSH

Jacques was on the official naproom rotation, but he slept here more than he slept in his own bed. Willingly. Because Kyrie had changed his life almost as much as Argent had. Turns out, Jacques was good with babies.

Sansa was overseeing naptime.

Whenever she did, the children had two options—sleep or do pushups. Which is why four of the bigger boys—a crew that included Timur—were toiling away in silence.

Jacques flopped onto the cushioned floor before her. "I'm home."

Sansa grunted. "About time."

Jacques was flattered. "You missed me?"

"If you are not sleeping, you push."

260
FIT

Jacques was no battler, but keeping up with crossers definitely helped a fellow stay fit. He joined their workout, though at half the speed of Sansa and the boys.

"Your form is good," she said mildly.

"Speed isn't everything."

"What else do you have?"

Jacques winked. "Staying power."

She laughed and lowered herself to the floor. "Then you stay, yes?"

Jacques flopped gratefully and kicked up his heels. "I have done something impetuous."

"And you need backup?" Sansa's dark eyes glittered. "What shall I bring? Polearm? Crossbow? Whip?"

"Lord." Propping chin on hand, Jacques sighed. "It's good to be home."

261

A GOOD BALANCE

I brought someone," said Jacques.

"You think I did not notice?"

"Well, I *can* be quite the distraction."

Sansa pushed easily to her feet. "Who is this that you bring me? This beautiful wolf is your impulse?"

"One of my better ones." Jacques accepted Sansa's hand up. "Sonnet can be your support. She has experience in the kitchen."

The wolf presented palms.

Sansa took hold and pulled Sonnet close, peering into those wide, whiskey eyes. "You will spoil them, yes?"

"Only in the nicest ways," Sonnet promised.

"Is good balance, yes?" Sansa inquired of Argent.

He huffed.

It was settled.

262

HOME FOR THE HOLIDAY

When Jacques turned back, Timur had coaxed Kyrie into his arms.

At fifteen, the young battler had matched his mother's height, and his jawline showed evidence of an inexpert shave. With an easy smile, Timur offered a hand. "Been a while."

Jacques marveled over the teen's calluses, but his grip was gentle. "Shall I take him?"

Timur cradled Kyrie closer and coaxed, "Stay with me for a bit?"

The boy peeped at his father, who said, "Indulge Timur. I have need of your uncle. Come along, Smythe."

Jacques was only too happy to be needed. Until he found out why.

263
ENCROACHMENT

With a hand over his gaping mouth, Jacques surveyed the upheaval in Argent's closet. "*Mon dieu*," he finally managed. "You are a menace."

"I had help."

"It looks like you turned Doran loose in here."

Argent sighed. "Mother visited. She overruled your selections and chose my attire for the week."

"What …?" Both hands were now over his mouth. "Which things?" He waved vaguely at a crumpled pile.

Jacques vowed, "I am never leaving your side again."

"That is highly unlikely."

"Then … I'll not leave until I'm confident you can dress yourself. Appropriately."

Argent candidly pointed out, "This, too, is unlikely."

264
OUT OF BOUNDS

Jacques set to work, putting things to rights. The clothes were exquisite, of course. He wouldn't have abided them here otherwise. But appropriate to the occasion? "Ward this room against her," he grumbled.

"Already managed," Argent assured. "Shall I ask one of the sedge to assist you?"

"Let me do it." Jacques tutted over castoff silk. "This is *my* job."

"You may have help whether you want it or not." Argent stalked doorward.

Jacques expected Kyrie to tumble in, the little barrier-wrecker.

But when Argent swiftly opened the door, he startled a different boy. "Nonny, you are out of bounds."

265

RASCALS ALL

Nonny stood his ground. "I needta talk to Jacques."

"And *this* is as good a place as any for a private word?" Argent challenged.

"Good thinking. Thanks, guv."

"*Tsk.* Brat."

It was Jacques' private opinion—and Nonny's good fortune—that the lord of the manor had been a rascally boy. Because Argent gave in to the bratty and the brazen far more often than the sensible ladies of Stately House ever did.

"Perhaps if you make yourself useful." With a hand on the half-goat's shoulder, Argent guided him inside. "Dichotomy Day is an *excellent* time to embark upon an apprenticeship."

266

BEST HOOF FORWARD

Argent excused himself, and Jacques ventured, "Do you even *want* an inside job? I've always thought of you as the outdoorsy type."

Nonny glared. "Because goats are livestock?"

"Because you're always tearing around with Gilen."

"Because we're chasing Jarrah," Nonny countered. "We're in charge of him, you know."

"And *he's* the outdoorsy type."

"Duh."

Sighing, Jacques sank to the fainting couch. "Hey, Nonny, nonny. Here, Nonny, nonny."

"What?" The boy sounded grumpy, though his posture was pliant. Hoofs picked lightly across the floor, never once treading on a castoff garment.

"Teach me, *s'il vous plait*. I need lessons in Nonny."

267
QUIBBLE

Nonny shuffled closer but mumbled, "Stop treating me like a kid."

"Is that a joke?"

The boy responded with a string of profanity.

Jacques laughed and pulled him close, hoping to stem the tide. "Are you sure *butler* is your calling? You swear like a sailor."

Nonny leaned into Jacques' side. "How're *you* supposed to teach butlering?"

"I believe the proper term is *buttling*. To buttle."

"You're a prissy tosh, but you're no butler."

"So ... I'm useless?"

"Nah."

Jacques was curious to know. "What do *you* think my job is?"

Nonny's eyes sparkled. "The guv says you're my new mentor."

268
INSIDE JOB

Welcome to the closet." Jacques gestured to his domain. "I'm a valet, of sorts. Lord Mettlebright's wardrobe is mine to manage."

Nonny gazed around, clearly unimpressed.

Jacques asked, "Do you like clothes?"

"Me?" The boy's expression was one of frank disbelief.

"*Non?*"

Nonny plucked at his thin cotton tee, the only one he ever wore. "When they brought me here, it was the first time I wore them."

Jacques whispered, "Should I be furious?"

"Nah." He gestured vaguely. "I have hair."

"Is there anything you *do* like about clothes?"

Nonny smiled impishly. "Nobody ever tried to make me wear shoes."

269
AT THAT AGE

Do we know how old you are?"

Nonny shrugged. "I'm about Gilen's size. He's nine."

Jacques cautiously suggested, "You're probably older. Goat clan runs small.

"You calling me puny?"

"More like … mature. Argent clearly thinks you're ready for new responsibilities."

"You allowed to use his first name like that?"

"Only behind his back."

Nonny's grin was the conspiratorial sort.

Jacques pointed between them. "You really want to work with me?"

"*If* certain conditions are met," he replied loftily.

"Right, then. Let's hear them."

Nonny kicked up his hooves, then clacked them together. "How come you only invite Gilen for baths?"

270
ROOM FOR ONE MORE

Deece and I were helping Gilen adjust to his new home."

Nonny rolled his eyes. "He's *fine* now."

"Care to join?"

"Duh."

"I'll let Deece know to expect you. Michael is sometimes there, too."

"He's all right."

Jacques explained, "We stay over at Deece's if he's due for tending."

Nonny hummed in a suspiciously disinterested way.

"You … know about tending?"

The boy snorted. "There's another condition."

Subject changed.

Jacques said, "Tell me."

"I get to keep calling you *Jacques*. No dumb titles or stuff."

"Continue apace," he invited graciously. Though he'd not noticed before. Nonny never called him *Uncle Jackie.*

271
PRIVATE ENTRANCE

Jacques ended chaos and sent Nonny off, promising to find him before the evening's grooming session. Then he strode to the ornate doors at the hall's end and touched the glowing sigil beside it.

A section of wall vanished.

So foxy. Intruders could batter the false door for days, never realizing the real entrance to Argent's den was two steps away.

Argent called, "Tsumiko, your delinquent student has returned."

"Is there tea?" she asked.

"All is in readiness." Argent sat in a rocker, shirt open, a baby curled against his bared blaze. "Now that he is back, Smythe can pour."

272
BUNDLES

Be there in a minute," called Tsumiko distractedly. She was bent over a book that was nearly half her height. Probably on loan from one of the dragon lords.

Jacques moved to the tea service. Argent waved away his silent offer and asked, "Nonny?"

"Not the most natural fit, but willing. Who's this then?"

"As yet unnamed," said Argent. "Naroo-soh brought two bundles for Christmas."

"Baby drop boxes working, then?"

"Too well. Of the nine children abandoned to us, only two were crossers."

"Humans?"

"Entirely ordinary," drawled Argent. "Cast upon the benevolence of the Amaranthine people."

Jacques sipped thoughtfully. "Good."

273

SILVER LININGS

Your reasoning?" Argent's gaze held a challenge. "In Japanese, if you please."

Meaning his private language lessons had begun for the day. Jacques ordered his thoughts.

"Ordinary people believe in Amaranthine benevolence. So much so, they think you could offer their children a better life."

Argent hummed. "Trust, albeit a reckless trust."

Jacques hesitated over a Japanese term. "The Waning?"

Brow quirking, Argent filled in the blank.

"Wouldn't there be Amaranthine couples glad to foster a child, even if they were entirely ordinary?"

"Perhaps."

"And the boxes *worked*. She found her way here. She's home."

Argent's gaze softened. "Well said."

274

POLYGLOT IN THE MAKING

Tsumiko had been a schoolteacher before Aunt Eimi found her, and under her tutelage, Jacques' grasp of Japanese was flourishing. Incentives abounded, not the least of which was an awkward hope to be useful to Argent.

"You will learn Spanish next."

"*Moi?*" Pouting, Jacques asked, "Who would teach me?"

"Sonnet is fluent."

"Really?"

"All the Starmarks are." Argent stood, passing Jacques the baby. "She is also conversant in Welsh."

Jacques eased back blankets, finding a woolly tail. "Planning for Welsh diplomacy?"

"*Tsk.* Would you withhold from any child the comfort of hearing their mother's language?"

Which encapsulated Argent's priorities beautifully.

275
READ AND WRITE

Jacques was better at conversational Japanese, but Argent had the highest of expectations. So Jacques was still toiling over a kanji quiz when a light rap interrupted the tail end of lesson hour.

Apparently oblivious to the many barriers in place, Michael leaned through the door. "Apologies for interrupting, but we have something of an … *event* underway. One that threatens to delay dinner."

Argent had unfurled nearly half his flourish before another word could be said.

"Ah." Michael raised both hands. "I don't mean *threaten* in the sense of a *threat*."

Nose to the air, Argent growled, "What *is* that?"

276
LAST TO KNOW

Jacques had to jog to keep up with Argent and Michael. Hardly his forte, so he missed some of their exchange.

"…seclusion?" asked Argent, whose tails were puffed double.

"Ginkgo may have colluded," said Michael. "Even Sansa wasn't sure until this morning, when Minx sauntered in and … well. As you can see."

Jacques needed a moment to sort out what was happening. Minx had laid claim to the kitchen table. She'd squeezed under it. To give birth.

Michael dropped to one knee beside Sansa, who was crooning in Russian to her Kith partner.

Argent huffed, wheeled… and hid behind Jacques.

277
CARRY ON

Jacques was curious about the imminent birth—or *births*—but he knew his place. Taking Argent by the elbow, he announced to the room at large, "Keep calm and carry on! We'll make alternate arrangements for the evening meal."

In the garden, facing the sea wind, Argent muttered, "Birthings...."

"I gathered. So! How about we go see Randolla?"

"Is this really the right time to be visiting one's tailor?"

"You say that as if there's a wrong time for visiting one's tailor."

Argent snorted.

Jacques quietly pointed out what would normally have been obvious. "The sedge has its own kitchen."

278
BIRD SANCTUARY

The sedge had arrived the previous summer. In keeping with the adage, *one man's trash is another's treasure,* Randolla Demoiselle had taken a shine to a scruffy meadow a few kilometers from Stately House. His clan diverted a stream, planted marsh grasses, and built thatched houses that looked like haystacks on stilts.

Far less rustic was Randolla's workroom. Jacques practically skipped up stone steps, bowing Argent through a heavy door and into a heaven that rivaled the finest Paris shops.

"*Jacques*! And Argent...?" Randolla's fingers fluttered. "Dear, dear. What's he spoiled this time? *Please* say it's not the Glimsleek brocade!"

279
POSITIVE REINFORCEMENTS

While it's true Argent's finery survives on a wing and a prayer, today's disaster is culinary in nature."

Randolla chuckled through Jacques' description of Stately House's emergency.

He perked up at the prospect of fitting denim to Starmark thighs.

And he begged an introduction to Sonnet, who arrived in a demure swish of skirts to serve Argent a steadying cup of tea.

He asked, "Is it over?"

"Not just yet." Sonnet lightly asked, "Do either of you cook?"

Jacques glanced at Argent, who sighed and said, "I do. And Smythe can manage with direction."

Sonnet beamed. "Roll up your sleeves!"

280
WINTER PICNIC

Jacques decided that cooking wasn't his thing. Menial. Messy. But even though others offered to take his place, he stubbornly stayed at Argent's side.

Sonnet and the cranes fried fish from the icy creek. Argent wielded chopsticks with expertise, turning tempura. Pumpkin slices and apple rounds sizzled in oil.

"You're good at this," Jacques remarked.

"Experience."

"You had to cook for … your people?"

Argent favored him with a sidelong look. "Are you forgetting who feeds your pastry addiction?"

Their crossers gathered, sharing the impromptu picnic, which did double as Sonnet's welcoming feast.

"Should I go back? Check?" Jacques offered.

"Do."

281
EENY. MEENY. MINY. MOE

Jacques marched toward Stately House, determinedly seeking information. He could have called Michael for an update, but Jacques was after more than a cub count.

Nonny had skipped dinner.

That wasn't like him.

In the kitchen, Jacques found a few of the missing. Tawny, with her finger in her mouth, curled against Sansa's side. Kyrie, who'd been coaxing for a kitten for ages, petted the sizeable newborn Ginkgo held. And Timur sprawled on his belly, stroking the smallest cub.

Three black. One brindled mahogany.

Jacques thought it an odd coincidence. "This one looks just like ...!"

"... his father," cheerfully finished Michael.

282
KITH SIRE

Deece hesitantly met his gaze, as if Jacques' reaction ... mattered.

"Many felicitations," he managed, just as cautious.

"Why be shy?" asked Sansa. "My Minx, she gets what she wants, yes?"

"I *am* here by arrangement," murmured Deece.

Michael cheerfully interjected, "This is all new to me, as well. I feel as if I've been let in on a grand secret. Help us keep it?"

"*Naturellement!*" And with more warmth, "Congratulations, Minx. Congratulations, Deece."

Ginkgo asked, "Who gets to name these cuties?"

"Minx has named her daughter. She is Wile." Deece beckoned Jacques to his side. "Help me name my sons?"

283
HANDFUL

So we went with Rasp for his kisses. And Rake for his claws … *and* the jaunty brindling he inherited from his sire. Then Fend, who will be a handful. Smallest of the brood, but already trying to fend for himself."

Argent remarked, "For someone who grasps complexities, you are surprisingly uncomplicated."

Why did that sound like an insult? Jacques defended himself. "My needs are *sophisticated*!"

"Your tastes are eclectic and expensive, but … you like kittens."

Didn't everyone? Jacques argued, "They're cubs."

Argent's mood shifted. "Smythe?"

"Yes, my lord?"

"I will be missing for a few days. Do not let on."

284
CALLED UPON

Jacques made one last circuit of the house before dragging upstairs. He needed a change of clothes, a cup of coffee, and help. Maybe Ginkgo's?

But Jacques found Nonny sitting with his back to Jacques' door. He joined the kid on the carpet. "I didn't forget. I wouldn't."

"You forgot Christmas."

"Nooo, I *avoided* Christmas." Jacques sighed. "It's not as if we'd made plans."

Nonny shot him a surly look. "Promise me next year."

Jacques frowned. "I'm sometimes called upon t–"

"*I'm* calling upon you," interrupted Nonny. "Promise!"

"Right. Christmas." They shook on it. "Now … let's see about that bath."

285
PERFECT AIM

Jacques warned, "It's not much of a grooming session without cats."

"You only wash if there's felines hanging about?"

"You're missing the midnight feast to welcome Sonnet."

"You trying to get out of this?"

"I'm giving you an out."

Nonny's eyes narrowed. "You want me out?"

Jacques wearily pointed to the filled tub. "In."

His apprentice obeyed.

"Hey, Nonny, nonny, wouldn't you rather have Ginkgo or Randolla or Tsumiko for a mentor?"

"I don't aim to be a gardener or a tailor or a … a lady."

"What *do* you want to be?"

"Cripes, you're thick. I want to be yours."

286
IF YOU CAN.T BEAT THEM

Oi, Jacques."

He snapped awake. Nonny was grinning down at him.

"I figured out why you never bathe alone. You'd drown."

Jacques sloshed upright and murmured, "Apologies."

"For sleeping through your promise?"

"Lord. Sorry. Been a long day."

He stuck to essentials, shimmying into silk, tousling oil into his curls, and patting on moisturizer. Turning from the mirror, he met Nonny's baffled stare.

"Want some? It's never too early to begin caring for your complexion."

"Not bloody likely."

Jacques advanced. "Trust your mentor!"

Nonny swore softly, but he submitted to a careless smear.

Which brought something unexpected to Jacques' attention.

287
GOOD LAD

Jacques pulled Nonny along, pausing at the head of a stairway to call, "Deece, are you nearby?"

Moments later, Deece joined them, concern plain upon his face.

"My room, I think. For privacy." Jacques shoved Nonny in ahead of him. "Is it warded?"

"Yes," Deece quietly confirmed. "Hello, Nonny."

"Cheers," mumbled the boy, scuffing a hoof into the carpet.

"Nonny's my new apprentice. Have a look, will you?"

Deece sat on the floor and beckoned.

"Go on, Nonny. There's a good lad. Our Deece is a daddy now, quite wonderful with children."

The crosser's cheeks flamed. "I'm not a child."

288
GROWING BOY

Deece murmured questions, tested limbs, sniffed uncertainly. Nonny submitted quietly enough, eyes downcast. He looked so small in the big feline's lap.

Finally, Deece asked, "Why are you concerned, Jacques?"

"When Nonny arrived just a few years ago, I could lift him, carry him. He was a little boy."

"He *was* little. Nonny was undernourished." Deece nuzzled the kid's hair. "It is better for you here."

Nonny muttered, "Think I don't know that?"

Deece began to purr. "You have gained ground with Sansa's cooking. The rest will come as you progress through your adolescence."

"And there it is," Jacques sighed.

289
WISDOM

How old would you guess Nonny is?"

"In Amaranthine terms or human equivalents?" asked Deece.

"Lord. I've only *been* human. Go with that."

"Thirteen...?" The cat smoothed a thumb under the kid's eye, which was smudged dark. "And needlessly depleted."

"Right. Can you stay?" Jacques folded back his duvet. "Tuck him in with me."

"Oi! I'm too old to be tucked in!"

"*Absurdité.* I *adore* tucking. Learn from me and be wise."

"Wise arse."

"Mind your hooves."

Nonny stilled, but his lip trembled.

Jacques pulled him close, kissed his forehead, and promised, "One never outgrows the need for beauty sleep."

290
PROFESSIONAL BEDMATE

Relax, Nonny. You're in the arms of a professional. Right, Deece?"

"Uncle does prefer him. As does Lapis."

Jacques asked, "Do you go deep?"

"No. I gotta sleep every night."

Once Nonny stopped squirming, he clung with force.

"I'm not going anywhere," grumbled Jacques.

"Liar. You go all the time."

"Part of my job."

"Well, *I'm* part of your job, now."

"Irascible goat. I'm as *here* as I can be. Get used to it." Jacques sighed. "You needn't grapple me."

"Get used to it."

"Brat."

"Prat."

"Lord. Why me?"

"Wish I knew."

Jacques diplomatically let Nonny have the last word.

291
YOU TRIED

I might know," Nonny mumbled in the vicinity of Jacques' breastbone.

"Know what, Nonny, nonny, hey?"

"Why *you*."

"Tell us, then. Assuming Deece is allowed to know the terrible truth." Nonny sniffled.

From his seat on the floor, Deece reached his arm around both of them and patted Nonny's shoulder.

"You lifted me up. You carried me." Another sniffle. "You tried to save me from a fox."

Jacques hummed. What else could he say? He wasn't any kind of savior.

But the mention of foxes brought other things to mind. Like his lord's vanishing act. Jacques asked, "Think Argent knows?"

292
HIMSELF

A rgent does not miss much," remarked Deece.

"Did he know about Minx?" challenged Jacques.

"Maybe ...?"

"I mostly steer clear of Himself," admitted Nonny.

"He'll have noticed that. Safe to assume he knows." Jacques dragged a finger over the downy hairs he'd discovered along the kid's jawline. "Maybe Argent's true reason for giving you to me was so I could teach you to shave?"

Nonny's laugh was a soft bleat.

Jacques checked, "You really don't know how old you are?"

Nonny looked up at him, wilted and weary. "They didn't give me *clothes*. You really think they threw me birthday parties?"

293
UNIFYING PALETTE

Early morning found Jacques returning to Randolla's. "You'll understand clothes' appeal if they're properly fitted."

"I *have* clothes."

"Your usual things are fine for usual things. But for *official* things, we'll splurge."

"On …?"

"Something tasteful. Something appropriate. I'm partial to greens, but blues would better bring out your eyes." Inspiration struck. "I wonder, would it be too *outré* for me to establish my own clan colors?"

Nonny snorted. "Clan Smythe?"

"Perhaps not. But we can still employ color."

"For what?" Nonny skidded on some ice and swore under his breath.

Tucking the kid's arm through his, Jacques promised, "You'll see."

294
COULD BE WORSE

Nonny cautiously reserved judgment and submitted to the tape measure. While draping lengths of different blues across the boy's shoulder, Jacques asked, "Do you have a clan name?"

"Not to know it. Not sure I want to."

"Were you kidnapped?" Jacques blinked. "Lord. That would be funny, except that it's not."

Nonny went all surly and silent.

More softly, Jacques asked, "Are you afraid you were abandoned?"

"Could be worse. Might be I was sold."

What a horrible notion. "Who rescued you?"

"Nobody." Nonny grimly reported, "Well-aimed kick turned into my lucky break. Trackers found me later. Dragged me here."

295
CLEAR AS MUD

We could look.”

“For what?”

“Your Amaranthine parent.” Jacques shrugged. “Clear up the mystery.”

“*Clear* is it? Like crystal?” Nonny challenged. “Or will you just drag some bloke through the mud.”

“Argent is discreet. I’ll grant you, indiscretions make for awkward conversations, but it’s not inherently bad to be … well.” Jacques couldn’t bring himself to say *bastard*. “It could mean a clan’s protection.”

“I have the guv’s.”

“You could claim an Amaranthine name and crest.”

“Got Himself’s.” Nonny rolled his eyes. “Or yours, if you do your *outré* thing.”

Jacques wavered. “But what if they’re *glad* to know of you?”

296
GOT IT GOOD

What if?” Nonny echoed, anger mixing with incredulity. “What if they took me away? What if getting a new name means losing the one I have? Then you couldn’t say, ‘h-hey, Nonny, nonny’ and mean *me*.”

“Nonny.” Jacques set aside suit samples. “I’m an insensitive brute.”

“Too right you are! I got a good place here. And a position.”

“And pants.”

The kid blinked, then narrowed his eyes. “If I didn’t want to be here, a well-placed kick is all I’d need to get myself gone.”

Jacques calmly moved his hands to cover his assets.

“Are you really that daft?”

297

COMMON GROUND

I'm rarely daft, but I feign it well." Jacques stooped to look Nonny right in the eyes. "I'll hear you out."

Nonny stamped a hoof. "I like it here!"

"So do I."

"I want to stay!"

"That's all I wanted, too, yet the first thing Argent did was try to toss me out again."

Nonny's brow furrowed. "I don't believe you."

"*I* was unwanted." Jacques remembered being this desperate. Had probably looked at Argent with the very same ... oh, lord. Well, damn.

"Why'd he change his mind?"

Jacques summoned up a rueful smile. "Because I belong here. Same as you."

298

VINTAGE APPEAL

D o you *prefer* shorts?"

"My legs don't get cold."

"You're beyond the Fauntleroy age, and I'm forbidding Lederhosen. But we're not trying to *hide* your heritage." Jacques addressed Randolla. "Newsboy knickers, poshed up a bit?"

The crane was soon pinning and basting. "Mind if I dip a wingtip in?"

"Huh?" asked Nonny.

"Goats *do* gallivant." Randolla knotted a thread. "Your clan mightn't be shocked that one of their bucks fathered a crosser. They may even be proud."

"O-oi!" Nonny blushed to the roots of his horns.

Jacques soothed, "All a man's secrets are known to his tailor and his valet."

299
COMFORT ME

Days later, Jacques sought out the one other person who *had* to know Argent was gone.

Tsumiko sat with a book across her lap as she gazed out the window. Two balls of fur curled at her feet—one raven, one brindle.

Though it was undignified, Jacques joined Rasp and Rake on the floor. Resting his chin on Tsumiko's knee, he lifted a mournful gaze and whispered, "How much longer?"

"Soon. I hope."

"Lord, I miss him."

"Trust him."

She petted his hair, and he hid his face against her skirt, letting her prayers and the cubs' purring comfort him.

300
SCRITCHIES

Just when Jacques' knees were beginning to protest, a rougher hand tousled his hair. He lifted his face to find Ginkgo smiling at him from across Tsumiko's lap.

"Hey. I thought *I* was the only one who came here for scritchies."

Tsumiko laughed and tugged one fox ear.

"That's the stuff," Ginkgo sighed. "So, Jacques. You seem in low spirits."

"Good of you to notice."

"Want to get out of here for a bit?"

Jacques made a face. "I'm terribly busy. Let me mope in peace."

"Ah-ah! Gonna have to insist," said Ginkgo. "Your lord and master has summoned you."

301

BOLT HOLE

Ginkgo's leaps were making Jacques seasick. "Lord. Where are we *going*?"

"I have a handful of bolt holes. Dad's borrowing one."

"And this is the only way to gain access?"

"Afraid so!"

"At least tell me this bolt hole is not a literal hole," Jacques begged.

"Nah. See?"

A cabin had been half-buried in brush.

Jacques ducked through the low door behind Ginkgo. When he straightened, there was already someone hurtling toward him. He caught the culprit, grunting under the unaccustomed weight.

Round eyes. Ginger hair. Throttle hold.

Jacques rallied. "*Not* my type, but I'm a fan of the tail."

302

UP TO NO GOOD

You asked for me, my lord?"

Argent hummed. "I want your opinion."

"About...?"

With a flick of his fingers, he indicated the crosser.

"Cute. Clingy. Not afraid of me. *Possibly* afraid of you." Jacques peered into eyes that sparkled with amusement. "Up to no good."

"Agreed." Argent's expression was thoughtful. "He is more than he lets on."

Jacques tried unsuccessfully to put the mischief-maker down. "What do *you* have to say for yourself?"

"Inti is Inti."

"Jacques is Jacques."

"*Tsk.* Take him to bed."

"Oooh, *scandalous!*"

Argent sighed.

"Am I watching over his long sleep?"

"Close. You shall dream together."

303

DREAMSCAPE

The dreamscapes Argent created were usually familiar. This wasn't. Scruffy grasses. Sour smells. Scrap metal. Strange pressure. Jacques turned and spied a bleak building behind a high fence topped with razor wire.

Inti stood staring at it.

"Do you know where we are?" Jacques asked.

"In a nightmare."

"Argent!" he called. "This is *entirely* inappropriate!"

And just like that, he was standing on the beach below Stately House, clad in his fundoshi. "Lord. Really?" Jacques flung his arms wide. "This is *questionably* appropriate."

But Inti crossed to him in a single bound, went up on tiptoe, and whispered, "Thank you."

304

LONG WALKS ON BEACHES

Jacques angled his head toward the water. "Any chance you enjoy long walks on beaches?"

"Not sure. Never tried."

He offered his hand. "Shall we begin the inquisition?"

"Inti is ready." He skipped the handholding, clambering onto Jacques' shoulders instead.

"Right. Well? What do you want to know?"

His passenger leaned precariously, searching his face. "Inti asks?"

"You haven't decided if you trust Argent yet, have you? I can fill you in."

"Jacques likes Argent?"

"*Non.* I love him."

"Jacques is biased?"

"*Non.* He brought you to the one person who can give an honest reckoning. Pick a question. Ask."

305
CLEVER BOY

I s your fox a good fox?"

"He's certainly good at being a fox."

"Tricky fox?"

"Argent embodies foxiness." Wading into the water, Jacques muttered, "Lord. This is convincing. And me without sunscreen."

Inti snickered. "Fussy, frisky fop."

"Guilty as charged. But you don't want to know about *me*."

"Maybe, maybe. Jacques is holding Inti."

"*Au contraire*. You're riding me."

Inti slid down far enough to dip a toe in the water. "Not here. There."

"Ah. You must admit, the bed's dreadfully narrow."

"Gentle, gentle, gentleman."

"And *you* are cunning enough to interest foxes?"

Inti's expression soured. "Guilty as charged."

306
OVERSIGHT

A re you *actually* afraid of Argent?"

Inti retreated into wary silence.

Jacques kept talking. "I didn't like to mention it earlier, but when you're wrapped around me, I can tell when you're trembling."

The crosser didn't deny it. He couldn't.

"Many of our newcomers get stuck on the fact that he's a fox. They get over it, though. Given time." Time Inti hadn't had. Time Jacques was clearly meant to make up for.

"Who comes? New comes?"

"Crossers." Jacques didn't think Inti's blank look was false. "Lord. Don't tell me he didn't tell you about Stately House."

"No, no, nothing."

307
REASONS

Jacques outlined Argent's entirely personal reasons for championing the rights and safety of crossers, including those living under his roof. *And* the necessarily proportional—though often underrated—importance of Lord Mettlebright's butler, valet, and confidante. "*Moi.*"

Inti boffed Jacques' chin with the end of his tail. "Not a reaver."

"Completely blasé."

"Why does he keep you?" Inti asked.

"I like to think it's an overflow of affection, though he'll deny it."

"Foxes lie."

"Mmm … *non*. He doesn't like to boast, which is ridiculous. Argent is *extraordinary*." Jacques nodded to himself. "But he'll look after you for entirely *ordinary* reasons."

"Reasons?"

308
SAFE AS HOUSES

Argent's reasons were probably really simple. Like giving you a safe place to go deep. And someone to dream with. Again, *moi*."

Inti slid from Jacques' shoulders to face him. "Inti is safe?"

"Exquisitely safe. Blissfully, even, since you're asleep in my arms."

"Safe with foxes. Safe from foxes." Inti shook his head. "He *stole* me."

"Wait a tick. Argent did? In a reprehensible way? Or in a rescuing way?"

"In a foxy way."

"I thought we'd established that foxiness isn't all bad."

"Pending, pending, depends."

"On what?"

Standing taller, Inti's whole demeanor shifted. "On what he wants from me."

309
HUNTING GROUND

Jacques nodded. "Shall we ask?"

For several moments, Inti considered him with unnerving calculation. But then he clambered onto Jacques' shoulders, clamping on like a monkey-boy helmet and slipping back into nonsense. "Ask, ask, ask."

"Right. At your convenience, my lord."

The scene shifted.

A classroom?

Jacques, now wearing one of his more sensible suits, strolled to the window. Cold daylight. Falling snow. Familiar territory. "This is Keishi."

"Which has become the hunting ground for a monster." Argent leaned against a lectern, tails flagging. "There are safeguards in place, but I like to be *thorough*. Inti will be my failsafe."

310
MEDIATION

Jacques guessed he was playing go-between. "Just to be clear, you stole this boy in order to hurl him into fresh peril?"

"You sound disappointed in me."

"Help me understand why I shouldn't be."

The scene changed, returning to Inti's nightmare.

"Crossers are not lab animals." Argent's tails lashed. "This boy's cries were my compass. I tracked him. I took him."

Jacques asked, "Why not bring him to Stately House?"

"Inti is … unique."

"Lord. Aren't we all?"

"Ingenuity. Subtlety. Fortitude. He shows promise with sigilcraft, and I believe he is a reach." Argent extended a hand. "My offer is apprenticeship."

311

TERMS

Jacques reached for one of the hands tangled in his hair, covering it with his own. "Do you understand the honor of what he's offering?"

"No." Inti's tail looped around Jacques' arm, holding it in place. "Make him tell."

"Ingenuity. Subtlety. Fortitude," Argent repeated. "These are qualities I admire; they are qualities we share. If you can find it in your heart to trust a fox, we would be well-matched."

"New terms. No terms. Hear terms," chanted Inti. But then his voice shifted as it had before, colliding into something canny and cunning. "Or do you think I'm a fool?"

312

SIMPLICITY ITSELF

Jacques opened his eyes to moonlight slanting through the cabin windows. He eased Inti into a more comfortable position, shushing and clucking all the while. If only he could banish *all* this boy's nightmares.

"Opinions?"

"Frightened. Desperate. Easily as sly as his new mentor. Optimistic."

Argent hummed. "Thank you for helping us come to terms."

"You'd have managed."

"Your simplicity inspired the necessary trust."

"I'm hardly *simple*."

"Am I to quibble terms with *you*, now?" Argent's tone mellowed. "Guileless. Authentic. Sincere."

"You're making me blush."

"You are too brazen to blush." His master smiled. "It is good to be home."

313

MUST BE CATCHING

Michael had never once asked for it, but that didn't stop Jacques from bringing the man tea at appropriate intervals. Sometimes, they shared the pot. Michael was generous like that.

Voices carried, and Jacques hesitated.

However, Michael waved him forward. "Jacques! Just the person. Keep Kurogi-kun company while I fetch a book?"

"Why the Japanese name? I thought your chat-buddy was American."

"He's my apprentice." Michael was all smiles. "Back in a tick."

"Mentorship must be catching." Jacques eased into camera range. "Long-distance learning?"

A young man was sketching looping patterns in midair. "Hi, Jacques! My friends call me Jiminy."

314

THE AMERICAN

Jacques slid into Michael's chair. "A ward."

"Sure am!" Jiminy left off twiddling to ask, "Are you one of First-sensei's students, too?"

"Michael's? Lord, no. I'm Stately House's butler."

"Fancy!"

"A bit." Jacques poured for himself and scanned Jiminy's setting—abundant books and crystals sprouting from cabinet drawers. "You're like him, then? Sigil savvy?"

"Yes. My placement's a real honor."

"I sometimes forget he's important-ish."

"Good." Jiminy shook hair out of his eyes. "Den isn't about digits."

Jacques decided he liked him. "Give me your perspective."

"On ...?"

"I've never managed an apprentice before. What might you consider mentoring *faux pas*?"

315
MENTORING STYLE

Jacques took delivery of a parcel from Uppington and immediately sought out Nonny. "My years in dressage left me with more than high boots and a riding crop!"

The kid warily inspected the box's contents. "What's all this then?"

"Grooming kit, hoof polish." He breezily added, "I checked with the mares, and they agree this will do you good. Smarten up your turnout."

Nonny looked queasy. "I'm not a pet pony."

"Granted. But mine is a doting sort of affection. Expect gifts, warm fuzzies, and pampering."

"And a hook knife?"

"You *do* need a trim." Jacques promised, "I'll be gentle."

316
SAY SOMETHING SOONER

They moved to the garden. Open air offered better lighting and the polish meant fumes. Nonny's grip on their chosen bench looked tight enough to crack the stone, and Jacques sighed.

"I *do* know what I'm doing."

"Says you."

"Calm down."

Nonny grumbled, "Who says I'm not?"

Just then, Ginkgo strode over, nose twitching. "What's up, you two?"

"Hoof trimming." Jacques indicated his supplies. "Then we'll add a bit of shine."

"So *that's* what's got you so skittish." The half-fox dropped to a seat beside Nonny. "Mind if I watch?"

Jacques wilted inwardly. "You're scared enough he could smell it?"

317

ANIMAL HUSBANDRY

I trust *you*," Nonny forced a leaky laugh. "It's knives I don't."

Ginkgo said, "Maybe explain things to me, first, Jacques. Ideally, without the knife in your hand."

He immediately surrendered the blade.

Ginkgo pocketed it. "So! Should I be shocked that our uppity lordling knows animal husbandry?"

"Ohhh, my stable boy fantasies were definitely tarnished by the muck and musk. But I found I liked animals. And the lusty looks a snug pair of breeches could inspire."

Ginkgo chuckled. "Not surprised on either score."

"I'm not an animal," protested Nonny.

"*Non*." Jacques tapped his knee. "These aren't goat's legs."

318

CLOVEN

What else *would* you call 'em?" Nonny snapped.

"Hirsute, I suppose. Or caprine?" Jacques showed his palms. "May I touch?"

"If it's you. Yeah."

"Here, see?" Jacques wrapped both hands around Nonny's thigh, kneading down to the knee. He lifted to bend it, then slid one hand further to grip Nonny's calf. "You have goat's hair, but this is a man's leg. Trust me, I know."

Nonny gulped.

"He's right," said Ginkgo. "The anatomy's human."

"Things transition here." Jacques framed Nonny's ankle. "Pasterns and dew claws. Very pretty flocking. And good, sturdy hooves."

Nonny's voice cracked when he echoed, "P-pretty?"

319
GOOD REFLEXES

aturellement." Jacques gave Nonny's flocking a fluff. "Even prettier once your hooves are neatly trimmed and we add a skim of polish. Perchance, are you ticklish?"

"Huh?"

Jacques pressed the pad of his thumb into the soft frog of one cloven hoof.

Nonny's leg jerked reflexively, and he swore. At himself. Then fumbled for an apology. "Did I clip you?"

"*Non.* Bear up a little longer." Jacques continued his inspection. "Who normally trims them?"

"Mare Alpenglow. Or sometimes Colt Withershanks."

"Would you rather go to one of them?"

Nonny gruffly confessed, "I hate it no matter who's holding me down."

320
TAKING RESPONSIBILITY

ord. They don't actually pin you, do they?"

"Someone holds me tight. Usually Deece. He covers my eyes so I won't see the knife."

Ginkgo asked, "You're connecting sharp instruments with … something bad in your past?"

"You could say that."

"Nobody ever mentioned you're having trouble!" Jacques softly exclaimed.

"Told 'em not to tell, didn't I?"

Reaching for Nonny's other hoof, Jacques kneaded in tandem. "That won't do. As your mentor, I'm taking responsibility."

"Oi. Don't blame me if you get kicked."

"Pish tosh. I *excelled* at gentling horses."

Nonny scowled.

Ginkgo chuckled.

Jacques smiled and went right on kneading.

321
HANDLE WITH CARE

Oi, Jacques. You got a thing for hooves?"

"Not especially. I definitely *do* have a thing for good grooming, though. You shall be *splendid*."

"Get on with it," Nonny complained. "I'll let you."

"Lord. Have some patience."

"Settle down, kiddo." Ginkgo turned on the bench so Nonny could lean into his chest. Resting his chin between the boy's horns, Ginkgo said, "Jacques is taking extra care because we know you were mishandled before."

"Who says I was?"

"Body language, mostly." Ginkgo softly added, "You drop the odd hint. We notice."

Fear sparked in Nonny's eyes, and his gaze slid sideways.

322
LOOK AT ME

Hey, Nonny, nonny, look my way," coaxed Jacques.

The boy complied, though there was rebellion in his stare.

"I'm going to trim your hooves, and I want you to watch me do it."

"Why?"

"Because I like the attention."

"That's crispy crackers."

"You're right. Let's be serious." Jacques urged, "Use all your lovely Amaranthine senses. Take in the sight of me, the scent of me, the sound of me. Feel the confidence in my movements. Watch for lies and see the truth."

"Dang, Jacques." Ginkgo cleared his throat. "Be careful with this one."

"Utmost care," he agreed. "I swear it."

323
UTMOST CARE

J acques was *good* at puppy dog eyes. They were one of the most potent weapons in his arsenal.

As it happened, Nonny was similarly equipped. He watched Jacques' every move with a heart-wrenchingly vulnerable expression.

There was trust here, but also the wariness of one who'd been wounded before.

Jacques was glad of Ginkgo's presence. The half-fox murmured to Nonny throughout the proceedings. This was essentially a pact, and Ginkgo made sure the kid knew it.

Nonny *needed* a promise this big, and Jacques wouldn't—couldn't—withhold it. Even though there'd be an awkward patch until Nonny outgrew his crush.

324
WHO BETTER

O nce Nonny ran off to get Gilen's opinion of the new sheen on his hooves, Ginkgo asked, "You knew?"

"Somewhat belatedly, but yes. I caught on."

"Happens. A lot. We're important to these children. Only natural they get attached."

"*I* did."

"You totally did," Ginkgo agreed.

Jacques fiddled with his cuffs. "Do you think Argent's laughing at me?"

"Nope. Dad's *trusting* you. Who better than Devotion to sympathize with a little boy in love?"

"Watch over him after I'm gone?"

"Slithering off somewhere?"

"*Non.* Never." Jacques knew what lay ahead. "But I'll be doddering before our *enfants terribles* reach maturity."

PART THREE

Summer of 5 N.S., also known
as "almost two years later,"
which coincides with the
beginning of the third book
in the Amaranthine Saga,
Tamiko and the Two Janitors.

325
PERMANENT RESIDENT

Jacques opened the front door and risked a whisper. "The remainder of the household is hovering in the vicinity of the kitchen door."

Akira's smiled sheepishly. "I thought this would be more … *official*, I guess?"

"I did the same when it was my turn. But where's your baggage?"

"This is it." He angled his head toward Suuzu, who wheeled a single case.

"For both of you? *Mon dieu*. I'll speak to Randolla about expanding your wardrobe."

"I don't want to trouble anyone …!"

"Stately House takes care of its own. Now! Manners, dear nephew. Where's your *tadaima*?"

Akira beamed. "I'm home."

326
CATCH AS CATCH CAN

Smythe. How much longer do you plan on monopolizing that young man?" Argent strolled forward, Tsumiko at his elbow.

"We've been caught." Jacques wasn't really surprised, but he pouted on principle.

"I am the only reason you remain unnoticed."

Tsumiko hurried into her little brother's arms, and Jacques moved to Suuzu's side. "Can you stay?"

"Until tomorrow." The phoenix's expression was pensive.

Jacques followed his gaze and thought he understood. "He's caught up."

Suuzu sighed.

With Tsumiko sharing Argent's years, she didn't look a day older than she'd been when Jacques met her. The seven-year gap between siblings had closed.

327

TOO SOON FOR SORROW

He's a man. I'll grant him that." Jacques took a soothing tone. "But he's a very *young* man."

Suuzu's voice was barely a whisper. "Years fly."

"They slow if you fill them. Make them sleek and fat. Laze in each day and enjoy it to the fullest." Jacques jostled the young phoenix in a friendly way. "Don't mourn his maturation. Wouldn't you rather have a man in his prime. *I* would."

Suuzu looked scandalized.

"Akira needs time. You have time. Argent will solve your problem." Jacques gestured to Tsumiko. "She's noticed, too. And my lord *hates* to see her sad."

328

STAMPEDE

Argent dismissed his mischief with a subtle flick.

Jacques reopened the front door, slammed it, and raised his voice. "*Mon dieu!* Look who it is!"

The predictable stampede left Akira surrounded ... and smiling. "Yes, I'm here for good. Is that all right?"

Approval was a carillon of universality.

Lilya rode in on Rake's back; Kyrie trailed after, leading Cusp, a cub from Minx's recent litter.

Nonny slipped into the hall, hooves clopping on tile. Instead of joining the throng, he crossed to Jacques and Suuzu, offering a casual, "How's it going?"

Suuzu did a poor job hiding his confusion. "Nonny?"

329
IN A HURRY

Yeah, yeah. Been a while." Nonny reset his hooves and squared his shoulders. "You look like Jacques just said something sketchy. Want me to make him take it back?"

Suuzu's posture shifted three ways before murmuring, "You … grew."

Jacques stated the obvious. "Nonny's been taking a more human approach to adolescence."

The kid was likely fourteen or fifteen. His face had lost its soft curves, and he was steadily gaining centimeters while the other crossers had stalled out.

The phoenix warbled mournfully.

"Aww, hell. Don't go all soppy on my account. I was in a hurry to grow up anyhow."

330
DRAGONS AND FOURS

The following Thursday, two more members of the Amaranthine Council arrived unannounced. Jacques found them in the front hall, not *quite* squabbling.

"But I cleared my schedule especially!" Lapis flustered easily when he was tired. "To slip away."

"Isla needed escorting," replied Hisoka. "My schedule is similarly open."

"I had hoped to have Jacques to myself."

"Understandable. I share your preference."

"I brought chocolates."

"I brought nephews."

Lapis whirled and draped himself piteously. "Am I supplanted?"

"He's only teasing," soothed Jacques. "He may even be pampering you."

Hisoka purred comfortingly. "If you share my hearth, your companions will be fourfold."

331

COMPATIBLE COMPANIONS

Though Hisoka and Lapis frequently came to Stately House for sleep, this was their first overlap. New possibilities. And challenges. Jacques caught Canarian's elbow. "Does Hisoka's usual suite have enough room for whatever you have planned?"

"With some small adjustments." He rubbed their cheeks together and murmured, "Leave the arranging to me and Cat."

"*Merci.*"

They went on ahead, and Jacques moved to shore up a listing Lapis. "Have you never groomed with felines? I should think you highly compatible."

"What? Dragons and cats?" he asked dubiously.

"Lord, yes. Flirting with dragons is exciting."

"Me? Exciting?" Lapis drooped pitifully. "Hardly."

332

JUST THE THING

Jacques guided Lapis to the kitchen. Sansa took one look and manhandled their guest into a nearby parlor. "Sit. I will bring something bracing."

Jacques feared it would be one of her diabolical doses.

Lapis slouched. "Everything in here is blue."

"*Oui.*"

"Coincidence?"

Sansa returned with a tray—steaming bowl, dainty spoon, and a sprig of forget-me-nots. The custard smelled of liquor and spice.

Lapis brightened, then blinked, looking up at Sansa with widening eyes.

"Is good, yes?" She put the spoon in his hand. "Do not leave a drop."

Lapis murmured, "*Not* a coincidence."

Fluting softly, he finally smiled.

333
GOOD ADVICE

Once the bowl was empty, Lapis was showing glimmers of his usual vivacity. Hisoka briefly reappeared, ushering Michael, and Jacques immediately surrendered his seat to the man.

"Hello, there! What's this, now?" Michael gathered up Lapis's hands. "You're terribly depleted, Lord Mossberne. Come to us sooner!"

Jacques collected the tray and eased out.

In the hallway, Hisoka spoke in low tones with Sansa. "Is Rilka here?"

"Not yet."

"Send for her," he urged.

Jacques gaped. "*Now?*"

"I think it best," assured Hisoka.

"And you brought my Isla," murmured Sansa, patting her belly. "Yes. Good. Now."

"Lord. I'd better warn Argent."

334
AVENUE OF ESCAPE

Canarian had just launched into a lengthy explanation about the nature of his association with Catalan when Jacques ducked out.

Nonny found him. "Aren't you supposed to be purring and prettifying?"

"*Oui*, but …!"

"Sansa sent for Rilka."

"You knew? Did Hisoka …?"

"Nah. The guv heard it from Doran, who heard it from Andor. Apparently. He mighta been having me on. Didn't know Doran *could* speak."

"Argent …?"

"Your bags are packed."

"Should I …?"

"All your faves. I swear." Nonny shooed him off. "I'll collect you when Himself's ready to do a runner."

"Lord, you're …!"

"Perfect for you? 'Bout time you noticed."

335
WOOING THE SCHOLAR

When Jacques returned to Lapis's side, Catalan was still hard at work, wooing the exhausted dragon. But Lapis immediately reached for Jacques and clung peevishly to his favorite.

"Come, my lovely," Jacques soothed. "Canarian's technique is *magnifique*."

Hisoka casually remarked, "Fortunate is the dragon who coils with cats."

Lapis managed to look scandalized. "That is *not* how the saying goes!"

But he gave in, which led to an excess of kneading, purring, and drowsy fluting.

Tucked snugly between Canarian and Jacques, Lapis mumbled, "Is it always like this?"

"Careful." Jacques kissed his brow. "The love of cats is uniquely seductive."

336
WHERE. O WHERE.

The four of you do not *love* me," protested Lapis.

"*Au contraire*! We are universally smitten."

The dragon squirmed closer. "I want a lady, you know."

Jacques did know. Lapis wasn't terribly subtle. "She will be the most fortunate of souls."

"Where is she, I wonder?"

"I'd wager Hisoka knows, if anyone does."

All attention swung to Hisoka.

"Despite popular opinion, I don't know *everything*."

"Lord. He's evading."

Catalan gasped theatrically.

Canarian began purring.

Lapis wibbled. "You would tell me if you could?"

"How could I do any less?"

Jacques' curiosity was doubly piqued, but Hisoka's tiny headshake begged discretion.

337
PATISSIER

Jacques made sure Lapis was deeply asleep before relinquishing the dragon into the care of cats. Following his nose to the kitchen, he found his lord presiding over a pâtissier course. Isla, who had more poise than a girl of fourteen should possess, and a vaguely beleaguered Michael were his students.

"*Tsk*. Finally."

Michael mildly remarked, "Argent's always resorted to baking during birthings."

"I intend to absent myself again. Can you leave?"

"*Oui*. Lapis is resigned to my absence," Jacques indicated the cooling racks. Chocolate croissants. A favorite. "May I?"

Though he huffed, Argent waved Jacques to the table. "Breakfast?"

338
INVOCATION

Having noted the kitchen's state of dishabille, Jacques inquired, "Where is Sonnet?"

"She's attending the birth," said Michael.

"Lord. With your blessing, I assume?"

Michael smiled crookedly. "I consider it an honor, Jacques."

Isla piped up. "She's close as a sister to Mum."

Michael gently added, "Ginkgo gave up his usual place so Sonnet could be the first to hold this newcomer."

Jacques accepted the coffee Argent brought. "Will that invoke some sort of custom?"

"Fostering," Isla declared with authority. "Any child born into Amaranthine hands is counted as clan."

Argent's tails twitched into view. "The blood of birthing binds."

339

AS GOOD AS GONE

Jacques spied another restless tail lashing the periphery. Argent's flourish was a bristling mess.

Michael noticed, too. "All right there, friend?"

"*Tsk*. This is a bright one."

"Another beacon?" asked Isla.

"Near enough."

Jacques preferred to breakfast at a more leisurely pace, but he had mercy on Argent. "We'll be off. However, I *demand* pictures."

Argent raised his voice. "Nonny, stop loitering."

With a soft clop of hooves, he entered, maneuvering baggage. "Just keeping handy. Here's your things."

Michael asked, "Did you want the car?"

"I want to be gone," retorted Argent.

Jacques knew what that meant. "Lord, have mercy."

340

WHEN TRAVELING BY FOX

Argent snatched everything from Nonny and marched out, leaving Jacques to follow. Amaranthine strength was certainly superior, and speed was a consideration. But this was necessary for another reason. Foxes didn't have a boot.

Argent shifted, and their baggage went wherever it was that his clothes and shoes did. Neatly stowed for the journey ahead.

Jacques propped a hand on his hip. "Have you increased in size? Again?"

Blue eyes narrowed, and a slender muzzle loomed large.

Pressing his hand to it, Jacques murmured, "Another tail, too? *Magnifique!*"

Argent hushed him by burying him in silver fur.

Jacques regretted nothing.

341
EVENT OF MY DEMISE

Jacques didn't mind flying in the first-class sense—soft music, strong libations, attentive stewards.

This might be faster, but white-knuckling a fantastical beast at great heights was far from relaxing.

"In the event of my demise, you must *swear* to hire a valet with taste!"

The world heaved to a halt, and Jacques groaned. Fur vanished, and he gasped over his sudden unseating. Argent caught him and carefully lowered him to the ground. For several moments, they simply stared at each other.

"Thank you for your trust," Argent drawled.

Jacques wasn't letting him off that easy. "Apologize to my hair!"

342
AHEAD OF SCHEDULE

Argent drew up short. "I smell dragon."

Jacques glanced between him and the welcoming committee. "Are you being rude to Sinder or obliquely ominous?"

"*Tsk.* There are *other* dragons hereabouts. Ones with whom I am not acquainted."

"Your timing couldn't be better," called Sinder. "Harmonious wanted you summoned. You're ahead of schedule. Welcome to the cabal!"

Jacques' heart lurched. "I can't attend a cabal looking like this."

Sinder's whistle wasn't the complimentary kind. "Damp and disarray really aren't your style."

"Juuyu! *Mon ami!*" Jacques pressed close. "*You* understand the needs of curls. Be a dear, and set me to rights?"

343

STORM BREWING

Jacques leaned into Juuyu's shoulder—pristine wool and starched cotton, soft tutting and sure fingers. "You use the same hair oil as Suuzu?"

The phoenix only warbled a chiding note.

Jacques was quite sure he'd been hushed.

"Something has happened?" Argent's question *demanded* an answer.

"It's the Four Storms. They're back with a vengeance." Sinder's mood shifted. "Can you smell the weather turning?"

"What? Trouble with the Chrysanthemum Blaze?"

"Nope. That one's safe enough. But Beckonthrall's in a snit over the loss of the Plum Cascade, and someone's gone and tried to take the Orchid Saddle from Lord Trystholm's trove."

344

IN A WORD

Argent's jaw tightened. "Why have they gathered while Twineshaft is away?"

"Oh, it's worse than that," said Sinder. "Lapis is down and out, yeah?"

Jacques stopped worrying about his hair when his lord growled. "*Mon dieu.* Lapis couldn't be safer."

"*That,*" snapped Argent. "Is not the issue."

"I think Hisoka is boycotting," said Sinder. "And Harmonious is too upset to think straight, let alone moderate a discussion. Argent, I need you in charge today."

"*Tsk.*"

"Here, now." Jacques needed information. "I missed something. What *is* the issue?"

Juuyu said, "Respect."

"Blunt much?" muttered Sinder. "You're not wrong, but seriously. Ouch."

345
FIGUREHEAD

Our Lapis?" Jacques asked, incredulous. "Lord Mossberne?"

Argent's lip curled. "According to the traditions of his clan, Lapis is neither a lord nor a leader. He is an academic with a reputation for mingling with humans. Broken. Expendable."

"Hey, now! Hisoka *did* handpick him," Sinder defended.

Argent wasn't impressed. "Dragonkind tossed humanity a scrap that would not be missed."

"Their loss," Sinder said firmly. "And not the point. We have a cabal simmering in there, and while they're *trying* to be polite, the air's thick with sway."

"*Tsk.*" Argent's fingers drummed against his thigh. "Very well. Jacques will do it."

346
TITLED AND ENTITLED

Pardonnez-moi?"

Juuyu's gaze sharpened. "How is he with sway?"

Argent sniffed. "Immune. Naturally."

Sinder rounded on Jacques. "Completely?"

"You're welcome to make an attempt." Jacques warmed to the idea. "Shall I kiss your nose?"

"Maybe later," Sinder muttered, clearly on edge. "Do you have *any* experience handling a roomful of people who are used to getting their own way. As in … always."

Jacques almost laughed.

Argent said, "Smythe generally gets *his* own way. Your cabal is outmatched."

Sinder looked skeptical.

"*Tsk.*" Argent held Jacques' gaze. "You should be capable of this much."

What else could he say? "Yes, my lord."

347

FACE YOUR DRAGONS

Sinder ushered them into a room, and Harmonious shouldered his way over. "Argent. *Please!*"

"I think not." Brandishing his flourish, Argent raised his voice. "I am entrusting you lot to Mr. Smythe. He will hear you out. *Do* try to confine yourselves to pertinent details. Tea will be served shortly."

"Smythe?"

"H-his human?"

With a genteel wave, he said, "I'm Jacques."

The door snapped shut, leaving him alone with eight dragons. It probably should have been alarming, but an instant later, Jacques faced eight kneeling supplicants, sheer layers and silky hair pooling upon the floor, faces hidden behind beringed hands.

348

BEG AN INTRODUCTION

Jacques was on intimate terms with two and a half dragons, but Lapis was a pariah and Sinder an outlier. However, Kyrie's bedtime stories held Jacques in good stead. This cabal was straight out of dragon lore. Right down to the players.

Dropping to one knee before the fellow all done up in browns, Jacques inquired, "Do I have the pleasure of addressing Lord Beckonthrall?"

Fingers parted enough to reveal cornflower eyes.

"And you've honored us with a full spectrum? These are your sons, yes?"

Hands fell away. "Bring Mettlebright back."

Jacques tapped Lord Beckonthrall's nose and cheerfully answered, "No."

349

IN AN ORDERLY FASHION

Somehow, Jacques had expected more trouble from a group that had raised Argent's ire. While not the eldermost of all dragons, Beckonthrall's sons were honored patriarchs—prismatic and prolific. If the stories were true, all thanks to their impish mothers.

Their abasement worried him.

"Where is Twineshaft?"

"Why is Mettlebright ignoring us?"

"Ignored? Hardly! *I* am proof that your concerns are important to the Amaranthine Council." Jacques sat upon the floor and offered his palms. "Come now, my lords. I must beg introductions. Will you deal with me in alphabetical order or by age? Or my personal favorite—rainbow order?"

350

BEAUTIES ALL

Jacques knew dragons craved compliments, so he didn't stint. Neither did he struggle. Dragons out-lustered crown jewels and spoke in stirring tones.

"Bless me. It's impossible to pick a favorite color."

Lord Trystholm's fuchsia-streaked carmine. Lord Shywind's peach tresses and turquoise eyes. Lord Yonkeep's deep greens and deeper dimples.

He may have been immune to sway, but Jacques didn't bother hiding his interest. And they posed and preened and played into his hands.

"Tell on," he coaxed. "Entrust your worries to me."

Lords Farsway and Winnowind wove sigils in a graceful dance. Only then did their father begin his tale.

351

DRAGONS OF YORE

Ancient aggressions. Escalating retaliation. Tentative peace. In short, peaceable dragons of yore had pacted with early reavers, teaching them the sigilcraft that meant holding their own against all Amaranthine. This unlocked the potential of remnant stones, leading to the creation of the Four Storms. Priceless artistry. Perilous weapons.

Plum Cascade.

Orchid Saddle.

Bamboo Stave.

Chrysanthemum Blaze.

"You taught humans how to kill you?" Jacques asked incredulously.

Lord Starsweep, the one with plummy hair and pale freckling, gently corrected, "We trusted them. Befriended them. And learned from them in turn."

"We made peace," said Lord Beckonthrall. "For our sake. And yours."

352

THE FATHERS ARE STRONG

The cabal barely noticed the arrival of tea, let alone that Argent brought it. Very foxy.

While he poured, Jacques coaxed for more details about the attempted theft of the Orchid Saddle.

"... the trove is *quite* near the hatchery," Trystholm fretted. "Six dragonlings and an egg!"

"Six?" interrupted Lord Deeptrove. "Ha-eun was carrying twins?"

Jacques tried not to roll his eyes as eight chuffed-to-bits dragons veered off topic. Again.

It hadn't taken long to sort out why the dragon lords were in a furor. They weren't chest-thumping brutes or greedy hoarders. They were doting dads, afraid for their children.

353
DEALING WITH DRAGONS

Setting a teacup before Jacques, Argent deployed a sigil and murmured, "Care to offer an early assessment?"

"Selfish. Imperious. Concerned. They remind me of you."

"Impossible."

"*Non?*" Jacques teased. "No retraction."

A silvery brow arched. "You will explain yourself. Later."

"Yes, my lord."

When *later* arrived, Jacques was summarily cornered and quizzed.

"Did they try to sway you?" Argent demanded.

"Unintentionally, I think."

"And...?"

"Impervious, as advertised." Jacques slyly added, "Now, if they'd *flirted* ...!"

Argent growled.

"Lord, I'm the *last* thing on their mind."

"And the first?"

"Safety. Stability. Security." Jacques advised, "Promise them those, and they *will* capitulate."

354
PERHAPS NOT ENTIRELY IMPERVIOUS

Throughout tea, Jacques attempted to steer the conversation, but he was only invulnerable to sway. Not to beauty or charm. And definitely not to Lord Deeptrove's honey-sweet voice.

He was half-lost in rainbow-hued fantasies when Lord Beckonthrall noticed. Capturing and kissing Jacques' hand, he coyly urged, "Speak for us."

"*Naturellement.* That was my lord's intent–"

"Consider us grateful," purred Lord Deeptrove, who pressed lips to Jacques' temple.

His eyes crossed. "R-right. But about ...!"

In lavish succession, the dragons bestowed affectionate caresses and lay soft kisses in interesting places. Jacques was rather enjoying the coercion.

Until Harmonious cleared his throat.

355
ON THE CONTRARY

Poor Harmonious. He looked properly scandalized. Understandable, given canine sensibilities.

The others had arrived, as well. Sinder's shoulders were shaking with barely-contained laughter as he hid his face against Juuyu's shoulder.

The phoenix calmly inquired, "Are we certain he has the correct interests at heart?"

Argent, who was covering his eyes, took his time finding words.

Jacques ventured, "We've come to an understanding."

Sinder tittered.

Argent glared.

Jacques promised, "The way forward is clear."

"Thank you, Smythe. But did you have to snog the entire cabal?"

"*Non.*" Jacques beamed at the assembly of dragons. "It was the other way around."

356
OLD ENOUGH TO KNOW BETTER

Argent herded Jacques to their rooms, insisting that his man needed to rest and refresh himself after a long-drawn day. Which was true. Still, Jacques was in new territory, with Argent testily playing valet.

"Did those dragons mishandle you?"

"*Non.* They were quite skilled."

"They are elders! Ancient and prolific."

"Many do say that an experienced lover is best!"

Argent scowled and sniffed each article of clothing as Jacques removed it.

Relenting somewhat, Jacques said, "They believe securing *my* good will means securing yours."

"They were toying with you."

"And I enjoyed the attention."

Argent's tails lashed. "You deserve better."

357
DRAWING A LINE

You will not—under any circumstances—use your body to barter on my behalf."

"Are you actually calling me a whore?"

"I am drawing a line."

"Lord. What's gotten into you? Foxes are *vastly* worse than dragons, always luring gentlemen into quiet corners."

"*Which* foxes?" Argent's eyes widened. "Have you been kissing my cousins?"

"Your cousins are beneath interest. There *was* that younger uncle, though. Turned up in my bed. We snuggled until morning."

"Aster?"

"The very fellow!"

"He is still in diapers."

"Had a nightmare, poor chap."

"Jackie, just ...." Argent's fit of pique faded. "You deserve better."

"I know."

358
WEIGHING RESPONSIBILITIES

Argent lingered, puttering about the edges of the suite, adding wards that were probably so redundant as to be pointless.

"Don't you have to go orchestrate peace on Hisoka's behalf?"

"Twineshaft is hardly in a position to criticize my methods."

Jacques smiled over Nonny's choices in *accoutrements*. "Do you wish to dress for dinner?"

"I am *thinking*."

"About ...?"

Argent huffed. "I intend to take responsibility for the Orchid Saddle."

"Will you bury their treasure at Stately House?"

"And endanger the children?" he countered acidly.

"*Touché.*" With a fond smile, Jacques whispered, "And *this* is why they remind me of you."

359

NEWS FROM HOME

Harmonious was presiding over a feast fit for dragons when the first text arrived. Jacques was well out of the limelight, so nobody noticed him stepping away. Except Argent.

"Well?" he demanded.

"News from home."

"Show me."

Ginkgo had sent through a snapshot. Sansa and Sonnet slouched together on a bed, looking sleepy and satisfied, a blanket-wrapped bundle between them. "All's well."

"So it would seem."

In the next photo, Kyrie delivered a careful kiss to downy golden curls.

Then a video arrived, and Michael beamed. "Come home, old friend. A son has joined the den. We've named him Vanya."

360

SEND A CAR

Argent must've entered into some sort of agreement with Lord Trystholm during the night, because at daybreak—*far* too early for Jacques' tastes—he was ready to go home.

"May I lobby for a less precipitous mode of transportation?"

"Already accomplished. Courtesy of Twineshaft."

"Mmm. Promising. How long do I have to make you presentable?"

Argent glanced down, seemingly mystified. "You were pleased enough with this last night."

"*That* was evening. *This* is morning. Whole new set of foibles." Jacques stretched languidly. "Will there be coffee?"

"Our driver is *well* aware of your preferences."

Jacques liked the sound of that.

361
WITH OUR COMPLIMENTS

Jacques felt *entirely* vindicated for lingering over his turnout, because when he strolled into the Starmarks' grand foyer, a familiar face was waiting. Canarian Evernhold lowered his glasses and swept Jacques with an appreciative gaze.

Distance closed, he inspected Jacques' glade green vest with his fingertips before tugging him close. "You're looking lively. Is it this color ... or the company?"

"Quite possibly the coffee. Is that for me?"

A travel mug exchanged hands.

"With our compliments. Catalan is waiting with the car." Canarian rubbed their cheeks together, but his purr tapered to a chuckle. "Or *was*. Cat can be ... impetuous."

362
THREE IS COMPANY

He turned as Catalan Evernhold sauntered into his arms and purred, "I love you."

Cat meant it. In his way. Deece's sexy older brothers were good sorts.

Jacques smiled and sneaked a sip of coffee.

Argent arrived and sighed. "If you would disentangle yourself from our driver, we can be on our way."

"I was just ...."

He waved that off. "Better this lot than those dragons."

Cat perked up. "You were canoodling with dragon lords?"

Jacques held up thumb and forefinger.

"Details!"

Not until Argent was out of earshot did Jacques admit that Lord Shywind had slipped him some tongue.

363
CANOODLE

Jacques sat up front with Cat so that Argent could use the car ride to confer with Canarian, who was no mere personal assistant. Whenever Canarian was involved, things got done.

"I hear you visited Evernhold." Cat remarked.

"Deece brought me 'round."

Cat took a leading tone. "Enjoy your visit?"

"Lord. What have you heard?"

"Nothing *too* specific. Next time, bring me along."

"Whatever for?"

With a sultry smile, Cat said, "You're not the only one who enjoys canoodling."

"You ... and your stepmother's consorts?"

"Wouldn't you?" His eyebrows arched. "*Did* you?"

Jacques held up thumb and forefinger.

Cat chortled. "Details!"

364
ALWAYS THE LAST PLACE

Back at Stately House, Jacques was having trouble locating his apprentice. He checked Nonny's usual haunts. Naturally, he was in the last and farthest from home.

"Lord. Why are you way out *here*?"

The half-goat's gaze was belligerent. "Those cats are here again."

"Yes, they've been enormously helpful." Jacques nodded to the bear who took up most of the shelter. "First with Lapis, then fetching me home."

Nonny snorted. "I'll stay here, thanks."

"Why? This is *barely* habitable! No offense, Doran."

The bear grunted.

"*Because*," grumbled Nonny. "I don't want to know what you're getting up to with those cats."

365
REDOLENT OF BEAR

I have no plans to *get up to* anything with Cat and Canary."

"This time," snapped Nonny.

"This time," Jacques returned evenly. He perched on the edge of a strawbale. "I intend to rejoin Lapis. Have a kip. Fit in some reading. All very chaste and proper."

Nonny managed to look skeptical and skittish. "What about grooming?"

"*Naturellement.* You know it's hospitable. They're Deece's brothers." He pointed out, "Hisoka will be there, too."

"And Deece?"

"And *you*, if you'll relent." Jacques held out a hand. "Come along, apprentice mine. You're redolent of bear. No offense, Doran."

The bear grunted again.

366
PARDON MY FRENCH

I hate them," Nonny muttered.

"No, you don't. You're just jealous."

"What's so great about cats, anyhow?"

"Mmm ... felines have a certain *je ne sais quoi*."

"Is that French for sexy?"

"Nonny, what's the rule we established with regards to my sex life?"

"It's none of my business." He grimly added, "Until I'm bloody well part of it."

"Stop appending." Jacques kept walking. "Your feelings are noted, and they are safe."

"If I wanted *safe*, I wouldn't have settled on you."

"Too soon for that. Your voice hasn't even fully settled."

Nonny swore, his voice cracking ... rather proving Jacques' point.

367
ADORABILITY QUOTIENT

Stop ignoring me!"

Jacques did stop, but only to pull the moody teen into a hug. "I never would, and I never will."

Nonny clung. "I hate you."

"Rage against me all you like, but *do* stop bashing Cat and Canary. They're quite respectable, and they think your whole satyr aesthetic is adorable."

"Am I?"

"*Adorable*? Lord, no." Jacques smoothed his brat's hair. "You're rude and stubborn and prone to flight, which leads to perpetually scuffed shoes and aching feet."

"I know what I want."

"I thought I did, too, when I was your age."

"Were you wrong?"

"Ah ... *non.*"

368
COMPLETELY IRRESPONSIBLE

You don't want a crosser," Nonny accused.

Jacques gazed into the sky. "Mmm. In my case, that's probably a point in your favor."

Nonny thumped him. "Are you stupid? Why are you telling me *that*?"

"Because it's true."

"But ... but it's so *irresponsible*!"

"I won't *lie* to you."

"You can't put me off, then say something like that! It's ... *confusing*."

Jacques attempted to clarify. "I was talking about *me*."

Nonny fidgeted. "So you'd consider a crosser?"

"Hypothetically? Or specifically?"

"Does the answer change from one to the next?"

Having already pledged honesty, Jacques could only say, "In your earshot? Probably."

369
DADDING

Jacques held Nonny's hand all the way back to the house, then used the connection to drag him—hooves skidding—to where Catalan sat at the kitchen table, holding the new baby while he chatted with Michael.

"... quite a few years since ours was this small," Cat was saying.

"You never considered enrolling them here?"

"With a little wooing, Ambrose might come around. For now, New Saga seems to be working out." Cat met Jacques' gaze, then took in the scowling teen. "Hello. You must be Nonny."

"S'right."

Cat's eyebrows lifted.

Jacques breezily explained, "He can't help it. He's fifteen."

370
STRANGER DANGER

Michael frowned. "You're not usually shy of strangers, Nonny. Come over here."

The kid dragged his hooves.

Hooking an arm around Nonny's waist and smiling up at him, Michael warmly asked, "You haven't held Vanya yet, have you?"

"S'right." And warily, "How come *he's* got 'im?"

"We're letting everyone get a whiff." Michael chuckled. "Not sure how Cat managed to get him away from Sensei."

"Canary distracted Uncle." Cat gazed at Vanya with the gentlest of expressions.

Nonny glared.

Jacques struggled to master his frustration over Nonny's stubbornness. "Cat *knows* what he's about, brat. He and Canarian are foster parents."

371
THEATRICALLY SPEAKING

Nonny hummed skeptically. "You have a kid?"

"Don't I look the parental type?" Cat grinned. "What type am I, do you think?"

There was challenge in his tone, and Jacques wondered if he should head off a confrontation.

"Kind of flash," said Nonny. "Bit lush. Right cheeky. And randy."

"*Nonny!*" Michael sounded scandalized.

Jacques covered his eyes … and felt a sudden sympathy for Argent. "Lord. *Really*, Nonny?"

Cat laughed. "What you see from the house rarely betrays what's happening backstage. You wouldn't guess it to look at us, but Canary's the 'fun dad.' A complete pushover. *I'm* the responsible one."

372
NON ISSUE

Cat lifted Vanya. "Here, Nonny. Want to try?"

"I've held babies before. Lots of times."

"So defensive." Cat's smile sweetened. "Then is it *me* you're afraid of?"

Michael covered Nonny's mouth, but he gestured his opinion.

Rising smoothly, the jaguar clansman handed off Vanya before whisking into Nonny's personal space. "You want to play? I'm good at games."

"Ruddy arse! You got a problem with crossers?"

"Why would I? Our brat's a crosser."

Nonny hesitated. "You've … got a crosser?"

"I'm perfectly willing to dote on you, too." Catalan's tone gentled. "Bury the hatchet, hmm? Jacques wants it, and I'm willing."

373
GETTING PERSONAL

Nonny sought Jacques' gaze, silently pleading with him to deny Cat's words.

Sympathy kindling, Jacques held out his hand, calling Nonny to his side ... and calling an end to hostilities. "Help me assess the newest addition to Michael's dynasty."

Catalan released him and hooves clattered. Nonny pressed close, muttering half-hearted profanities until Jacques discreetly tweaked his tail.

Shocked into wide-eyed silence, the boy blushed.

"Not in front of the baby," Jacques softly ordered.

"You're not supposed ta ...!"

"Insult guests?

"But ...!" Nonny's gaze darted to the others. "This's *personal*, like."

"As were your remarks toward my friend." Jacques quietly demanded, "Apologize."

374
CORRECTION

You're taking *his* side?"

Lord, why was everything so damnably *monumental* when you were fifteen?

Jacques shifted into a dominant posture, but he also wrapped his arm around Nonny, keeping him from bolting. "I won't command trust or peace, but I *will* insist upon courtesy. Apologize."

"Sorry," he mumbled to the floor.

"*Non.* That's not how cats apologize."

"I'm not a cat," Nonny muttered.

Catalan looked on, no trace of teasing or triumph in his gaze. He was definitely in dad mode, and he was backing up Jacques.

"Right, then," chimed in Michael. "Shall we take this to the baths?"

375
BY THE BY

Along the way, Jacques acquainted himself with Vanya. "Welcome, young master."

He was definitely Michael's—rosy fair, with blond fuzz that would probably lengthen into ringlets.

"You're the toast of the In-between, by the by. Few people have been prenatally propositioned as much as yourself. Universally, I might add. As many boys as girls, what with reaver parents hedging their bets.

One eye squinted. Jacques placed his wager on brown.

"However, your preferences are entirely moot, since your mother is swift with a blade and quick with a match."

The other eye opened, and Vanya glared.

"I'm your Uncle Jackie."

376
FOR THE SAKE OF HEARTH AND HOME

Michael called for Deece, who fetched Hisoka and Canarian. The bathing chamber quickly filled with stripping felines.

"They *all* hafta be here?" Nonny grumbled.

"I don't make the rules," countered Jacques.

Michael said, "From what I understand of the feline courts, a lady mistress's consorts *must* get along, so any friction is dealt with swiftly. Ideally with all barriers removed."

"And a generous amount of bath oil involved," Jacques helpfully added.

Nonny wadded his shirt and chucked it into the corner.

"Perhaps Deece should demonstrate?" suggested Michael.

"I'll do it." Gilen's tail lashed. "*I'm* Nonny's best friend. I'll do it."

377

THE TIGER AND THE GOAT

Jacques retrieved Nonny's crumpled shirt and hung it alongside his own things.

The kid sat disconsolately on a bath stool, head bowed against his best friend's shoulder while Gilen lathered blond hair, quietly talking into Nonny's ear.

Jacques was fond of the half-tiger, who'd been one of the first to cling to him. Gilen *adored* Hisoka and was training with Deece in order to be useful to him. Jacques could easily envision a tiger-striped bodyguard in the Twineshaft cortege someday.

Gilen gazed at Jacques over Nonny's head, a troubled light in eyes.

The lad probably thought him a poor choice.

378

SET STRAIGHT

Canarian beckoned, so Jacques slid into hot water at his side. They'd always gotten on, due in part to a mutual appreciation for fashion, theater, Hisoka, crossers, and Catalan. Not necessarily in that order.

Jacques tensed when Canary pulled him closer. "Nonny will misunderstand."

"Cat will set him straight."

"Lord, are you *trying* to be ironic?"

"Trust us." Canary purred comfortingly. "We'll win Nonny over."

"One look, and he'll throw a tantrum because your hands are on me."

"And Cat will tell him to take a longer look, to learn how you like to be handled."

"That's optimistic."

"That's cats."

379

APOLOGIZING TO CAT

After much dawdling, Nonny sent Jacques one last, longing look, clearly hoping for a reprieve.

Jacques simply nodded.

Resignation turned to resolve, and Nonny presented himself to Catalan.

"*Mon dieu*," Jacques breathed.

Canarian hummed inquiringly.

He could only shake his head and whisper, "Later."

Instead, they watched Cat beckon Nonny closer.

Cat spoke in undertones, and Nonny tensed. So did Jacques.

With a finger to his lips, Canary held him back, gaze intent.

Hoping for some hint about what was being said, Jacques looked to Michael, who'd stayed close to Cat, probably to mediate.

Michael's surprised smile gave Jacques hope.

380

I MUST PROTEST

To Jacques' increasing mystification, Cat coaxed Nonny into his arms, and their exchange continued well beyond a simple apology.

"He's *good*," Canarian murmured admiringly.

"Care to fill me in?"

"Wait and see. Nonny will let you know his decision."

"Is your partner propositioning my apprentice?" Jacques drawled, only half kidding.

Canarian's brows arched. "And if he is?"

"Depending on the nature of the offer, I might wish to file a protest."

"Cat's acting as your friend."

Jacques trusted these two, but he still muttered, "True friends stab you in the front."

Canarian nuzzled his ear and cheerfully reminded, "That's cats."

381
MON DIEU

I t's later," prompted Canarian, who'd kneaded Jacques into a blissful fog.

"Hmm?"

"What inspired your earlier oath to the Maker?" He quietly reminded, "You said *later*, and we are alone for the moment."

Jacques sighed. "Nonny made peace with Catalan. He hated everything about the idea … and did it anyhow. For me."

"Nonny trusts you."

"But I'm not the trustworthy type!" Jacques waved a hand. "I lack moral fiber."

"Beg to differ."

"Lord. Listen, I have to be good. *Better* than good. Upstanding! And I'm rather more used to being disreputable."

"Again," said Canarian, whose eyes sparkled. "Beg to differ."

382
HEART TO HEART

N onny found him sleepless in the naproom.

"Thought you were going to be with Lapis," he quietly accused.

"Changed my mind." Jacques wasn't exactly hiding. Neither was he stashed behind a barrier.

"Room for one more?" mumbled Nonny.

He simply lifted the corner of his blanket, same as always.

Nonny barged right in, which was also the usual.

Jacques remarked, "You certainly underwent a change of heart…?"

"Guess so."

"Have you been with Catalan this whole time?"

"I suppose he was hanging about for most of it." Nonny finally sought his gaze. "I was having a talk with the guv."

383

FLEETING YOUTH

Went over my head, did you?" Jacques accused mildly.

"Guess so."

"Are you going to leave me in suspense?"

"Might do. It'd serve you right." There wasn't much sass in the token retort.

Jacques was sorely tempted to apply his considerable powers of persuasion to the situation, but his scintilla of moral fiber forbade. "Did you at least apologize?"

"Yeah. Right off. But that cat had this barmy idea ...." Nonny's expression was impossible to read by nightlight. "He thought maybe—since I'm the right age just now and everything—that I might like to go to a proper high school."

384

PULLING STRINGS

School?" Jacques echoed faintly.

"New Saga High School. Same place Isla and Akira went."

"So you're leaving?"

"For a bit." Nonny fit his arms around Jacques and held tight.

Jacques tucked his boy under his chin. "I thought they had a rigorous application process."

"Canarian'll pull some strings. I'd go through the grades like the human students. Graduate in three years."

"Where would you live?" Jacques ventured, "With Harmonious?"

"Dorms," he corrected. "So you know, I'm *not* done being your apprentice. And I'm not done with ... how I feel. I'll come home grown up and sweep you off your feet."

385
A LOT CAN HAPPEN

Are you threatening me?"

"I'm promising."

Jacques knew Nonny meant it, but he knew what going away could mean. "A lot can happen in three years."

"You doubting me?"

"I'm speaking from experience." Jacques steered the conversation. "Honest question. What does Gilen think of your stubborn attachment?"

"Thinks it's understandable. He admires you a lot."

Jacques gaped.

"Your face," Nonny teased. "Don't get all high and mighty. Deece is way more popular. Though most of 'em love Ginkgo best. The crazy ones crush on Argent."

"Don't *any* of you pine for Tsumiko?"

Nonny's expression instantly gentled. "We all love Lady."

386
ONE OF THE CRAZY ONES

But *you're* my choice. Wish you'd believe me." Nonny grumbled, "I can't exactly stop."

"Did you know I love Argent?"

"How thick do you think I am, *Devotion*?"

"I'm talking *grand passion*, here. I was fervently, sordidly smitten."

Nonny snorted. "Can't be."

"What makes you so sure?"

"Scent and … that thing you do with otherwise innocent words."

Jacques chuckled.

Nonny definitely blushed.

"Hey, Nonny, nonny?" he coaxed.

"Wut."

"Argent disappointed all my hopes, but he somehow managed not to break my heart in the process." Jacques gently said, "I won't think less of you if your love also changes shape."

387
WORN OUT

After a sleepless night, Jacques was more than ready to join Lapis. Hisoka yielded his place with a grateful smile, and Jacques ferried away a jumble of paperbacks and biscuit tins.

Pulling a pliant Lapis into his arms, he was mildly surprised when the dragon crooned and nuzzled his neck. Already waking?

"Let's have a little lie-in, shall we?" Jacques begged.

Lashes fluttered, and Lapis murmured, "Why so fraught? Are we out of biscuits?"

"I've worn myself out. Shelter me?"

Lapis pulled the comforter up over their heads. "I'll hold them off if you'll hold me."

Balance achieved, both slept.

388
EMPTY BELLY

Jacques woke to the reassuring scent of Lapis's perfumed oil. A soft clink—cup meeting saucer. A papery whisper—the turn of a page. So peaceful.

Then another sound chided him—the rumble of an empty belly.

"Lord, you're famished, and I'm keeping you from breakfast."

"Good morning, Uncle Jackie. Sonnet was just here, bringing tea and promising trays. And full of news."

Jacques propped up on an elbow and spied the reason Lapis had uncled him. Vanya curled against the dragon's bare chest, whiffling in his sleep.

Sapphire eyes sparkled. "I had to swear not to eat her fosterling."

389
BREAK WITH TRADITION

Jacques decided that dragons could bask in more than the sun. Lapis was suited to moments like this.

"Curls, do you think?" asked Lapis.

"Unavoidable, really."

"Ringlets are wondrous things."

"Spoken like one who's never had to deal with them. Do all dragons have straight hair?"

"Probably. Although, in theory, a half-dragon could break with tradition."

"Maybe someday, you'll introduce me to a child with blue curls."

"I would not mind that sort of someday."

"And then I shall have to teach you how to properly care for curls."

With a shy glance, Lapis murmured, "I shall rely upon you."

390
JUST ANOTHER DAY

The following morning saw a return to ... well, Jacques would never go so far as to say that life at Stately House was *normal*. He breezed into Akira's room, intent on rallying some much-needed support.

"Wakey, wakey!" Jacques swept aside the drapes, mostly for the drama of it. "Show a leg, me boyos. Or *more* leg. Lord, are you getting taller, Suuzu?"

The phoenix had the world's mildest glare. Barely creditable.

Jacques proceeded to steal blankets.

"Mmmornin', Uncle Jackie." Akira showed no signs of leaving the protective circle of Suuzu's arms. "Whassup?"

"Andor's special friend is here. Unofficially, of course."

391
BETTER TOGETHER

Akira's hands held Suuzu's. It was always adorable when he tried to protect his comely bird.

"It's not like you to hold a grudge," Jacques said, mostly teasing.

"I'm not. It's just ... this is Suuzu's last day."

"And you want to keep him all to yourself?"

Akira hesitated.

Suuzu hid his face against his nestmate's shoulder.

Jacques came to sit on the edge of the bed. "Andor looks forward to Caleb's visits. He can't get away nearly as often as either of them would like."

"Caleb's nice," Akira said quickly. "But... well...."

Suuzu's trill was resigned. "He never travels alone."

392
PET THEORY

Josheb's ... a lot. And Suuzu didn't like his questions."

"I think Josheb was *intrigued*. There aren't many like us." Jacques rested his hand over Akira's and Suuzu's tangled ones. "While the Amaranthine offer peace, it's not the same as friendship. Few unendowed humans are invited into a den or nest."

"Caleb was," pointed out Akira.

"He's an unregistered reaver, so Andor's interest makes sense. By comparison, we have nothing to recommend us. Yet here we are."

"I didn't do anything worth *investigating*. Suuzu and I just ... happened."

Jacques had a pet theory. "Maybe Josheb wishes it would happen to him."

393
SLOW TO TRUST

Jacques rejoined Argent, who was entertaining.

"Sooo ... kitchen!" Josheb rapped the tabletop. "Can't be where *everyone* eats. You've got ... how many students?"

"That information is not public," Argent said blandly.

"But we're not *in* public." The American beamed. "I made it inside the house this time. Doesn't that mean you trust me a little?"

"This is your fourth incursion," said Argent.

"Harsh," muttered Josheb.

"Up until now, you have not boasted about, reported on, or otherwise leaked any details about us."

"Hey, I wouldn't do that!"

"More importantly, you did *not* do that. So I will trust you. A little."

394
BETTER PART OF VALOR

Argent announced, "Today, you will be permitted to mingle with some of our students."

Josheb leaned forward. "No kidding? But that's huge! They're just kids, right?"

"Most. Yes."

"I almost never get to hang out with children of Amaranthine descent."

Jacques was favorably impressed. Although Josheb blundered through his interactions with Amaranthine during old reruns of *Dare Together*, he'd gained some polish.

Respectful postures. Proper terms.

"Also, my bondmate would like to meet you."

"You'll introduce me to Lady Mettlebright? That's ... wow."

"Later. Yes." Argent beckoned for Jacques to get the door. "But first, my son. He is ... a fan."

395

YOU ARE CORDIALLY DARED

Jacques eased open the door, and Kyrie peeped through.

Josheb failed to hide his surprise. Or his delight. That was good. Honesty was the surest road to trust.

Pushing back his chair, Josheb showed his palms. "Hey, little mister. Don't be shy. You watch me and my brother on television?"

"Yes." Kyrie grabbed Jacques' hand and pulled him along, as if not wanting to leave his uncle out.

After introductions, Argent prompted, "You had an invitation to issue?"

"A *dare*," Kyrie corrected.

"Oh, yeah? We Dare brothers take those pretty seriously. What'll it be?"

"Please, come swimming with our club?"

396

ASK BETTER QUESTIONS

Jacques led Josheb into a nearby room to change.

Once the door shut, Josheb ventured, "I thought Ginkgo was Lord Mettlebright's only son."

"So inquisitive. And about all the wrong things."

"What *should* I be asking about?"

"Your *entrée* into the Fundoshi Swim Club." Jacques genially confided, "There's a dress code."

"And my next question would be …?"

"What's a fundoshi?"

"I'll bite. What's a fundoshi?"

Jacques raised his voice. "Sonnet, be a dear? Help me gird our guest?"

A light rap preceded Sonnet into the room. He was already dressed for the beach.

Josheb gaped. "That's … a lot of skin."

397
DARE TO BARE

Y ou'll wear one?"

"*Naturellement*! I am the swim club's founder and primary lecturer."

Josheb peeled out of his shirt. "Does that rig come in blue?"

"*Oui*. I know *just* the shade." He selected the one that would best set off the American's eyes. "Pants. Off."

"Umm...."

"Feeling shy?" Jacques glanced back and lightly remarked, "Sonnet and I do know what little boys are made of."

Josheb's gaze had a pleading quality.

Jacques sighed. "Are you wary of me? Trust yourself to Sonnet, and I'll keep my back turned."

"It's not *that* ...!" With a sheepish look, Josheb muttered, "Caleb doesn't know...."

398
SHOW ME YOURS

J acques' interest piqued. "A gentleman's valet keeps his secrets. You may confide in us ... if you dare."

"Unfair!"

"Entirely." Jacques approached, carefully gauging Josheb's reactions. "You've won Argent's trust. Let us prove ourselves worthy of yours."

"I ... have a tattoo."

"Do tell! Better yet, *show*." Jacques bartered for its baring. "I recently added my sixth tattoo. Mine were wrought with the aid of the First of Wards. Experimental sigilcraft."

"You're what? A test subject?"

"A willing one. Haven't you ever wished to see the things your brother does?"

Josheb slowly nodded.

"Then we must chat! Say ... during tonight's grooming session?"

399
HIGHLY IRREGULAR

Before agreeing to anything, Josheb raised his hand and said, "Hey. Did I *do* something to make you think I'm wary of you?"

Jacques thought back. "Not specifically. Many are, so I'm accustomed t–"

The last thing he expected was for Josheb to haul him close and hug him. "I'm sorry you were hurt by enough people that you expect more of the same."

This was highly irregular.

American enthusiasm?

Amaranthine adaptation?

Jacques tried to think of something witty to say, but then Sonnet got involved, enfolding them both and crooning, "You're both good boys. Let's all get along."

400
LEND BALANCE

Josheb's hopeful smile faded. "I'm making you uncomfortable, aren't I?"

"Uncomfortable? Lord, no." Jacques frowned thoughtfully. "Although I've never been quite this close to an excess of facial hair."

"Oh. The beard. Not your thing?"

"Very not."

Josheb tried to pull away, but Sonnet didn't let go. He softly said, "I was raised to be modest, so I'm more self-conscious than most wolves. It's especially shocking to bare my blaze, but if it would lend balance to our trust …?"

Jacques had thought it amusing to consign Josheb to a fundoshi. It wasn't funny, now. "Sonnet, why have you never protested?"

401
MARKED INTEREST

The children invited me. How could I refuse?" To Josheb, he added, "They are *such* dears. But more to the point, if you're willing, I'll help you cover your tattoo."

"*Sonnet*," Jacques cut in.

The wolf's tail tucked.

"Have we been imposing on you all this time?"

"No. You make it easy to be brave." He shyly added, "I'm curious, though. About your tattoos."

Jacques blinked. "Mine?"

"What has you curious?" quizzed Josheb.

"His tattoos have a faint scent, and it stirs me up a little." Sonnet fluttered a hand over his heart. "Like the anticipation of a good chase."

402
TONIGHT

Nobody's mentioned that little detail before." Jacques searched Sonnet's whisky-gold eyes and ventured, "We'll *also* have to have a chat. Later."

"Later," agreed Sonnet.

"But not any sort of vague, putting-me-off later. *Tonight*."

"There's dinner to prepare. And our guest to consider."

"He doesn't mind," Jacques drawled.

"I don't mind," Josheb quickly assured. "Count me in!"

Sonnet hesitated, but in the way of someone who doesn't know how to be greedy. Jacques knew just how to coax him. Up on tiptoe, he delivered a *pudding please* that would've made Ever proud.

"Vanya …?"

"Bring him," urged Jacques. "*And* his illustrious Papka."

403
SIDELONG

Jacques intercepted Josheb's sidelong looks while Sonnet played valet. "No need to hold back. I'm not shy."

"Can I get a quick peek?"

"So eager." Jacques pulled his hair away from his nape. "This one's oldest. It allowed me my first glimpse of Ephemera."

In a hot second, Josheb was breathing down his neck. "How's it work?"

"Who can say?" Jacques softly admitted, "I've always thought it must be magic."

Fingertips traced over sensitive skin. "Is Lord Mettlebright taking volunteers?"

There was so much longing in Josheb's tone. A twinge of envy Jacques understood all too well. "I'll ask."

404
FLEX AND HOLD

Josheb struck a pose but immediately wilted. "They confiscated my phone."

"You've no place to put one," Sonnet pointed out.

"Lord. Let me." Jacques fetched his.

"Send the pictures to me?"

"Flex and hold. No, not your arms." He twirled a finger in the direction of his derriere.

Josheb sighed but gamely complied.

"Will you feel better or worse if I remark upon the cut of your hipbones?"

He snorted. "Do you ever switch that off?"

"I do." Jacques paused. "Is that a request?"

"Nah. You do you."

"And you be your charming, rough-and-tumble self. For the children, of course."

405
SWOOP

O h, man! Oh, *wow!*" Josheb ran ahead, leaping onto the wall edging the long drop to the beach.

Sonnet hurried after, protective as ever. Jacques took his sweet time.

Suuzu, in truest form, banked into a showy turn that revealed Nonny and Akira clasped in his talons. He swooped to cheers, then beat his wings, suspending them for a moment before dropping his passengers into the sea.

"Nonny always goes with a buddy," Jacques explained. "He's not our strongest swimmer, but he can never get enough ...."

But Josheb wasn't listening.

"Over here! Suuzu!" Josheb whistled and waved. "Do me!"

406
IMPERTINENCE

W ell, that's one way to make an entrance," Jacques murmured.

Sonnet hummed and reached for his hand.

"You're not mothering me, are you?"

"No." The swing of his tail brushed pleasantly against the back of Jacques' thighs.

"About your blaze." He blundered forward. "I don't know the protocol, so you'll have to forgive my impertinence, but... to my knowledge, I've never seen it."

"Do you want to?"

"Not if it's an imposition."

Sonnet smiled and shyly changed his question. "Will you look?"

"Look, as in *don't touch?*"

With a soft laugh, he turned, lifting aside the length of his hair.

407

LIVING GOLD

"Lord, you're tall," Jacques complained.

Sonnet sat upon the wall, giving Jacques better access to an intricate pattern of amber swirls that gleamed softly against bare skin.

"In a way, I've never seen my blaze either." Sonnet peeped over his shoulder. "Only in mirrors. Or… reflected in your eyes."

"May I touch? Or … too personal?"

"It's certainly personal, but you may."

Jacques traced Sonnet's blaze, admiring the artistry. It was as if he'd been inset with living gold.

Sonnet's tail puffed and settled.

Jacques glanced guiltily. "Too much?"

"No." With a low laugh, Sonnet confessed, "I'm not impervious to compliments."

408

APPROPRIATELY FESTIVE

Sonnet patted the wall. "Sit beside me?"

Jacques settled in, politely ignoring the feel of cold stone against bare buttocks.

Again, Sonnet took his hand.

"Something's happened, hasn't it?" Jacques kissed Sonnet's knuckles. "Spill."

The wolf's gaze turned soulful. "I should tell my parents about Vanya."

"*Naturellement.*"

"But … *how*?"

"Photograph? Phone call? Letter by herald would be appropriately festive."

"No … I mean … how do I explain that a bond of sisterhood is at the heart of this honor? And that I'm proud to be this boy's second mother?"

"Did you need me to jot that down? Because it's well said."

409
SAFE SPACE

Sonnet's whine nearly broke Jacques' heart.

"Bring them here? If Michael can't charm them, Sansa will browbeat them."

The wolf bit his lip, kicked his feet, and finally asked, "Have *you* ever wanted to invite your family here?"

Jacques' eyes widened. "*Mon dieu.* I shudder to think what would happen if Bon-Bon were to sneer upon all I hold dear. Or for Maman to belittle my feelings or criticize my choices. It would be *horrible.*"

A tear slipped down Sonnet's cheek. "I *knew* you would understand."

"Shall we bring your news to them? I would be pleased to escort you."

410
NOVELTIES

Josheb whooped overhead, having challenged Ginkgo to a cannonball contest.

Meanwhile, Jacques asked, "Will you take a turn?"

"Flight isn't a novelty for me."

"I almost can't picture you flitting about."

"I prefer to run."

Jacques still couldn't picture it. Sonnet was all aprons and rolling pins and rocking chairs. "I'd like to see that."

"Next time?" He smiled tentatively. "*I* could escort *you.*"

"What is appropriate attire for running rampant?"

Sonnet gazed thoughtfully toward the moon, which showed pale in the blue sky. "Something more … rugged …?"

"Rugged," Jacques echoed, testing the word. "I don't think I've ever attempted rugged."

411
IN A PINCH

Michael lounged in the shallows with Gilen and one of Stately House's newbies. Arnaud's diaper had been adapted to make room for a long, spotted tail. The little crosser gave up patting at lazy waves the moment he caught wind of Jacques.

Toddling over, hands upraised, he lisped in delight, and Jacques' lips twitched. Baby talk was especially cute in French.

"What's he saying?" asked Michael, who'd taken to watching over their club's little guys.

Jacques didn't like to brag.

Gilen bumped shoulders with Michael and offered a teasing translation. "We do in a pinch, but Papa Zha-Zha is best."

412
SPLENDID ACQUISITION

Jacques stayed with Arnaud so Gilen could have a turn in Suuzu's clutches. Josheb was queued up, and he offered his hand to Gilen. The American's methods were very different from Jacques' *suavité*, but Josheb commanded an audience in his own way.

"He would make a splendid acquisition."

Michael hummed. "Too much a wanderer, don't you think?"

"I'll still mention it to Argent."

Ever since Jacques brought home Sonnet, he'd been given *carte blanche* with regards to new hires.

"By the way, he wants you to tattoo him."

"*Really?*" Michael's eyes took on a shine. "I'll talk to Argent, too."

413

NO CONTRADICTION

Laughter drew Jacques' attention to Nonny, who had buddied up with Sonnet. Their game made no sense—lunging, dodging, circling, and growling. Wolf versus goat, but without a hint of danger.

Sonnet was as comfortable here as he was in the kitchen. Tail flagging playfully, the wolf's laugh deepened as he casually tossed Nonny, then dove after him. Powerful. Protective.

Jacques liked the way Sonnet embraced his contradictions. Or maybe it was truer to say there were none. Every part of Sonnet was part of Sonnet. He was at ease with himself, and that put Jacques at ease with him.

414

EVERYTHING AND NOTHING

Right, then!" Jacques firmed his stance. "Suuzu needs a break."
There were groans and whinging, but Deece arrived with a couple of coolers, neatly diverting everyone's attention.

Suuzu glided in and shifted, and Akira splashed into the shallows. As Suuzu pulled him close, Akira talked animatedly, leaning into his nestmate's side like it was nothing. Even though Jacques knew it was everything.

They'd earned more than that fleeting moment, but Josheb the Gregarious squelched their way, arms flung wide, bottles of iced drinks in both hands. Exultant. Grateful. Oblivious.

Michael cheerfully inquired, "Shall we?"

"Lord, yes. You get the American."

415
DOUBLE TAKE

Jacques routinely helped Argent, Ginkgo, Deece, and Sonnet serve at table during the evening meal, making himself available to cut food into bite-sized pieces or reach second servings. Or thirds. Crossers had big appetites.

Tonight, the Americans were holding court on opposite ends of the table, telling a highly-entertaining tale that *hadn't* made it to television, regularly interrupting each other to set the record straight.

Midway through, while Caleb was speaking, Jacques saw Sonnet reach past Josheb to replenish a platter. Josheb glanced up to thank her and did a befuddled double take. "Sonnet ...?"

The apron-clad wolf smiled serenely. "Yes ...?"

416
REWARDING GOOD BEHAVIOR

If Jacques' mind hadn't already been made up about the American, Josheb would have swayed him with his next easy smile. "I *wondered* where you were!"

"The kitchen. I'm a cook, you see."

"Did you make these?" Josheb lifted the cotton towel from an empty basket.

Sonnet's eyes took on a shine. "You like my rolls?"

Josheb coaxed, "Any left?"

"I'll see what I can find!" She fairly skipped to the kitchen.

Jacques circled the table to grip Josheb's shoulder. "I could kiss you."

The man's eyebrows jumped, but he tapped his cheek. "Put 'er here."

Jacques took that dare.

417
PETITION

Normally, Argent was swift to enforce rules, but when Kyrie and Lilya stole from their chairs to approach Caleb Dare, the fox turned a blind eye.

So he was ready to yield?

Jacques moved to oversee.

Caleb read a petition signed by *nearly* everyone at Stately House, then asked, "What would you advise, sir?"

"I cannot think of a finer way for a man of your reputation to use his influence."

"I'm more of a dog person, but sure. I'll sign."

Which is how the Dare brothers—at least on paper—swayed Lord Mettlebright on the proposal "Kittens for Crossers."

418
SANCTUARY

Deece's technique with massage was as potent as ever. When Josheb's soft snores signaled a release from the day's obligations, Jacques sought the sanctuary of his rooms only to find them too empty. So after his nightly rituals were accomplished, he trod the familiar path to the nap room.

All the usual culprits were variously curled and cuddled amidst the pillows and furs, and rockers swayed in triplicate. Spying Tsumiko, Jacques knelt to lay his head on her knee, and she petted his hair.

This.

This was probably why he'd never wanted Sonnet mothering him.

This belonged to Tsumiko now.

419

PLANS DASHED

Jacques hadn't realized he'd fallen asleep until a stealthy blanket settled around his shoulders. Strong arms were pulling, lifting, carrying, but he couldn't see. He fumbled and found smooth skin, then traced along a collarbone.

"Oh, it's you," he murmured, for he'd know that collarbone anywhere.

"You made me promise. *Tonight*, you said. No putting-me-off *later*."

"Lord. I did." He admitted, "I left Josheb with Michael and Deece."

"And Vanya is with his mother."

"Plans dashed." Jacques ventured, "Where are we off to?"

"Bed."

"Together?"

"You *did* promise."

Jacques missed a beat. "I did?"

"Your tattoos," Sonnet reminded. "Show me?"

420

COMFORT ZONE

Sonnet's rooms smelled a little of starch and a little of candle wax and a little of tea. He stole Jacques' dressing gown and hung it beside a fresh-pressed dress and apron. Fluffed fur topped the bed, but the sheets beneath were crisp and smelled of lavender.

"Have your way with me," encouraged Jacques.

"Are you sure?"

"Quite." He doubted anything Sonnet had in mind would push him past his comfort zone.

"Then ... I will."

"Beg pardon if I fall asleep on you."

Sonnet was suddenly looming over him, his posture utterly dominant. "Beg pardon if I keep you awake."

421
TAIL TUCKED

Jacques relaxed into a smile and a submissive posture. "Why so grim?"

"This feels … inappropriate?"

"Which part? Because I thought wolves kipped in company."

"That's … true."

"Is it me?" checked Jacques. "I've been called inappropriate on many occasions."

Sonnet's tail tucked, butting against Jacques' thigh.

Jacques carefully pushed loose hair aside to try to read Sonnet's expression. "Did we cross a line earlier?"

"No."

"Did you *want* to cross a line?"

Sonnet finally said, "Maybe that's it. This feels like … trysting."

"But it's not?"

"No …?"

So much uncertainty.

"If you're curious about more than my tattoos, I won't be miffed."

422
NEW MOON FESTIVAL

Come, now. Confess."

Sonnet flopped to the mattress, all pretense of posturing gone. Jacques rolled to face him and lifted an arm.

Scooting closer, the wolf hid his face against Jacques' pajamas and mumbled, "The moon."

"Mm-hmm?"

"There are wolvish festivals."

"So I've heard. Isn't the next one for unattached males such as yourself?"

Sonnet crooned a mournful note.

"The Elderbough pack will be observing."

"I don't want *them*."

"You want me?" Jacques fitted pieces together. "Is *that* why you invited me to run with you?"

Sonnet tensed.

"Will you accept a verbal *répondez*?"

"*S'il vous plait.*"

Jacques promised, "*Oui.*"

423
RUGGED ENOUGH TO REVEL

I do have a question about appropriate attire," Jacques said. "How would you define *rugged*? Buckskin? Denim? Lord, please tell me you don't mean flannel."

Nothing.

Only quiet breaths.

Jacques tried again. "I *do* wonder what revelries young wolves get up to on moonless nights."

Sonnet whined.

Jacques tweaked the tip of his ear. "Is there something about this festival that scandalizes your nobler sensibilities?"

"A little ...?"

"Then I'll probably enjoy it."

Sonnet tightened his hold but offered no further elucidation.

"Moving along. Shall I *show* you my tattoos, or is it more sporting to make you hunt them down?"

424
NO HARD FEELINGS

Jacques had been in his fair share of compromising positions, and this one was decidedly picturesque. Candlelight did lovely things to Sonnet's complexion and put fire in amber eyes. But the reason Jacques' ankle was propped on his shoulder was entirely innocent. And that made the whole situation funny.

Sonnet nosed an inked sigil, making the grumbling, growly noises that all wolves seemed to lapse into when talking to themselves.

"Is it really that interesting?"

"No ...? I don't know," Sonnet muttered distractedly. Then his tongue swiped skin.

Jacques hummed appreciatively.

Sonnet looked shocked, mostly at himself.

Jacques blew a kiss.

425
TOO KIND

Discover anything?"

Sonnet's gaze dropped. "That you trust me. And that I cannot trust myself."

"I feel doubly complimented."

"This is awkward."

"It needn't be."

Gesturing around them, Sonnet said, "I brought you into my den."

"Lapsing into euphemisms again? A weary friend happened to drop by. You're guilty of nothing more than hospitality."

Sonnet radiated contrition. "You're tired."

"I am. But I've given up a night's rest for men who held far less of my regard."

"You're too kind."

"Self-indulgent is closer to the mark." Jacques didn't mind admitting, "I quite enjoy being at the center of your attention."

426
VIVE LA DIFFERENCE

You have always been kind to me," Sonnet insisted.

"Because I am a gentleman."

"Are you actually *un*kind?" There was a challenge in that tone.

"I should hope not." And Jacques proved it by redirecting his friend. "May I stay over?"

Sonnet drew himself up. "Of course!"

"*Bon*. Lie here. And while I sleep, you can muddle with *this* tattoo. It's what the others usually do."

Moments later, Sonnet nuzzled his nape.

Jacques leaned into his larger frame. "Don't you crave this kind of closeness?"

Sonnet ventured, "We have the children."

"This is different."

Eventually, he conceded, "This is different."

427
FASHION THYSELF

Jacques had never been a morning person, and none of his former acquaintances would ever have called him dedicated to anything but fashion. But devotion could drive a man to unforeseen lengths.

Still clutching a coffee cup, Jacques dragged himself across the garden at the ungodly hour of nine-thirty to undergo the daily rigors that kept him fit to be tailored.

True, he could have gone to Sansa, who put their energetic young crossers through their paces, but Jacques preferred a kinder, gentler taskmaster.

"Lord, I hate this," he grumbled to Deece.

"I know. But we look forward to it."

428
DOJO

Deece patted his back, let him complain, stole his coffee cup, and made him stretch. All while his sons watched with feline fascination. Or in Fend's case, disdain.

"*Must* they stare?"

"They like you." Deece quietly added, "They are jealous of you."

"Because they aspire to sit-ups?"

"Because I am with you in different ways than I am with them."

Jacques caught Rake's eye and said, "Your sire dotes on all of you. Me, he tortures."

"They think you're my favorite."

"Don't drag me into your sibling rivalries."

"They don't think of you as a brother."

"Uncle?"

Deece winced. "Pet."

429

PET NAME

Should I be insulted?"

"I hope not. You've always been part of their lives, part of our hearth." Deece reasoned it through. "I guard you, I groom you, I hold you while you sleep. And Minx thinks it's … cute."

It had never occurred to Jacques that Minx might object.

Rasp scooted closer and licked Jacques' cheek.

Rake began to purr.

Deece cleared his throat. "*She* calls you my pet, in teasing."

"Is that why you all toy with me, *mes amis*?" Jacques pressed wrist to brow.

Fend ambled closer and nosed Jacques' belly.

"So strict," Jacques complained, but sit-ups resumed.

430

TASKMASTER

Jacques eyed Fend. "What must the pet endure today?"

"The boys were hoping for a run."

Jogging on the beach sounded so picturesque, but Jacques knew he'd be chased back and forth across the sand by this trio of capering beasts.

"The boys?" Jacques narrowed his eyes. "Or Fend?"

Fend bared his fangs in a dangerous smile.

But then Deece's attention swung away, and Rake slunk toward the open door.

Stately House's dojo housed a small arsenal, so a combination of barriers and illusions kept it—and Jacques' calisthenics—neatly under wraps.

No crossers allowed.

Yet a five-year-old exception appeared.

431
TALE BRINGER

Nobody had noticed at first. Why would they? Kyrie rarely strayed. But out-of-bounds incidents kept adding up.

By some quirk of heritage, barriers were useless against the boy. He strolled right past them.

Kyrie offered his hands to Rake, who butted him affectionately.

Deece asked, "What's happened?"

"The Elderboughs are early."

"Did they need help?"

The boy shook his head and cast a longing look at Jacques, who was only too happy for an excuse to leave off crunching his abdominals. "Well?" he prompted.

"Ninook and Joonta brought two new children." And in an awed whisper, "One is a *baby*."

432
PRESENTABLE

How did you find Deece's dojo?"

Kyrie said, "It is next to the garden."

"You can see it?"

"I can *feel* it."

"Which part?" Jacques opened his closet.

"The purples and blues."

"I see. Well, I *don't*. But you've always liked crystals."

"They sing for me," Kyrie shyly shared. "You cannot hear them?"

"Alas, no. Though I hold out some hope." Jacques knotted his tie. "There. Do I look and smell more like myself?"

"Yes!"

"Excellent! Now, what sort of baby did the wolves bring us?"

"American."

"*Inhabituel*. What's their clan?"

Kyrie tugged his hand to hurry him along. "Coyote."

433

WOLVES AT THE GATE

The Elderbough pack visited often enough that they'd claimed a patch of woods alongside the little-used driveway. The number of wolves at Stately House's gate had recently increased, thanks to a large-scale evacuation of Kith from America.

Adoona-soh's bondmate sat a little apart with Sonnet, deep in a conversation that cut off.

Jacques hesitated. "Are we interrupting?"

"You are Jacques." Ninook's tail swayed. "I have been remiss. Come, tell me about yourself."

Jacques caught Sonnet's furtive glance. Lord. Now what?

She blushed and nodded to the bundle in her arms. "It's fine. She'll need a whiff of her Uncle Jackie."

434

RIGHT TO IT

Ninook asked, "How did you and Sonnet become acquainted?"

"A bit of weather-provoked serendipity. I was caught in the rain. We shared a pot of tea."

"And became close?"

"Not especially. My duties keep me with Argent, and Sonnet works alongside Sansa. We do overlap in the naproom."

"We both like cubs," murmured Sonnet, who offered their newcomer.

Jacques cradled the coyote crosser, who gathered breath to wail.

"*Non*. None of that. You're not carried off, *mon petit*. Here is your trusted one." Moving closer to Ninook he coyly added, "Get your whiff and learn that I am quite harmless."

435
BENEATH NOTICE

Ninook took that for invitation and pressed close, inhaling deeply, but also making certain that the baby could see him and—perhaps more importantly—smell him.

"May we twist a bit of your hair for a bracelet?" Jacques inquired. "It helps. Sometimes."

"Perhaps a braid, three strands from her three minders," Ninook suggested. "I'll give the task to Torloo."

Kyrie tugged at Ninook's tunic. "Torloo came?"

"Oh! Kyrie. I did not see you there."

"I know." He went up on tiptoe. "Does she have a name?"

"Losi," said Ninook, his expression warming. "The boy who found her named her Losi."

436
TOO LITTLE

Kyrie crooned over the baby in that musical way dragons had, and when he showed her his hands, Losi lifted hers.

"And here you thought no one could be as wonderful as Ninook," Jacques drawled, surrendering her.

Sitting beside Sonnet, Kyrie asked, "Is she too little to be afraid?"

"No, love. She's too little to be anything but wise."

Jacques tended to agree. "Trust at first sight."

A leggy young wolf loped over, licking Ninook's chin before flopping at Kyrie's feet.

Losi made little hooting, howling noises.

"Lord. What's set her off?"

The wolf shifted to confess, "It was me."

437
ELDERBOUGH TRACKERS

Torloo!" Kyrie sprang up.

The older boy gamely crossed his legs, creating a seat for him. Hooking his chin over Kyrie's shoulder to smile at the baby, Adoona-soh's youngest started a friendly thrumming that was a far cry from a grown wolf's rumble.

Adorable.

Losi gurgled back, hands waving excitedly.

Doubly adorable.

Jacques *liked* Torloo. The kid had been one of a long line of Elderbough trackers who'd turned up to get a whiff of their quarry's son, but Torloo hadn't confined himself to duty.

Kyrie considered Torloo-dex Elderbough his friend.

And bless his loyal heart, Torloo considered Kyrie his.

438
ONE OF YOURS

Jacques hadn't forgotten that Ninook was well within his personal space and—practically—breathing down his neck. But he pointedly ignored the posturing.

In fact, it was *because* he was gazing off in a bored way that he caught sight of a stranger on the grounds, drifting in the general direction of the house.

Jacques pointed. "Is that one of yours?"

"He runs with us, yes."

"There were no humans on the guest list we approved." More to the point, "Did you *tell* Argent?"

Ninook hesitated.

Jacques sighed. "You'd better collar that fellow before ...."

But it was already too late.

439

CROSSING PATHS

Should I go?" asked Torloo, whose tail had puffed double at the precipitous arrival of an enormous silver fox.

"Naroo-soh is already there," soothed Ninook.

Indeed, Adoona's eldest had pushed his way between the young man and Argent's muzzle. Naroo-soh was talking fast, but he paused to snap something over his shoulder.

Their unanticipated guest actually went full grovel. Jacques would swear he was grinning.

"Where'd you find *him*?"

"In America," said Ninook. "Our paths crossed soon after the Emergence ... under dire circumstances. His quick thinking saved many lives, including Torloo's."

Torloo helpfully added, "Coop's the one who named Losi."

440

INCONTROVERTIBLE

Thoroughly distracted, Kyrie returned the baby to Sonnet, and he and Torloo ran to help Roo-nii. Ninook was not so easily turned aside.

"Lone wolves may not run with a pack, but they are not without support."

Jacques agreed. "Everyone adores Sonnet."

"Yourself included?"

"Incontrovertibly."

Sonnet's soft whine was definitely a protest.

Ninook's posture shifted, and he handed off Vanya to Jacques. "I will say it again, Sonnet. You are welcome to run with us."

"I understand."

With a final sniff for Jacques and smile for the baby, Ninook strode off.

"Sonnet?"

"Y-yes?"

Jacques sweetly asked, "What was *that* about?"

441
HACKLES

Ninook is a dex. They look out for lone wolves. My grandsire probably asked him to check on me."

"That sounds like Harmonious, but *something* must have raised Ninook's hackles where I'm concerned."

"I told him you would run with me during the new moon."

Jacques guessed, "A shocking departure?"

Sonnet sighed. "I shouldn't have asked him for advice."

"About me?"

"Among other things."

"So Ninook disapproves of the wild revelries you've planned?"

She went quiet.

Jacques had been *joking*. "Maybe you should tell me more about new moon traditions."

Sonnet blushed and whispered, "Not in front of the children."

442
SCAMPER

They strolled toward the house in a silence that Jacques refused to prolong. "This is awkward for you."

"Mmm."

"But we'll run." Whatever that meant.

Sonnet's gaze remained fixed on Losi. "Mmm."

"Shall I do my own research? Discreetly, of course."

"You'd do that?"

"I'm the willing sort. Well, I draw the line at flannel, but I can be otherwise rugged and ready to revel." And because Jacques knew just enough to be dangerous, he asked, "By any chance, are there salacious overtones to our upcoming scamper?"

Sonnet looked incredibly embarrassed but a tiny bit relieved when she answered, "Mmm."

443
NO POSITION TO CRITICIZE

In the kitchen, Sansa and Michael sat across the table from Adoona-soh. Conversation immediately lulled. Déjà vu.

"The dears are both hungry," Sonnet murmured.

"Bring them," urged Sansa.

Jacques started forward with Vanya, only to pivot when the woman bared a breast. "Lord. Warn a fellow."

Sansa's chuckle was entirely unapologetic.

When Michael came to fetch his son, he smiled ruefully. "Have you seen Argent?"

"He's out front. Making a point."

"I am here." Argent stalked in.

"The American boy?"

"Ordinary. And exhaustingly eager. But I cannot fault their choices."

Michael's hand settled against Jacques' back. "That *would* be hypocritical.

444
NEEDED

This one knows what she needs," crooned Sansa.

"People generally do," remarked Adoona-soh.

Jacques risked a glance. Sure enough, Adoona was looking right at Sonnet, whose tail lifted.

Argent asked, "You needed me?"

"If you can spare the time," Michael began tentatively. "I need to arrange for a series of crystals for Kurogi-kun. Something just off-key, so he'll have to bring them into balance. I'd prefer to choose them myself."

"You need a ride."

"To Glintrubble."

"When?"

"I could go get my coat …?"

"Rearrange my calendar, Smythe. I will be away." Gazing off after Michael, Argent blandly added, "Family emergency."

445
VALISE

J acques chivvied Argent to his closet. "Fresh shirt!"

"This one is fine."

"That tunic is barely acceptable even when it *is* clean."

Argent glanced down, possibly for the first time in hours. "Ah."

"Good grooming is only slightly contagious, and you show no symptoms."

"I hardly spit up upon myself."

Jacques extended a semi-formal tunic in the Mettlebright colors, then packed two others.

"Surely luggage is not required."

"I'll not let you slight Dwennon or the First Herd." He held out silver-stitched breeches. "Attire is a subtle, unspoken compliment. Very fox-worthy. Trust me."

Argent sighed. "This is why I do."

446
MORE THAN A MATCH

L atching the valise, Jacques eyed Argent critically. "You won't leave this house until Tsumiko tidies your hair."

His lordship managed to look beleaguered.

"Bid her *adieu*. I'll see if Michael wants to borrow my new aviator goggles."

Argent snorted. "Surely not."

"The contents of a gentleman's wardrobe should be a match for *any* occasion."

They parted ways, and Jacques found Michael, adjusted his cloak pin, then gave him passing marks. "*Do* try to keep him tidy."

Michael laughed. "No promises. Glintrubble's collection will have me thoroughly diverted."

"Right, then." Jacques warned, "I'll be calling you at regular intervals. Pick up."

447
DANCE ATTENDANCE

Jacques took himself to the blue parlor, where Lapis lounged, head tipped back, expression blissful while Kyrie brushed his hair. Isla was also dancing attendance upon Lord Mossberne, adding gold leaf to his pedicure.

"Your meeting has been postponed," Jacques announced. "Michael needed his lordship, and they'll be away for the rest of the day."

Lapis opened an eye. "No matter. More time for amateur theatrics."

Isla spoke up. "Uncle Jackie, May I go over Sensei's calendar with you?"

"In French?"

"Would you mind?"

"Hardly. It's all the same to me." He impulsively asked, "Shall we use your father's office?"

448
COMPARE NOTES

They've added several new words to the French dictionary!" Isla was now fluent enough to talk at full speed. "Most are specific to the In-between, and I need to know them all."

"Show me the list. We can practice."

Isla whisked to her father's desk and set out her books. "We shall! But first—and this is top secret—Kimi's set the date for her next kiss, which is why Sensei's schedule has changed."

They compared calendars and renegotiated sleep schedules. But before Isla could return to lexicial interests, Jacques casually asked, "How much do you know about the packs?"

449

INDEPENDENT RESEARCH

Lots, but far from everything. Wolves have a distinct language, complex traditions, and unique lore."

Jacques ventured, "Like … oh, say … moon festivals?"

"Yes! I've been memorizing the Seven Score Moons, the basis for the wolvish calendar, but it's complicated. There are several migrating moons, and certain moons are only named as they occur."

"So if I needed to research a specific moon …?"

She straightened. "Which one?"

"Perhaps the upcoming new moon."

Isla frowned. "I've only studied the full moons!"

"Alas."

"*Non*!" She reached for the ON button on her father's computer. "We can ask Reaver Foster. He's bound to know."

450

YET ANOTHER AMERICAN

As Michael's computer whirred softly to life, Jacques protested. "Think of the time difference. Jimsy may well be tucked safe in his den at this hour. And we can't simply commandeer your father's apprentice."

"Papka won't mind!"

"*Au contraire*." In his periphery, the computer screen winked on, and a window popped up, revealing a redhead pulling off *rugged* like it was easy. In French, Jacques muttered, "Did you do that?"

"Oh!" Isla blinked and straightened in her seat. "You're not Mr. Foster. Who are you, please?"

On the other side of the world, the freckle-faced American cautiously answered, "I'm Kip."

451
PRETTY BOY

sla Ward of Stately House. This is Uncle Jackie, our butler.”

Jacques was intrigued. Since when did squirrel clansmen flash tails? “You haven’t answered Isla, pretty boy. Why are you in Jimsy’s room? Are your intentions honorable?”

If they weren’t, Jacques was prepared to be doubly intrigued.

“Behave,” chided Isla.

Kip was a good sport, smiling through the banter. Isla was so easy to tease. But there was a point.

“It’s a matter of some delicacy.”

“My favorite,” murmured Jacques.

That’s when Lapis turned up looking the farthest thing from rugged. “Why have the two of you commandeered Michael’s desk?”

452
YOU MAY BE EXCUSED

apis had swathed himself in sheer fabrics that shifted between navy and gold as he moved, offering mesmerizing glimpses of hip bones, collar bones, and so much skin. Lord, dragons were ornamental.

A fleeting touch acknowledged Jacques’ appreciation, but Lapis was saying, “Are you a Woodacre? You *look* like a Woodacre.”

Moments later, Jacques and Isla were excused.

As sigilcraft banned them further, Isla murmured, “I wonder if Kip wants to come to Stately House? For school, I mean.”

Leave it to Isla to assume all interests were academic.

Jacques sighed. He’d missed his chance to ask Jimsy about Sonnet.

453
DEAF AND BLIND

J acques was intensely curious about Kip's *delicate matter*, but Michael's return from Glintrubble thoroughly distracted Lapis. The dragon helped unpack arrays of crystals, caressing their facets and coaxing out their lingering melodies.

Deaf and blind to such wonders, Jacques turned to Argent. "Is this Jimsy's final thesis?"

"A reasonable comparison, though attainment is not limited to academic achievement. Michael is overseeing one facet of a larger rite of passage. Jiminy will be recognized as an adult male of his pack."

"What was yours?"

Argent hesitated. "A journey."

"Where did you go?"

He turned the question back. "Where would *you* go?"

454
PROVING JOURNEY

A re you serious? Or are you keeping me from chasing tales?"
Argent's gaze held amusement. "Both."

"Right. Well." Jacques finally answered, "I can't think of anywhere else I'd rather be, so we can safely assume that *my* journey brought me here."

His lordship huffed. "You can be surprisingly sensible at times."

"What other sorts of things do you suppose Jimsy has to do? As a wolf, I mean."

"I hardly know. Traditions vary by pack." Argent's brows arched. "If you want a lecture, ask Isla."

Jacques pouted. "What if my questions are too ... delicate?"

Argent blinked, sat, and said, "Ask."

455

COLD FEET

The appointed day arrived for Jacques to escort Sonnet to Keishi. Caffeinated and cashmered, he let his carpet bag swing gently ... and hummed.

She arrived in a clatter of low heels, travel dress swirling modestly about her calves, overnight case in a white-knuckle grip at her side, tail far too low.

Of course Sonnet was nervous.

But Jacques was a superlative event organizer. Offering his arm, he said, "Michael's bringing the car around."

"Mmm."

"Sonnet, love. How are you with sigils? I'm pants with them, of course."

"I learned from Mum. *Yours* are ... oh." Sonnet blinked. "What's Lord Mettlebright done?"

456

BAGGAGE CLAIM

Jacques lifted the bulging carpet bag. "His lordship placed a sigil hereabouts. Can you banish it?"

Sonnet searched his face, extended a finger, and gasped.

"Gone?"

"Vanished." Sonnet's nostrils were as wide as her eyes. "What have you *done*?"

"Packed for the trip."

Her fingers trembled as she unbuckled the fastenings and eased open the bag. Vanya gurgled and kicked. "You can't pack a baby!"

"I can," argued Jacques. "I did!"

"But ... but this is kidnapping!"

"*Non*. This is trust. He's coming with Sansa's blessing. Your claim's the *surest* sure thing. Sentinel and Rampant will be so proud of you."

457
HANDLER

All other qualms forgotten, Sonnet fretted and fussed and crooned over her fosterling.

Jacques cheerfully endured her scolding while navigating the roads to Keishi in one of the estate's poshest antiques. Lord, he loved a Rolls.

"Mark's expecting us."

"Who?"

"One of your strapping uncles. Valor will meet us at the gate, and Rampant knows we're coming. Your mother felt it would be best *not* to tell your father. I think she likes to rile him up. And really … can you blame her?"

"Da …?"

"I'll handle him. Handling things is … well! This sort of thing may be my actual job."

458
SUCH A GENTLEMAN

They made one last stop. Sonnet fed Vanya a bottle, but her mind was elsewhere. Eventually, she asked, "Am I ridiculous?"

"I find you wonderful. Is that enough?"

Sonnet considered. "Is there more?"

"There can be." Jacques twiddled his fingers at her travel dress. "While you're far from Rubenesque, you're a handsome enough woman. What's the usual term? Statuesque."

"Do I look like a mother?"

"Every inch," he staunchly assured.

"You're not just … being a gentleman?"

Jacques struck a pose. "I am *always* a gentleman. Which is why I need you to slip out of your shoes for a moment."

459
SHOES OFF

M y shoes?"

"If I may?" Jacques knelt before her chair and tugged at ribbons. "Fear not. I'll put you back to rights."

"Why must I be barefoot?"

He patted an ankle before glancing up. "Because I don't kiss women."

Sonnet's eyes widened.

"Most of the ladies in my life get air kisses and harmless remarks that pass as compliments. Hmm. Stockings on or off?"

"Leave them. I'll be male for you."

Jacques rose and stepped smartly into Sonnet's personal space. "Then if I may ... paraphrase?"

Sonnet's tail quivered, his posture receptive.

"My wolvish is unrefined," warned Jacques. "Pardon my accent."

460
PARAPHRASE

C upping Sonnet's face to encourage a better angle, Jacques pressed a careful kiss to the underside of Sonnet's jaw. In wolvish—assuming he'd done it correctly—it was the sort of gesture shared by packmates on the cusp of a hunt.

A friendly gesture.

A kiss for courage.

Sonnet blinked against the extra shine in his eyes and exhaled shakily.

"We're denmates belonging to Stately House." Jacques promised, "We'll be fine, you and I. How do you say it? Everything you need, I will be."

A soft gasp.

A warming of cheeks.

Both of which inspired Jacques to improvise further.

461
OPEN TO INTERPRETATION

Jacques kissed the corner of Sonnet's smile. To strengthen it. Or maybe because while Sonnet could be a lady, he was also unabashedly masculine, especially while stripped to his fundoshi.

"That one probably didn't translate."

Sonnet's nostrils quavered. "It did."

Jacques brazenly kissed the opposite corner. "For balance. Now. Feeling braver?"

A strong arm pulled him closer, and Sonnet pressed his lips to Jacques' jaw, lingering there. Jacques' heart leapt when Sonnet added a little nibble. He had no idea what it meant, but he hoped the wolf would do it again.

Sonnet's eyes sparkled. "That probably didn't translate either."

462
WELL SUITED

A baby? Whose baby?"

Jacques would swear Rampant *squeaked*.

"Mine." Sonnet firmed her stance. "Vanya is mine."

"Another fosterling! And such a beautiful soul. Oh! He's one of Michael's, isn't he?"

Rampant was in the midst of a thorough sniffening when the door snapped open, rattling the room's painted screens.

Sentinel warily eyed his son's dress, then his son's escort.

Jacques twiddled his fingers.

"Eloquence will want a whiff!" exclaimed Rampant. "Ever, too."

Sonnet managed a backward glance as her mother bustled her out. Jacques blew a kiss, waved, then casually remarked, "Motherhood suits Sonnet."

Sentinel sank to the floor.

463

SAD HUDDLE

Jacques sat before Sentinel, whose gaze was entirely mournful. His eyes were the same amber as Sonnet's. A Skybellow trait.

"I'm glad we've a moment alone. Argent suggested I have a word." From an inside pocket, Jacques withdrew a crystal and held it out on his palm.

Sentinel slowly uncurled a fist to cover it.

"Have I ever actually *told* you that you're adorable when confused?"

If anything, Sentinel's mood took another downward spiral.

"Aren't you happy for Sonnet?"

"Fostering I can understand. But ... why mothering?" Sentinel hunched miserably. "Is the reason he doesn't want to be a father ... *me*?"

464

THAT CERTAIN SWAGGER

Lord. You're probably the reason Sonnet became a wolf."

"I'm a dog."

"A practicing dog. With wolvish swagger." Jacques lowered his voice. "How could Sonnet *not* admire you?"

Sentinel's bafflement only increased. "My son wears dresses. He aspires to motherhood."

"Aspired and achieved," Jacques countered. "And admired for it."

"You admire him?"

"*Her*," he gently chided. "At the moment, *her* is the appropriate pronoun."

Sentinel eyed him. "What do you think of my son?"

"*Moi*? Sonnet is someone I'd hate to disappoint." Jacques supposed there was nothing else for it. "Which is why I wanted a word. About wolvish traditions."

465
ALPHA MALE

Jacques *knew* he liked Sentinel Skybellow.

Though he'd left the packs to become Rampant Starmark's bondmate, Sentinel hadn't shed *all* his wolvish aesthetic. He dressed the part of a kinder, gentler canine, but he'd retained most of his wildness. No doubt wolfsong still ran in his blood. All very alpha male.

And once he'd gotten over his initial surprise, Sentinel proved to be refreshingly frank.

"Lord." Jacques was almost giddy. "And here I thought wolves were straightlaced."

"Such traditions have a practical side." Sentinel frowned vaguely. "But why *you*?"

Jacques suspected, but he wasn't about to dish. "Why *not* me?"

466
CONGRATULATIONS

Jacques mostly hung back, letting Sonnet bask in the warmth of her clan's congratulations. With Vanya in her arms, she was courage itself.

Brava.

Hands down, Jacques' favorite moment was when Eloquence swooped in, stole Vanya from Harmonious, and settled the baby in Sentinel's arms. There was some good-natured ribbing about becoming a grandsire, and he scowled. But Sentinel also inhaled slowly, no doubt adding Vanya to his heart and his den.

"Are you surprised, Da?" Sonnet quietly asked. "That they trusted someone like me?"

"No," Sentinel's gaze lifted. "There is no place safer than the heart of a wolf."

467
RESOURCES

The sun dipped low, and Harmonious urged Jacques to make use of one of the guest pavilions. Carpet bag in hand, he strolled along a covered walkway, admiring the leaves falling at twilight. When a golden ginkgo leaf drifted to a stop at Jacques' feet, he hastily fished out his phone.

Mon dieu, I am an idiot

> **My sympathies**

You ran with wolves, yes?

> **You know I have**
> **Still do sometimes**

I need a discreet favor

> **Sure thing**

Lord
It's important

> **Still sure**
> **What's the thing?**

This next festival, I plan to run

No response.
And then Jacques' phone rang.

468
MORE THAN ORNAMENTAL

Jacques exited the bath to find furs already spread ... and Sonnet seated upon them.

His dress hung neatly from a peg, and his hair fell loose around bare shoulders. Vanya draped limply along his forearm, snoozing contentedly in jonquil yellow jammies.

"I'll watch over your sleep." Sonnet tentatively added, "If I'm welcome."

"I do more holding than being held."

Sonnet's tail rustled against the bedding. "I could hold you."

"How much privacy do we have?"

Rising, Sonnet handed off Vanya, then moved around the room, turning crystal columns that weren't just ornamental.

Sonnet returned, his gaze expectant. "It's just us."

469
SPOONS

Merci." Jacques arched his brows. "Are you going to tuck us in together?"

Sonnet waved at the bed he'd prepared. "I'll keep you warm."

"Both of us?"

He collected Vanya but stayed close. "Are we not denmates?"

"Some of Stately House's finest," Jacques agreed, loosening the tie on his dressing gown. "I don't usually retire this early, but ... we should talk."

"We *should*." Sonnet beamed. "Vanya likes the sound of voices. He'll go deep knowing we're near."

Which was both beside the point and entirely Sonnet. He fussed until Jacques was on his side, sheltering Vanya, then slid in behind.

470
CASTING CALL

Jacques remarked, "Most people wouldn't dare get between a mother and his baby."

"I trust you with him."

He could feel the compliment. He could also feel the hand at his hip and breath against his shoulder, right through the silk. "We'll return home tomorrow."

Sonnet nuzzled Jacques' nape. "Yes."

"Apologies for the lackluster quality of my soul."

"Don't be daft. You are charisma itself." Sonnet whispered, "I think you're brilliant."

Jacques cleared his throat. "About the festival. I've begun preparations, but there's something I need to know."

"Yes?"

"Which of us will be playing the part of the moonbeam?"

471

VIVID IMAGINATION

It makes a difference in the *accoutrement*. I'd thought *rugged* was required, but before I consult with our tailor, I need to know my part." Jacques eased more onto his back. "Am I the noble wolf or the moonbeam he seduces?"

"I ... umm ... *oh*. Really?"

"I'm not opposed to role play."

Propping up on an elbow, Sonnet whispered, "I want to be the wolf."

"*Naturellement.*"

His voice deepened. "I want to give chase, to pursue."

"Lord. There goes my heart."

Sonnet winced. "I'd never *hurt* you."

"This isn't fear, love. I'm only imagining what you'll do once you catch me."

472

NO HOLDS BARRED

Jacques wasn't going to make this hard for Sonnet. "No need to hold back. I'm looking forward to an encounter with your wild side."

In the softness of candlelight, Sonnet's gaze turned contemplative. "You'd let me do whatever I want?"

"Probably. I'm easily caught up in the moment." Jacques touched Sonnet's flushed face. "You're younger than I realized. I'm your senior, aren't I? In relative years and in experience?"

Sonnet slowly nodded.

"And younger wolves turn to their older packmates to learn about ... well. The birds and the bees doesn't quite fit. You want to learn the lore of lovers."

473
ALL THAT MATTERS

You rather put this off," Jacques murmured. "Was it for lack of a suitable partner?"

"I've been ... busy."

"I keep busy myself." Jacques chose to be straightforward. "You know I sometimes seek the company of cats?"

"I knew."

"Is that part of why you chose me? You wanted an experienced lover?"

Sonnet tensed.

"We need to be clear. Our game of hide-and-seek will stir instincts, and I'm responsible for the consequences." Jacques sighed. "I'm aware that I'm an unusual choice for a caper through the woods, but if you trust me, if you want me, that's really all that matters."

474
FRONT SEAT. BACK SEAT

During the drive home, Sonnet was quieter than usual.

Jacques didn't mind. When it came to wolves, words weren't the thing.

Dipping into his repertoire of postures, he did the best he could, given his lack of tail.

Sonnet responded, easing into a slightly bewildered, if receptive attitude.

Pleased, Jacques hummed and drummed his fingers on the steering wheel... and let his imagination run a little wild.

Sonnet seemed intrigued.

Then Jacques turned the tables, adjusting into a feline pose that probably translated just fine.

"J-jacques ...?"

"Hmm?"

She leaned forward. "Are you ... doing that on purpose?"

"Entirely. Is it working?"

475
CONTEXTUAL CLUES

Jacques angled his chin just so.

Sonnet was staring, and not in a way that begged him to stop.

So he went one better, adding a hand gesture. Feline again, but Sonnet had enough contextual clues to catch his meaning.

"Is …? *Jacques!*"

"Hmm?"

"Not in front of the baby!"

"Pish tosh. Vanya will be glad to know he was born into a loving home."

She gasped, then tittered, then finally relaxed into a sheepish smile. "*Must* you tease?"

"It's only teasing until you slip out of your shoes."

Her jaw dropped.

He chuckled.

Then Sonnet whispered, "Right, then. They're off."

476
PARKED

Jacques hit his turn signal and pulled to the side on a country road that saw almost no traffic. Turning and lowering his sunglasses, he said, "I'll be needing some confirmation."

Without breaking eye contact, Sonnet reached down, hooked his shoes, and passed them forward.

"Right. Shall I join you? Or do you fancy a stroll?"

"Here, please."

Jacques obliged, sliding into the back seat.

Sonnet asked, "What did you offer? Exactly."

"This?" Jacques repeated the gesture. "Do you want the literal meaning? Or the highly euphemistic one, popular among feline consorts?"

Sonnet went all dominant and politely ordered, "Both."

477
MINDING

They gossiped about cat customs. Consorts were bold about things that made Sonnet blush, but his curiosity doubled. "They don't mind? I might mind."

"*Naturellement.* Because wolves. But if you need more in the way of closeness, cats make good companions. Deece, for instance."

"Oh, I couldn't!"

"He's a denmate. And a tribute."

Sonnet wilted. "Are you putting me off?"

"Lord, no. I'm reminding a lone wolf that he isn't so alone. Let us care for you."

His posture shifted. "If it's you...."

"Feel free to presume at any time."

Sonnet still hesitated. "Because you don't mind."

"Because I *care.*"

478
ONLY NATURAL

Jacques understood the trap of comparisons, but clearly the hedonism of the feline courts was helping Sonnet put his own urges into perspective.

"It's only natural to want things."

Sonnet's sigh ruffled his hair.

"Some of us even need to be wanted." Jacques remained squarely upfront. "Even if it's only for one night."

That earned a stammering protest.

"I know, love. I do. But I'm giving you permission to embrace wolf tradition and indulge your curiosity. Chase me, catch me, and I'll do what I do best."

Rather predictably, Sonnet asked, "Which is ...?"

Jacques didn't like to brag. "Exceed expectations."

479

JOSTLE

Sonnet had shimmied out of stockings, so he strode through the kitchen door barefoot … and stopped so fast, Jacques jostled into him.

Lord. What had tucked his tail?

There was plenty going on, but given recent dishing, Jacques supposed it *had* to be the cats.

Kyrie hurried forward, a kitten cradled to his chest. "They're new! We're naming them!"

"The petition worked? *Magnifique*."

"Oh!" the boy gasped. "That's a good one!"

Lilya, who presided over a basket of mewing fuzzballs, exclaimed, "Yes! Perfect, Uncle Jackie."

"Rather doggish," remarked Catalan, whose gaze rested on Sonnet.

Canarian hummed. "French names are lovely."

480

NEED A MINUTE

Hisoka was also there, his chair pulled close to Michael's, their hands curled around steaming mugs.

Sonnet tried to back up. Straight into Jacques.

"Right, then." Stealing the baby, Jacques yielded Vanya to his papka. "We'll just freshen up. Won't be a minute."

He caught Sonnet's hand and pulled him along until they reached Jacques' own suite. Door secured, he asked, "Sonnet?"

The wolf whispered an apology.

"Why?"

"They'll know."

"What will they know?" Jacques tried teasing. "That your name is French and therefore lovely?"

"That I'm all stirred up." Sonnet softly amended, "That you have me all stirred up."

481

SIFTING AND SHIFTING

Jacques promised, "Cat and Canary rarely tell all they know. They're good friends of mine."

"And more …?"

"Sometimes." He gently tapped Sonnet's nose. "I gave up keeping secrets from Amaranthine ages ago. Do you want me to explain to them …?"

Sonnet's gaze was mournful.

"Oh, lord." Jacques hated to ask. "Don't tell me you're jealous, too."

"Too?"

"Nonny."

"Ohhh." Sonnet's expression softened. "No."

Jacques tried to sift out the truth. "What then?"

"They're so fond of you. There's so much trust." He fidgeted. "It's lovely."

Startlement slowly shifted into understanding. "Well, then. Shall we invite them to a grooming session?"

482

ALL IN THE UPBRINGING

Breathless moments passed before Sonnet's tail quivered upward. "Yes…?" he whispered, sounding a little shocked at himself. But then his stance firmed, and his gaze steadied. "And Deece, too?"

"How are you so brave?"

"*Is* it bravery?" Sonnet softly admitted, "I'm curious."

"If anyone will understand your curiosity, it's cats. They embody it." Jacques was quick to clarify, "They're gentlemen. And … well. Because of their upbringing, they know a good deal more about females."

Sonnet blinked, clearly baffled.

Jacques backed up. "This festival. The mock chase. The traded intimacies. I was given to understand they're … *preparatory*."

Sonnet simply blinked again.

483

GO ON

When Sentinel had explained, Jacques had been so grateful for information, he'd questioned nothing. But he should have. Sonnet wasn't a typical wolf.

"*Mon dieu*. Once again, I'm an idiot. Sonnet, *why* do you want to chase a moonbeam?"

"I want to run …?"

"So you said. And a fine rollick we'll have, but … most males take what they learn and go on to pursue a she-wolf."

Sonnet shook his head. "I don't want to be a father. I want to be a mother."

"I know. You mother *beautifully*, but … isn't there an eventual goal?"

Sonnet's head tilted. "To catch you."

484

PUT ANOTHER WAY

Catch me … as in catching the sort of moonbeam Paltry did?"

Sonnet took a patient tone. "Such encounters are *rare*."

"But … what I mean … his partner's *male*." Jacques took a deep breath and forged ahead. "If I'm meant to guide you … oh, *blast*. Readying you for a male lover is *vastly* different from coaching you on the needs of a female one."

Sonnet frowned. "Is it?"

Jacques frowned back. "Isn't it?"

Gaze thoughtful, he asked, "Wouldn't my lover's needs be guide enough?"

"Lord." Sinking to a seat on the edge of his bed, Jacques repeated, "*Lord*. There goes my heart."

485
CUTTING CORNERS

Sonnet came to kneel before him, concern clouding his face.

Jacques waved a hand. "You don't need me, not really. You'll be marvelous, no matter your choice."

"But ... I'm not looking for a bondmate." Sonnet dropped to a whisper. "I thought it would be all right, since you aren't either."

Jacques kept a protest in check. Sonnet wasn't entirely wrong. Neither was he entirely correct. But this wasn't about what Jacques wanted.

"It *will* be all right," he promised.

Sonnet touched his chest, his cheek. "Why are you stirred up?"

Jacques' explanation cut a few corners. He just kissed him.

486
EXTRACURRICULAR

Jacques was fairly certain he'd been making a point. Or possibly using a kiss to avoid a conversation. But when he drew back, Sonnet followed.

"No ... *wait*. I wasn't ready!" He pressed a pleading kiss to Jacques' jaw. "Again?"

Oh, this was premature.

And potentially problematic.

When Jacques didn't immediately respond, Sonnet tried a nudge, then a nuzzle. "I want to try."

"And I want you to succeed." Jacques put a finger to Sonnet's lips, gently fending him off. "Only a little, though. And try to keep perspective."

Sonnet whispered, "We can start ... now?"

Jacques hummed. "We started *ages* ago."

487
PRELUDE

We did?" Sonnet's brow puckered. "You mean … in the car?"

"Before that."

"Last night? All I did was hold you."

Jacques hummed. "The day I touched your blaze, I think. Then we held hands. Since then."

Sonnet's tail shivered into a low sweep.

"Or maybe it was when you came to my rescue in the rain." He smiled at the memory. "Bundled me off to your cousin's tea shop and stole my pants."

"You were soaked through!"

"And you were downhearted."

Sonnet's expression warmed. "And you invited me here."

"One of my better impulses." Jacques urgently repeated, "Only a little."

488
ONLY A LITTLE

Jacques believed that kisses shouldn't be perfunctory. Sonnet might have no interest in bonds, but he deserved affection. So keeping lustier impulses carefully closeted, Jacques stayed soft and chaste.

Sonnet pressed nearer, peeping through his lashes.

Smiling, Jacques kissed the corner of his mouth.

A low whine.

"Hmm?"

A whispered confession. "I … I want a taste."

"Is that wise?"

Nearly cross-eyed with closeness, Sonnet asked, "Does it have to be?"

"I *am* trying to be responsible."

Sonnet grumbled, "I can be a gentleman, too."

"Oh … damn." Jacques really *was* too easily carried away.

Sonnet huskily promised, "Only a little."

489
SOMETIMES

Sonnet's grumbling murmur was back, and Jacques left himself open to the wolf's careful lapping. Sonnet probably *needed* this. Instincts and all.

Jacques knew that he was a safe partner for sleep and for play. Nothing reaverish to tempt or trap, no strings attached. Picked up, yet always put back.

Still, he couldn't really complain. Neither could he resist. Kissing with fangs in play? *Lord.*

Sonnet drew back—hazy, happy. "It's nice, kissing."

"Yes … rather."

"May I kiss you sometimes?"

Jacques hesitated.

Sonnet reasoned, "You give Catalan and Canarian *sometimes*."

"*Mon dieu.* That's … it's different!"

Utterly radiant, Sonnet whispered, "Good."

490
COUNTDOWN

Jacques took extra care with albeit hasty ablutions. Tattle-tale scents banished, he made an appearance.

Catalan immediately stepped into his arms. "Mmm. This *simmer* … is it for me?"

"I'm always glad to see you," Jacques fondly assured.

With a knowing smile, Cat arched up to nuzzle behind Jacques' ear.

Still at the table beside his uncle, Canarian pointed toward the door.

Hisoka raised a hand, then began lowering fingers. *5 … 4 … 3 …*

The clop of hooves came close enough for human ears to hear.

"Lord. You utter tease," Jacques whispered.

Cat kissed his cheek the same moment Nonny walked in.

491
UTTER TEASE

Jacques' heart clenched to see injury on Nonny's face.

Cat immediately relented, capturing the disgruntled boy. There was a lot of rubbing and whispering and purring.

Nonny's irritation quickly changed to exasperation. "Gerroff, already. Oi, watch where you're putting your hands! Jacques, take him back!"

Jacques wrapped his arms around both of them. "Hush. He's only teasing you."

"Thinks he's funny. What a riot."

"Miss me?"

"You? Guess so. Him? Not so much. I can't stand cats!"

"Nooo. Do not say it," begged Catalan, who enfolded Nonny. "Let me dote."

Rolling his eyes, Nonny addressed Jacques. "Himself's asking for you."

492
NEW ARRIVALS

Argent lounged beside an unremarkable door, his gaze cool and assessing.

Jacques stood a little straighter. "My lord?"

"There were arrivals while you were off gallivanting. Keep them occupied."

He glanced at the door. "I'll certainly ... ah."

Argent had vanished.

Right, then. Jacques rapped and let himself in.

"Uncle Jackie!" Isla exclaimed. "*Do* close the door. We're not meant to be here. At least, not *officially*. Do you remember my mentioning the other members of my triad? Well, it was more of a quad, I suppose...."

She rambled through introductions even though Jacques certainly *did* know Inti and Tenma. Unofficially.

493
CLAY WARDS

B amboo skewers and a jumble of metal instruments that looked suspiciously like lockpicks strew across a table. Jacques eyed Inti, who smiled sweetly while kneading a gray lump.

"*Mon dieu.* Tell me you're not messing with plastic explosives."

Inti snickered.

"It's clay, of course," Isla corrected. "A traditional medium for sigilcraft. Inti's been showing us since clay wards are his mentor's specialty."

Jacques' brows lifted.

"She means Goh-sensei," offered Tenma.

The monkey-crosser extended an intricately-pierced disk, inquiring, "See?"

"Alas, I can only really see the magic when Michael holds my hand."

Inti hopped up. "Can he, can see, can we?"

494
KNOW IT ALL

I sla brightened, but then her face fell. "Papka might be interested, but we're meant to stay out of sight."

Jacques indicated the table. "These are impressive enough to interest the First of Wards?"

"They're *amazing*!" She warmly assured, "Inti's amazing."

Isla might be clever, but she could be oddly obtuse. Jacques found her innocence endearing. "So they *work*?"

"Oh! Ohhh. But Uncle Argent was adamant." She quailed at the very suggestion of disobedience. "Sensei is the only other person who knows we're here."

"*Non.* I know." Pulling out his phone, Jacques added, "And Michael has met Tenma. I'll text him."

495

BIT OF MISCHIEF

Inti climbed onto Jacques' back to eavesdrop on his texts.

Up for a bit of mischief?

> **What did you have in mind?**

If I were to allow Inti to smuggle us over
Would we be interrupting?

> **You know you're always welcome**
> **Answering emails can keep**
> **Bring that bit of mischief**

Minutes later, the monkey-crosser hunched like a gargoyle on the corner of Michael's desk, skewer flashing into clay until it resembled lace.

"Extraordinary!" Michael held out a hand to Jacques. "Come see."

Fingers brushed, then locked as Michael pulled him closer, banishing one man's blindness as if miracles were simple.

496

YOUR WISH IS MY COMMAND

While Michael and Isla analyzed Inti's first sigil, the crosser asked, "Want, wish, what?"

"*Pardon?*"

"What can Inti make Jacques?"

"Lord, I don't know." He considered. "Can you make a sigil that hums a lullaby?"

Inti slowly straightened, then scurried closer. "Could be, should be, maybe. If Inti had the right stone."

They applied to Michael, who seemed as intrigued by the prospect as Inti himself. The ward rummaged through a chest of small drawers. "Right. I'll yield a remnant on one condition."

Inti's tail quirked into a question mark.

Michael beamed. "Might my apprentice and I watch the process?"

497
SMILE FOR THE CAMERA

Can you see, Kurogi-kun?"

"Think so!" Jiminy gave a thumbs up. "Don't move too fast, okay Inti?"

The monkey crosser batted his eyes at the camera, then whispered something to the orange stone Michael had surrendered.

"What was that? Did you start?"

"Nope, *nein*, *nyet*," Inti answered, earning a soft giggle from Isla.

Jiminy sighed. "This is so much harder when I can't feel the stone's song."

"*I* never know what's going on until I walk into a barrier."

"That must be … umm. Sorry, Jacques."

"No need for pity or apologies. I can't miss something I've never had," lied Jacques.

498
DEMONSTRATIONS

Inti's gaze sharpened.

Jacques knew he'd been caught out, but he pasted on a smile.

Gripping Jacques' shoulder, Inti pulled Jacques back to Michael's side. "Here, here, hold."

The ward offered half his chair.

Jacques sat and stayed quiet, savoring the casual closeness when Michael slipped a paternal arm around his back and reclaimed his hand.

Inti patted his head and plunked down to pinch and pull.

Smooth dome. Scalloped edge. Shallow depression.

As Inti added details, Jiminy squinted, "Wait. What?"

After repeated interruptions, Jacques drawled, "Just ship monkey-boy to America. Like an exchange student."

Michael laughed. "I'll ask Argent!"

499
SINKING FEELING

Jacques' reserves were entirely depleted by the time he ushered Sonnet to the onsen. Cat and Canary were in fine form, and Jacques settled back to watch them work.

Sonnet's shyness melted like bath salts, and he was soon trading confidences with Cat and sighing under Canarian's kneading hands.

Tête-à-tête and massage *à trois*.

The wolf *did* keep glancing his way. Amber eyes.

Jacques offered a hazy smile. "Not to be gauche, but I *knew* you'd get on. *Très bien.*"

Canary's gaze turned thoughtful, while Cat's glittered with possibilities. Flame. Emerald.

Jacques hummed appreciatively and sank lower, then listed sideways.

500
CATS AND CADS

Jacques roused enough to know he was in his own bed, with a purring Catalan for a pillow. "Mmm ... what did I miss?"

"Daring advice, impetuous kisses, and a bouquet. Your wolf favors lavender."

"Were you good to him?"

"Sonnet trusts easily, learns eagerly. Is this envy? I could be twice as good to you."

"I can't be jealous. He needs your sort of friendship."

Catalan kissed him softly. "Canines don't understand dalliance."

"You've seen how he is. How he'd be. I refuse to be the cad who breaks his heart."

"Because you're inconstant as a cat?"

"Because I'm *human.*"

501
ROMANTIC

Dogs were never meant to be alone.”

"Sonnet's a wolf.”

"He's a romantic. Wearing your colors. Wearing your scent. You *enjoyed* this trip.”

"There's ... this festival.”

"Oh, we wheedled *that* out of him. Among other things.” Catalan's next kiss lingered. "Felines inspire intimacies. And we're very good at secrets.”

"There's no secret here. Just curiosity and ... coming-of-age explorations.” Jacques sighed. "I'm a one-off.”

"I *like* thickness in a man, but you're too much, even for me.” Catalan drew back. "Sonnet wants us, yes? To make peace. To share trust.”

"*Oui.*”

"To be part of your circle of friends. *Your pack.*”

502
UNFAMILIAR VOICE

The next morning, Jacques was intent on having a quick word with Ginkgo about certain arrangements. Michael directed him toward his own office, where the fox-crosser was apparently serving as translator for Tsumiko.

Preparing tea for all involved, Jacques swept through the door, ears straining for any tidbits of gossip, but an unfamiliar man said, "Kip's not here ....”

Then Jiminy's voice. "Allow me.”

Beyond curious, Jacques circled the desk to peer over Ginkgo's shoulder. "Kip?” he echoed.

Jiminy glanced his way and grinned. "Friend of ours. There, that's done it.”

Tsumiko gasped, and Jacques' amazement matched hers. *Lord. Wings.*

503

GOT A SEC

Jacques listened with growing incredulity. An unregistered reaver and a crosser who'd make her his nestmate. Willing to go public. Jacques stole half of Ginkgo's chair and murmured in French. "Bold prediction. The whole world will develop a feather fetish."

Ginkgo rolled his eyes, leaned back, and hollered, "Hey, Dad. Got a sec?"

On screen, Tami started and began trembling. Sensible woman.

Tsumiko sweetly called, "Argent?"

And in a fluid rush, the fox was simply there, arms around his bondmate.

"Oh, sure. Her you'll answer."

"*Tsk.*" With a gentle tug for his son's ear, Argent calmly demanded, "Explain yourself, Jiminy."

504

SPLENDID STUFF

The audacity of Tami's scheme just kept getting better. Jacques was practically swooning. He looked to Argent, sure he'd be pleased.

"I do not require baiting."

The fox's gaze connected briefly on Jacques', and his crabby demeanor fell away. Triumph sparkled in Argent's eyes, and he let Jacques see it.

The Sunfletch-Reaverson courtship would sway American sentiment. Splendid stuff. But for Argent, this was much more personal. Ash was a *crosser*.

One who would command a following.

One who would influence public opinion.

One whose courage would protect all crossers.

Argent called, "Twineshaft, do you have a moment to spare?"

505
LOVELORN

Once the international call ended, Argent hooked Jacques' arm and steered him straight into the conservatory. "Tell me."

"It'll work."

"Tell me something else."

Jacques hesitated. "Jiminy's smitten ...?"

"One does not require sharp eyes to spot a wolf in love. Rather, who is *Kip*."

So Argent had been present far sooner than he let on. Sly thing. "Squirrel clan. He hijacked Jiminy's computer, seeking advice on a delicate matter. Lapis turned me out before I could learn anything truly enticing, but ... Kip radiated *lovelorn*."

"Since the topic is broached." Argent's arms folded. "Perhaps you should also tell me about Sonnet."

506
RENT BOY

Jacques stood silent.

"I value privacy, and I will respect yours if you insist. However, entanglements can affect an entire household."

"I was ... approached. Engaged, really. I'll be performing a service of sorts. Lord, that makes me sound like a rent boy."

Argent growled.

"Oh, do calm down." And Jacques wearily spilled out everything.

Silvery tails surrounded them. "Sonnet is not the first to place an enormity of trust in you."

"*You* were first."

"*Tsk*. You deserve more than I can provide."

"I haven't forgotten."

"... Inti has designed a sigil for your next tattoo. Perhaps *this* time...."

Jacques stood silent.

507
FINAL FITTING

The following afternoon, Jacques invited Sonnet to Randolla's. "I know it's late to confer. Mere hours until sunset, but this was a rush job."

Sonnet's eyes widened.

"*Non*? Too much?" Jacques spun on his heel, and trailing scarves swirled. "It's a trifle cold for me to be clad in 'naught but moonbeams,' so ... compromise! I think Randolla's captured the romance of wolvish lore. Or ... no ...?"

Sonnet cautiously fingered a filmy layer.

"Am I chase-able? Or did you have your heart set on rugged?"

"You're *luminous*."

"All but my boots. They're kind of...."

Sonnet interrupted by gathering him close and sniffling.

508
CATCH AND RELEASE

Ah, ah!" Jacques kept his tone light. "*Far* too soon for me to be caught. I shall require a head start. And probably several second chances. Do wolves subscribe to a catch-and-release philosophy?"

Sonnet murmured, "I would let you go if it meant I could catch you again."

"Then we'll cut blazes along formerly empty trails. All traditions begin somewhere." Jacques wrapped his arms as far as they'd go around broad shoulders. "Tonight, you can create your pack's lore."

"You're just so ...." Sonnet's voice caught, and he busied himself nuzzling at Jacques' hair before finally murmuring, "I'm glad it's you."

509
HAVE A CARE

Shortly after dinner, Argent cornered him. "Have a care."

"I did prepare." Jacques clarified, "For *eventualities*. I borrowed a bolt hole. Ginkgo won't be far, and he'll be discreet."

"Sensible."

"I'm occasionally capable."

Argent's tone shifted. "Will you be all right?"

His feelings curled protectively in on themselves. "I know how to satisfy a playmate. Do you really want to know my plans?"

"Not in any great detail. But … *wolves*."

"They have beautiful ideals." Jacques sighed. "Sentinel gave advice. As did Ginkgo. I *do* understand my role."

Argent softly repeated, "But will you be all right?"

"Piffle. I'll be brilliant."

510
FINISHING TOUCHES

The sun set while Randolla fussed over finishing touches. Then the beaming tailor escorted Jacques through a private door. Ginkgo waited outside, offering a lamp that glowed blue.

"I set up more, but not many. You'll still be the brightest thing in our woods."

"*Merci*."

They walked … but Ginkgo stopped. "Hey, Jacques?"

"Mmm?"

"Did Dad tell you to be careful?"

"More or less."

"If Sonnet wanted careful, he wouldn't have turned to you." Ginkgo eyed him approvingly. "You hired a tailor. You secured a den. You put glitter in your hair. Don't skimp on the rest. Be your sexy self."

511

REALLY VERY WOLVISH

Y ou think I'm sexy?"

Ginkgo chuckled. "Sure. Sexy and sulky and sultry and salty. And you pull off the silver eyeliner way better than I do. More to the point ... you feel things deeply, which is really very wolvish."

"Most people compare me to cats."

"Look, I *know* wolves. They embrace everything, even the sad stuff. And what they feel gets woven into their songs. That sorta ... changes it. Elevates it. Or maybe just *accepts* it."

Jacques pointed out, "Everyone feels things."

"Not everyone *considers* those feelings. Or feels for someone else." Ginkgo strolled on, saying, "It's really very wolvish."

512

BRAZENING HIS WAY

J acques muttered, "I can't be here for him always."

"Did he *ask* for always?"

"Only for tonight."

Ginkgo's ears pricked. "That bothers you, doesn't it?"

Jacques couldn't even scrape up a smile.

"Oh, man. Okay. Look, Sonnet *isn't* a lone wolf. He's definitely been a *lonely* wolf, but he put some spin on that, probably to make it easier. He found friends and raised some kids. Believe me, that *also* makes it easier.

"Here, now, Sonnet's making a bold move. Brazen, even. He wants to run with you, to be part of your pack. That's *us*. So ... bring him in."

513
ROMANTICIZED

There's *no* romance?" Jacques was skeptical.

"Oh, I wouldn't say *that*. This is Sonnet we're talking about. He romanticizes gruel." Ginkgo nodded in the direction of the Elderbough pack. "Since it's you, I'll be blunt. Every young wolf that's running tonight is pairing off, maybe even getting off."

"These festivals. You've done them before."

"Sure," Ginkgo admitted easily. "Silver hair looks the part. And, well ... *foxes*."

"Clearly, I was too circumspect earlier. I demand details!"

"You *would*. Fine. Here's one. Ponytail *entendre* is a thing. Give him one and give it a tug." He smirked. "You can thank me later."

514
ALL YOU GOTTA BE

We've kissed. Sonnet and I."

Ginkgo didn't look nearly as shocked or as concerned as his father had been. "Wolves always want a taste."

"But this felt like a kiss."

"Then it was." Ginkgo slowed. "Y'know, wolves aren't very good at explaining themselves. Words aren't their first language. Or second. Or third. But this stuff doesn't need words."

"Granted."

"You're gonna be all Sonnet can see tonight. That kind of focus ...? It's pretty addicting." Ginkgo added, "It's also really rare for outsiders, but ... really simple, too. No bluffs, no lies, no hedging. With wolves, all you gotta be is honest."

515
CRAZY ABOUT

Jacques couldn't resist asking, "Your tastes run to wolves?"

"I mean … what's not to love? No such thing as a bad wolf. Or dog, for that matter." Ginkgo's ears angled in the direction of a faint howl. "Wolves were my way to rebel. To become someone else. To be part of something good."

"An honorary Elderbough."

"Nothing *honorary* about pack." He casually added, "Just like there's nothing halfhearted about devotion."

Jacques dodged. Sort of. "What do the Elderboughs think of Sonnet?"

"You kidding? They're crazy about him. And no wonder." Ginkgo searched his face, then asked, "Ever hear him sing?"

516
SHAME ON YOU

Non. The house is warded against howling."

Ginkgo nudged him with an elbow. "*Howling?* Shame on you."

"I'm hardly conversant in wolvish." Jacques shivered as a thin note reached his ears. "The nuances are lost on me."

"Wolfsong steals from the soul. It's a heist that reveals the heart."

Feeling as transparent as his ensemble, Jacques asked, "What does Sonnet sing about?"

"You know what? Ask him. It's almost as big a compliment as asking a wolf what their name means. Ever done that?"

"I *know* what a sonnet is."

Ginkgo nudged him again and softly repeated, "Shame on you."

517

CAROUSE WITH IMPUNITY

Sonnet knows I'm here. That might calm any jitters, knowing there's a ... well, I'm like a referee. Making sure things don't go too far."

Jacques asked, "How do you define *too far*?"

"Loosely. Nights like this, the boundaries are down. Bond-building isn't a danger, so all's fair."

"Carouse with impunity?"

"Be your sexy self. And ... he'll probably be extra careful, but if by some fluke, things take an uncomfortable turn, I'm there."

"Literally? Good thing I have exhibitionist tendencies."

Ginkgo snorted. "I'm no voyeur. My wards are tuned. Just say the word." And leaning close, he whispered, "Pompadour."

518

LOVELY STUFF

Alone, Jacques only took a few steps toward the fairy lights in the distance before asking, "Are you here?"

"Here." Sonnet stepped into view, clad in loose pants that swished softly to his ankles. Several necklaces looped his neck. He drummed his fingers just below them and confessed, "I'm all .... Aren't *you* nervous?"

"Come here." Using Sonnet's loose hair, Jacques pulled his head down. "Get a whiff. Anticipation is lovely stuff."

Sonnet knelt, burying his nose in Jacques' belly. Then he lifted his face, gaze rapt.

"Ready to run?" Jacques asked.

Hands falling to his sides, Sonnet breathlessly ordered, "Go."

519

MOONLESS NIGHT

Lord, it was dark. Jacques blessed Ginkgo's foresight as he stumbled toward the beckoning fairy lights. The flutter of cool cloth against his skin was inspirational, but moonbeams were probably a lot lighter on their feet.

Holding his tiny lantern aloft, Jacques lengthened his stride, only to falter to a stop. A meadow? Had it always been here?

Crystals drifted temptingly overhead, more blue.

Tinier sparks hid amidst ankle-deep grass, pale gold.

Skybellow colors.

Leaves rustled, and Jacques glanced back as a large wolf slipped from the shadows, stealing up behind him.

Smiling coyly, Jacques blew a kiss … and *ran*.

520

FAMILIAR TERRITORY

Sonnet was all pounce and tussle. He leapt and spun and pinned his would-be moonbeam before letting him up to run anew.

It was flirting. Familiar territory for Jacques.

Truest form wasn't ideal for *other* pursuits, but a shift was coming. Sonnet wouldn't be able to resist for much longer. Not with that ego-stroking intensity shining in amber eyes.

Pursuit would lead to capture.

And then Sonnet would be caught.

The wolf thrummed with a daringness that tipped his hand. Sonnet might be good and sweet and noble, but he was no more interested in remaining chaste than Jacques himself.

521
FEELING IT

With a grunt, Jacques hit the ground. Again.

Cold seeped up from behind, even as warm fur pressed over him. He gratefully buried frigid fingers in Sonnet's ruff. Lord. He'd be feeling this tomorrow. Repeated pouncing *wasn't* the reason he'd thought he'd be acquiring aches, but ... the night was young.

"There are more interesting ways to wear a man out."

Finally—*finally*—Sonnet shifted. "You're cold!"

"A bit." Jacques asked, "Will you warm me?"

Sonnet looked doubtful. "Out here?"

"I arranged a den. And snacks. I shan't complain if you abscond with me."

"A den?" Sonnet swayed closer. "For us?"

522
CONSIDER ME WILLING

Moonbeams shine brightest in a wolf's shadow." Jacques looped his arms around Sonnet's neck. "Wolvish lore is riddled with delicious euphemisms."

Sonnet's gaze sharpened, and his voice went all husky. "I want to hold you."

"I look forward to a night in your arms."

"I think I want to ... to ...."

"You may consider me willing. Though I'd prefer *retreat* to camping rough." He confided, "After touring a few of Ginkgo's bolt holes, I chose the most *apropos*. It's little more than a cave. Very earthy. Very den."

"*You* ... wanted a cave?"

"All the better to bring out your wild side."

523

SLEEPING FURS

Cave chic had been the right choice, and Ginkgo had seen to other details. Sonnet spent several minutes grumbling and huffing his way through the blankets heaped on the sleeping platform.

Jacques asked, "Problem?"

"Wolf. Cat. Bear. Dog." Sonnet's smile was tremulous. "Even fox. These are from... everyone."

"Sounds crowded. Will they distract you from me?"

That earned him a chiding look. "Get in. You need warming."

Jacques unlaced and unbuttoned.

"Uhh ... *oh.*"

"Steady on," Jacques murmured, shedding moonbeams while Sonnet doused the lights.

Then the world narrowed to ticklish furs and a breathless silence as two hearts beat faster.

524

BE HONEST

In an attempt to be the responsible one, Jacques had prepared a lecture—largely anecdotal, geared to intrigue, and ... entirely superfluous. Sonnet proved he'd never needed a teacher, and Jacques went from being responsible to simply responding.

Sonnet lingered over him, attentive and generous.

Jacques had always been weak to slow kisses.

Holding back became impossible, and Jacques knew he couldn't hide anything either. Without a word, he confessed all.

Sonnet lapped up the truth. A growl rattled through Jacques with exquisite authority. He arched and groaned and praised.

Then Sonnet was crooning over him in a *sotto voce* howl.

525
MORNING AFTER

Jacques woke alone.

Well, not truly. Ginkgo lounged on the floor, elbow propped on the sleeping platform. "Morning."

"Lord. Did something happen?"

"Sonnet went to fix breakfast for everyone."

"Back to normal?"

"What happens when the moon can't see stays secret." Ginkgo patted Jacques' shoulder. "I'm here to spare you the walk home … and to break some news. You're leaving for the States. Almost immediately."

"Without a word?"

"It's pretty typical. Most packs find ways to separate festival partners." Ginkgo shrugged. "To prevent bond-building."

"Which is why I'm being shipped off to a foreign city?"

"It's more of a farm."

526
MUTUAL APPRECIATION

Ginkgo piggybacked Jacques toward home. "You're escorting Inti to Jiminy's enclave. But first, we're hitting the nearest bathtub."

"You're coming with me?" asked Jacques. "That's rare."

"Not much choice. Or did you *want* me to deliver you to Dad looking like sex and smelling like a threesome?"

Jacques snorted. "You're straight."

"Yep, but you're not the first guy to help a good friend over an awkward patch." He quietly asked, "You gonna be okay, Jacques?"

"I'm going to be *grateful*."

"I get that. I mean … *wolves*."

Jacques murmured, "Lord, yes." But his appreciation was far less generalized after last night.

527

TOO SOON

The claw-footed tub in Jacques' suite fit two. Barely. And only because Ginkgo cut a trim figure. Sonnet would have spilled over, all on his own.

"Dad wants you to go after Kip."

"Fetching as he was in freckles, it's a little too soon for another affair."

Ginkgo's hands slowed against Jacques' scalp. "You will, though. Have more …?"

Jacques hunched his shoulders. "That's what you'd expect from someone like me."

Gentle scratching resumed. "Did Sonnet … *say* anything?"

"I suppose. I don't know. I'm not conversant in wolvish."

Ginkgo was quiet for too long. Finally, he asked, "Sonnet … *sang* for you?"

528

ALWAYS IMPORTANT

Jacques was honestly afraid to ask. "Is that important?"

"Always." Ginkgo leaned to the side and turned Jacques' face to meet his gaze. "Wolfsong is *always* important. And in that context? You did good."

"I did very little. *He* was the one …."

"Yeah. I get that. But I still say you took the right kind of care of our Sonnet. Wish I'd been there to hear. But … it won't matter."

"I thought you said it'd be important."

"Oh, it is. I just meant I didn't really need to *be there*. If you've changed Sonnet's song, I'll hear it. Everyone will."

529
FRAUGHT WITH POTENTIAL

When Jacques—eventually—arrived in the foyer, he wheeled a trunk behind him.

Argent eyed first him, then it, before remarking, "Is that all?"

"*Non.* I sent the larger one ahead with Ginkgo, though he was skeptical it'll fit in the boot."

"You couldn't have economized?"

"Sacrifices *were* made," Jacques loftily assured.

Just then, Argent strolled up. *Another* Argent. "Leave off, imp."

A third Argent tapped Jacques' shoulder. "We are very nearly late. And certain brats grew bored."

"Idle tricksters *will* make mischief," a fourth Argent blandly agreed.

"Lord. Does Tsumiko ever ...?"

It seemed a reasonable question.

Jacques would have.

530
MISSED A SPOT

Three of the Argents went very still, their expressions carefully—dangerously—neutral. But the fourth giggled and flung his arms around Jacques' neck. Which was utterly absurd for the fraction of a second before several illusions met a swift end. There was a queer *pop* and then there was so much ginger fur.

"Jacques is always Jacques, and Inti likes it that way." The crosser nuzzled close and whispered, "Didn't Jacques wash behind his ears?"

"Ah. Did I miss a spot?"

Eyes the color of conjac warmed with the smile that creased their corners. "Some things do not wash off."

531
UNATTENDED

My lord, this is becoming ridiculous."

"In what sense?"

Argent could be so peevish about conventional means of travel. While observing the letter of international law, he was giving the particulars his own personal twist.

"I would like to sleep. For that, I need a drink, but every one of these highly capable flight attendants seems to be ignorant of our presence."

"I refuse to be fawned over." Argent coolly suggested, "I could induce sleep."

"I need a drink." Drumming fingers on his seat tray, Jacques amended, "*Drinks*. Preferably a cask of star wine."

"Drowning sorrows?"

Jacques softly assured, "*Non*."

532
SET ME UP

Jacques inspected his nails, which still shimmered with pearly polish. "You've never asked about my assignations before."

"You've never taken up with another member of the household before."

"Sure about that?" he challenged.

Argent's briefly calculating look fell away, and he unbuckled, glided down the aisle, and returned with a single flute and a bottle of champagne. "Best they can do."

"Beggars can't be choosers."

Playing the sommelier, Argent uncorked and poured.

Jacques sipped, slouched back in his seat, and stared out the window.

Eventually, Argent said, "I *am* sure. Of you."

"Right." Jacques raised his glass. "Keep them coming."

533
INCOGNITO

S mythe? *Tsk*. Wake up, Jackie."

"Mmm. Hmm?" Jacques pushed up his eye mask and squinted blearily at Argent.

"We have arrived. Customs must be endured, and there will undoubtedly be press."

Jacques automatically checked Argent's shirt for stains. Mercifully, there were only crumbs. "You'll need the other suitcoat, the one with your crest. And your *good* shoes."

"If you insist."

Jacques turned on his phone. "Jiminy checked in. Nothing from Inti."

"Juuyu and Sinder are escorting him. They'll meet us at an...." Argent hesitated. "Sinder called it an airbnb. It's in an ordinary neighborhood, so we can fade from notice."

534
WELCOME TO FLETCHING

T heir covert base of operations was a trite little two-bedroom condominium a ten-minute drive from Bellwether's campus. Juuyu had stashed Inti with Jiminy, and for the sake of appearances, Argent made several.

Meanwhile, Jacques unpacked trunks and flipped through a three-ring binder with laminated menus from local restaurants. Tacky ... but informative.

He set up the cheap coffee maker in the kitchen, then stepped outside to contemplate the sky. Argent's clan colors were stunning on cloudy days, but the new smoky gray ensemble would be dead sexy in full sun. Decisions, decisions.

Someone gasped, and a tentative voice asked, "Jacques Smythe?"

535

BEING NEIGHBORLY

Neatly groomed. Nattily dressed. Jacques' desultory once-over snapped into focus at the demitasse cup and saucer in the man's hands. "Lord, is that an espresso?"

"Yes! Oh, my. Would you like one?"

Jacques decided to be neighborly.

The man was flustered, yet clearly delighted. "It's an *honor*!"

Jacques clasped his hand and held on. "People don't usually recognize me."

"Ah. I'm afraid I'm a *bit* fanatical about all things Amaranthine."

Jacques noted the tiny pumpkins on the man's bowtie and decided to be charmed. Bowing over his hand, Jacques murmured, "I would *love* coffee. Your name?"

"It's Harrison. Harrison Peck."

536

MAKE YOURSELF AT HOME

I won't be intruding?"

"No, not at all. It's just me." Harrison gave a little tug, pulling Jacques across the threshold. "I'll just set up my machine. Make yourself at home."

Harrison's condo had the same uninspired floorplan as next door, but personal touches abounded. Crayon drawings of a bowtied Mr. Peck littered the walls. "You work with children, perhaps?"

Steam hissed. "Yes! At the elementary school."

Jacques paused before an imposing wall chart, scanning sticky note dates and translations. "Are you *actually* learning the Seven Score Moons?"

Harrison brought the promised espresso. "I'm muddling along. In my spare time."

537
TOE TO TOE

A m I keeping you from your work?" Jacques moved forward to accept the coffee and stayed toe-to-toe.

"Not today. It's Saturday."

"Is it?" He sipped and sighed. "An appointment, then? Or some … assignation?"

"Nothing that can't wait."

Jacques lightly tapped the knot of Harrison's bowtie, *not* a clip-on. "You're dressed to impress."

"I need groceries." He shrugged. "This is how I always dress."

"Sit with me," Jacques invited. "Tell me more about yourself, Mr. Peck."

"Me?" Waving from chart to coffee to crayon masterpieces, Harrison said, "What you see is what you get."

"Sit with me," Jacques insisted. "I'm *intrigued*."

538
SMALL WORLD

Q uite coincidentally, Harrison was the attendance clerk— whatever *that* was—at Landmark Elementary, the same place Tami Reaverson worked. He was unattached, intelligent, and inquisitive.

Coffee turned into an offer of breakfast, and Jacques waited to be quizzed about Argent. And waited. When Harrison remained solidly in neutral territory, chatting happily about nuances of clan customs and culture, Jacques' estimation of him soared.

"Would you like to come to Stately House?"

"Wh-what …?"

"I like you, Mr. Peck. I think you'd fit right in." Jacques wistfully added, "It wouldn't be the first time I hired someone simply because they were perfect."

539

EXCELLENT JUDGE

But I'm a complete stranger," Harrison protested.

"I'm an *excellent* judge of character." Jacques confided, "His lordship trusts me."

"Well, yes. I *know* he does. I mean, you've moderated several televised press conferences for the Five." Then, more softly, "Oh, my. I don't know if I could leave."

"You *did* say you were unattached."

"To a single person, yes. But I'm part of a community." Leaning forward, Harrison grew suddenly formal. "Mr. Smythe?"

"*Jacques*, please."

"Are you busy this evening?"

"What did you have in mind?"

Jacques wondered how the man could pack so much happiness into one word.

"Bingo."

540

GAME NIGHT

Jacques supposed he was willing to try anything once. "Does *bingo* count as a night on the town here in Fletching?"

"It does in Archer." Harrison reeled his hands. "Most of the town gathers together, and I host a game that's intended to encourage peace between humans and Amaranthine. Would you come as my guest?"

A red flag was already flying. "Were you hoping to put me on display? I need to be discreet."

"I *see*." Harrison considered him thoughtfully. "You can't help but stand out, being new and being … well, being *you*. But can't you hide in plain sight?"

541

IF THE WARD FITS

do love a man who knows how to be creative." Jacques weighed the risks against his impulses. "It *could* be arranged, but … lord. I'd need permission."

The man leaned forward and breathlessly asked, "From Lord Mettlebright?"

"Him and a few others." He tapped a quick message to Sinder. "All very hush-hush."

Harrison murmured, "It's like you're a spy."

"That's probably just the accent." Jacques pocketed the phone and sat back. "There. Text sent. We'll see if my friends decide you're a security risk."

"Will it take long …?"

"All depends, really."

Someone knocked.

"Ah." Jacques beamed. "Not long at all!"

542

SECURITY BREACH

o all it takes to lure you out is an espresso machine?"

Jacques guided Sinder forward. "Stop pretending to be upset and meet Harrison, who's been most hospitable."

The man's eyes were bright, his hands already on offer.

"Hello. Charmed, I'm sure. Harrison, was it? I'm Sinder."

"May I ask which clan …?"

"Sure. Why not? Do you believe in dragons?"

"Oh! Oh, my," he breathed. "I'm quite beside myself. Please, make yourself comfortable! Coffee?"

"Okay, sure. Thanks." And once he'd gone, Sinder shook his head. "He's no reaver, Jacques. I'm almost afraid to ask. Why'd you say Harrison has potential?"

543
FIGURE OF SPEECH

Jacques couldn't quite let that pass. "Is a reaver bloodline required for humans to distinguish themselves?"

"What...? Oh, for storm's sake. That's not what I meant!"

"Potential is in the eye of the beholder."

"Yes, yes. And I'm sure you're both brimming with it." Sinder grumbled, "Stop pretending to be upset and tell me why I'm here."

"What would it take for Stately House to abscond with Harrison?"

"You want to kidnap this man?"

"Figure of speech. He's a natural. The children would adore him."

"Sounds familiar." Sinder glanced kitchenward. "I suppose it depends on what you want him *for*."

544
LOADED QUESTION

Jacques patiently repeated, "For the children."

"Not for yourself?"

Jacques was taken aback. "What gave you that idea?"

Sinder raised a finger but hesitated. "I don't think I can answer that without insulting one of you. Or both of you."

"I don't target *every* gentleman I meet for debauchery."

"I know, okay? I messed up, and I'm sorry."

Jacques took a more dominant posture. "You misinterpreted *something*."

"I'd rather not say. Would you settle for groveling? Please?"

"*Non.*"

"Shit. Fine. He's cute. You'd noticed. And he's noticed you noticed. Satisfied?"

Jacques was intrigued all over again. "You think Harrison's cute?"

545
NOTICEABLE

Lord. I didn't even know you *noticed* men. Do you have a type?"

"*Now* who's jumping to conclusions?" Sinder rolled his eyes. "It's my job to notice people. *And* to keep you out of trouble."

"So do you find *me* attractive?" Jacques was mostly teasing.

"Seriously? You know I don't." Sinder's eyes narrowed. "Are you deflecting? I don't really care *what* you get up to. Argent's the one who'll–"

"Lord. I'm not trying to bed him. I'm trying to employ him."

Harrison had returned, a fresh demitasse in hand.

Jacques sighed. "Not that you *aren't* bedable."

Harrison breathed, "Gosh."

546
FASHION STATEMENT

All right, fine. I get the picture." Sinder held out a hand. "Give me your phone."

Jacques caught Sinder's arm. "You didn't have to do that."

The dragon winced. "Sorry. Slipped out. Hey, Harrison. I'm working a little technological magic. This'll give you a direct line to Jacques. You can be text buddies or whatever."

The man sank to a seat. "So ... I pass?"

"Let's call it the first hurdle." Jacques sat beside him. "Pray tell, is there a dress code for bingo?"

A smile bloomed. "Whatever's comfortable. It's very come-as-you-are."

Sinder warned, "Tonight's fashion statement had better involve sigilcraft."

547

LOOPHOLES

Y ou two have fun." Sinder hesitated on the threshold and raised a warning finger. "Responsibly."

Jacques innocently asked, "*Moi*?"

The dragon worriedly reminded, "Argent will put a knot in my tail, then shave my mane if anything happens to you."

"That *would* be a crime against nature. However, I doubt Harrison has anything untoward in mind."

"And you...?"

"This is hardly the time to indulge my little whims."

Sinder frowned. "Will that stop you?"

"Does anything?"

"*Why* are you speaking in loopholes?"

"Because I *like* you, and that always leads to bedevilment." Jacques relented, promising, "Best behavior. On my honor."

548

AT EASE

A lone again, Jacques faced Harrison. "What must you think of me?"

He candidly replied, "I've always thought you have a flirty sort of smile."

Jacques relaxed. "What a lovely thing to say."

Harrison simply smiled back, absolutely, positively at ease. Which only firmed Jacques' opinion. Stately House needed people like this. Perhaps he did, too.

With a man like Harrison, he'd be on equal footing. He could almost picture it. A chest of drawers for bowties might just fit alongside the armoire where he kept his dressing gown collection.

Shared passions. Shared lifespan.

"Jacques?" Harrison offered his handkerchief. "What's wrong?"

549
BEYOND HELP

Jacques bravely admitted, "I haven't the wherewithal to seduce you."

Harrison didn't look shocked, only concerned. "No need to go out of your way."

Accepting his handkerchief, Jacques blotted unforeseen tears. "What must you think of me," he glumly repeated.

"Mostly, I'm intrigued. What can I do?"

"I am beyond help."

Like a gentleman, he didn't pry. "Then may I distract you …?"

"Are you even gay?"

"Oh! Bi, actually. Although recent fascinations have me suspicious that I'm pan. But that isn't what I meant." From the inside pocket, Harrison produced a folded paper. "I'll let you hold the grocery list."

550
PRODUCE SECTION

They chatted about the Twineshaft Initiative and bingo strategy. Jacques learned that Harrison took ballroom lessons on the sly. Something to do with a co-worker at Landmark.

Harrison's name rang out—*again*—and he traded salutations with yet another local.

"Do you know *everyone*?"

"If they've had a student at Landmark in the last decade, then yes. In fact, some of my first kids are now sending their children to us."

"I can't even imagine."

"It's only natural."

"For humans. My children will always be children. At least during my lifetime."

Harrison searched his face. "Is *that* why you're downhearted?"

551

LEND AN EAR

Harrison added oranges to the trolley. "I deal with lonely kids all the time."

"You … think I'm lonely?"

"Oh, my goodness! I shouldn't be making–"

"*Non.* Don't apologize." And cautiously, "You're not wrong."

"My job? Listening might be the most important part. Kids always need someone to ask after their pets, remember their favorite color … and hear them out when no one else will listen."

"My favorite color is green."

"I'll remember." Harrison nodded at the touch of silk Jacques had added to his ensemble while dressing. "And I'll listen. If you like."

Jacques marveled at his good fortune.

552

SPARE ME

Jacques held out a frosty blue suitcoat, the one with the Mettlebright crest stitched in silver. Argent would be mingling with local dignitaries—or the American equivalent—at an impromptu gala at Bellwether College.

The fox sniffed. "Who were you with?"

"Sinder didn't tattle? I'm shocked." Jacques turned Argent to smooth lapels and tie. "I met our neighbor. We have plans … if you can spare me."

Argent's brows drew together.

His concern made Jacques smile. "Not *those* kinds of plans. Though I will need protection."

Silver tails exploded around them.

Jacques bowed his head. Truly, he was a fortunate man.

553
EXEMPTION

Jacques suspected he was glowing with sigilcraft—both Juuyu's and Argent's—not that he could tell. Nor would anyone else, which was rather the point. He was somewhat miffed that nobody would recall the gorgeousness of his new wool-cashmere suit, but ... needs must.

Harrison's initial puzzlement melted into delight. "So you *can* ward a person!"

"I can interact normally with people, but their memory of me will be fuzzy." Jacques tucked a blue crystal into Harrison's vest pocket and gave it a pat. "This makes you exempt."

The man beamed. "Shall we?"

From behind Jacques, Argent drawled, "Not just yet."

554
WHAT ARE YOUR INTENTIONS

Harrison's gasp was pure delight. He gave Jacques a meltingly grateful smile before offering his hands to Argent. "Good evening, Lord Mettlebright. This is truly a pleasure."

"You will not remember meeting me."

"Oh!" Harrison's smile didn't waver. "If you think that's best, sir."

"It is. For now. If my man has his way, you *will* see me again. In the meantime ...."

Jacques held his peace while Argent hassled Mr. Peck with increasingly personal questions.

Harrison answered candidly.

Finally, Argent inclined his head.

"Satisfied?" inquired Jacques.

"Carry on, but do not forget. You need to locate that Woodacre for me."

555

WHEN IN ROME

Harrison smuggled Jacques into a booth at the back corner of the hall where bingo would transpire. People were already claiming seats and ordering snacks.

"Do you want something from the concession stand?"

Jacques suggested, "You choose."

"It's nothing fancy."

"No matter. Although I draw the line at imitation cheese."

"Noted!" And with a teasing air, Harrison asked, "Would you like your frozen lemonade stirred or shaken?"

"When in Rome. Guide my choices, sensei."

Harrison beamed. "If you want the *good* stuff, we could hit up Swifty's after."

"Haute cuisine?"

"Archer's finest," he promised. "I'll bring snacks, but save room."

556

LIKE BEES TO HONEY

Jacques watched the coat racks fill and the stage lights go on. Noise levels increased enough to drown out a popcorn cart, and all arriving children made a beeline for Mr. Peck and his cloverleaf bowtie. They bounced in place or smiled bashfully, and it made Jacques homesick.

So he snapped a picture of his all-American snacks and the bingo cards and dried kernels of field corn he was meant to use to cover squares.

Wish me luck.

Nonny's reply wasn't long in coming.

Since when do you eat corndogs?

Immediately followed by...

Oi.

I think something's wrong with Sonnet

557
EFFICACIOUS

Jacques needed a moment, so he took it.

Can you be more specific?

> **She burnt the gruel this morning**
> **Keeps calling me Florent,**
> **whoever the hell that is**
> **Tail might be permanently tucked**

Did something happen?

> **Nah**
> **Been quiet**

Was it possible? Jacques didn't like to presume, but....

Does Sonnet know where I've gone?

> **NOBODY knows where you've gone**
> **The guv said to stay mum**

Pass along a message for me?

> **Easy**
> **She's right here**

I was spirited away by foxes
But I'll be home anon

> **I gotta actually say *anon***
> **Who talks like that**
> **Oh**
> **It worked**
> **Wag's back**

558

SECOND OPINION

Jacques startled when someone slid into the seat across from his.

"Easy, Jacques. Lord Mettlebright placed a call, and Jiminy volunteered me." He offered a hand. "Lou Booker, though my denmates call me Rook."

Jacques brightened. "You're a wolf."

"And that makes you happy." Rook's expression warmed. "A refreshing change of pace."

"Did someone decide I needed a bodyguard?"

Rook lifted his chin toward Harrison. "I think your boss wants me to decide if he's worthy of you. Not that Argent *said* as much."

Jacques tried to hide his smile behind his corndog.

Rook chuckled. "Which *also* makes you happy."

559

TRIVIAL PURSUITS

Rook and Jacques went toe-to-toe on Harrison's trivia contest. Privately, of course.

"What new primetime television drama has made history by casting Pim Moonprowl, an openly Amaranthine actress?"

Rook made a ready sign. So did Jacques. Tied.

"What's one name for the wolvish calendar?"

Jacques rolled his eyes. "Too easy."

"For Betweeners, sure. But most of these folks are learning something new every time he asks a question."

"Which of these Amaranthine are *not* part of the cozy clans? A, cat. B, mouse. C, cow. D, chicken."

"Keep naming them," challenged Jacques. "First one who can't loses this round."

560
PENNY DROP

What do Amaranthine of the turkey clans exchange during the Vernal Equinox?"

Jacques frowned.

Rook held up his hands. "I know plenty of pheasant lore, but none of my acquaintances are turkeys."

"Pheasants?"

Rook grinned easily. "Longtime friends. Part of our enclave."

Harrison announced more bingo, and Jacques and Rook agreed that the final round of trivia would be winner-takes-all.

And then the penny dropped. "Perchance, does your enclave include squirrels?"

"That's right."

"Do you know ... Kip?"

"Cheeky brat. But a good friend to have."

Of all the foxy ...! Jacques was here under false pretenses. Argent had never needed help!

561
TO GO

Lord," Jacques drawled reverently. Swifty's produced hot pastrami sandwiches that required the removing of one's jacket *and* the rolling up of one's sleeves. "Pure decadence."

"I know, right?" Harrison opened two more bottles of beer. "Half the county points to Swifty's as their guilty pleasure."

"What does the other half do for fun?"

Harrison didn't even hesitate. "Gert's Pies."

"Are these sublime pies *also* sold out of the back of a petrol station?"

"Nooo, but her husband runs the bait shop next door. Do you like fishing?"

Jacques sincerely doubted it, but no matter. "My good man, it's a date."

562

SQUIRREL IDENTIFICATION

They repaired to the living room, and Jacques loosened his tie and loitered.

"I'm going squirrel hunting tomorrow. Or the next day. Soon."

Harrison raised his bottle. "Tallyho!"

"About them. What do you think? Are squirrels cozies?" It was a silly question. Was he drunk?

"Probably. They're in every backyard."

"Friend of mine argued that they're one of the trickster clans. Wait a tick. I'm not sure that nickname's intended for a general audience."

"No, you're okay. I've heard it used. Coyotes are tricksters."

"*Bon.* So? Cozy or trickster?"

"How do *they* identify?"

"Mmm. When I catch mine, I'll ask."

563

BUT SOFT

Pardon my intrusion."

Jacques opened an eye and huskily drawled, "But soft, what bird through yonder window breaks."

Juuyu's gaze was carefully averted. "You did not return home."

"Are you actually flustered? You needn't be." He gave Harrison's shoulder a squeeze. "Come, sir. Show proof of my innocence, lest yon phoenix suspect debauchery."

"Jacques? Mmm. Morning. Wait. Did you say ... phoenix? Oh, gosh. Hello!" Harrison threw aside his half of their shared afghan—proving he was fully dressed—and hurried to greet the stranger crouched on his windowsill. He earnestly assured, "No debauchery here. Though Swifty's counts as hedonism. Coffee?"

564
LOOK AT THE TIME

A smile creased the corners of Juuyu's eyes, and he reached across to gently rearrange Harrison's sleep-rumpled hair. "I must decline. Jacques will be late if we do not leave immediately."

"Before coffee?" complained Jacques.

"Coffee or a change of clothes. Choose."

Wardrobe won that particular round. "Lord, look at the time. Parting is such sweet sorrow, etcetera, etcetera. Also, I'm holding you to your promise."

"Did I promise something?"

"I'm struck through the heart! It was a solemn vow between friends."

"Remind me."

Jacques bussed Harrison's cheeks. "Your summer holiday belongs to me. I'll see you at Stately House."

565
TOUGH NUT

A rmed with a to-go cup from Founders, personally poured by Rook, Jacques entered the bakery next door, where redheads ruled the day. Only to realize—quite belatedly—that he *knew* the person transferring muffins into the display case.

"Welcome to Tough Nut Bakery!" And in teasing tones, "Your face."

"Spokesperson Woodacre," he murmured. "I didn't realize you … baked."

"Denny. Please." One of the most prominent Amaranthine in America offered his hand and asked, "What can I get you, Jacques?"

He skipped to the crux of his visit. "Kip."

"That rascal? He doesn't drop by often, but hey! You're in luck."

566

COMMON GOOD

Jacques took a seat in one of the bakery's booths, snapped a picture of his selection, and texted it to Nonny.

> **No lovely lie-in for me**
> **But here's a bright side**

It didn't take long for Nonny to respond.

> **Cor. You eat MUFFINS?**

> **Came highly recommended**

> **Good if I show Sonnet?**
> **She's hovering**

> **Do**

Moments passed, and Jacques' suspense grew.

> **You actually *like* them?**
> **You're all about fancy pastries**
> **Muffins are for commoners**

> **I'm smitten**
> **Perhaps it's the hint of cardamom**
> **Elevates the experience**

A longer pause. Then Nonny texted,

> **NOW look what you've done**

And sent through a picture.

567
MIDNIGHT MUFFINS

Sonnet bent over a cookbook, a finger pushing loose tendrils from her coiffure behind one pointed ear. Several spice jars were already on the counter, alongside the basket in which Vanya was no doubt asleep.

> **Sonnet's chuffed**
> **Argent's the only one who knows**
> **how to make your fancy favorites**
> **but she can do muffins**

Another snapshot followed. Sonnet had glanced up, her lips parted in soft surprise. An expression Jacques had inspired before, though under very different circumstances.

> **It's a trifle early to be making me muffins**
> **Argent isn't done conniving**

A selfie followed. Nonny grinned cheekily. Sonnet looked ... good.

568
FANCY

Jacques didn't even care that somewhere across the world, Sonnet was currently wearing shoes. He'd happily steal them in a capricious reversal of the Cinderella story, then lure him into some quiet corner. Or better yet a snug den.

Caught up in wolf-inspired fantasies, Jacques nearly missed his squirrel.

Jacques strolled over and took several moments to enjoy Kip's perusal ... and bewilderment. Good boys were so much fun to tease.

Only once understanding dawned did he say, "Found you."

"Aren't you supposed to be in Japan?"

Deep down, Jacques agreed. But he played his part. "His lordship fancied a trip."

569
NATTER

Jacques allowed Kip to steer him out the door and into an alley.

"You're not a reaver." His confusion seemed to be getting in the way of courtesies, but no matter.

"You're not wrong." Hooking one of Kip's beltloops, he murmured, "Where do you keep your tail?"

The ploy worked. Kip cracked a smile. "You're very comfortable with closeness."

"*Naturellement*. Stately House is overrun with crossers, and I'm the little beasts' favorite uncle."

Jacques could practically see Kip's twitching whiskers, so he nattered on, giving the squirrel clansman reasons to trust. And to relax his guard.

Because Argent was descending.

570
LOOKING AFTER

Jacques rarely saw Argent in flight, at least … not in speaking form. So while he was very generously offering to foist Jarrah on this distant kinsman, he was—peripherally—enjoying his lordship's graceful arrival.

Kip caught on quicker than most. He skittered, and Argent streaked after him, abandoning Jacques to the alley.

Hands in pockets, he gazed after them with a regretful sigh. His part in the proceedings was over.

"Pardon me?"

Jacques half-turned.

An oddly familiar man with exquisite taste and tailoring beckoned. "Lord Mettlebright dropped by earlier. He suggested I look after you while he's occupied with Kip."

571
FITTING PASTIME

On the sly, as it were," continued the man. "Best not to rile the wolves with what amounts to a friendly game."

Jacques considered the unmarked alley door. It offered no hints to what lay beyond, but he was curious what Argent had deemed appropriate for his *looking after*.

Mounting the stairs, he lightly asked, "You have plans for me?"

"Several!" A speculative gaze swept Jacques from head to toe, and light fingers tested the silk of his scarf. Up on tiptoe, eyes fairly sparkling, he happily revealed, "Tyrone Sunfletch. We're tailors, my brothers and I. Care for a fitting?"

572
CYRIL.S BOYS

Find Me was exactly the sort of boutique that Jacques gloried in, and the three very pretty shop boys didn't hurt. Jacques adored Tyrone's instinct for lines, Faisal's sense of drama, and Giuseppe's eye for color. He was in the hands of artists.

Giuseppe unrolled and draped.

Tyrone wielded tailor's chalk.

Faisal sought the perfect accessories.

He let them doll him up, dote, and otherwise distract him until Argent suddenly stalked through the door. Everyone stilled as the fox trailed a finger over the detailing on Jacques' vest.

Taking a deep breath, Argent relaxed visibly and lightly asked, "Having fun?"

573
MUTUALS

After years of careful tailoring, Jacques' devotion *fit*. Closing his eyes, Jacques basked in the knowledge that Argent both knew him well … and genuinely cared. Theirs was a mutual attachment.

"I've had the *loveliest* day. Thanks to you."

Argent gave his shoulder a light pat. "You cannot go without greeting Jiminy. He has offered his den for the night."

"Are you trying to keep me from Harrison?"

"No. You have *always* chosen well for yourself." Argent held Jacques' gaze until he could do nothing but believe him. "Your presence was specifically requested. It seems a mutual acquaintance is in town."

574

BECAUSE WOLVES

Jiminy's smile was the same as usual, but he was as jumpy as a cricket. Jacques finally asked, "Am I making you nervous?"

"Tiny bit. No offense."

"How can I put you at ease?"

"Well … I'm a *wolf*."

A simple fact that had Jacques smoothly adjusting his posture. "I'm not opposed to wolvish practices. Do you need a whiff?"

"Sorry."

"Lord, don't apologize. I'm the farthest thing from shy."

Jiminy took a dominant stance and opened his arms.

Jacques stepped into a firm embrace.

At a soft scuffle from the doorway, Jacques held out an arm to welcome one more.

575

PETAL MOON

Torloo-dex Elderbough skipped forward, tail flagging. Jiminy grinned and made room, and slim arms wrapped around Jacques' middle. Adoona-soh's youngest was a capable hunter, but Jacques was in a position to know that he was also as much of a cuddler as Kyrie.

Torloo wriggled closer, breathed deeply, and sighed his way to a smile. "Hello, Uncle Jackie."

"Hello, Petal Moon."

Blue eyes shone with delight over Jacques' nickname for him. Such endearments were treasured by wolves, who valued them as a reflection of the bonds that inspired them.

Lord. Why had he never come up with one for Sonnet?

576
FASHION ADVICE

Argent left, an appointment to keep. Tyrone dropped by with something scrumptious for Jacques to sleep in. And Inti joined the club, clambering onto Jiminy's shoulders. While Torloo led the way toward Jiminy's den, Jacques checked his messages ... and found one from Harrison.

Tomorrow: which one?

The accompanying photo showed three bowtie options—fire hydrants, butterflies, or a black-and-white bovine print.

There's this wolvish saying
I'm glad our paths crossed

I've been smiling all day

Jacques realized that he was smiling, too.

The tie?

Moo

Spot of tea?

"A moment," Jacques begged of Torloo, hanging back to place a call.

577

TEMPTING TERMS

While I'm very much a tea and slippers kind of friend, I must decline for this evening. Can you forgive me?"

"It's fine. I know I can't monopolize you."

"You're welcome to try." Jacques breezily added, "I have to sleep somewhere."

"Oh? And where are you sleeping tonight?"

"Alas, I can't go into any great detail."

"Question withdrawn. I shouldn't have even asked." Harrison's tone shifted. *"I've been considering the contract your dragon friend brought over."*

"Quick work! What's the offer?"

"Two months. Annually. With the option to stay longer."

"Tempting terms?"

"Gosh, yes."

"You'll come?"

Harrison laughed. *"Gosh, yes."*

578

PILLOW TALK

Jacques lolled among the furs that lined Jiminy's den and watched embedded crystals winking like scattered stardust. Argent might like to add something similar to the naproom's ceiling. Jacques would bring it up. Michael could sort it out.

Inti wriggled closer and whispered, "Why is Jacques awake?"

"Because I cannot sleep."

"Same for Inti."

Actually, Torloo wasn't sleeping either, but he'd taken truest form and lay across the den's door.

Inti's hand found Jacques' and a crystal slid against his palm. "Tell Inti all about it."

"All about what?"

The crosser kissed Jacques' cheek and begged, "Trade secrets with me?"

579

MATURE CONTENT

Jacques let go long enough to pull Inti close, then linked their fingers around the crystal. The monkey-crosser might be more mature than he let on, but nobody was too old to seek comfort.

"You sure you want to know the things I *don't* say?"

Inti snickered into his chest.

Jacques kneaded one slim shoulder, worried over the tension he found there. "Tell Uncle Jackie all about it."

"Inti has a reaver class. Inti is a reach."

"I … haven't much context. Congratulations …?"

The crosser offered a surprisingly succinct explanation before relapsing into childishness and whimsy. "Inti thinks trouble is near."

580

THE TRUTH WILL OUT

Why?" Jacques frowned. "How can you tell?"

"Little whispers. Distant songs."

"And … who sings to you?"

Inti drew back, shrewdly searching Jacques' face. In the faint light of the softly twinkling ceiling, he glared warnings. "Do not laugh."

"Lord, you know I won't. You're too much of a handful to take anything but seriously."

Patting his cheek, Inti crooned, "Good, good, good man."

"Good? Hardly." Drumming his fingers lightly over Inti's ribs, he warned, "Like the true cad I am, I'll tickle the truth out of you."

There was a smile in his small voice. "*Stars*. Inti sometimes hears stars."

581
TRUTH BE TOLD

Is it nice, listening to stars?"

"No. Yes. No." Inti sighed. "They have beautiful voices. But they tell the truth, and Inti doesn't always want to hear it."

Jacques kept his tone light. "Did you learn a terrible truth about yourself?"

"Inti did."

"And you're hiding it from Argent?"

His short laugh ended in a sigh. "Jacques is too good at this game. Can you keep a secret?"

"From Argent? *Non*."

"Not *from*. *For*. Keep a secret for Inti?"

Bumping noses with the monkey crosser, Jacques reissued his invitation. "Tell Uncle Jackie all about it."

"Inti is afraid of foxes."

582
AU REVOIR

Jacques only had to stave off his homesickness for a little longer.

There was pie from Gert's, and a vintage travel case arrived from Find Me, all mahogany and leather straps, brimming with tailored finery.

Snowflakes danced in the wind when he bid *au revoir* to Harrison, who hugged him hard and begged him not to be a stranger.

Jacques navigated the banalities of travel, and once aboard their flight, Argent's hand found his.

"Yes, my lord?"

"I am *tired*."

Doing the math, he sighed. "How much longer ...?"

"You will do." And nestling against Jacques' side, the fox fell asleep.

583
HOLD TIGHT

The enormity of Argent's trust was flattering, but Jacques had concerns. Tucking his lord and master under his chin, he gazed pleadingly into the camera, sent the selfie, and thumbed a plea.

Argent wore himself out
I shall need reinforcements

Canarian Evernhold was already responding.

How secure are you?

Probably spectacularly warded
Assume we're safe

Hold tight
Making calls

Jacques turned so Argent's ear rested over his heart. He petted silver hair and thought devoted thoughts until Canarian's next text pinged.

How many taskforce members
do you know about?

More than I'm supposed to

Sinder?

Sinder

You'll be meeting Colt

584

TARMAC

A warm hand patted Jacques' cheek, bringing him out of a dozy haze. He pulled Argent more firmly to his side and peered around the empty plane. "Ricker Thunderhoof, I presume?"

"Call me Colt."

By the time he'd successfully disentangled Jacques, his partner was there to receive Argent.

Jacques moved stiffly to the plane's dinky WC and emerged feeling more ready to face their journey's next leg. "Well, gentlemen? How do you want me?"

Colt asked, "Do you ride?"

"Are you asking after my posting ... or preferred positions?"

Hallow blushed.

Colt's smile widened. "It seems Sinder wasn't exaggerating about you."

585

PROTOCOLS

Canarian awaited them alongside a customs officer, who verified their identities and stamped their passports. Couriers were sent for luggage, and a mini-bus with darkened windows pulled up to the curb to whisk them away, Keishi-bound.

Jacques perched on the edge of Argent's bed, holding his hand. "With all this." He waved at the luxurious interior. "Why did you ask if I could ride?"

Colt said, "Once the sun sets, we're taking to the sky."

"This bus will become a decoy," added Hallow, whose cheekbones were mesmerizing.

"Expecting trouble?" Jacques asked lightly.

"Argent was," Colt replied. "This is *his* plan."

586

PRIVATE ENTERTAINMENT

Dressage really hadn't prepared Jacques for straddling someone of Colt's girth, but the stretch was satisfying in its own way. He relaxed into an easy rhythm that carried him higher.

Lord, he loved horseback riding. The *entendre* wrote themselves.

He refrained from telling Hallow, who somehow managed to be drop-dead gorgeous, assassin-level dangerous, and exceedingly virginal, all at the same time.

As city lights receded below, Jacques willed his thoughts away from leather, laces, and that tantalizing peek of wing folds. His success rate was roughly two-out-of-three. "Do bats ever–"

Hallow silenced him with a finger against his lips.

587

UNDER COVER OF DARKNESS

Hallow wordlessly transferred Argent into Jacques' arms, stood upon Colt's broad back, and began weaving sigils.

Jacques peered around, but it was wretchedly dark. Rather the point.

Also, it wasn't as if he could *do* anything about a hypothetical attacker. Argent's safety was up to Hallow and Colt, both capable swordsmen. *Non.* The only thing Jacques could do was protect Argent's rest. Moods mattered, and—all *entendre* aside—he knew how to set one.

So Jacques distracted himself by relaying several saucy schoolboy anecdotes that were foundational to understanding his ever-expanding packing list for Nonny, who would soon be dorm-bound.

588

PROBABLY NOTHING

When Colt ambled to a stop in woods, Jacques assumed they'd reached Stately House's outermost barrier. His extremities were numb, so when Ginkgo sprang onto Colt's back to take his dad, Jacques had trouble letting go.

"Easy does it," Ginkgo murmured, gently prying cold fingers. "You did good."

"Nothing to it," he assured wearily.

"Good thing Deece is here." Turning slightly, the half-fox quietly ordered, "Better carry Jacques." Then took off.

Jacques asked, "So ... were we followed?"

Hallow hesitated. "It was probably nothing."

"Lord, have it your way. But was it nothing like a dragon? Or nothing like a fox?"

589

GOOD NEWS TRAVELS FAST

Jacques hissed as he swung a leg over, then slipped down into Deece's waiting arms.

Colt shifted into speaking form and answered, "Something was there, and we avoided it. Under the circumstances, we couldn't risk a closer look." Big hands framed Jacques' face. "More importantly, how are you feeling?"

"Good of you to ask. Nothing a cup of tea and a long soak won't put to rights."

Deece said, "Cat and Canary are readying the bath for you."

Jacques perked up. "They're here?"

"They will be. Often," said their younger brother. "Uncle approved their plan. They are joining the enclave."

590

RIDERS

O ur needs are simple," Catalan assured. "Tracks for the train. And a theater, of course."

"Of course," Jacques agreed. "Simplicity itself." Then Canarian began kneading his left thigh, and Jacques groaned into the folded towel serving as his pillow.

Deece ventured, "Argent agreed to a railroad?"

"Why not?" asked Cat. "The children will love it."

"It might be fun," agreed Gilen. "If we can ride …?"

"In grand style!" Cat promised. "Tomorrow, we'll get up a woodland expedition. Scout possible routes."

"We can help," Gilen swiftly volunteered. "Right Nonny?"

Nonny, who'd been unusually quiet, asked, "You're *really* moving here? For Jacques?"

591

DEDICATION

J acques tensed, and Canarian tutted, kneading firmly until he was once more limp and pliant.

Meanwhile, Cat sloshed to Nonny's side and wrapped an arm around his shoulders. "Yes, we're *really* moving here. And being near friends and family …? *Very* attractive. But why would you think Jacques alone swayed our choices?" Nuzzling Nonny's ear, he asked, "Is my favorite satyr jealous? Come, be teacher's pet!"

"Teacher …? *You*?"

"Beginning after the Dichotomy Day festivities," Cat confirmed. "I'll be dedicating myself to Stately House's bright future."

"You're gonna teach crossers?" Nonny looked to Canarian for confirmation, then gruffly accused, "You're such *dads*."

592

WEE HOURS

Hours later, Jacques was up late, doing a little extra pampering, when someone tapped on his door. Leaning out of his *en suite*, he checked the clock. One in the morning? He slipped into a dressing gown and softly called, "Yes?"

"Uncle Jackie?"

He opened immediately. "Kyrie? Lord, is anything wrong?"

The boy appeared momentarily befuddled, but he whispered, "May I come in?"

Swinging the door wide, Jacques bowed him through. Then tried to decide if it was a bad sign when Kyrie traced a sigil on its back before speaking again.

"Why are you all ...." Kyrie cautiously finished, "Green ...?"

593

CLEANSHAVEN

Facial." Jacques waved at himself. "I skimped while we were away. I was about to peel. Coming?"

Kyrie asked, "May I help?"

"By all means." And he directed the boy through the final four stages. "It's never too early to take care of one's skin. Or scales."

"So smooth!" He patted Jacques' cleanshaven cheek.

"Mm-hmm. So is that why you dropped by? To trade facials?"

Kyrie gasped, then went all tongue-tied.

"Were you meant to be delivering a message or something?" Jacques guessed.

"No, but ... I think you are wanted."

"By whom?"

The boy sheepishly pointed toward Jacques' balcony. "Sonnet."

594
DAMPENING EFFECT

Kyrie hastily explained, "I think Sonnet has been trying to get your attention for a while, but Dad's barriers …. You cannot hear him from inside, but a wind brought me a whisper."

Jacques crossed to the double doors and opened them, letting in a gust of cold air. "Are you sure?"

"I am. I could make an opening for you," Kyrie offered.

"Is he down in the garden?" Really, Jacques couldn't see. Or hear a call. Or a howl, for that matter.

Kyrie reached out, slipping both hands into … nothing. "Sit on the rail. And when I say *go*, jump."

595
MEET ME IN THE GARDEN

Pardonnez-moi?"

"I will open the way, and you will jump through."

"You're vastly overestimating my courage."

"Never underestimate wolves."

"Sonnet's there?"

"He is."

Jacques swung one leg over the railing, then the other. "They say trust is beautiful."

"You are," Kyrie assured, humming as he pushed at … nothing.

Suddenly, Jacques heard a mournful crooning. "Sonnet?" he called in an undertone.

"Go," Kyrie urged.

Jacques wasn't sure which of them was more startled when he collided with Sonnet in midair.

"You fell!" he exclaimed in consternation.

"More of a leap, actually."

"You jumped?"

"Neatly caught."

Sonnet whined softly, then kissed him.

596

SURE THING

Jacques had been missing this, so he made certain the kiss lingered. Sonnet drew back with obvious reluctance, and Jacques laughed breathlessly when the wolf moved on to sniffing and grumbling.

"That was *dangerous*."

"Was it, though?" asked Jacques. "Wolves are the surest of sure things."

"You trust me that much?"

"*Oui*." Jacques let himself be happy.

Sonnet looked away. Was he being shy? Jacques toyed with a loose lock of Sonnet's hair while he waited to see if this homecoming would land him on lavender-scented sheets.

But Sonnet's voice had changed when he said, "Jacques ...? We need to talk."

597

THE THING IS...

He *knew*. Jacques had been through this so many times before. Usually, he saw it coming.

Sonnet tentatively asked, "May I confide in you?"

Somehow, Jacques summoned up a smile. "You may put your faith in both my insatiable curiosity and my discretion."

"I heard from my daughter."

"One of those lovely orphans you raised?"

"Hazel. She's ... in the family way. Again."

"Lord, you're a grandmother? You must be excited."

Sonnet's hold on him tightened. "The thing is ... it wasn't meant ... mmm. They didn't plan to have more than three children. Everyone's in a to-do, and ... Hazel wants her mother."

598
APOLOGY

O f course she'd want her mother. Any child would. Well, I certainly never wanted Maman, but if it was *you*, I know I'd want...." He stopped himself.

Sonnet stole a kiss.

Not a proper one.

It was an apology.

Jacques knew how these things were supposed to proceed. Knew how to be generous. "You'll go to her. You *must*. Hazel will be relying on you."

"She *is*," Sonnet whispered.

"I understand. I do."

"But...."

Jacques wondered if Sonnet didn't want to leave in much the same way he didn't want to be left behind. He dared to ask, "How long?"

599
A LITTLE WHILE

T welve seasons, and everyone's frantic since crosser births endanger the mother."

"Confide in Argent," Jacques advised. "Or Harmonious, since Lady Anna managed with Ever."

"Yes, of course. I'll write them."

"Your departure's imminent?"

"Tomorrow."

"Ah."

"It's only for a little while," Sonnet said. "I'll come back. Someday. I will."

Jacques was keenly aware that *a little while* meant something different to people whose lifespans never ended. Sonnet's *someday* would be years from now. Possibly decades.

Jacques had been through this so many times before, so he didn't ask Sonnet to stay.

And Sonnet didn't ask him to wait. The end.

600
BACK TO WORK

Jacques needed a few days, and he spent them hiding in Cat and Canary's room. They didn't ask questions, only purred over him and filled in for him. But when Argent slept past his scheduled return, Jacques wrestled his butlerish armor into place and went back to work.

Meetings to attend.

Letters to answer.

Calls to make.

Disappointments to bury.

In some ways, it was a relief that nobody had known. Well, *almost* nobody. He'd nearly found the courage to text Harrison when Argent shuffled from the bedroom, barefoot and rumpled, stomach growling.

"Have Sonnet bring a tray? *Several* trays."

601
SORT IT OUT

I'll just ... see to it, shall I?" Abandoning the mail, Jacques hurried for the door.

The fox was in front of him in a wink, frowning. "Jackie ...?"

"Please, don't ask."

"You cannot hide anything from me."

"Then you don't *need* to ask. You'll sort it out."

Argent let him go.

In the kitchen, Ginkgo helped him load trays.

Feeling the half-fox's gaze, Jacques stiffly inquired, "Something to say?"

"Nah. Words never help." And he just ... gave his back a single pat.

Jacques' lips trembled, but he firmed the line, stacked his share of the trays, and followed the half-fox upstairs.

602
STARS TELL THE TRUTH

Jacques knew something was wrong the moment Argent turned from the table, letter in hand. "When did this arrive?"

"Not sure. I've been … out of pocket." He set aside trays, found the envelope. "Doon-wen Nightspangle?"

"He is gone."

"Who's gone?"

"Inti."

Jacques missed a beat. "Where did he go?"

"Heaven knows. He was taken."

"From *Bellwether*?"

"Inti felt eyes on him, so he left campus. To lead them away."

"Was it those foxes?" asked Ginkgo.

"There is no proof." Argent's frown deepened as he gazed at his son. "However, someone has been quietly, methodically stealing crossers. And they have Inti."

PART FOUR

Early in the spring of 11 N.S., a little more than a year before Kyrie and Lilya will attend summer courses at Wardenclave, which means Stately House is setting up for the fourth book in the Amaranthine Saga, *Mikoto and the Reaver Village*.

603
TAKING A CALL

Michael was looking unusually discombobulated when Jacques opened to his knock and beckoned him through. He'd been mired in correspondence all morning, so Michael's arrival was a welcome break from the tedium. Except for one tiny detail.

"Lord, you're shaking."

Argent strode forward. "What has happened?"

"I just took a call," Michael said, holding up his phone. "From Timur."

"Is he hurt?" Argent asked darkly.

"No, no! No, he's fine. Well, not *fine*."

Silver tails unfurled as Argent firmly guided Michael to the sofa, "Sit. Tell us. What has you addled?"

Michael's gaze pleaded with Argent. "Timur .... He was *crying*."

604
DOING HIS PART

Argent growled, and Michael quickly said, "He's not in *danger*. Timur's ... well, he's sad."

"Why?" Argent's tone promised death.

"Let me back up. Old friend, it would seem that I'm a grandfather. Twenty-four times over. With another baby on the way."

Argent looked totally confused. "How?"

"At some point, he decided to ... do his part."

Jacques couldn't even imagine. Actually, he was doing his best *not* to think about the mechanics of singlehandedly kicking off a Spomenka baby boom.

"And Timur ...?" Argent pressed.

"... was hoping to settle down."

Jacques lowered his gaze. That one? Oh, yes. That he could imagine.

605
REJIGGING SCHEDULES

I am going." Argent wavered. "*Can* I go?"

Jacques flapped a hand. "Lord, it's fine. I'll handle the fall-out. Clear your schedule and shore up any gaps."

"I will get to Timur. Reassure him. Michael, pack and be ready tomorrow. After that, Ginkgo will want a turn." Argent grimly swore, "He will not be alone."

Again, Jacques lowered his gaze.

"How far along …?"

"In her fifth month."

Jacques was grateful that human pregnancies only lasted nine. He shied away from the attendant knowledge that Amaranthine pregnancies took thirty-six months. And that Sonnet had been gone twice that long … and longer.

606
VOLUNTEER

Jacques resigned himself to four months of utter disarray. *Everyone* wanted a turn sitting with the forlorn father-to-be, who'd stranded himself in the English countryside.

Jacques wondered if Glintrubble was anywhere near Merritt House.

And then he distracted himself by polishing the silver tea service.

Which was why he was in the vicinity when Deece approached Argent, who was about to dash off again.

"Fend wants to pact with Timur." Resting a hand atop his Kith son's broad head, Deece quietly added, "If you bring him, he will stay."

Argent's tension eased somewhat, and he bowed to Fend. "*Thank you.*"

607

MARCH

Jacques meandered snow-edged paths, hunting for signs of spring. Hardly the sort of thing he'd done in Uppington, but if Jacques brought Argent a sprig of this or that, the fox would set aside his agenda, just to gaze. Then he'd bring it to show Tsumiko.

Today, Jacques crouched before a patch of snowdrops. White petals. Peridot freckles.

His contemplations were interrupted by Kyrie, who was far too light on his feet.

"Are you busy today?" asked the eleven-year-old.

"I certainly find ways to stay busy. But I'd let you overturn my plans."

"Fairlee says a calf is coming today."

608

SINGLEHANDED

The Evernholds' arrival had benefited the entire enclave. Their vintage railroad was mostly a novelty, but it had brought Fairlee Longbrawn to Japan. He was an old friend from their theater days, and after singlehandedly laying tracks, the bovine clansman had asked to stay.

Jacques still hadn't decided if Fairlee was a preservationist or a hobbyist or a hedonist. But Stately House now boasted a dairy barn, a creamery, and a small herd of cows—all Kith, each with different ancestry.

"Where's Lilya?"

"She ran ahead. I came back for you." Kyrie offered him a hand. "Be mine for today?"

609
CALVING

Do I seem the sort to hang about in barns?"

"No, but you like babies."

"I suppose I do." Jacques arched his brows, sure there was more.

Kyrie asked, "Are you going to visit Timur?"

"There are many other people he'd be far happier to see."

"You do not think you could cheer up Timur?"

"I haven't seen him since he was, what … sixteen? We're practically strangers."

"Are you feeling shy about him?"

"Lord, I don't know. Do you really think he'd want his gay uncle dropping by? We can't have much in common."

Kyrie pointed out, "You like babies."

610
HONORARY UNCLE

Jacques faced himself and decided that *yes*, he *was* feeling shy about Timur.

Like most reaver kids, Michael and Sansa's oldest boy only returned to Stately House for the odd reaver festival or Dichotomy Day celebration. Once a year at most, since he'd had regular classes, summer courses, and apprenticeships.

Timur had his mother's build and his father's smile. Fun and funny and fearless. Already growing into exactly the sort of man that Jacques could easily fall for.

So he'd unobtrusively distanced himself. It wasn't that Jacques didn't trust himself, but … lord. His own nephew? He'd *never* tread that path.

611
PRACTICALLY STRANGERS

In a twist Jacques probably should have seen coming, Argent told him to pack for a long weekend.

His trepidation was easily matched by that of the strapping young battler who answered his knock. Brown eyes peered at him from under unruly curls with a wary sort of resignation. "You … needn't have come. Fend's here."

"Argent insisted."

"Ah. Sorry for the hassle. Come in …?"

Snug knit and a battler's physique were a devastating combination, but Jacques did his best to face the man head-on. So he noticed Timur's deepening blush.

Jacques realized something important. "Lord. I'm hardly one to criticize."

612
HAVE IT ALL OUT

Right, then. Let's have it all out so we can move past any unnecessary mortification. I'm *aware* that you've nobly done your part for the In-between, and I'm not bothered by your heavily euphemized contributions."

Timur looked away, tears welling.

Had nobody addressed Timur's obvious shame? Even though it'd kept this bleeding-heart battler from asking for much-needed help.

"Since it's a matter of record, I can say with certainty that I've slept with more people than you have. I like sex. You like children. I think we both know which of us is more likely to be called a whore."

613
HITTING HARD

Timur looked shocked. And ready to argue.

Jacques wasn't finished. "Sacrifices are personal things, and you've made several. Twenty-four, if I recall correctly. It must be hitting you hard about now, knowing how many little ones you gave up."

His face crumpled, tears spilled, and with a strangled sob, Timur hauled Jacques into his arms. Bodily.

Wingtips dangling above the floor, Jacques folded his arms around Timur's shoulders and spoke soothingly, murmuring encouragements in all the languages they had in common.

"You'll not have my hate, only my expertise." Jacques tugged a curl and promised, "I'm treating your hair later."

614
ALTERNATIVE MEDICINE

Lord, you're big as a wolf," Jacques complained in admiring tones. "Now set me down. I brought remedies for heartbreak."

"Who said anything about heartbreak?"

"*I* did. Just now. I'm a past master of the art." Jacques crossed to his baggage, which included an insulated bag. "For starters."

Timur unzipped it. "Ice cream?"

"Gelato. Fairlee's been dabbling for my sake."

"You … brought me gelato." Timur seemed amused.

"Much safer than plying you with liquor, which only leads to strip poker and the sorts of dares that would leave you with a whole new set of regrets."

Timur finally cracked a real smile.

615

HALF A DOZEN

Timur read labels. "Lemon-lavender, cherry blossom, panna cotta...."

"Oooh, *mine*!" Jacques beckoned for that one. "While I've never been vanilla in *other* areas .... Here, just a bite!"

Timur hummed around the spoonful Jacques thrust upon him, showing signs of his old sparkle. "Strawberry-basil, chocolate, and ... gumball?"

"Children are Fairlee's usual clientele. He runs the enclave's ice cream shop, one of the most popular stops on Stately House's railroad."

"A lot has changed ...?"

"And continues to change."

Timur tentatively asked, "May I offer some to Manya?"

"Do!"

As soon as Timur left, Fend set one big paw across Jacques' knees.

616

SACRIFICES WERE MADE

How are *you* faring? This is a long way from your father's hearth."

Fend's eyes narrowed.

"I meant no insult. But I won't ignore *your* sacrifices, either." Jacques asked, "Do you want a share in the spoiling?"

Timur returned minutes later. "Are you actually feeding him from a silver spoon?"

"I forgot to pack my runcible one," Jacques answered breezily. "Eat your gelato. Or did you want me to spoon-feed you, too?" He offered the next bite.

"Didn't *you* claim this one?"

"Panna cotta is a longstanding favorite."

Timur eyed Fend. "You have a wicked streak."

Fend began to purr.

617
PARTIALITY

Jacques wrapped Timur's treated curls, then daubed mud on his un-stubbled cheeks. The young man submitted without any protest. In fact, he looked serene.

"You're a good sport."

"I'm familiar with ... well. This." Timur asked, "Can you keep a secret?"

"Your every confidence is safe with me."

"I've spent a lot of time with dragons. They're partial to hot pools. And hot mud. And hot oil." His quietly confessed, "I've been a bath attendant and everything."

Heedless of the newly-applied mud, Jacques cupped Timur's face. "I know this weekend is supposed to be all about you, but ... lord. Do me?"

618
MAN ON A MISSION

Maybe Timur was just glad of a project. Maybe he needed to get out of the little house he and Manya managed to share without ever really seeing each other.

"The Thunderhoofs are healers," Timur explained as he rummaged through their supply room. "I talked to Bavol first thing. We can use his preparation room."

While Timur teased the right temperature out of a bed of embers, Jacques chatted about safe things—cuisine and scenery. But then he asked, "Are you looking forward to .... mmm. I suppose you *are* a father, biologically speaking. But are you looking forward to fathering?"

619
FIRST NAME BASIS

S o much. It's the *only* reason ...." His voice caught.

Jacques redirected. "Son? Or daughter?"

"Shouldn't matter."

"It certainly could!"

Timur sought his gaze. "Would it matter to you?"

"I wouldn't enjoy explaining to a daughter why she couldn't join the Fundoshi Swim Club."

"A good point. Sons, then?"

Jacques only shook his head. Fatherhood wasn't in his future. "Will your youngster call you *papka*?"

"I'd like that. Yes."

"And will they call me *Uncle Jackie*?"

When he hesitated, Jacques wondered if he'd presumed too much.

But then Timur answered, "*They* will, but ... would you mind if I called you Jacques?"

620
LEFT WANTING

W hile Timur's dragon goo cooled, he gave Jacques a tour. "Papka's lineage traces to Glintrubble's first crystal adepts. Ancient history, but many people here loved Willem Ward ... and miss him."

Jacques supposed that was a kind of immortality. "Ever consider wooing an Amaranthine?"

"Nobody's ever wanted me before. Why would that change?"

"You're a reaver."

"And ... you're not?"

"People only want me in a passing-fancy sort of way." Jacques shrugged. "I'm everyone's favorite uncle."

"A little like ... always the bridesmaid, never the bride."

"*Exactement!*"

Timur looked away, looked back. "Awful, isn't it?"

Jacques patted Fend. "Usually only when I'm alone."

621

DRAGON STYLE

Timur's fingers slid confidently along Jacques' spine, pinching and plucking. "... even better if they can raise their ridges in speaking form."

He'd entered lecture mode. Like father, like son.

"The oil's hot. Ready?"

"Do you worst."

Timur prattled on about instinctual responses to stimuli while Jacques became a blissful puddle.

"Lord. This is the sort of male bonding I can get behind. Or on. Or under."

"You're very ... upfront."

He had no idea.

Or maybe he did. "If you were Amaranthine, I'd also be tending you."

"Wouldn't that...? It *would*, wouldn't it? Celibate caste my ass."

Timur's laugh rumbled pleasantly.

622

WHAT WILL BE, WILL BE

Jacques explained, "This is another of my remedies."

"Pancakes?"

"Not simply *pancakes*. This is very specific. These are late night pancakes in the drawing room."

"This is a drawing room, then?"

"Close enough. Eat."

Timur forked a mouthful of their midnight snack, and Jacques poured more batter, which sizzled and puffed. Argent would return for him tomorrow, so they were prolonging their final day.

"I'm not heartbroken, you know. Over Manya." Timur stared at his plate. "I was *willing* to fall in love, but she never gave me the chance."

"*Qué será, será.*"

Timur asked, "Why did your heart break?"

623

TAKES ONE TO KNOW ONE

I already told you. I fall in love too easily. Heartbreak is the usual upshot."

Timur pointed out, "You didn't fall in love with me."

"*Non.* You're safe." Which suggested an uncomfortable truth. "I suppose that means I'm not over him."

"Well, it felt like Devotion was mine these past few days." Timur's smile faltered. "I didn't fall in love either, but … I failed. And I feel foolish."

"But not especially gay?"

He chuckled. "No, Jacques. Not especially gay."

"Then tonight's commiseration is limited to pancakes. More's the pity. Someone someday is going to be *very* lucky."

"Your someone, too."

624

UNSOLICITED ADVICE

While Argent conferred with Dwennon Thunderhoof, Jacques tweaked one of Timur's now-lustrous curls. "Unsolicited advice time. If you really, truly want to *keep* your child, come home to Stately House. Your parents refused to send Lilya and Vanya away, yet they lack for nothing."

"Papka *did* say I'd be welcome."

"Understatement."

"I have … obligations."

"Even members of the Order of Spomenka have to call someplace home."

Timur frowned. "How …?"

"I know just enough Russian to be dangerous." Jacques promised, "Your secret's safe, friend."

Timur hauled him off his feet and gruffly promised, "Winter, after the baby's weaned from mare's milk."

625

DUE IN JUNE

Somehow, they kept Timur's predicament and plans a secret from the children. Then again, the young ones mostly ignored adult matters. The periodic absences caused by their rotation through Glintrubble drew as much attention as Spokesperson Mettlebright's other travel for the Amaranthine Council. Which was to say ... none.

The kids were far more excited about a very different due date. Because June meant summer courses and bingo nights and bowties.

Harrison Peck dropped his bags, flung his arms wide, tried to hug everyone at once, greeting every blessed child by name, and generally making Jacques proud to be his friend.

626

HOME AWAY FROM HOME

Jacques and Nonny finally waded through the crowd to collect the man and his bags.

"C'mon, now" Nonny grumbled. "He's here all summer."

"Yes!" Harrison gazed around. "It's *so* good to be back."

"The guv won't complain if this is the summer you decide to stay."

"For now, I'm just going to enjoy being with people I care about."

Jacques claimed his hug and kissed Harrison's cheeks for good measure. "Fair warning, *mon ami*. You aren't the only one who considers this their second home."

Nonny's eyes sparkled. "You'll just hafta share the limelight."

"With ...?"

They pointed.

Harrison whispered, "Gosh."

627

SHARE THE LIMELIGHT

Josheb ambled forward, hand outstretched. "So you're the Harrison all these kids are crazy about! The American who wears a different bowtie every day."

Caleb, who was famous for interjecting little-known facts on episodes of *Dare Together*, added, "Uncle Jackie's best friend."

"Gosh! I'm... *hi*. This is a pleasure!"

Caleb made totally unnecessary introductions, then came to stand beside Jacques.

Predictably, Harrison skipped straight past fanboy to friend, expounding on his research into little-known Amaranthine children's games, the basis for one of his summer courses.

Once they were engrossed, Caleb bumped Jacques' shoulder. "Would you like to meet a star?"

628

LUMINARIES

I daresay you and your brother count." Jacques blandly pointed out, "I'm surrounded by luminaries."

Caleb lifted a palm.

Jacques missed a beat, but he covered the crystal resting there. Caleb gave a squeeze and lowered his arm, hiding their connection.

"You wanted to hold my hand?" Jacques inquired lightly. "Not that I'm complaining."

"I'm ... spoken for."

"Ah, well. I probably wouldn't have liked a long-distance relationship."

Caleb's gaze softened in a way that made Jacques feel seen. As in ... exposed.

"My star wants to meet you. Sometime during our visit, if you can find the time. Nights are best."

629

THREE WAYS

Star ... as in an Impression?" Jacques whispered.

"Yes. Eri's an imp."

"*Your* star. But I thought you and Andor .... I mean, he's the possessive sort, and he doesn't hide it well. But lord. You're actually a throuple?"

"Well, it *is* a three-way pact." Caleb's expression gave away nothing.

"*Details*?"

The man dished, but not about the things Jacques wanted to learn. "Josheb knows about Andor, but Eri has always been my secret. We're confiding in you."

"I'm honored, titillated, and the teensiest bit frustrated. But ... why me?"

"Eri likes you. They wanted me to invite you to a wine tasting."

630

BEDROOM EYES

Humming happily over his date with a star—tentative, since Jacques wasn't sure when he'd have an evening free—he let himself into Akira's room without knocking.

Upon the bed, arms shifted, and long fingers flexed against pale skin. From over Akira's bare shoulder, Suuzu's flame-colored gaze locked with his—sulky and surly.

Jacques had yet to catch them at anything more suggestive than a snuggle, but he held out hope.

When would Akira finally notice that he was never more than a heartbeat away from being devoured by someone *Clannish* had recently named one of the world's sexiest bachelors?

631
NEWS OF THE DAY

Jacques didn't throw open the drapes, only parted them enough to let in a sunbeam or two. He sat on the edge of the mattress. "I bring news."

Akira stirred, smiled sleepily, and murmured, "Morning, Uncle Jackie."

"*Afternoon.* Up until all hours?"

"Mm-hmm. Suuzu felt like singing."

"The Dare brothers are here, and Harrison's arrived. None of them have the good sense to be jetlagged, so the day promises to be noisy. If you wish to hide, I'll aid and abet. If you wish to participate, welcome feast preparations are underway."

Akira brightened and tried to rise.

Tried and failed.

632
GOOD GRIP

Akira tried again, but the blankets shifted along with Suuzu's grasp. Sunlight lit flames in orange eyes, lending heat to his mutinous gaze.

"Josheb will be flipping burgers, and Harrison promises pie. I'm off to the kitchen next to help peel apples."

"Sounds great." Akira made another bid for escape, only to abruptly freeze. "Umm ... Suuzu?"

Jacques would've loved to know what was happening under the covers.

"I think we'll ... be a little longer," said Akira.

"Tray?" he offered.

Suuzu pulled the duvet over both their heads.

Akira's voice held laughter when he answered, "No thanks. We'll be there. Eventually."

633

CONSPIRATORS

The peeling party was already underway by the time Jacques reported for duty. Harrison had conspired with Fairlee, who'd lugged two bushels of apples to the kitchen table.

"Room for one more?" Jacques inquired.

Gilen scooted over, and he squeezed in between him and Tawny.

"Do you like apple pie, Uncle Jackie?" asked the tiger-crosser.

"What's not to love? The best I ever tasted was from a little place in America. Harrison brought me."

The man promised, "These will be just as good as Gert's!"

"Bold assertion."

"Bold, but not baseless." Harrison radiated *joie de vivre*. "Gert gave me lessons!"

634

VANISHING ACT

Energy levels at Stately House were still running high a few days later, when Hisoka arrived with a small cortege. Isla had somehow contrived to accompany him, and Canarian stayed close, looking especially beleaguered. He shot a pleading look Jacques' way, then created an opening.

Without a word, Jacques essentially scruffed Spokesperson Twineshaft and steered him through Argent's conservatory doors.

Hisoka sagged into ready arms.

"Lovely to see you, too." Jacques dared to pet pewter hair.

He sighed and stroked his thumb over the tattoo at Jacques' nape. Slowly, Ephemera winked into view. A small gift from a grateful person.

635
HOW MUCH

Hisoka had trouble settling, which was going to be a problem this close to Dichotomy Day. Jacques decided a change of pace was in order. "How much do you trust me?"

"More than I let on."

"Run away with me?"

Hisoka peeked out from under the arm he'd flung across his eyes. "Pardon?"

Jacques tapped a finger to his lips, slid from the enormous bed in Hisoka's usual suite, and held up his own dressing gown.

Clearly curious, the cat knotted it, took Jacques' hand, and followed him along hushed halls, like a couple of naughty children out past curfew.

636
SHARING

Jacques hustled Hisoka through the door to his own rooms, stole back his dressing gown, and nudged the cat into his bed. He slid in after and whispered, "All right so far?"

"Are we going farther?"

"You know me so well."

Hisoka peered around with interest. "You take good care of your things."

"And I'll take good care of you."

"This room only smells like you."

"*Naturellement*. It's my room."

"You don't ... share."

"I'm sharing now." He propped chin on fist. "We're going to be in so much trouble with Canary."

"Ah. Yes."

"Do me a favor?"

"Hmm?"

"Trust me."

637
INSTINCTUAL LEVEL

rust your nose. Trust your instincts."

"I'm Amaranthine. That's our very way of life."

"But do you trust your instincts where *I'm* concerned?" Jacques ran his thumb over one of Hisoka's knit brows. "Will you believe them, even if it means believing in me more than anybody else?"

"What are you after?"

"I can't tend. Or surrender a whisker. But we need that level of trust."

Hisoka looked so doubtful.

"And for this to work, you'll have to let your guard down. All the way down."

"Why?"

Jacques answered, "Because she's getting to you, and not in a good way."

638
RUNAWAY

isoka's hand found his mouth, covered it.

Jacques caught his wrist, pulled it aside. "We've run away. You think I don't know who we're running from?"

He dully said, "What she wants ...? I can't."

"Then don't."

As if things were ever that simple.

Hisoka hissed softly. "She ...."

"Lord, I know." Jacques pulled the blankets up over their heads, then tugged Hisoka close, speaking into his ear. "She isn't Michael."

He flinched.

"Look. Cat told me how he and Canary dealt with this sort of thing. Their friend took charge, commanded them. Prior commitments are powerful." Jacques offered, "Pact with me."

639
PROMISE ME

Hisoka radiated reluctance. "What exactly are you proposing?"

"Promise me that you'll consider my feelings above anyone else's. No other person, no matter how dear, shall obligate you without my consent. Put simply, my orders trump hers. That should work, *n'est ce-pas*?"

"It … might. But such a promise would leave me at *your* mercy."

"An ideal situation, since I don't have any designs on you."

"What if that changes?"

Jacques diplomatically skipped past issues of compatibility. "It won't change. It can't. In part *because* prior commitments are so powerful. Your heart is somewhere else, and my devotion belongs to another."

640
WORDS TO BIND

A pact," Hisoka finally agreed. "I'll look to you. No one else can command me."

Jacques handed down the only order they needed. "Consider me first, knowing that I'll always want what you want."

There. Neatly done. That created a loophole that would protect Hisoka. Only … he seemed to be waiting for more.

"Did I forget something?"

"About … Michael. Did I do something that led you to think …?"

"*Non.*" Jacques couldn't really point to anything specific, yet Hisoka's preference for his former apprentice clearly ran deep. "You are subtlety itself."

Hisoka hesitated too long, and Jacques pretended not to notice.

641
SIGNIFY

After rearranging twice, Jacques asked, "Is the bed too soft?"

Hisoka spoke from the vicinity of his breastbone. "It's customary to signify a pact in some way."

"Like … exchanging tokens?"

The cat's head lifted. "A kiss is traditional."

Jacques blinked. "*Vive la traditionnel.*"

Hisoka stretched up, delivering a quick, careful kiss before retreating.

"*Mon dieu*! I wasn't ready."

"What's done is done."

"Half-done at best. I didn't get to kiss you back!"

"I thought you didn't have any designs on me."

Jacques rolled Hisoka onto his back and loomed over him. "Even between unromantically-involved intimates, a pledge should have balance."

642
A PACTMATE IS HERE

Are you actually testing boundaries? I don't have many." Jacques leaned down and claimed a chaste kiss. "Do what you like. It isn't as if I'd get the wrong idea."

"You want what I want," Hisoka said, echoing Jacques' own words.

"*Mais oui!*" Jacques asked, "Is it true that you're always in the right place at the right time?"

"Yes."

"Even now? In my bed. In my arms."

Hisoka's posture subtly shifted. "Yes."

So Jacques tested boundaries, respecting all he found.

All they really did was snog, but Hisoka began purring, and Jacques supposed he was finally on the rebound.

643
PLAYDATE

A few days before the summer solstice, Argent had Council business in Keishi. On his way, he escorted Kyrie and Lilya to Kikusawa Shrine, where Jacques would oversee their playdate with Ever.

Dress-up. Cookie-baking. Doggie-back rides.

Leaving the kids to Starmark oversight, Jacques took to the gardens, wanting to avoid Kikuko Miyabe, who reminded him a little too much of Maman.

Spying Dickon on a bench under Kusunoki, Jacques veered his way. Another man was with him, lean and angular, with traditional clothes and a topknot.

Jacques brightened with sudden recognition. "This is an unexpected pleasure! You're Sho Woodwend's father."

644
IN THE NEIGHBORHOOD

I hope Sho has been behaving himself?"

"Oh, he and Jarrah—our squirrel crosser—are sources of endless mischief, but it's nothing Argent can't handle." And with a guilty start, he looked between the men. "I hope I haven't spoken out of turn?"

"Not at all," Dickon assured. "Junpei is a neighbor."

"My bondmate's village is nearby, so I visit often." Pointing up, he added, "Our older boy Matsu is playing chase with Kyrie and Kusunoki."

Jacques peered up, blinking when tiny red petals caught in his lashes. "Is that safe?"

"Perfectly safe," Dickon assured. "Kusunoki won't let them fall."

645

NO MISUNDERSTANDING

Jacques nodded, then shook his head. What an odd thing to say. He turned the words over in his mind, but they scattered like so many flower petals.

"You let children climb this tree?"

"Yes," said Dickon. "Even Ayaka and Aoba have been up among his branches."

Jacques couldn't believe it. Crossers were natural climbers, but Dickon's and Noriko's children were *little*. "Am I misunderstanding something?"

The men traded a speaking glance. Junpei said, "It is not easy to explain."

And then there was another person standing in front of Jacques—tall and wide and solemn. He asked, "Uncle ... Jackie?"

646

THERE AND GONE

Are you the one Kyrie calls Uncle Jackie?"

Jacques had to look way up to meet eyes like glittering green stones. "*Oui*. Yes ... err. *Hai*."

Cascading red flowers looked amazing against the inky gloss of his hair.

Jacques knew what that meant. "Kusunoki?"

The tree imp lightly touched his shoulder. "Kyrie is a good boy."

"That's gratifying to ...."

But Kusunoki was simply gone again. Jacques shook his head at the suddenness of it, then noticed the two men who stood gazing at him with sympathetic smiles.

Jacques brightened with recognition. "This is an unexpected pleasure! You're Sho Woodwend's father."

647
TOO CUTE

When Argent came to collect them, Jacques hung back with the fox while Kyrie and Lilya bid their goodbyes. Jacques remarked, "Kimiko is really showing."

"It *has* been two years," Argent rejoined, sounding supremely bored.

"Quen's hovering is adorable. Have you ever seen someone so in love with the idea of fatherhood? Well, I suppose there's Timur. And Michael. But when you add in a clannish protective streak ...? Too cute."

Argent's expression soured.

So Jacques cheerfully inquired, "Will you every be this adorable, my lord?"

Argent's gaze went as steely as his tone. "And what do you mean by that?"

648
MAKE A NOTE

I wasn't being cryptic."

"*Tsk.*"

"Lord, I wasn't questioning your virility. I only thought it might be exciting, getting ready for a baby right from the beginning of everything."

"Stately House is not running a maternity ward."

Jacques leaned closer. "Should we be?"

Argent hesitated. "Make a note, Smythe."

"Yes, my lord."

"In the meantime, feel free to spend more time with Sansa when she and Michael next decide to add to their flourish."

Jacques repocketed his phone. "I don't have a death wish."

With a significant look, Argent said, "Neither does Tsumiko."

"Aha! You're protecting her. *Quite* adorable."

"*Tsk.*"

649

ADVENTURES IN POCKET SQUARES

Jacques and Harrison were having proper tea-and-slippers evenings, and by day, Jacques let Harrison's insatiable curiosity take the lead.

"Today … knots!"

"Wolf knots?"

"Knotting ties." He tapped the day's bowtie—seahorses. "Randolla thinks he can add to our repertoire!"

Soon they—and twenty-odd crossers—sported bowties, ascots, and Windsor knots, and Harrison was getting adventurous with pocket squares.

Life was good.

Really.

Suddenly, Harrison was hugging him hard. Then the crossers mobbed them both, and Jacques chided himself for being maudlin. Harrison was here, the best sort of friend. One he wanted to keep. *Oh.*

"Ever consider getting a tattoo?"

650

JUST TO PASS THE TIME AWAY

Suuzu was gone on a whirlwind tour of interviews and Dichotomy Day appearances, so Akira was free to roam.

Jacques eavesdropped shamelessly while he chatted with Harrison. After five summers, Harrison was easily as fluent in Japanese as Akira was in English, so their conversation drifted unchecked between two languages.

With a rumble and cheery clang of its bell, the *Cat's Canary* puffed around the bend, pulling a flatbed heaped with wood. While the crossers manhandled bonfire-fodder onto handcarts, Harrison led out with an American folksong about working on the railroad, which Fairlee took up.

Life was good.

Really.

651
HONORARY MENTION

The Elderboughs were joining the festivities this year, which thrilled Josheb. "No cameras, but who cares? Two whelps have reached their attainment, and a couple are establishing a den. Plus, I hear there'll be a few pack names handed down."

"Hoping for one?" Ginkgo asked.

"You think I don't already have one?"

"No kidding?"

Caleb said, "Over the years, we've received our fair share of honors. Most feel pretty honorary, though. It's not like we have close ties to any of the packs."

While everyone else tried to guess Josheb's pack name, Caleb tapped Jacques. "Tonight work?"

"*S'il vous plait.*"

652
SLIP AWAY

Revelers fanned out along the beach, where twin bonfires blazed. Nobody noticed when Jacques slipped away and climbed stairs to the garden above.

Caleb stood waiting. "Sorry to take you away from the festivities."

"A quieter celebration suits my mood just fine." They strolled in the direction of the woods.

Andor lumbered out of the shadows. "Caleb," he greeted. Then he bent close, searching Jacques' face. "Peace."

"Lord, yes. Peace and respect and the unchecked admiration of a devotee. We've been on excellent terms since my first sip of star wine."

With a smug little smile, Andor rumbled, "Good man."

653

BEHIND THE SCENES

After hauling Jacques and Caleb into his arms, Andor strode into the woods with a definite spring in his step.

"So ... how did you meet?" asked Jacques. "I mean, *everyone* knows how you met Bigfoot. No offense, Andor." Jacques dropped a kiss on the bear clansman's eyebrow.

He grunted in an amused way.

"But by all accounts, imps are rare!"

Caleb spilled details that never made it into the pilot episode of *Dare Together* until Andor reached the small cabin he shared with his twin. Doran was out somewhere, but somebody else was there, filling Andor's kitchen with a warm glow.

654

STARRY EYED

Caleb announced, "Eri Skypact is a vintner and a descended star. Eri's pronouns are they/them."

They'd caught Eri setting the table. Light shone through the two heavy goblets they hugged to their chest, brightening the honeyed yellow glass. The imp held very still, up on tiptoe, wide-eyed and ... hopeful?

Jacques was trying to sort out a name for the color of Eri's hair—cream, ivory, beige? Words that failed to imply the luster of a precious metal. "I'm ... staring. I apologize if I've made you uncomfortable." Jacques managed to blink a few times. "Lord, I can't seem to look away."

655

DAZZLED

Caleb crossed to his star. "I'm not sure if you'll be able to hear Eri's voice. If not, I'll play go-between."

"Right. Not a reaver," Jacques murmured. "Sorry about that."

Gently nudging Eri, Caleb prompted, "Didn't you want to meet Jacques?"

Sensing his cue, Jacques bowed and extended a hand, as if inviting Eri to dance.

The imp's glow subtly intensified. Setting aside the goblets, they padded over on bare feet to set their hands in his.

Jacques's fingers closed, but it seemed a shame to shutter even that much of Eri's light. "Lord, I might actually believe in angels."

656

ARDENT ADMIRER

Jacques skipped along to the most important bit. "I'm an *ardent* admirer of star wine. Thank you creating one of my favorite things."

With a little shimmy and skip, Eri flung their arms around his neck, which left Jacques holding a star to his heart.

Caleb was talking. "Nooo, I don't think they're getting through. Too bad. Early on, I found that the closer our connection, the clearer Eri's voice grew. And ... I'd swear that the more star wine I drank, the better I could hear the stars."

Although he already felt tipsy, Jacques suggested, "Somebody pour me a drink?"

657

FIGMENTS

Jacques was on his third glass when Andor left briefly, returning with something that he set at the center of the table.

Caleb was saying, "One secret is celestia bumber nectar."

An Ephemera? Jacques admitted, "I can't quite see."

"That's all right. Most people can't."

Caleb touched his hand, a sympathetic gesture, and it was like the whole room suddenly snapped into focus. Jacques could see the fuzzy blue-and-white bee that purred upon the table, and he could hear a lilting voice, only ... not with his ears. It welled up inside him.

"Should I kiss him? That worked with you."

658

THAT THING YOU DO

With a kind look and a small headshake, Caleb ignored his bonded's question. "Just like on the show, I'm not very good with creepy-crawly things. Josheb swears that bumbers are cute as kittens, but I don't really understand the appeal."

And he withdrew his hand.

Or started to.

Jacques didn't let him.

"Don't run off *now!*" He grabbed the other man's wrist. "Not when things were just starting to get interesting."

"Are you kidding me? The thing works with you, too?" Caleb locked fingers with Jacques, looking to Andor. "But why would it?"

"Lord, I don't know. But ... don't stop?"

659
TICKLISH

Weave *my light into a sigil for him?"* suggested Eri.

Caleb said, "You *know* we need Michael for that. But I agree it's worth trying."

Jacques dared to ask, "Were you really going to kiss me?"

Caleb laughed. "You *would* hear that part. It's one of the 'closer connections' I mentioned earlier. Nowadays, our bond has strengthened, and it's amplified by both crystals and sigilcraft."

"Ah. Maybe that's it? I'm a bit sigil'd."

Which began a very ticklish inspection. In the middle of it, Eri's voice came again, full of portent. *"You are greatly loved, Jacques Smythe. You are* expected.*"*

660
HERE AND NOW

Andor brought him home, but Jacques turned right around and started walking. What had Inti said about stars? Beautiful, but bringing truths that were hard to hear.

Loved, was he?

Greatly loved.

But by whom?

Was this some airy-fairy reference to the Maker? Or was there really someone out there? If so, why weren't they *here*. Jacques needed someone *here*. He was tired of vague hopes and empty words.

Tripping over a railroad tie, he caught himself against a train car.

Then Catalan was there, lending support, asking if he was drunk.

And Jacques demanded comfort in no uncertain terms.

661

A FRIEND IN NEED

Now will you speak?" asked Cat. "What brought this on?"

Jacques sighed. Any number of excuses would do, and most were true. "I was lonely."

His friend hummed in a way that asked for more.

So he evaded. "Will Canarian be angry?"

"Only that he wasn't here when you needed us." With a languid stretch, Cat located his phone on the bedside table, checked his messages, then let the thing slip from his fingers. "Rest. He'll be here within the hour."

Guilt blossomed. "You sent for him?"

"Mm-hmm. We three can talk. Or not talk. Maybe a little of both?"

662

LONG TIME COMING

Canarian was very good at taking charge.

In the aftermath, Jacques voiced a lingering suspicion. "Did Argent bring you here as a replacement for ...?"

"Ah, here it is," murmured Cat. "Say it."

"*Non.* I'm over him. Let me rebound in peace."

"Oh?" Canary asked.

"Ohhh," Cat breathed as they traded a long look. "How long since you last visited Evernhold?"

"A while."

"Don't be coy. You *must* remember. Our fathers are not so forgettable."

The answer was too telling. "Seven years, more or less."

Canary whispered apologies.

Cat pressed closer. "Shall we plan a trip? To Evernhold."

"*S'il vous plait.*"

663
TRICKY QUESTION

Jacques lounged against the garden wall, sipping coffee. Across the way, Deece was guiding Nonny's courses. While away at school, he'd gotten it into his head to learn to fight. Nonny was proud of his newfound proficiency, which lent a formidable edge to his promise to always protect their crossers.

"Uncle Jackie?" Akira made his way over, leading six-year-old Vanya. "He has a tricky question, and I thought you could help me explain ...?"

"All right." He dropped to one knee to better meet the boy's troubled gaze. "What's on your mind, Vanya?"

"Is it true that I have another mother?"

664
ALL ALONG

Lord, boy. You have more mothers than most, especially if you include the well-meaning mothering of your older sisters."

Vanya nodded and shook his head and tried to explain. "Papka was talking on the phone, and he said something about *Mama Sonnet*."

Jacques closed his eyes.

Akira knelt by his side and stole his coffee cup. "I thought if *anyone* could explain Sonnet ...? I'm sorry, Uncle Jackie. Should I have gone to Ginkgo?"

"It's fine," Jacques lied. Because nobody ever spoke of Sonnet, other than to pine for her cooking. But ... had Michael and Sansa been in contact all along?

665

BELONGING TO A WOLF

Uncle Jackie?" asked Vanya.

Jacques moved to a seat against the garden wall. Patting spaces on either side, he pulled both his nephews close. Dropping a kiss on Vanya's golden curls, he began, "You were very little when your Mama Sonnet went away. You were born into her hands, and that means you belong to a wolf."

He told about smuggling Vanya from Stately House in a carpet bag.

"You *didn't*!" Akira exclaimed, leaning in and laughing.

Vanya beamed. "I was kidnapped?"

"*Non.* Not really." And because it was the truth, Jacques added, "I'm sure Sonnet thinks of you often."

666

APPLICANT

Early in July, Kyrie came to sit with Jacques in the naproom and held out his arms to take the toddler lolling against his shoulder. Jacques arched his brows. "Plenty of crossers to go around."

That's when his phone vibrated.

"Did you know that would happen?"

Kyrie just smiled a secretive smile and walked away.

Jacques answered. "Timur?"

"*I'd like to file an application for a new member of the Fundoshi Swim Club.*"

"A boy! All's well?"

"*Yes. Rilka's here, and she made sure. Manya's resting, and ....*" Timur's voice quavered. "*I'm holding my son.*"

"His name?"

"*I'm calling him Gregor.*"

667
EN ROUTE

It was September before Jacques could visit. "Looks just like you," he declared. "How's Papka's little battler, hmm?"

Timur radiated a weary sort of contentment. "You can't stay?"

"*Non.* Catalan and I are spending a week at his fathers' place. Bit of a holiday, now that Harrison's gone back to the States. You were on my way."

"I'm sorry I haven't gotten to meet Harrison."

"There's always next summer."

"Maybe. Maybe not." Timur asked, "Do you have time to talk?"

"I'm all yours."

"I received an offer from Glint Starmark."

"*Not* another bid for paternity?"

"A teaching post. At Wardenclave."

668
FAMILY TIES

Jacques recommended bringing Catalan in on the discussion. Cat sauntered in, stole Gregor, and sat with Fend, murmuring, "Greetings, kinsman."

Timur perked up. "You're family"

Jacques pointed out, "Cat is Deece's older brother."

"I'm *also* jaguar clan." Slouching into Fend's flank, he added, "Minx is a relative. She requested—by which I mean *demanded*—that I oversee her sons' training. So we're old hunting partners, Fend and I."

Jacques hadn't made that particular connection before and immediately felt stupid for ever assuming that Cat and Canary had come to Stately House for him.

They'd relocated for Deece and his boys.

669
FOSTERLING

They talked through Glint's offer, comparing pros and cons. Timur wanted to keep Gregor with him, if possible, but his son would be a toddler in need of constant attention.

"You're a fosterling," Cat pointed out. "Use *that* to secure the help you need."

Timur frowned. "I'm not."

"You take so much for granted. But it's a child's job to be spoiled." Amusement sparkling in his eyes, Cat asked, "Who raised you? Who ran with you? Who readied you to be the father this boy needs?"

Jacques watched Timur start to answer, then rethink his answer. Then finally realize. "Ginkgo."

670
HE WILL HATE THE IDEA

A whole summer without Ginkgo? Ah, but we *do* have Harrison, now. Our meadow mice might be willing to temporarily take over the garden. And other members of the enclave could pitch in variously."

Timur brightened.

Jacques warned, "Argent will hate the idea. And so will Kyrie."

"He adores his brother," agreed Cat. "But Argent adores his sons. Fend thinks you can use *that*, too."

All eyes swung to Fend.

Jacques thought he saw it. "What if Kyrie went along? As a camper."

Fend began to purr.

"Lord, if Kyrie asked, Argent would find a way to make it happen."

671
AWKWARD QUESTION

Jacques reclaimed Gregor, if only to check out his accessories. Beads sparkled at his ankles. "Already warding him?"

"Everyone agreed it was for the best. Papka came and tuned them himself."

"Is Gregor a beacon."

"Not quite."

"But close," interjected Cat.

"That's the consensus." Timur's smile wavered. "Say. Do you mind if I ask something potentially awkward?"

Jacques beckoned for more.

Timur came to his side and opened his phone's gallery. "Maybe it's because I've been away. Of course I'd expect Papka to be Papka." He tapped a folder and slowly flicked through snapshots. "I'm not imagining it, am I?"

672
PHOTOGENIC

Jacques hadn't seen any of these pictures, which were mostly candid shots. "Who's been playing paparazzi?"

"Ginkgo sent most of these. Keeping the family connected."

Michael in the naproom, reading to the crossers.

Michael at the kitchen table, chatting with Lapis.

Michael on the beach, holding hands with Sansa while a bonfire burned.

"This one I took. See?" In it, Michael smiled softly down on his newborn grandson.

Timur looked honestly confused, and Jacques couldn't understand why.

Lowering his voice, Timur said, "Jacques, Papka turns *fifty* this year."

"Are you sure ...?"

"How long has it been since Papka stopped aging?"

673

COMFORTABLE DISTANCE

In November, Hisoka dragged in weeks late, barely coherent from lack of sleep. Lapis and Catalan maneuvered him to bed, where Jacques took charge.

"You're in no fit state to lead."

"Perspicacity Smythe." Hisoka murmured, eyes already closed.

"People shouldn't ignore your needs."

"Mmm ... questioning my stamina?"

"You're in no fit state to flaunt, either."

"Never learned."

"And you call yourself a cat."

There'd been no repeat of intimacies since their pact, nor had any awkwardness cropped up. If anything, Hisoka came more easily into Jacques' arms. Even more gratifying, he'd regained his former poise. When in a fit state.

674

SKIMPING ALONG

Nobody was surprised when Hisoka overslept. Canarian and Isla rearranged and rescheduled. Harmonious and Lapis filled in. Contrary to popular belief, the world *could* skimp along without him for an extra week.

When Hisoka finally stirred, he kept nuzzling one of Jacques' newer tattoos, a delicate whorl that curved along his hipbone. Jacques petted his hair and kept turning pages.

Until Hisoka gasped sharply and scrambled onto hands and knees. He swayed there. "Jacques?"

"Here."

Hisoka pushed aside blankets and lifted cloth, as if needing to reassure himself that Jacques was himself. "All here."

"Were you dreaming?"

"Someone was ... singing."

675
HERALDRY

Hisoka stared as if seeing him for the first time. Old and sad, his gaze left Jacques feeling oddly uncertain, then genuinely concerned when Hisoka crawled up to kiss the corner of his mouth.

Why apologize?

"What's going on, Posy?"

"I'm not sure. But … do you perhaps have luggage with a crest on it?"

"Do you mean Argent's crest?"

Hisoka shook his head. "Do the Smythes have heraldry?"

"Lord, yes. There should be several grand old pieces in the attic at Uppington."

"Send for something large and showy. Please. You'll need it."

"For what?"

"I'm not sure. But … do it."

676
CLASSIC

Jacques jotted off a quick note for Bon-Bon, which he carried to the foyer so it would catch the next outgoing herald.

Hooves clattered, and Nonny stepped into his personal space. "So … about *Christmas*!"

Jacques lapsed into a smile. Ever since that *one* time when Jacques spent the holiday in Keishi, Nonny had been extracting promises.

"You'll be here, yeah?"

"I promised, didn't I?"

"Too right you did. Which is brilliant because …!" Nonny presented a script.

"A Christmas classic." Jacques skimmed a partial cast list. "Hey, Nonny, nonny?"

"Wut."

"*Please* tell me Cat and Canary are casting Argent as Scrooge."

677

HOLIDAY PLANS

Jacques wasn't sure what was at the heart of Nonny's unwavering dedication to Christmas festivities, but the whole household benefited. He'd been in charge of holiday plans even before Cat and Canary began amping up the pageantry.

In the kitchen, Nonny appealed to Sansa for extra baking days and special menus for several parties.

"Do you need help?" asked Jacques.

"Mori and Mei are always with me, and the mares are here, but for this, I am missing...." Dark eyes sought his, and she reached across, touching his face. A motherly gesture. Perhaps an apology.

For almost speaking Sonnet's name.

678

EXPECTATIONS

Jacques leaned into Sansa's touch, accepting all it meant. She wasn't the most demonstrative mother, but Jacques found the lack of drama refreshing after Maman. No meddling. No manipulation. Sansa expected her children to be as strong and independent as she was. Full stop.

Nonny shuffled his papers. "Don't forget the cake."

"You think I forget my precious children's birthday?"

They quibbled, and Jacques looked on with the strangest sense of loss.

Funny he'd never noticed about Sansa either. It was too outré to remark upon a woman's age, but Jacques feared that in a few years, he'd catch up.

679
BIG AS LIFE

Timur's unannounced arrival at Stately House caused a stir among the children, *especially* with Lilya. The big brother she'd mostly loved from afar was suddenly there, big as life and bursting with good news. Jacques could tell she was genuinely surprised about Gregor, though he was sure that Kyrie had always known.

Fend slunk to Jacques' side, ears flattened against his skull.

"Don't be a grump. You grew up here, so you *know* how this will go. Any second now, someone will suggest a party."

Right on cue, Ginkgo did.

"Lord, it's official. Everyone up past bedtime. Mayhem until midnight."

680
PARTY ORGANIZERS

Somehow, Nonny was in charge. "Invite the wolves, Ginkgo. I'll tell the cranes. Who'll get the mice?"

"What about Hachi?" called Tsumiko. He was one of their newest members, a preservationist. And shy.

"I'll go," offered Michael. "Don't forget Andor and Doran."

Jacques perked up. "At least there'll be star wine."

Fend's gazed up at him hopefully.

"Lord, I don't know. How old are you in panther years?"

Fend reared back and planted big paws on Jacques' shoulders.

"Right. I'll slip a saucer into my pocket, but I'm confiscating your car keys."

They sealed the deal with a nose boop.

681

PUT ON THE SPOT

When Andor arrived with two casks, his gaze sought and held Jacques'. With a determined air, he crossed the room, crouched slightly, and gruffly said, "Come for a visit."

Jacques hadn't been back. Not that he'd ever frequented Andor's place before, but they both knew he'd been avoiding Eri for … lord, was it six months already?

"I want to." And because it also was true, Jacques whispered, "I don't want to."

"Make peace," Andor urged.

He drew a shaky breath and nodded.

To his consternation, the bear clansman picked him up and walked out the door.

"*Now?*"

Andor simply grunted.

682

PADDLE

Andor bypassed his house, aiming for the low structure beyond, where star wine was made.

Eri turned from their work, eyes widening.

Andor set Jacques on his feet and stepped back.

After a moment's hesitation, Eri offered Jacques their paddle, pointed to the vat they'd been stirring, and twirled a finger.

Jacques took over. Or tried to. Andor came up behind him, repositioned his hands, then guided him through the correct motion. Once Jacques showed he could manage, Andor grunted and ambled off.

Jacques was helping with a batch of star wine? Lord. He … smiled.

Eri saw. And smiled, too.

683
MAKE PEACE

Without Caleb there to bridge the gap, Jacques and Eri worked in an enforced silence. Until he realized the only reason for the hush was him. Nothing was stopping Jacques from talking.

"The children are all excited for Christmas," he offered.

Eri's gaze sought his, and they took a receptive posture.

Oh. Of course. He was a dolt, and this didn't have to be difficult. Jacques shifted into an apologetic stance.

Eri turned their face away in a return of regrets.

And then Jacques was once again holding a star to his heart.

Across the room, Andor grunted in approval.

684
BASIN

Jacques was saying, "Then they cast me as Bob Cratchit. Bit of a stretch, but it'll be a lark," when Fend slipped in, tail lashing, only to still at the sight of Eri.

Andor growled.

Fend had the good sense to grovel.

"My fault entirely! I promised him a saucer of star wine."

Then Eri was petting, and Fend was purring rapturously.

Andor brought goblets and a basin.

Jacques whispered, "Who slipped you past the wards, hmm?"

Fend only licked star wine from his whiskers.

But Jacques thought he knew. Did Stately House have *any* secrets from Kyrie?

Probably not.

685

THE GREENING OF THE FOYER

The wolves helped Nonny gather boughs for the greening of the foyer. Once the mice maneuvered a lofty Christmas tree into position, the room smelled like a forest.

Torloo hurried over. "Uncle Jackie …?"

"Hello, Petal Moon."

The boy clung long enough for Jacques to wonder. Kneeling, he asked, "Is something wrong?"

"Boon's gone tracking." Torloo's tail tucked. "Alone."

"Where's Moon-kin?"

"Talking to Argent."

Half-formed plans to barge in on that meeting were interrupted by another of the Elderbough dexes.

"Jacques," she said, voice urgent. "We have unexpected guests. Could you let Lord Mettlebright know that Lord Beckonthrall wants a word?"

686

HERE THERE BE DRAGONS

When Argent finally called for Jacques, he expected to be briefed about Lord Beckonthrall's reasons for demanding a private meeting.

Instead, Argent announced, "I have changed my mind. Ginkgo will escort the children to Wardenclave for summer camp."

"They'll be thrilled," Jacques assured.

Argent waved that aside, as if his reasons were the farthest thing from indulgence.

"I need to take several trips."

"Very good." Jacques asked, "Should I pack?"

"I will be traveling alone, incognito, and illegally."

"May I know why?"

"To tour several galleries." Argent grimly revealed, "I am going to build a trap for the Gentleman Bandit."

687

UNDOCUMENTED ABSENCES

After Timur's return, Jacques had expected things to finally settle down, but Argent's clandestine trips were wedged into every scrap of spare time.

Jacques began keeping two calendars. One listed plausible—yet fictional—appointments to explain where Argent Mettlebright was on any given day. The other tracked the truth for him and Tsumiko. Not in any detail, of course. But Argent was always back when he said he'd be, so Jacques found the wherewithal to carry on.

At the end of May, Stately House saw off their campers.

And Harrison was to arrive any day to liven up their summer.

688

CHASING TWO RABBITS

Nobody could have foreseen that summer. One groundbreaking event after another.

The birth of Quen and Kimi's daughter.

News of Lilya's contractualized engagement.

Mikoto Reaver's induction ceremony and marriage.

An adoption application from Waaseyaa.

A proverbial message in a bottle from Inti.

Argent holed up in his closet with Jacques and complained, "One or the other I could have dealt with, but both together?"

"Wait for Sinder's information. Then you'll know what you're dealing with."

Someone knocked.

It had to be Nonny. Nobody else could *find* Argent's closet.

He leaned in. "I wasn't eavesdropping, guv. There's a delivery for Jacques."

689

ATTIC RELIC

In the foyer, Akira perched atop a wooden crate, cheerfully kicking his heels. "It's from England. Uppington."

Argent pried boards, and Jacques exclaimed, "Lord, I'd forgotten!"

A grand old steamer trunk lay within—polished wood, soft leather, and buckles as gold as the crest emblazoned on the front.

"What's it for?" asked Nonny.

"Travel."

"Don't be an arse. Why's it here?"

"I sent for it. Ages ago."

"Whatever for?" asked Argent.

"Hisoka said I'd need it."

"Did he?" Argent's gaze jumped from Jacques to the trunk to Akira.

Jacques witnessed Argent's moment of clarity.

Then twenty-odd tails flailed into view.

690

CONTENDER

Stay calm."

Jacques rolled his eyes. "That's by far the least reassuring thing you've *ever* said to me."

Argent paced a conservatory footpath, tails practically in knots. He swore softly.

"And that's a contender for the *second* least reassuring thing. Lord, it's just us. Blurt away."

"Boon called in a favor."

"What does that even mean?"

Argent's jaw works. "It means that if I cannot come up with something else, I am going to have to ask you to do something awful."

"You know I'd do anything for you."

With an expression of regret, Argent whispered, "You say that now."

691
I GOTCHA

Hours later, Jacques was still horrified. And incensed. Sick at heart ... and to his stomach. And he needed someone to know it, and yet he didn't want anyone to ever find out. Yet he knew where he wanted to turn. "Nonny...?"

It came out weak.

He tried again. "*Nonny?*"

His voice broke.

"Hey, Nonny, nonny, are you near?"

And there were hoofbeats, then a handkerchief, then a hand in his. Nonny had the good sense to get them inside Argent's closet before demanding, "What is it? It's bad, yeah? I'm here. I gotcha. What in the bloody hell happened?"

"Argent."

692
ROLE OF A LIFETIME

Jacques tried to think where to even begin. "I have to pretend to be someone's lover. And I need the act to be convincing. Help me sort out how to do that?"

"Can't you ask Cat?"

"I ... don't want him to know what I'm going to do."

Nonny's face scrunched up. "You're embarrassed? *You*?"

"It's like ... my playing Bob Cratchit was a stretch, right? Nobody in their right mind would believe I'm a family man. But nobody will bat an eye when I'm cast as a pedophile."

"Stop right there! Budge over. And start this back at the bloody beginning."

693
FAMILY MAN

First off, Bob Cratchit wasn't a good fit because you can't pull off *poor*. And you were the gayest family man *ever* since Cat played Mrs. Cratchit."

"He was in a dress."

"Sonnet wears a dress, you fucking moron! You were perfect, or didja miss that all your kids were crossers? Hell, you got more applause than Ambrose!"

"That's … really not the point here."

"Jacques, I know better'n anyone that you wouldn't touch a kid. I *tried*. Also, Akira's an adult."

"He's my nephew."

"You're not fucking related. And you don't actually wanna fuck him."

"But what if I do?"

694
WHAT IF I DO

Nonny hesitated. "Do *wanna*? Or do *fuck him*? Wait. Why is that even a thing?"

"Lord, have you met me? Being in love and being in bed—they're intertwined."

"Should we be breaking our rule? Your sex life's none of my business. But … you *have* one," Nonny pointed out. "Even though you're not in love."

"How can you tell?"

Nonny clammed up.

"I'm serious. How can you tell I'm not in love? Is it Amaranthine sensitivity?"

"Well, yeah. But also no. Fuck, this is so stupid." Nonny's eyes began to water. "Jacques, I know what you look like in love."

695
LOVE SHOWS

I'm *not.*

"Well, when you *were*, it showed."

Jacques asked, "Showed *how*? I need to know for Akira's sake."

"I hate you so much right now." But Nonny painted a startlingly clear picture—postures, expressions, tones, endearments, scents, even shoes.

"Am I really that obvious?"

"Nah, you don't really let on, but ...." Nonny sighed. "Do you *know* how long you were the only person I could see?"

"Right. Sorry."

"Don't belittle my feelings."

"You don't love me anymore."

"Right. Sure. Just like you don't love Argent anymore?"

Jacques realized. "Lord. I'm going to have to fall in love with Akira."

696
EASY

You can't!"

"It's easy," countered Jacques. "I've *always* been easy."

"You *idiot*," Nonny exclaimed. "You can't have him, and it'll fucking wreck you. Again!"

"Will you be here when it's over?"

He muttered, "Yeah, of course."

"That'll help." Jacques patted his arm. "Try to make sure I don't embarrass myself?"

"Don't be stupid!" Nonny was beginning to sound alarmed.

"I have to think how to do this without hurting anyone. Especially Suuzu. I won't come between them."

"What about *you*!" Nonny shot to his feet. "I'm gonna kill the guv!"

"Don't. Please. He hates this, too. And ... he needs me."

697
NEEDS MUST

Argent's plan progressed. Juuyu swept through Stately House and carried off Akira, who had no idea what was in store.

Then came another knock in the night on Jacques' door.

"Jackie? I need assistance."

He yanked the door open and gasped, "Good lord."

"I need to wash." Argent heaved a shuddering breath and dully corrected, "*We* need to wash. Before Tsumiko sees."

Blood on his face. Blood in his hair. Blood on the coat he's *promised* to keep tidy. Because he'd wrapped it around … well, then. Needs must.

Jacques hustled him through to the *en suite*, then demanded, "Show me."

698
BROCADE

Blood streaked pale skin and matted dark hair. It flaked away when Jacques' thumb caressed freckled scales and the dainty point of one ear. He unbundled the tiny newborn, opened his dressing gown, settled her against his bare chest, and pulled the heavy brocade closed again.

"There we go, sweetheart," he murmured. "I'm your Uncle Jackie. Let's run a bath for your daddy, hmm?"

Argent was watching him almost like he was proud.

"You *hate* birthings," Jacques remarked.

Shuddering, Argent began stripping stained clothes.

Jacques eyed his bloody claws and asked, "Was she born into your hands?"

"After a fashion."

699
BIDE A WEE

"Did I ever tell you how Ginkgo was born?"

Jacques' heart wrenched. "So … the mother was past help."

"She may have been bait. Or a taunt. Or simply brutalized and abandoned."

They cleaned her child. Jacques even oiled her expensively before diapering her with a handkerchief and swaddling her in a pillowcase. Kissing purple fuzz, he promised, "Won't be long, love. Bide a wee."

Jacques changed the water, found his nail brush, and set to work on his listless lord.

He'd changed the water again before Argent broke the silence, whispering, "In trying to fix *this*, did I lose you?"

700
BRAZENING ON

"Nonsense. There's no getting rid of me. And not to brag, but I see the compliment. Your plan *hinges* on me. Very flattering!"

Argent blinked. "You were *angry*."

"Lord, yes. At first. But I've had time to rally." Argent needed him. Needed this. "*Speaking* of changes. Your plans are masterful, but they don't take wardrobe into account. May I shop?"

Argent blinked again. Then something brighter and sharper and *right* rekindled in his eyes. "You think you can improve upon a fox's scheme?"

"Oh, I know I can." Slipping into confiding tones, Jacques asked, "How do *you* feel about pastels?"

excerpted from *Fumiko and the Finicky Nestmate…*

Akira texted Uncle Jackie.

Do me a favor?

Within reason
I'm feeling rather favored out
Actually, nevermind
Favor away
This will help me slip into character

What?

Favoritism
I'm embracing it
I will be so good to you

Akira had always thought he and Tsumiko were alone in the world. So when Jacques Smythe had sashayed into their lives and demanded favorite uncle status, Akira had wholeheartedly embraced the novelty of an extended family.

They had real ties. Sort of. Jacques was related to the husband of the previous owner of Stately House, the lady who'd left everything to Sis. Also, Jacques was cousin to the husband of the woman who'd given birth to Kyrie. That lady had given Kyrie to Sis. For keeps. And somehow or other, they'd also inherited Jacques. Definitely also for keeps.

I love you, Uncle Jackie

You say that now
How do you feel about pastels?

I have no strong feelings

You say that now

"Have you ever wanted to invite your family here?"

Jacques' eyes widened. "*Mon dieu*. I shudder to think what would happen if Bon-Bon were to sneer upon all I hold dear."

Lord Mettlebright's Man

SUUZU
AND THE
NINE NIPPETS
OF LEGEND

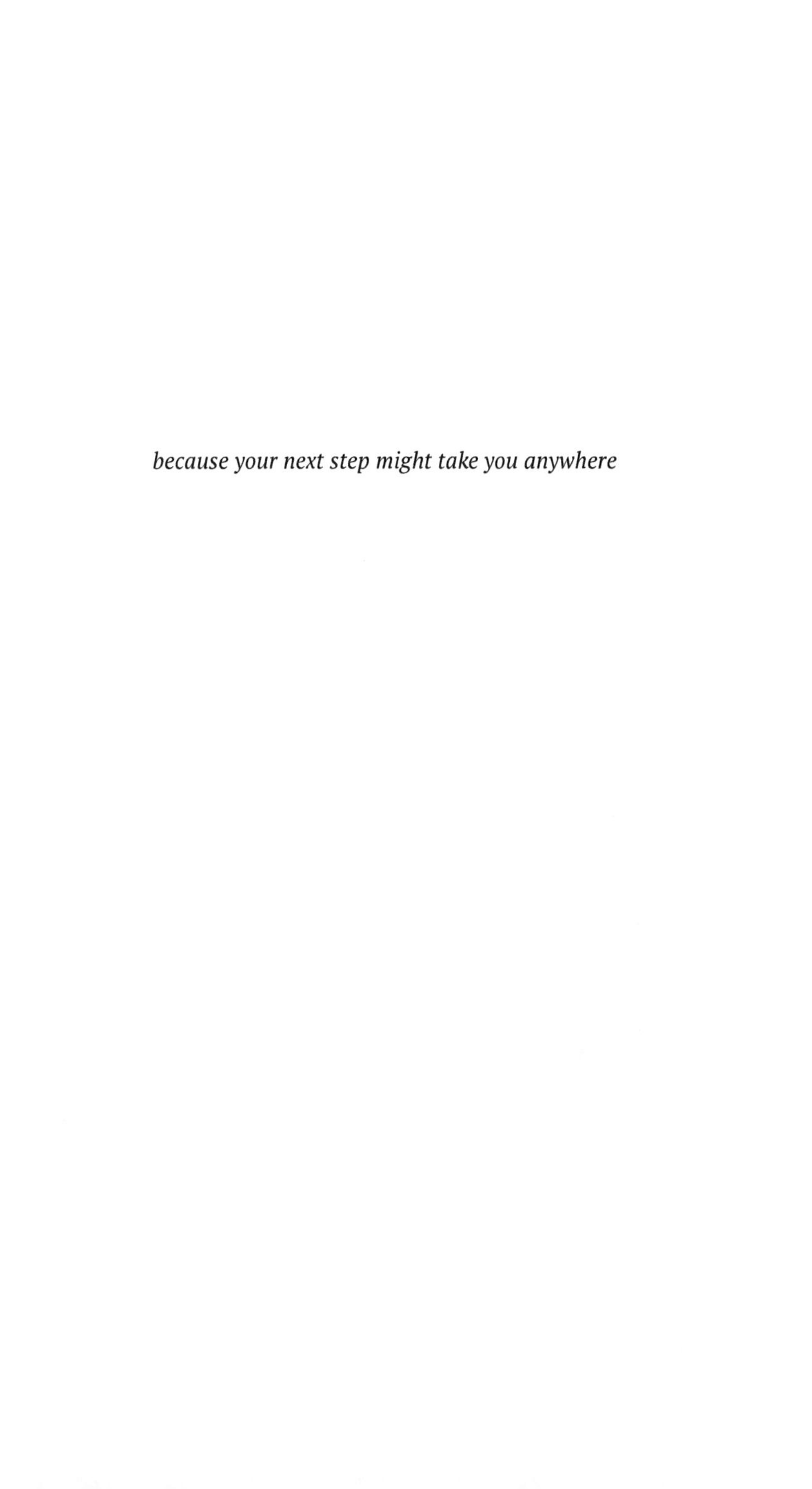

because your next step might take you anywhere

TABLE OF CONTENTS

SUUZU AND THE NINE NIPPETS OF LEGEND

BY FORTHRIGHT

1

THE PROMISE OF A PROMISE

Suuzu kept his eyes on his feet as he followed Argent along a hall that wasn't familiar. He had a vague sense that they'd been nearing the room he normally shared with Akira, but ... no. The carpet here was different. Slate strewn with silvery ginkgo leaves, speckled with tiny red flower petals that seemed to leap from the underlying pattern. Wait. He blinked, trying to focus. The petals looked real.

"Come closer." Argent held out a hand. "Suuzu? Are you quite well?"

He shook his head. "I cannot hear Juuyu any longer."

"He saw you safely here, but he could not linger. His home is with Fumiko. Yours is here." Argent crossed to him, peering up into Suuzu's face. "You have not been abandoned."

A soft groan surprised Suuzu. His face heated.

"Are you in any discomfort?" With traces of worry, the fox took a gentler tone. "Suuzu?"

"I am well. I think." He dragged his gaze from the petal-strewn floor, letting it drift over their surroundings. "Where is this?"

"Some areas of Stately House are private." Taking his elbow, Argent guided him toward a set of double doors. "Place your hand here," he directed.

Suuzu's palm pressed wood that might have been plain if not for the intricacy of the sigilcraft lacing its surface. Fox magic. While Argent waited for the patterns to shift, Suuzu stared at the ring that gleamed on his little finger. Rosy-orange glass. Fragile, yet real. Everything that had happened after Akira slid it there hadn't quite sunk in, but the ring was meant for a reminder.

Jacques had given his word.

And then he'd taken Akira away.

No. That wasn't quite right.

Akira had gone away with him.

Leaving Suuzu alone.

No. That wasn't right either.

Akira hadn't abandoned him.

Suuzu's free hand lifted to the pin that Akira had encouraged him to wear, even though the gift had yet to be properly given. Akira had taken his necklace, promised to return, and accepted his kiss. He closed his eyes, revisiting the moment, needing it to be true.

His best friend. His lifelong friend. His nestmate.

A hand touched his cheek, and Suuzu blinked his way into the present.

Argent let his hand fall to his side, then angled his head away, speaking to someone else. "Hajime, can you help me understand what is going on with this boy? Is anything amiss?"

Suddenly, they were three, for a stranger stood with them before the double doors. "Akira's phoenix? We left him in California."

"Juuyu brought him. He says there will be a child."

Suuzu cut a sharp look at Argent. It wasn't like the fox to spill secrets. How had this stranger come to be here, within Argent's innermost wards? Only Jacques was privy to all and everything. Had Argent taken new counsel in his absence? Did Hisoka know?

But wait. Red flowers. And the name. Wait. Wait! *Hajime.*

Because Akira was tree-kin. How could he have forgotten?

"I know you," Suuzu whispered.

"You do. And one day soon, you will remember that you do." A smile creased the corners of eyes that were a deep, dark red. "Did you open the puzzle box?"

He nodded.

Hajime took Suuzu's hands and stretched up to kiss his cheek. The scent of flowers intensified, as did a sense of ... home. Suuzu knew, since he'd been raised among trees and their kin, how often seeds were hoarded away or scattered abroad. Only a few trees ever took root near their parent. Frivolous as tree imps might seem, they were more than capable of doting.

Suuzu relaxed when strong arms slipped around him. This tree imp would watch over him, both for Akira's sake and for the sake of the child.

Because there would be a child.

It became difficult for Suuzu to breathe. Juuyu had been proud, but he was grove-bred and grove-born. Both their parents and most of their extended family were tree-kin. They had context for such things. But what would Akira think?

"He has been sprigged. One of mine."

Argent sounded startled. "*Yours.* How?"

"A seed found its way into his hands, and he accepted it. What else matters?" Hajime radiated approval and pride. "This is a good place to begin a grove."

"As I mentioned before, we will see our first Scattering in

springtime. Any advice you can give would be invaluable, but Suuzu is a much more immediate concern."

A door opened, and another voice filtered through the haze. "Why are you standing in the hall? Oh, my. Bring him inside, Haji-oji."

Suuzu shuffled along and stumbled to a stop the moment he realized where he was. Argent's private rooms. The ones he shared with his bondmate. Even knowing he was here by the fox's invitation, Suuzu quailed inwardly.

"Peace, Suuzu," Argent murmured. "I would not have brought you in if I did not think you belong here."

He nodded meekly. It would have been easier to take this in stride if Akira had been at his side. Absence. It left him lost, even in someplace that should have been familiar.

Tsumiko took his hand and drew him to a sofa for two. Akira's sister was a small woman, but her presence was staggering. Even with formidable wards in place and Argent shuttering her soul, Suuzu could tell that Lady Mettlebright held a beacon's classification. She let go and sat, gazing up at him with Akira's eyes. Sister and brother had the same coloring, and it made Suuzu wonder if they both took after the father that Akira had gone off to find ... and hoped to rescue.

Realizing that she was waiting on him, hands folded in her lap, gaze full of sympathy, he lowered himself to a seat at her side. "Lady," he began. It's what all the children here called her.

She shook her head. "I told you before. You may call me Tsumiko. Or even 'Sis,' like Akira does."

"Honored sister," he managed, not quite ready to lapse into Akira's brand of familiarity.

Tsumiko accepted that with a smile.

Suuzu knew that he needed to tell her, that she didn't know

yet. Argent was giving him the chance to speak for himself, to tell her why his heart and soul were in utter disarray. There would be a child. That was important to tell. But a very different confession tumbled past his lips.

"I love him."

Tsumiko's eyes really were so much like Akira's, her gaze so steady. It flustered him.

Suuzu clarified, "Akira. He is my choice."

"Yes. I know." She gently added, "It shows."

He needed her to understand the place he wanted in her brother's life. Suuzu recklessly admitted, "I kissed him."

Her lips curved into a smile that could only be called … fond. "Was he shocked?"

She didn't mind? Suuzu had braced himself for more in the way of censure.

"Akira can be pretty oblivious," she offered.

"I … he … yes … well, no. Not entirely …? He said he was willing, and he prepared this." Suuzu lightly touched the pin he wore. "While not a promise, it is the … the promise of a promise."

"How beautiful! May I?"

Unwilling to yield it, Suuzu scooted closer and angled his body so she could see. Tsumiko kept her hands folded in her lap, but she leaned in for a look. "Are they real?"

"Nippet eggs."

"Such pretty colors! Did you see, Argent?"

The fox came to sit on the arm of the sofa beside her. "There are nine named varieties of nippets worldwide, some rarer than others."

"And how many of the littlest of avians are in your collection?" she inquired lightly.

"All of them. Naturally. However, I was not aware that a nippet's eggshells could be as distinctive as their feathers." Argent casually inquired, "Akira understands the significance of his gift?"

"I believe so." Suuzu shyly explained, "Egg shells have a prominent place in avian courting tradition."

Tsumiko brightened. "Oh, of course! Like how a feather from Zeriel's nippet came to mean, 'loved from afar.' Are the messages the same for the eggshells?"

Suuzu hunched his shoulders. "What?"

Her smile dimmed somewhat. "I'm sure I read about it, though that *was* a few years ago now. It was among the stories I uncovered … since there's a connection to dragon lore. Zeriel's special someone was a dragon. Mind you, it's not common knowledge. The dragon part, I mean. I've only ever seen the one reference. In fact, the note was scribbled in the margin of a collection of ballads the Kimiko found for me."

Argent lightly cleared his throat.

"Oh. Sorry. Setting all that aside, I *do* believe the meaning of a red feather remains to this day." She glanced between him and Argent. "Am I wrong?"

The fox shrugged. "I was only obliged to learn the language of flowers. Twice, since the meanings vary between Japan and England. The finer nuances of feathers and eggshells are probably exclusive to the avian clans."

Lord and Lady Mettlebright looked expectantly between him and the gift Akira had—not quite—bestowed. And Suuzu could only confess, "I do not know."

2

TRYING TO BE WISE

Tsumiko served Suuzu tea and draped him with blankets, trying to fend off a chill he didn't really feel. Then she excused herself with murmured apologies and a promise to bring something more nourishing. He couldn't imagine eating. Was it possible the golden seed was sustaining him? That was part of the original story, in which Auriel of the Golden Seed used a handful of them to save the lives of a group of starving runaways.

Suuzu had no appetite. None.

But he should probably eat.

Wouldn't that be better for …?

He still shied away from the idea, but Suuzu needed to get used to it. There would be a child, and they would need nourishment and a nest. Yes, a nest would be necessary. Hadn't Akira said he could begin plans for a nest? Something for the two of them. Only … now there would be three.

A nest for three could still be cozy.

And now there was a golden seed for Akira.

In the puzzle box Fumiko had given him.

If Akira planted it, he would gain a tree's blessing.

Their pact would be kept, and they could remain together. Always.

But Akira was far away. Pretending to be a paramour.

What if something happened before Suuzu could give him the seed?

Argent moved to sit at a table under the window, quietly opening mail and scanning letters. Though he didn't look Suuzu's way, the fox remarked, "This is Jacques' place. Correspondence is one of his many duties. He made me promise to make an effort."

Jacques Smythe. Lord Mettlebright's man. Of course he'd be welcomed into Argent's private spaces. His place was here. His place was empty.

Suuzu lowered his gaze and stared morosely into his cooling cup.

"*Tsk*. Of all the …!"

Suuzu glanced up.

"Tiresome thing. I suppose I will have to respond, if only to fend him off. Not that he can reach us here." Argent tossed the letter onto the table. "Things have changed since the days when I was at the beck and call of every Smythe in Uppington."

"Except Jacques."

Argent paused, then sniffed. "I suppose I do let him goad me into this and that."

"Are you worried?"

"About Jacques? No," he said firmly. "He will be fine. *They* will be fine, Jacques and Akira both. I have done everything in my power to make certain."

Suuzu didn't mean to let the next words slip. "Except to send them."

Argent slouched in his chair and scowled at the letters before him. "Yes. I did. But how could I ask anyone else to risk their lives while selfishly holding back our best chance at success?"

Thrashing free of the blanket, Suuzu stood swaying. "You *took* him, my nestmate! You took my choice away, and now I am–!" His voice cracked, and he closed his mouth against the rest of his resentment. Only asked, "How could you?"

"Hisoka agreed this was the best course, as did the members of his taskforce. Jacques went willingly." Poking at the letter he'd tossed aside earlier, he grimly admitted, "I do not wish to lose him, either."

"Taskforce?" Suuzu's stomach roiled. "My brother knew?"

"There is more at stake than *us*. There are more reasons we decided to proceed than I am at liberty to enumerate. But those reasons were *good*. And the necessity pains me." Argent sighed. "I am *trying* to be wise."

For his part, Suuzu was trying not to panic. Or vomit. Or weep. Or shift. Because the urge to take avian form and fly after Akira was clamoring at him with increasing insistence, but to do so was to risk the child. Until they were safely delivered, he'd need to remain in speaking form. Suuzu's wings were effectively clipped.

Argent asked, "Would you be more comfortable in your usual room, or do you need a neutral space?"

"I do not think I can ...." Suuzu shook his head.

"I understand. I will have Nonny ready one of the guest rooms." Argent sighed and raised his voice. "Nonny, are you *quite* done eavesdropping?"

"Just hanging about in case you needed anything. Jacques is better at knowing your mind, guv." Nonny sauntered forward, gaze alert. "You're looking kinda puny, Suuzu."

"Apologies," he managed.

In the next moment, the goat-crosser shoved up under Suuzu's arm. "Lean on me, there's a good lad."

Suuzu mustered a warble of protest.

"Oh, I know you've got the years, but I'm getting on in my own way. Nabbed my attainment *ages* ago, not that I'll be pulling rank or disrespecting a spokesperson. Jacques has always been strict about manners. So with all due respect …!"

Despite the differences in their heights, Nonny hauled Suuzu off his feet, cradling him against his chest.

"*Nonny.*"

Argent's threatening tone was enough to quell Suuzu, but the crosser brazened through. "He's quaking like a firstie during one of Catalan's casting calls. I really *was* the only thing holding him up."

The fox came close, frowning as he searched Suuzu's face. "There is no need to put on a brave face for me. We are essentially brothers."

As silver tails fanned out, encircling the three of them, Suuzu only managed a weak chirp. Truly mortifying. A spokesperson should be able to find the words in any situation. But this had rattled him more than he'd wanted Juuyu to know, and … there was something in the air. Faint, yet familiar. It doubled his longing for Akira, then multiplied it again.

Nonny didn't seem to notice. "That's the guv's way of saying he–"

"I am *quite* capable of speaking for myself."

Argent's gaze flitted between the two of them, and Suuzu was only too familiar with its considering quality. Nothing could dissuade Lord Mettlebright once he'd settled on a plan. Except perhaps Jacques, but he was otherwise embroiled. With Akira.

"Suuzu." Argent took his hand, pulling Suuzu out of his circling thoughts. "Juuyu insisted upon a companion, and I cannot be so constant. Would you accept Nonny?"

Suuzu glanced at the crosser, whose expression was both

intent and open.

Argent apparently read hesitation into his lack of response. "Or perhaps Deece? He is a tribute as well …?"

Suuzu took a longer look. Unlike Tsumiko, Nonny looked nothing like Akira. But he was similarly brave. Maybe foolishly so. And right now, Suuzu wasn't.

Nonny's eyebrows lifted. "What d'ya say?"

Suuzu lowered his gaze. "If you are willing …?"

"That's that, then. Suuzu Farroost, I'm your man!"

3

NATURAL ENEMIES

Argent asked, "May I bring in some people who wish to reassure themselves with regards to your wellbeing?"

From the sofa where Nonny had tucked him back in, Suuzu cautiously asked, "Which people?"

"I asked Tsumiko to take Michael into our confidence. And Lapis happens to be here. Shall I open the door?"

"Do I have a choice?"

"Yes and no. Spokesperson Farroost cannot simply vanish for three years without a word of explanation. Choose allies. To begin, I suggest Lapis, Harmonious, and myself. And Isla. In the face of Spokesperson Twineshaft's *vacation*, she and her staff have shown remarkable poise and creativity in keeping speculation to a minimum. All while providing palatable alternatives for the dozens of diplomats and organizers Hisoka has disappointed."

Suuzu recalled his own clogged calendar, which Argent had helped to clear in order for him to travel to California before

Akira's departure. "I have inconvenienced so many."

"Harmonious and I have moved up the induction of three new members to the Amaranthine Council. The excitement will distract the masses from certain absences. And we can redistribute the workload." He gently reminded, "There will finally be another avian."

"Cheren Fellstrike." Suuzu had put forward the eagle clansman's name himself. While not as internationally famous as Cyril Sunfletch or Zonda Shore, Cheren was respected within the closeknit community of preservationists responsible for tending the eldermost groves. "He will assist you in upholding the rights of both Kith and tree-kin."

"Hmm." And twirling a finger toward the door, Argent asked, "*Will* you let Michael and Lapis see you? They do mean well."

"Ah. I apologize. Yes. I would be grateful."

Argent gestured, and several sigils spun in answer. A light tap sounded from outside the door, and Nonny hurried to yank it open. Michael strolled in, a tray held high, and Lapis drifted after him, gazing about with the curiosity of a newcomer. If not for Suuzu's infringement, would Argent have willingly allowed the dragon into his personal space?

"I apologize," Suuzu whispered again, feeling increasingly anxious.

"Here, now. Budge over," Nonny ordered, wedging himself in with Suuzu before rearranging the blankets. When he caught Suuzu's puzzled gaze, the goat-crosser said, "Grab hold if you need to. 'Cause you look like you need to. Hey, Michael. Whadjya bring?"

"Not sure. Lapis requested it, and Sansa seemed pleased to be asked." Moving a tuffet closer to the sofa, Michael perched there, and Argent wordlessly whisked away the tray. "Hello, Suuzu. Good to have you back with us."

Suuzu liked and trusted Michael Ward, but his grip on the edge of the blanket tightened.

"It's all right, friend." Michael's good humor remained intact. "What little I can do can wait, but you know how Argent is. Strict with private matters. We're here instead of the mares, not that any of them have the right sort of experience. I understand congratulations are in order. You've become our first brush with old grove miracles. It's a pleasant surprise."

Michael left off his soothing patter when a clawed hand touched his shoulder. Lord Mossberne stayed behind the reaver, gaze alight with interest. Still, the dragon lazily drawled, "Hello, sprigged boy."

"Lapis," Suuzu whispered. The two of them worked well together. Had done for years. Yet Suuzu was grateful that Michael was between them. Like a shield. Which was nonsense, since few souls were gentler than Lapis Mossberne. Suuzu warbled in weary dismay.

"Instincts, I imagine. Fresh and fraught." Lapis's posture shifted into apology. "What knowledge I have is largely based on oblique references in ancient chronicles, but your experience is firsthand. What would the good phoenixes of your colony want for us to do for you?"

Suuzu tried to think.

A hand found his, and under cover of the blanket, Nonny gave a squeeze. "Suuzu's had a long day, hasn't he? Travel and time zones and whatnot." And catching Suuzu's eye, the goat-crosser asked, "Trust these guys? Or should I give 'em the hoof?"

While he was trying to form an answer, the door opened again, shutting quietly behind Tsumiko ... and Kyrie, who offered a small wave before disappearing through a different door.

"Let me," Tsumiko offered.

Michael yielded his place to her.

Tsumiko said, "I spoke with your brother. Briefly. Let's follow

Juuyu's advice."

Suuzu's grip on Nonny firmed, but he nodded. Argent silently rearranged things, leaving Tsumiko seated on the tuffet, holding the bowl Michael had brought. And then Suuzu was staring at a spoonful of something unfamiliar poised before his lips.

"Ahhh," coached Michael, who now sat cross-legged on the floor. "It's apparently an old dragon recipe, but what's good for the drake is good for the gander."

Nonny snorted, "Isn't it rude, comparing a phoenix to a goose?"

"Cock then," Michael amended, which set off a round of genial squabbling over appropriate terms and polite society.

When Suuzu parted his lips, Tsumiko neatly deposited the first bite of food he'd taken in ... how long? It had been *days* since Zuzu stood over him, watching carefully until he'd nibbled his way through the paper tray of doughnut holes that Fumiko brought to tempt him.

This was also sweet, but in a different way. Custard laced with ...? He accepted a second bite to help him decide.

Michael kept right on talking. "This apparently counts as comfort food, although it has considerably more liquor in it than Sonnet's gruel, which has been dearly missed. She raised Vanya on the stuff, which *may* account for the sweetness of his disposition."

"Little guy just took after you, is all," said Nonny.

With a laugh, Michael said, "Anyway, we can look forward to more gruel in the near future. When is Sonnet expected, Argent?"

"Sometime next week."

Nonny said, "Be good to get some of her gruel into Sansa. Like ... immediately."

Michael arched his brows. "Hoping to sweeten her temperament? Or the twins?"

"Both. Because if their mum's mood is any indicator, they'll be a couple of terrors."

"In any case, gruel can be your first meal," Michael cheerfully proposed. "Just the sort of thing for a wake feast."

Suuzu balked.

From across the room, Argent mildly said, "You *need* sleep, Suuzu. Juuyu said as much, too, though anyone with eyes can tell how ragged you are. Michael will help you to go deep, and I will ensure your safety."

That hadn't been a suggestion.

Tsumiko murmured, "I have huddlebud. Is it safe for someone in your circumstances?"

"Yes." He turned his face from the next spoonful. Really, he shouldn't be letting her feed him. For adults, this was courting behavior. Which meant she was treating him like a child. Did she also think his attachment to Akira was a child's fancy?

Nonny waved her off and asked, "Where're you putting him?"

"Kyrie's room." Argent nodded toward the door through which the boy had gone. "He has been moving his things so you can be here. With us."

Argent's motives might be mingled with strategies, but Suuzu couldn't deny that there was no safer place. He bowed his head and hoped his posture told enough.

Then Lapis was there, beringed fingers beckoning for him to take hold. "Allow me …?"

Suuzu tipped his head inquiringly.

"In the absence of both Akira *and* Jacques, will I do? I know our clans are traditionally at odds, my being phoenix prey and all. But perhaps that will soothe your instincts. As will the trust we've shared since your appointment to the Council."

"I would never harm you," Suuzu vowed.

"Nor I you." With another twiddle of fingers, Lapis murmured,

"Argent will feel better once we're safely tucked in and warded so well, even the winds will not know how to find us."

Suuzu spared Argent a glance, only to realize that the fox's silver tails were still on display … and weaving in restless agitation. "I apologize," he mumbled. Again.

Lapis pulled him to his feet, and Nonny got up under his arm again.

Argent led them along a short hall off the master suite to a small room—ceiling high, walls lined with bookshelves. Definitely Kyrie's space. There were no windows, which normally made Suuzu restless, but for once, he appreciated the sense of snug security. Like boring into a hollow tree in order to build a nest.

Nonny got him moving, walking him around the perimeter before asking, "Tidy enough? You'll be able to relax?"

"Yes." The room was uncluttered and orderly, with both crystals and sigilcraft lending the space an aura of peace. Mildly startled to find it true, he whispered, "I could sing here."

"Can I tell Kyrie that? He'd be chuffed."

Suuzu nodded, and Nonny herded him toward bed. "Off with the outer layers, yeah?"

But when the crosser reached for the pin, Suuzu quickly covered it.

"Be a shame if it was damaged. Let's find a safe place to hide it. How's this?" And taking a handkerchief from inside his vest, Nonny murmured, "Unpin Akira's gift. Good. Now, hold out your hand."

Spreading the crisp linen across Suuzu's palm, Nonny directed him to place the pin there, then he slowly and carefully folded the handkerchief around it, like an origami packet. Nonny said, "Jacques taught me this trick. It'll do, yeah?"

Suuzu closed his fingers over it, not sure he'd be able to let it go.

Lapis was already under the bedcovers, all silken and sparkling and smelling faintly of fruit and flowers. The dragon silently opened his arms, and on some level, Suuzu's instincts decided that the offered safety would be enough. He crawled awkwardly into Lapis's embrace and huddled there.

"Would a little tending help you go deep?" asked Michael, who came to sit on the bed's edge.

Suuzu knew it would and nodded.

With a little rearranging—the bed was narrow for two—Lapis curled against Suuzu from behind. Once everyone else exited, Michael took Suuzu's free hand. Souls sought each other.

Michael's eyes widened. "I can *tell*."

Suuzu searched the man's face, waiting for more.

He changed positions, kneeling beside the bed and taking Suuzu's hand into both his own. Eyes closed as he focused on something intangible, he finally whispered, "Extraordinary. I haven't had much cause ... no close ties with an Amaranthine while they were carrying. You're my first, and I can *tell*."

"I cannot." Suuzu admitted. "It does not seem real yet. It does not show yet. Although I have not checked since Juuyu carried me here."

"How long before ...?" began Michael, though he faltered to a stop. "Actually, I'm more curious *what* shows."

Lapis asked, "May we see?"

"Now, Lapis," chided Michael. "We shouldn't intrude."

"I won't pretend I'm not curious. And I won't be offended if Suuzu refuses to indulge me." Lapis slipped his fingers into Suuzu's hair, carefully pulling and petting. "I might even be envious. Is there a waiting list somewhere for those who would welcome the blessing of a tree?"

Suuzu gathered his courage and rolled onto his back. Draping an arm across his eyes, he clutched Akira's courting gift and mumbled, "Go ahead."

The dragon propped up on an elbow, and there was a tugging

and lifting of cloth. Then a warm, dry hand settled over Suuzu's ribs before passing lightly over his belly. "Nothing yet," Lapis reported.

Suuzu let go of Michael to roll into Lapis again.

With a soft trilling, the dragon pulled him close, helping him to hide his tears.

Michael wryly offered, "The first one's always like this. Uncharted territory and all that. For what it's worth, this will be old hat by the third time around."

Suuzu warbled a muffled protest.

Lapis dropped a kiss atop his head and invited, "Command us, sprigged boy. What do you want?"

Suuzu wanted Akira. Desperately.

A mournful note tore from his throat.

"I know. Yes, of course he's the one you want. But ... some lesser boon?" Lapis ventured, "Would you like a song?"

"Sing me a song of trees?"

With a low laugh, the dragon promised, "Every one I know."

4

FRUSTRATED TRAVELER

Boniface Smythe was perturbed. And not the mild perturbation of being served an inferior blend of tea or being seated next to that second cousin who'd gone abroad *once*—twenty years ago now—and *still* insisted on trotting out amusing anecdotes that had aged poorly. No, this was the perturbation of a man who'd traveled a great distance—at no inconsiderable expense—only to be thwarted on the final leg of the journey.

"Who do I speak to about a missing road?"

The receptionist—or whatever—eyed him like he was mad.

Knowing full well that his Japanese was flawless, Boniface looked down his nose at the man and said, "It's very irresponsible, you know. And *rude*. How am I meant to get to my destination if you've gone and lost the way there?"

"I'm very sorry, sir." The man spoke slowly and broadly, which caused Boniface's eyebrow to tick up a notch. "Do you need directions? Do you need a translator?"

"I need a road! Lord, are all the locals imbecilic?" And switching back to Japanese, he reiterated his problem for the third time that afternoon. Because the postal clerk had sent him to some sort of town hall, whose secretary had quickly shunted him to *this* pokey building, which housed several boring little prefectural offices.

"Look, I've been here every year for absolute ages, so I know what I'm talking about. There used to be a perfectly suitable road from this *quaint* hamlet of yours to an extensive seaside estate. My aunt's place, as was. And now everyone in the vicinity insists there never was such a road, let alone a house. So I rented a car, because I … know … the … way! Only it's gone. The whole route. It's probably all Argent's doing, and I want it set to rights. Immediately."

The receptionist—or whatever—blinked in surprise. "Argent?"

"Yes, Argent. Argent bloody lord Mettlebright. The utter arse."

"I see, I see." Clearing his throat, the man pointed. "Try the Office of Ingress, please. At the end of the hall."

"Lovely. Just lovely." And turning on his heel, he eyed the signs jutting above each door. If this took much longer, he'd need to find tea. And not the godforsaken stuff that came in vending machines.

Turning in through the appropriate doorway, he scowled at the various signs plastered around a sparsely furnished waiting room.

"Do you need help, sir?"

Boniface was startled to be addressed in French, then wary when he realized that the man behind the little desk beside the door was Amaranthine. "I *know* Japanese," he muttered.

"As you wish," the greeter murmured, smoothly switching back to the local language.

"What made you think I was French?" he demanded in his primmest English.

The Amaranthine smiled benignly. "Your suit, sir. Did you have an appointment?"

"*Non.* Lord, this is absurd. *You* have to know he lives nearby, surely. The mail certainly gets through. Look, my brother's there!"

"Where is your brother, sir?"

"Stately House! How many times do I have to go over all of this?"

"Your name, sir?"

"Boniface Smythe. Of the Uppington Smythes. Jacques is my younger brother, and Argent has him on a leash. Or vice versa. I don't really *know*, since Jackie's always so damnably *coy*."

With a slight lift of his brows, the Amaranthine said, "You're in the right place, sir. Please take a number."

"Can't you *do* something? The day's getting on."

"Yes, sir. As I said, you're in the right place. Please, take a number."

"Oh, bloody hell." And turning to the dispenser bolted to the desk, Boniface jerked a ticket free, stalked to the other end of the room, unbuttoned his suit coat, and sank wearily to a seat.

On the wall opposite, a screen played through an endless loop of advertisements. The usual pap about integration and etiquette, liberally sprinkled with "fun facts" and the safe, simple checkup that could determine if you, too, were a reaver.

The loop played through three times before Boniface's number pinged onto the display, directing him to Booth #2.

"Good afternoon. I'm Reaver Kominka." She smiled sweetly and offered him a clipboard and pen. "Fill this out, please."

"What for?"

Her smile didn't waver. "Background check."

"Hear, now. This is totally unnecessary. You're familiar with Argent Mettlebright, surely."

"Certainly, sir. He's a member of the Amaranthine Council."

"Yes, well, he *knows* me."

The woman's smile widened. "Yes, sir. Of course, sir. Thank you for filling out the form in its entirety before returning it to me."

Boniface skimmed the form, which was going to take forever to fill out, but he couldn't think of any other way to get at Jacques. So he returned to his chair, tossed the plebian ballpoint pen onto the seat beside his, and withdrew a fountain pen from an inner pocket.

He was only a quarter of the way through the tedium when someone else entered the waiting room. He glanced up, then did a double take.

An unaccountably tall woman in a neat travel dress spoke in low tones with the receptionist. Her head came up, and she spun on one kid heel, giving him a better look at both her and the child propped on her hip. He quickly lowered his gaze to his clipboard, though not before he spied a tail wagging under the hem of her skirt. Wolf, then. He knew *that* much.

Before he could sort out the next question on his form, those shoes entered his field of vision, and he sighed, because manners dictated he stand.

Rising, he looked *way* up into a pair of wide golden-brown eyes. "Well?"

She was … sniffing.

The endless loop of Amaranthine etiquette hadn't covered sniffing. He wasn't sure if he could take offense or not. Too tired to be awed by his close encounter, he grumbled, "*Lord*. What do you want?"

"Oh, I do think … yes, it must be true." And bending so they were nearly nose-to-nose, she kept right on speaking in well-modulated—if somewhat husky—English. "Pardon me, love, but aren't you kin to Jacques Smythe?"

5

BIG BONED WOMEN

ou know him?" asked Boniface, trying not to let on how relieved he was.

The wolf beamed.

"Right. Of course you know him. But how did you know we're family?"

"Scent." And with a look that swept him head-to-toe, "Style."

That shocked him. "Jackie and I dress *nothing* alike!"

She smiled knowingly. "If shoes could run in the family, you're closeknit."

Touché.

He couldn't quite bring himself to offer his palms as the looping video repeatedly suggested, but he did give his name. "Boniface Smythe of the Uppington Smythes. I'm the elder brother."

Practically glowing, she murmured, "Brothers!"

He simply wasn't sure what to make of her response. "Are you and my brother … close?"

That brought an interesting mélange of expressions—

wistfulness and yearning and pride. With demurely downcast eyes, she said, "I do hope so. Yes, I'd like that."

Which was only confusing. Big-boned women weren't Jackie's type. "Who are you to him?" he ventured.

"I'm Sonnet." And setting down the child, she briskly said, "Hold Uncle Boniface's hand while I send word to Stately House." And to him, "I'll just let them know there are three of us, shall I?"

Boniface should have been grateful. Progress at last. But then light fingertips skimmed across the back of his hand, reminding him that there was a child. He tried to look casual, slipping his hands into pants pockets. Something he considered gauche, so it felt forced, awkward. And a trifle cowardly.

The little girl folded her hands in a way that hid her claws. Blinking wide gray eyes with slender pupils, she said, "You don't have to be afraid. We're nice."

"I'm not afraid." He glanced after Sonnet before cautiously asking, "You know Jackie? Jacques, I mean."

"Only stories. Many stories." She smiled sweetly. "I'm Linnea Rimestead, and I'm almost six."

"You're Amaranthine ...?"

"Half." She went up on tiptoe and shared, "I'm going to go to school at Stately House."

"And that lady ...? She's your escort?"

"She's Gram."

"You're a wolf?" he asked doubtfully. Comparing the two, the little girl's complexion *might* pass, but her shoulder-length hair was spun silver. Nothing like Sonnet's brunette.

"Da's mouse clan," she proudly reported. "Gram raised my mum and Uncle Alfie. And I have an Uncle Wyn and an Uncle Pennythwaite. And there's Uncle Triggs and Uncle Beck. And now you, Uncle Boniface."

"I'm *not* your uncle."

"Gram said you are." The bitty girl went up on tiptoe again. "That means you're pack."

"I'm a *what* now?"

"Pack. A packmate. It means you're *family*."

She was an articulate little thing, but Boniface wasn't about to let an almost-six-year-old talk him into a corner. "*Non*. It's impossible. We are perfect strangers, and besides …!"

Sonnet returned then, skirts and tail swishing. With a chiding sort of smile, she firmly declared, "Nonsense. You're Jacques' brother!"

Like that settled the matter.

Granted, it was much easier to put an almost-six-year-old in her place than a woman whose advantages included a scant meter and several stone. Boniface had to resist the urge to go up on tiptoe in order to announce, "I won't be bullied."

"I'll guarantee it, love. We wolves are very protective." And before he could summon up a cutting enough insult to match his indignation, she went right on. "I spoke with Nonny, but he can't bring the car around. The boundary's only a short run, but … well. I'm not sure I can carry you, Linnea, and our bags. I assume you have luggage?"

Boniface frowned. "In the boot of my rental."

"You have a car? *That* simplifies matters!" She gestured for him to lead the way.

In the parking lot, he indicated the only vehicle he'd been able to secure. It was no more intended for big-boned women that Jacques was. He grudgingly asked, "Where are your bags?"

"Sent ahead. By herald. Well, Linnea? Do you want to ride with Uncle Boniface or with your Gram?"

The little girl clasped her hands. "Oh, I want to ride in an automobile! Please, Gram? May I?"

Sonnet smiled indulgently. "Of course, love. You certainly may."

Without so much as a *by your leave*.

Boniface unlocked doors and stood back while the wolf fastened the child's seatbelt. Linnea acted like this was some amusement park ride. He decided he was still perturbed, but for reasons of presumption this time. "I'm not a chauffeur," he grumbled.

Straightening, Sonnet softly inquired, "Are you capable? A safe driver? If you're not confident in your skills, I'll figure out something else."

She was all concern and condescension.

"Lord, I can drive. Quite well, thank you very much."

"*I* should be thanking you." She stepped closer, her gaze roving his face. "This is a rare treat for my girl. And for me. Jacques never mentioned he had such a lovely brother!"

Boniface sourly pointed out, "You won't fit in the car."

"Oh, that's no trouble at all. I'll run ahead. Try to keep up, love. There's a trick to some of the turnings."

"You're going to *run*?"

"I suppose it'll have to be more of a lope. Automobiles have their limits."

Boniface looked her up and down. The kid heels. The classically elegant dress. The upswept hair. This woman didn't look ready for a jog down back-country roads.

She made a little shooing motion. "In you go, and we'll be off."

If he hadn't been half-mad from lack of tea, Boniface might have refused her on principle. He didn't take orders. From anyone. But he swept around to his side of the car, took a seat, and put the key in the ignition.

The child wriggled in what he hoped was excitement. It would be inconvenient if she suddenly announced she needed a WC.

But then Boniface shifted into reverse and put an arm across the back of the seat, turning to check that the way was clear … and … squeaked.

An enormous wolf stood with head lowered so that it could peer through the back window.

Boniface made another strangled sound.

The brown wolf angled its head and peered at him out of the corner of its eye, blinking almost … shyly. The thing wagged its tail and offered a low wuff.

"Bloody hell!"

"That's Gram," Linnea announced. "Truest form."

Golden-brown eyes narrowed, and Boniface swiftly faced forward. His voice came out embarrassingly high. "Why is she growling?"

"You used a bad word. That's not allowed, Uncle Boniface. It's a *rule*."

Knuckles white on the steering wheel, he managed. "Too right. Bad form. Very sorry."

And then he backed out of his parking slot, hit his blinker, and followed a trotting wolf up the road out of town.

6

POLITE DISTANCES

Boniface didn't notice at first. He'd been keeping what he hoped was a polite distance from the Amaranthine wolf who kept checking over her shoulder to make sure he was still following. But he'd spent the better part of half an hour staring at Sonnet's butt.

Finally, he asked, "Are you sure that's your grandmother?"

Linnea, who leaned as close to her open window as the seat belt would allow, answered, "Quite sure."

He lowered his voice. "Because that wolf definitely has ... that is to say. Oh, blast." He tried to put it more delicately. "That's a *boy* wolf, isn't it?"

"Yes." She patiently explained, "There's a rule. It's easy. If Gram is wearing shoes, use *she*. Without shoes, use *he*."

"But ... why ...?"

Linnea smiled sweetly. "Because that's Gram."

Up ahead, the wolf swung around, and Boniface hit the brakes, worried she—*he*—had somehow overheard his questions and deemed them inappropriate. But Sonnet only nosed in the shrubbery alongside the road, then looked back their way, tail wagging.

Boniface peered around and muttered, "It's about right. There was a bridge across a ditch at this point. At the beginning of the drive."

"I can smell the sea," Linnea announced.

"It's off that way." He waved lazily, then leaned out the window to catch a breeze that lifted the hair from his cheeks and brought back memories of dressing in kimono and fawning over cherry blossoms. Maman had pushed for Boniface to play the part of a dutiful nephew in the hope that Aunt Eimi would find him charming enough to settle her fortune on him.

Useless in the end.

Thanks to Tsumiko.

And Argent, who'd become world famous about the same time that the Smythes were no longer invited to Stately House. Jacques had somehow made it back here, though. Called the place home. Sent cheeky gifts and little notes on stationery embossed with the Mettlebright crest. Notes that drove Maman crazy because they never did say why Jackie was shacking up with Argent bloody Lord Mettlebright.

Oh, she *loved* that her son was on the telly.

Always on the sly fox's arm.

Always fussing with his tie.

And Argent *let* him.

Jacques, who'd embarrassed Father and Maman by having inconvenient inclinations. Yet somehow, everybody in their set always found the scandalous brat so very charming. Enough to overlook Jackie's chatting up their chauffeurs and stable boys and sons.

"Uncle Boniface ...?"

He drew himself up and glanced at his passenger.

"You need to drive." Linnea patiently pointed ahead. "Gram is waiting."

"About time somebody tracked down that dratted road." Easing off the brake, he hit his blinker and haughtily announced, "I reported it earlier. Very irresponsible. Roads shouldn't be allowed to go missing."

Linnea giggled softly and said, "You're so funny, Uncle Boniface."

Lord, he hated children.

Boniface rolled forward, any sense of triumph buried under fresh qualms and a growing sense of dread. Wolves everywhere. Big as life. Some even bigger. And showing a lot of skin, despite the snap of autumn in the air.

What's more, the estate had changed. Drastically. Sometime in the years since his last visit, a village had sprung up. And not the human sort. Houses and gardens and windmills and walls. He spied a theater. Lord, they even crossed railroad tracks, and he spied a gaudy yellow antique locomotive and vintage train cars parked on a siding.

Gravel crunched under tires as he entered a circle drive and came even with the double row of trees with autumn-gold leaves that now lined the front walk. That's when he spied Argent on the step, Tsumiko at his side. Waiting.

The dread was back.

Boniface may not have panted after Argent as Jackie had done, but neither had he been especially ... nice. What if the high and mighty Lord Mettlebright held a grudge?

Sonnet opened Linnea's door and collected the girl, whispering something in her ear before smiling at him. "Come along, love. Home sweet home!"

He couldn't manage the protests he should make. This wasn't his home. He wasn't her love. And he bloody well knew the way. But all he could do was try not to look meek as he trailed after Sonnet, who presented herself to Argent and Tsumiko, tail a blur.

"Jacques has a brother!"

"I was aware."

"His name is *Boniface*."

"Yes."

The gaze Argent flicked over him certainly hadn't changed. Aloof. Calculating. It made Boniface feel like a little boy. A naughty one at that. Hardly fair. He determinedly stepped up, wanting to eliminate Argent's advantage. He had no right trying to loom. They were practically the same height.

Tsumiko smiled softly, which was better. But ... lord, she didn't look a day over ... well! They'd thought her a child, but she should be thirty by now, surely. Odd, that.

"Good afternoon, Uncle," she offered pleasantly. "This is such a surprise."

In far less welcoming tones, Argent bloody lord Mettlebright drawled, "What are you doing here, Bon-Bon?"

7

FAMILY RESEMBLANCES

oniface was actually grateful when Argent pulled him aside, out of the path of a mob of children who clearly knew—and liked—Sonnet. The fox steered him firmly into a parlor and closed the door before rounding on him. "An answer, please. What are you doing here?"

"*Jackie's* here," he pointed out peevishly. "I'm checking on him."

"Concern for your brother? This is rather belated. He has been here twelve years." Icy blue eyes narrowed. This *wasn't* bringing back good memories. "The truth."

"Oh, why else? Maman sent me to snoop." Boniface hastily added, "Jackie recently asked for a trunk with the family heraldry on it. I trust it arrived safely?"

Argent's stare was impassive.

Boniface stubbornly met it. "You *know* how she is."

To his utter amazement, Aunt Eimi's former butler grimaced. "Are you seeking refuge from Yvette?"

"Lord. Is that an option?"

"*No.*"

He'd been joking. Mostly. It wasn't as if he'd ever turn to Jackie if he needed refuge, but the refusal still stung.

Argent said, "Jacques needed the trunk because he intended to travel. He is not here at the moment."

"Where's he gone?"

"I really could not say."

"But ... he lives here?"

"He does."

"Will he be back soon?"

"I really could not say. And I cannot have you spilling details about our private life to your precious Maman ... or anyone else."

"Do you want me to sign a non-disclosure agreement or whatever?"

Argent smoothly said, "You cannot spread secrets if you never leave."

Boniface didn't like the fox's tone. Utter arse.

"Will anyone miss you? Any wife? A child or two?"

"No," he snapped. Then felt like a fool for wearily adding, "Maman would miss me."

Again, Argent surprised him by almost—almost—smiling. "You? A confirmed bachelor? I would have thought Yvette would have arranged something for you by now."

"It's not that she doesn't fancy the idea of grandchildren, though I'm quite sure she'll refuse to answer to Grandmere. But ... well. You know how she can be."

"Nobody is good enough for her precious Bon-Bon?"

Boniface could only mutter, "It isn't funny."

"No. It is not." And then Argent moved to the door and let Tsumiko in.

She was all politeness and poise when she said, "Uncle

Boniface, you must be tired after your trip. I can show you to one of our guest rooms."

"Just put me in Jackie's," he suggested.

Argent countered, "Impossible. His suite is next to mine, and guests aren't allowed in the family quarters."

So Jacques was family, then? And Boniface very pointedly wasn't. Again, the distinction stung.

Then Tsumiko asked, "Would you like to meet Kyrie?"

"Who?"

She turned toward the door, presumably to collect this Kyrie person, but Boniface was distracted. Argent had begun sprouting tails, which was both new and alarming. When Boniface dragged his gaze back to Tsumiko, there was a boy. And suddenly, Argent's display made a strange sort of sense. It was a warning.

Boniface's polite smile faltered. Because of course Kyoko's baby would be here. The cursed child. Tsumiko stood with her hand resting lightly on the boy's shoulder, and they both watched him carefully.

Then Argent stepped between them, and Boniface wasn't sure which of them he was sheltering from the other. The fox made the introduction. "One of my sons, Kyrie Hajime-Mettlebright. Kyrie, this is Jacques' brother. Perhaps you recall your Uncle Jackie referring to Bon-Bon?"

"Oh!" And with a soft smile, "Oh, yes. How do you do?"

And his smile was just like Kyoko's, despite the red eyes and purple scales.

"Please, do not be alarmed. I will not come any closer." The boy sounded every bit as cultured as Argent, and his voice was pitched to soothe.

Boniface frowned. "I'm not afraid. I was only surprised."

"Why?" challenged Argent. "You knew we'd taken him."

"No, I know. It's not that. It's just ... well, he looks like .... He reminds me of Ceddy. A bit."

Boniface shot a nervous look at Argent, hoping for some signal if he should stop, but he received a small nod. Right then.

"Stewie and Kyoko have a child. Ceddy—short for Cedric, of course. The second. Named for our grandfather. He's not as ... well, it's only natural he's *not*, since he's fully human. But technically ... biologically ... Ceddy would be your half-brother."

A smile bloomed anew, and the boy asked, "Do you have any pictures?"

"I ... well, yes. I suppose I do." What was the harm, really? It wasn't as if this boy could usurp Ceddy's place or steal his inheritance. He wasn't Stewart's child. Pulling out his phone, he flicked through the gallery and found a picture of Ceddy on his pony. "This is recent-ish."

Kyrie hadn't moved. "My I come closer?" he asked.

"Lord. I'm over the shock of you," he groused. "I'm not so high strung that I need to be handled with kid gloves."

Still, he was grateful that Kyrie approached slowly.

At his suggestion, they sat together on a little settee, with Argent and Tsumiko looking on. She stood in the circle of both the fox's arms and his tails, looking at peace with the world.

"Who is this, please?" asked the boy, pointing with a gilded claw.

"My cousin Stewie. Stewart, really. He married Kyoko after ... well. She was your ...." He couldn't bring himself to say *mother*, since she'd thoroughly abandoned that role. Kyoko pretended this boy didn't exist. That the years she'd lost had never happened. "It was difficult, you understand?"

"Yes. I do not blame her."

His voice was so polite, so pleasant, Boniface wanted to believe him.

Red eyes roved his face, and Kyrie said, "You are not much like

Uncle Jackie. Although the color of your eyes is the same."

"*Non*. I look like my mother, who looked like her mother. But Jackie resembles our maternal grandfather. Lord, what a scamp. According to Grandmere, he made the most of his puppy dog eyes and curly mop."

The boy smiled Kyoko's smile again. "I take it back. You *are* a little alike. Your inflections. Your expressions."

"I'll try not to be insulted."

"Do I resemble my half-brother? Somehow ...?"

"Ceddy? Not at first blush. But if you don't mind my saying so, you're ... uncanny."

Kyrie's expression softened. "Should I go back to Mother, now?"

"Do stop. You're no weirder than that mouse girl I met earlier. Or that wolf with special rules who sniffed me out. And I grew up with Argent bloody lord Mettlebright sneering at the state of my handkerchief. Trust me, that puts iron into a lad's soul."

Across the room, Argent said, "Language."

Boniface hesitated. "Oh, blast. Did I swear?"

"A little." Kyrie lightly touched his arm. "Be more careful in front of the children."

"Aren't you a child?"

"I am nearly thirteen." And with a searching look, he pressed, "What did you mean? When you said I am uncanny."

"Your inflections, they're pure Argent. Only I think your expressions are more like Tsumiko's. But ... your smile. It's hers. Kyoko's." And with an uneasy glance at the two who'd raised her baby, he lamely repeated, "It's been difficult, you understand? But she *can* smile again."

"Good," said Tsumiko.

Argent didn't contradict her.

Kyrie asked, "May I call you Uncle Bon-Bon?"

"Don't be ridiculous. My name is *Boniface*."

Undeterred, the boy asked, "Uncle Boniface?"

This was a bit different from when Linnea tried to claim him. That girl had no right to him that he could fathom, but this boy ... with his good manners and his soothing voice and his prettified claws. This boy that smiled with Kyoko's smile and whose hand was warm in his and whose scales were smooth as silk. And there were freckles. They were purple, which was a shocking color, but they were such an ordinary, people-like thing. Boniface freckled whenever he forgot to apply sun cream.

Oh.

His thumb swept across the back of Kyrie's hand again.

When had he begun touching the lad? He hadn't meant to.

"It is all right to be curious." Kyrie said, his voice so gentle. Such a little gentleman. "Curiosity can be a compliment."

Boniface checked on Argent, who looked on without protest. In fact, something about the way his tails were swaying kind of seemed ... almost ... pleased?

"Uncle Boniface?"

"Mmm?"

Kyrie relaxed into a smile and said, "I am very glad you came."

Dropping the boy's hand, Boniface mumbled, "Are all dragons so ... vivid?"

"Yes. Mostly." And with a hopeful smile, Kyrie announced, "Lapis is here. Would you like to meet him?"

"Lapis ...?" Boniface shot a worried look at Argent. "Lapis ... Mossberne? Good lord."

The fox held out a hand. "Let us begin our non-disclosure agreement with the immediate surrender of your phone, camera, and any other recording devices."

Boniface sulkily dropped his phone onto the fox's palm. "I

never once told on you."

"True. Which is why I will suffer your presence a little longer. For Kyrie's sake."

"Until Jackie gets home?" he ventured.

Argent's brows arched. "I really could not say."

8

MEMORY LAPSE

When Suuzu woke, Nonny was speaking in warning tones. "Oi. How'd you get in here? Wait. Did you …? You've been here before … maybe?"

"Have you begun to remember me? Good. Peace is so much easier when the initial confusion loses hold. I am Hajime, and we *are* acquainted. Once you grow more accustomed to the scent of my flowers, you will not forget so much. And you will notice me more often."

"You've been here the whole time?"

"This is not the first time I have checked on Suuzu. Or did you mean here at Stately House? Argent brought me with him from America."

"I know the guy collects Ephemera, but … you're kinda big for one."

"I am rather small for my kind."

"You're … a *tree*, ain'tcha?"

"I am a tree. And this young phoenix belongs to my son. Suuzu …?"

He opened his eyes and twisted enough to peer over his

shoulder. A tree smiled faintly at him, deep red eyes crinkling at the corners. "I belong to your … son?" Suuzu whispered, startled that the words felt true.

"Do you remember me?"

Tiny red flowers didn't belong to any variety of tree that Suuzu knew, not that the grove his colony harbored was terribly diverse. They only had a few varieties, the majority having purple flowers.

Hajime prompted, "You opened the box. You found what I hid there."

Hazy recollections aligned themselves. Of the delight with which Akira had told him about meeting his father. "Akira is tree-kin."

"Since when?" exclaimed Nonny.

Hajime smiled. "And Suuzu is the child of a grove."

"I am." Suuzu rolled onto his back, though Nonny didn't let him go, like he was afraid Hajime would carry him off. Placing a hand over the two clamped around his chest, Suuzu murmured, "It will be all right, Nonny. Hajime is family. I had forgotten, but parts are coming back to me."

"You will acclimate sooner, given your sprigging. I *am* pleased. Even proud. I usually cannot stay for long near my leaflings, but I am looking forward to meeting the child you will raise with Akira."

"What's he on about?" demanded Nonny.

"Hajime is one of Akira's parents. He is also the parent of my child."

Nonny's face screwed up. "Well, that's very soap opera of you. Does Akira know you're up the duff?"

"No."

"Can I be there when you tell him?" Nonny grinned. "The look on his face is gonna be priceless."

"If … I need moral support."

"Yeah, of course!" Nonny rolled his eyes. "He'll probably go all soppy about having a baby and all."

Suuzu hummed uneasily.

Nonny's eyes narrowed. "Oi. He'll be happy!"

"Are you showing?"

They both jumped and turned to blink at Hajime. Suuzu had honestly forgotten he was in the room. Judging by Nonny's muttered oaths, he had, too.

"And the other seeds? Are they safe?" prompted Hajime.

"They could be safer." And seizing upon inspiration, Suuzu asked, "Will you keep them?"

Hajime brightened. "That would be wise. Until the time is right."

Suuzu moved to get up, but Nonny hauled him back. "You stay. I'll go. Tell me where to look."

"I am not an invalid."

"No, but you're not unaffected. Tell me where."

So he directed Nonny to the bag someone had left near the foot of the bed.

"You mean something priceless has been sitting here this whole time? *Could be safer*, he says. Yeah, you weren't kidding. This ain't safe at all. Or wouldn't be if Michael and Lapis hadn't laced this room tight-shut. Although ... *you* got through."

Hajime simply smiled.

After a quick rummage, Nonny found the puzzle box. "This it? Nice! The shells are pretty."

"You may give it to Hajime."

He handed it off, saying, "Mum's the word, now."

"You will not remember," said the tree. "I do apologize. It may be months before all who live nearby retain any memory of me."

"Does Argent know you? To remember you, I mean?"

"Not entirely. But he keeps me close, and Tsumiko reminds him often." Then Hajime repeated his earlier question. "Suuzu, are you showing?"

"How many days have passed? How long have I been asleep?"

"This is the eighth day," said Nonny. "Me and Lapis have been taking turns. He should pop back in soon. He went down to the kitchen since he said you were getting close to waking. Should be back with a tray or two."

Eight days. Certainly long enough. "I ... yes. I should be showing."

"Showing *what*, exactly?" Nonny asked.

Suuzu's fingers plucked at the soft cloth of his clothes. "I am male, so there will be a ... it is reminiscent of a seed pod? Or some compare it to a chrysalis. It will grow here. Upon my abdomen."

"Can I see?" And when Suuzu made no move, Nonny asked, "You don't want a look?"

"I *should* ... confirm ...."

Nonny glanced between him and Hajime. "So you're having a baby tree?"

"And a phoenix," Hajime said. "It does put my heart at ease, where dragons are concerned."

Suuzu confirmed, "The child will be a phoenix, and they will be born with a golden seed in their hand. Their tree twin."

"Gotcha. So it really is like the stories. Plant the seed by your front door ... and all that." Nonny nodded wisely. "We've got a Scattering coming, so tree lore has been part of bedtime stories ever since summer. Seemed far-fetched, though. But I guess it's good. Your kiddo will have plenty of company."

"I am ... most fortunate."

"So can I sneak a peek?"

Suuzu rolled onto his back and covered his face. "You may."

Blankets folded aside, and cloth parted. For several long moments, there was only an awful silence. Then Nonny asked, "If it's pink, does that mean it'll be a girl?"

"What?" Suuzu exclaimed in alarm, propping up on his elbows

in order to check. Because an off-color could mean that the sprig had sickened. But there it was, a deep, vibrant green, nearly glowing with health as it curled around his navel.

"Made you look," Nonny teased. His blunt-nailed fingers brushed lightly over brown skin, not quite touching the addition. "This is a good beginning, yeah? Everything normal?"

Suuzu knew from both lore and from experience that the shoot would take hold and flourish. Supple. Sturdy. Resilient. But there *were* a handful of guidelines that would be useful for his valet to know. Taking a deep breath, Suuzu began, "No saltwater."

9

AMATEUR DRAMATICS

You gonna want to hide from the kids?" asked Nonny.

Suuzu slowly shook his head. "For three years?"

"Yeah, not happening. Come on, then. They need to know their Uncle Suuzu is back home where he belongs."

He balked at the door. "Where are we going?"

"Kitchen. You barely touched the trays Lapis brought, and Sonnet needs to know if there's stuff you can or can't eat."

"Sonnet arrived?"

"Only just, and it's great. She hasn't stopped cooking almost since she walked through the door. Musta really missed us."

Suuzu thought back and shook his head. "She departed so suddenly. Vanya cried for days."

"*Weeks*. But she had a good reason. In fact, Sonnet brought her along. She's fostering a granddaughter!"

"Dog clan?"

"Mouse crosser. Seems those orphans she raised way-back-when made some pretty interesting matches. Ask her about it. It's a good story, and you know wolves. Proud of their pack."

As they neared the kitchen, Suuzu murmured, "I am not hungry."

"Not having an appetite's not the same as not needing food." Nonny tucked Suuzu's arm through his own. "Teach me how to take care of you. I'll do a good job if you guide me. It's just until Akira's back. Then I can go back to tormenting Jacques."

Suuzu lowered his gaze.

"Hey, they're fine. This is Jacques we're talking about. He'll carry this off with all kinds of style." Nonny paused, then changed tacks. "Speaking of style ... I maybe have a good idea. Are you acquainted with Randolla?"

"The tailor? Passingly."

"We'll visit him. Like ... next."

"It will be some time before any of my clothing will need to be adjusted."

"But he's avian."

Suuzu wanted to protest that Randolla was a crane, hardly close kin to a phoenix, but that's when Ginkgo found them, a crosser propped on his hip.

"And here's Nonny, one of our big boys. He's a good one to ask if you have questions, since he also came to us from England."

"Big boy?" countered Nonny. "I'm not a kid any longer."

"Gentleman goat, then," Ginkgo amended. "And this is your Uncle Suuzu. He's several kinds of fluent, which is perfect if you need a translator. Guys, this is Sonnet's granddaughter Linnea."

Introductions were cut short by a screechy shout from further along the hall.

Ginkgo rolled his eyes. "Can't leave him for more than a minute, can we?"

"We cannot." Linnea cheerfully confided, "Uncle Boniface is *so* funny. About every little thing."

Nonny took the lead. In one of the small parlors, they found a newcomer teetering on a footstool, his hands in the air while their little cobra-crosser wrapped around his ankles. "*Mon dieu*, a satyr. What will they think of next?"

"Sorry, sorry. Be'el-garva is good at getting around barriers. Aren't you, bae?" Ginkgo added, "Like I said, the children are curious. And they all miss their Uncle Jackie."

"Come to Nonny, sweetheart. We need to be considerate of Uncle Bon-Bon. He's an ordinary sort of bloke, so he's not used to Amaranthine."

"See here!" the man protested, but then his gaze fixed on Suuzu. "Lord. You look just like Spokesperson Farroost."

"Peace. There is no danger here." Suuzu offered his hands to the newcomer.

Ginkgo interceded. "He's Boniface. Jacques' older brother. And yeah, Suuzu's a member of the Amaranthine Council."

Boniface smelled of stress and cologne and exhaustion ... and kinship. Suuzu helped him from his perch and kept hold of the man's hands. Half a head shorter than Suuzu, Boniface wore his straight hair in a sleek, shoulder-length bob, nothing like Jacques' artfully tousled curls. But the resemblances *were* there, in the shape of the hand that clung to his ... and in the careless way with which he wore expensive things ... and in the color of the eyes that pleaded silently for shelter.

Suuzu surprised himself by asking, "Would you like to meet Jacques' personal tailor? We were going there next."

"Will there be any half-squirrel, half-mouse, half-raccoon types loitering about, waiting to pounce?"

Nonny said, "Oi. Sho is half-tanuki, and you're being an ass. Be'el didn't mean to scare you."

"Lord, I'm not afraid." And to the girl, "For pity's sake don't cry. I'm sure you're very sweet. Gorgeous colors, by the way." And looking to Suuzu, Boniface muttered, "I'm pants at children. How do I smooth this over?"

And suddenly, Suuzu was in familiar territory. Peacemaker. Spokesperson. "That is easily done. First, tell her you are sorry."

"I *do* apologize," Boniface immediately said, in tones that rang with dignified sincerity.

"Now meet her palms. Show him the way, Be'el."

Boniface was monumentally awkward, but in an honest way, and that had always fostered trust. Soon the little girl moved on to Linnea, who cooed over Be'el-garva's copper scales and turquoise hair. In the easy way of small children, they'd already declared themselves best friends when Nonny angled his head toward the door.

They escaped. And when they set off along the path to Randolla's shop, Suuzu had Boniface Smythe by the hand.

10

PERSONAL TAILOR

Suuzu made certain that Boniface was comfortable with Randolla's kinfolk, who exclaimed over the man's suit and coaxed him to consider one of their own designs. Only then did Suuzu allow Nonny to pull him into a curtained alcove where the crane clansman had offered a private consultation.

"We're alone, and there are safeguards in place," said Randolla. "Anything you share here won't be overheard."

"I ... am a tribute of the Farroost clan," Suuzu announced, needing to work up to the next part. "And I have ... consumed a golden seed."

"And he's courting a fellow," Nonny put in.

Suuzu warbled a protest.

"What? Jacques is always saying that a man has no secrets from his valet or his tailor, and that's the two of us. Besides, Randolla's avian. Use your resources!"

Suuzu admitted, "I never did learn much about courtship. No

need. Being a tribute."

"I see! Yes, I see. May I ask about your lovely accessory?" Randolla gestured to Akira's courting gift. "Is that from your suitor? Did he pin it in that exact way?"

"No." Suuzu cupped his hand over it. "I put it on myself."

"Ah! Then there's no message. Unless you're *sending* one?"

Nonny raised a hand. "Hold up. How you wear the pin means something?"

"Oh, certainly! If one egg or another is given, the message is fairly straightforward. But all nine nippet eggs? That alone sends a message—a many-faceted attachment. And such a token lends itself to a courting game."

"It does …?" Suuzu flushed and lowered his eyes. "I am not so sure. Akira may have simply thought it was pretty."

"How's it work?" asked Nonny.

"Note that the topmost egg is yellow." Randolla explained, "That's the egg of a honey nippet. In avian lore, they're associated with Auriel of the Golden Seed. You know his story?"

"I do." With a small shrug, Suuzu recited, "When the eldermost groves were first planned and planted, none could have guessed that some of the golden seeds would not take root in the ground … but in people. Auriel's mercy saved twelve souls, who in their turn carried twelve souls *and* twelve seeds. His gift is still unfolding, for it was in the eldermost groves that power first found its way into human lineages."

Randolla nodded approvingly. "Forefathers of reavers, treasured for their startling strength and alluring sweetness. Those who nurture bonds with the distant descendants of Impressions taste a bliss that can become help … and strength … and joy. And this has led to the various meanings attached to yellow feathers. And to yellow eggshells."

"How come *various*?" demanded Nonny. "Doesn't it get confusing if there's more than one possibility?"

"A courting couple will decide upon a meaning together. We learn the traditional meanings as a matter of course, but secret messages are one of this game's delights."

"So what's Suuzu's pin saying now? Traditionally?"

Randolla said, "Yellow represents sweetness of soul. At least, that's most common meaning. But it can say, 'this bond is sweet,' 'my need is met,' 'you are my help," and … 'irresistible connection.'"

Suuzu wanted nothing more than for *all* of them to be true.

11

ANY PORT IN A STORM

oniface wasn't the clingy sort. It wasn't dignified. But Stately House was full to overflowing with strangeness, and he'd grown everlastingly weary of people telling him not to be afraid. He wasn't! At least … not when he was with Spokesperson Farroost.

Maybe it was because he knew Suuzu from the telly. He'd done all those announcements during the Miyabe-Starmark courtship.

Maybe it was the quiet ways Suuzu found to reassure him. Granted, the hand-holding had been a little embarrassing. But even now, the spokesperson's hand rested lightly on his back, and Boniface appreciated the guidance. And the sense of security.

Or maybe it was because Suuzu didn't prattle on about Jacques at every opportunity. Lord, it was getting old.

So when they finished at the tailor's, Boniface kept close to Suuzu, despite that Nonny fellow's broad hints that he could shove off at any time. But the spokesperson made bird noises, and goat boy raised his hands in surrender. And Boniface was relieved.

They returned to the main house through the kitchen door, because apparently Spokesperson Farroost was in need of a meal. Boniface's stomach had unclenched enough that his interest was piqued.

Mercifully, there weren't many people in the kitchen. Sonnet bustled back and forth, having changed into a simple blue dress and a capacious apron. Her gaze sought his, and her tail fluttered in the vicinity of her hem, but all she said was, "You boys sit. I'll bring something."

Suuzu guided him to a long, sturdy table. A man was already there, helping a toddler to eat. The man grinned in an easy way and said, "I remember you."

Boniface drew a blank.

"I'm Timur. A member of the family that was hanging about on the fringes whenever your family visited."

"Aunt Eimi's staff ...?"

"That's right," the man said, sounding amused. "I'm one of the chauffeur's sons. And this is Gregor. He's mine, and he's *very* glad Sonnet's come home. Her gruel is brilliant, especially with a cup of good, strong tea."

"Already steeping," announced Sonnet, who set out bowls and nudged the three of them into chairs.

"Is there enough for one more?" inquired someone else.

Boniface turned, mostly to make sure the newcomer wasn't toting any spare children. Gregor was human enough to be dismissible, but he didn't fancy being coiled up with another cobra-child or lectured by another mouse-girl.

Only the new arrival wasn't a child.

Shooting to his feet, he muttered, "Lord."

"*Lapis* will do," he said with a benign smile. "Suuzu, really. Is that all you're taking? Gregor eats more!"

And thus dismissed, Boniface sank to the edge of his seat.

Sonnet leaned over him, depositing teapot and cup in easy reach before sliding another steaming bowl in front of Lapis bloody lord Mossberne. "Tuck in, love," she urged. "If there's one thing I'm confident about, it's my gruel. It'll hearten you."

"Too kind," Boniface managed, stealing glances at the spokesperson for the dragon clans. They'd said he'd be hanging about, but Boniface hadn't truly believed it. He'd lapsed into actual staring when Lord Mossberne slowly turned and smiled in the very same way he did on magazine covers, only it was more … slow and knowing and sexy.

"Boniface, isn't it? What's on your mind?"

He blurted, "The telly doesn't do you justice."

Then he shoved a mouthful of glop into his mouth to keep from saying anything further … and hummed in surprise. And delight. Good lord! The woman called *this* gruel?

Across the table, Timur grinned and said, "I know, right? Sonnet, you're a treasure."

"Oh, go on," she murmured. But she circled the table to peck his cheek, then tousled Gregor's ringlets.

Boniface ate determinedly and was about to pour himself a cuppa when he noticed that Suuzu was lagging behind them. He hadn't touched his gruel. Didn't he know it was ambrosia?

Nudging his arm, Boniface urged, "Take a bite."

Suuzu gazed at him for a long moment, but he obeyed.

Boniface couldn't understand why something so lovely seemed to stick in his throat. So he poured a cup of his own tea and passed it to him. "Drink."

With traces of reluctance, Suuzu accepted the cup, gazed mournfully into its contents, then quietly downed the drink. That's when Boniface noticed that everyone else had gone weirdly quiet, determinedly minding their own bowls.

Only then did he realize that Argent had turned up again. The fox prowled around the table so that he was facing him and Suuzu. His gaze was cool, calculating, and Boniface felt like a child who'd been caught out of bounds. It was deucedly hard not to squirm.

"Spokesperson Farroost," Argent began. "I have need of your unparalleled diplomacy."

At his side, the phoenix shifted in his chair and murmured, "Ask anything."

But Argent's gaze slanted to Boniface. "I have work."

"Don't let me keep you."

He inclined his head. "Tsumiko is similarly occupied."

"Ah. Of course." Was he about to get the boot?

"So until your departure, I am placing you in Suuzu's care. Bring any concerns or questions you have to him."

And then he walked away.

Timur offered a solemn wink.

Nonny signaled for another serving of gruel.

Sonnet brought it and hovered. "Timur, dear? I don't think our Boniface is used to Amaranthine. Shouldn't you give him some advice? As a reaver and all."

"You're a reaver?" Boniface asked, since this was the first he'd heard of it.

"Runs if the family," Timur replied easily. "And there's nothing to it, really. We're all people, so basic courtesies apply. That goes for Fend, too." And raising his voice slightly, he warned, "Don't toy with the man!"

"Do you like kitties, Bon-Bon?" Nonny asked in teasing tones.

Almost at the same time, Suuzu urgently inquired, "Are you aware of Kith?"

Boniface turned to see what the fuss was about.

A black panther, big as a horse—well, nearly so—was slinking closer, tail lashing.

Then everyone was talking at once, hurling advice at him and pleading with the cat. Boniface managed a weak oath before the thing mauled him. Only ... when the world righted itself, he was two rooms and a long hall away from the kitchen, being carried by Suuzu.

The phoenix calmly asked, "Which room is yours?"

Nonny trotted after them, grumbling, "You can't get out of eating forever, you moody chicken."

12

TIME HONORED TALE

Suuzu asked for the room adjoining Boniface's. Actually, he insisted.

"But why?" Nonny asked. "I have a whole suite ready for you. Moved your clothes and everything."

"Argent made him my responsibility." And more softly, "He … startles easily. I want to remain accessible."

"Guess we can make this do until we're shed of him. You okay with the tiny *en suite* in here? You can't go into the onsen until I check on stuff like mineral content." Hooves shifted restlessly on the hall carpet. "And … you won't keep your secret long if you help us with the kids' baths like usual. They'll notice and ask questions. They'll talk."

"Allow me?"

Suuzu hadn't realized that Lapis had followed them.

"Is Boniface settled?" the dragon asked.

Nonny jerked his chin. "Next door. And Suuzu wants this one."

"Very sensible. May I add a few sigils? Perhaps something to alert you if he becomes distressed ...?"

"The guv already marked Bon-Bon," said Nonny. "Same basic tracer we put on all the kids."

"I will ask him to carry a linked crystal. Tomorrow." Waving at the door, he added, "He is fatigued. He locked himself in."

"So ... here's the thing," said Nonny. "With both Jacques and Akira gone, Ginkgo needs my help overseeing the little guys. And it's getting to be that time."

Lapis fluttered his fingers. "Do what must be done. I can see to Suuzu's needs." And seeking his gaze, the dragon said, "I needed to discuss some upcoming appointments, which Isla moved from your agenda to mine. Which means our evening will be part business meeting, part pampering."

To some degree, Suuzu was grateful. His friends were already covering for him.

And yet ... he wanted to protest. To have a voice and to make his own choices.

Something must have shown on his face, because Lapis gathered his hands and softly inquired, "Did you not sleep safely in my arms?"

Suuzu bowed his head. "My trust has long been yours."

With a soothing warble, Lapis promised, "I will not leave his side, Nonny."

"You're the best. Back after a bit." Before rounding the corner, he called back, "With a tray."

The room included a miniscule *en suite* mostly crowded with a small claw-footed tub. The thing was meant for one … but Suuzu guessed it would do nicely for him and his child. And all at once, he could see it. Him in the bath, supporting his little one while Akira draped his arms along the tub's edge, making faces until their baby giggled and reached for his other papa.

Oh.

It was the first time Suuzu had allowed himself to picture his future as a parent.

Cupping his palm over his stomach, he let himself want small, ordinary moments like that one, raising a son or daughter here at Stately House. With Akira.

"Suuzu …?" Lapis softly called.

He opened his eyes, which had fallen shut while the dragon played bath attendant. There were tiny red flower petals mixed in with the soap bubbles on the surface of the water.

Lapis quietly announced, "We are not alone."

Suuzu raised his head and stared into the face of the tree imp who'd draped his arms along the edge of the tub.

"Good evening, Suuzu. Do you remember me?"

"Hajime."

The tree's expression brightened.

Lapis resumed the careful kneading of Suuzu's lathered scalp. "Will you introduce your friend?"

"Hajime is Akira's parent."

"Tsumiko's, too. Good evening, Lapis." With an apologetic smile, Hajime promised, "The more often we meet, the sooner you will remember that I am here."

Lapis said, "That … seems like a thing I've heard before."

"It is. Thank you for your gentle handling of my son's phoenix." And with obvious pride, he added, "I am also parent to Suuzu's leafling."

"Quite the plot twist. But such are the stories of trees."

"Dragons collect stories, do they not? Suuzu is interested in stories about nippets." Hajime trailed his fingers in the bath water. "Do you know any?"

"Nippets?" Lapis sounded intrigued. "Does this have anything to do with the lovely pin you were so reluctant to set aside?"

"Akira gave it." Suuzu tipped his head back, seeking Lapis's gaze. "I only recently learned that there are messages carried by each type of egg. Randolla told me that a yellow egg means, 'irresistible connection.'"

"And Tsumiko mentioned that red nippets having something to do with dragons ...?" Hajime added in a leading tone, "Do you know why?"

"As it happens, I do. Give me a moment to gather my thoughts."

Moments turned into minutes, but Lapis insisted on helping Suuzu from the bath, swathing him in robes and tucking him into a chair near his hearth. Dragons always *did* try to banish chills. Only after Suuzu's hair was dry and brushed and treated with oil did Lapis sit on the sofa opposite, Hajime's hand in his, as if trying to hold onto the memory of him.

"Nippets with red feathers are known as Zeriel's nippet. It is their formal name in all the records of preservationists and ephemerologists. And in certain types of courting lore, including avian. Zeriel's is a time-honored tale, which I suppose means ... it's very old."

"Will you tell it?" Suuzu asked, his fingers smoothing over the yellow egg, then moving on to the red one.

"With pleasure. Ah! Strictly speaking, Zeriel's story is not a romance. However, many of the meanings attached to the red nippets *are*." With a careless shrug, Lapis added, "I've always liked romantic subtexts. Perhaps that—and your own hopes—will color my account."

Hajime leaned against Lapis and said, "Zeri's story has always been one of my favorites."

"You know it?" Lapis asked in surprise.

"I do."

"Then why didn't you tell Suuzu yourself?"

"Because he will not forget your words. And you will tell it true." Hajime patiently explained, "You sympathize, I think."

Lapis trilled softly and smiled at the tree. Then seeking Suuzu's gaze, he said, "A bard could unfold this with more grandeur, but I can provide context for the answer you seek."

Suuzu could only nod.

"There once was a star who loved a dragon, for the dragon had a way with words. His songs drew Zeri close, and his stories held him captive. Other stars noticed and remarked upon Zeri's obsession, but he followed wherever the dragon went, becoming little more than a drifter.

"The dragon *also* noticed, and he called out to the star. In the course of things, the two became friendly. Zeri would have done almost anything for the dragon. Almost. Because he couldn't bear to leave the sky.

"The dragon didn't think this a slight. Instead, friendship became such a source of strength—for both of them—that in the fullness of time, the dragon summoned forth wings. For the sake of his star, a dragon regained the sky."

Suuzu pondered that, and eventually inclined his head.

Lapis nested his fingers together, and his tone took on a lilt. "Red nippets are held dear by those who understand unrequited love. The meaning of a red feather—and presumably the red eggshell—is 'heart's call' and 'loved from afar.' There are also traditions that lend a more nuanced meaning: 'passion beneath the surface,' 'patience and perseverance,' 'closing distances,' 'overcoming obstacles,' and more personal messages." Eyes out of focus, the dragon offered two. "'My heart beats for you.' Or ... 'my blood sings for you.'"

Suuzu privately favored one of the earlier interpretations.

Loved from afar.

13

JUST JACKIE

Suuzu stood before the window, lost in thought. There were many trees surrounding Stately House, and any might do for building a nest. Akira had asked for a treehouse. He should look for one to suit their needs. Although a house on the ground might be better, since the child would want to plant their golden seed beside it. That was traditional. But ... surely that would require Argent's input.

A small noise made Suuzu turn.

The door that connected his room to Boniface's swung partway open. He stood there, barefoot and uncertain. "I ... can't seem to fall asleep. And there was a light."

Suuzu extended a hand. "You may enter."

Boniface edged forward, peering around Suuzu's room. "Where's that Nonny person?"

"He needs sleep. As do you." Taking a coaxing tone, he urged, "Join me."

The man tiptoed fully into the open. "I'm not intruding?"

"Do you know about Amaranthine sleep patterns? I will not need to rest until next month." Suuzu crossed to a deep couch which held an inviting array of blankets and pillows. Perfect for nest-building. With a twitch of fingers, he invited, "Come here by me."

"What's that?" asked Boniface.

On a low table, Nonny had left a tray. The assortment of nibbles had failed to tempt him. "Would you like something? Help yourself."

"You didn't eat again?"

"I was not hungry."

Boniface eyed him critically. "Everyone keeps trying to get you to eat. Why won't you?"

"I ... was not hungry."

"Well, I'm not sleepy. But we both know I need it."

Suuzu fussed with the arrangement of pillows, then shook out a blanket. "Perhaps I will manage something if you will share with me ...?"

Boniface clutched a dressing gown over silk pajamas. "To be clear ... I'm not gay. That's my brother."

Inclining his head, Suuzu said, "That was not the kind of comfort I meant to offer. I am promised to someone."

"And you take your promises seriously."

"I do." And more softly, "I miss him."

Boniface blinked. "So ... you're gay?"

"The one I yearn for *is* male. But I am not like Jacques, who finds things to admire in many kinds of people. For me, there is only Akira."

"Jackie's always had flings and fuck buddies, but that doesn't mean gay chaps can't be monogamous." Boniface generously added, "There's probably a flag for your sort of queer. There are flags for everything. I'd find it for you, but … Argent nicked my phone."

Suuzu sat and patted the space at his side. "Rest a while. Keep me company."

This time, Boniface closed the distance, sitting so near their arms touched. "Do you like my brother?"

"I do not dislike him."

"I still can't get my head around it. Why is everyone so gone on Jackie?"

"Jacques is a good man."

"Is he, though?"

Suuzu hated that Jacques was probably touching Akira, teasing Akira, and most especially sharing a bed with Akira. But he believed every word when he retorted, "Jacques is one of the finest men I know. Might *ever* know."

"Are you putting him on par with diplomats and world leaders?"

"He surpasses them."

"But … *why*?"

Unsure how to explain, Suuzu withdrew his phone and opened up a folder in his photo gallery. He asked, "How do you see your brother?"

"Jackie is eccentric and expensive and exhausting. Flippant with those who are due respect. Polite to waiters and wastrels and waifs. A total hedonist with a knack for getting into pretty boys' pants. The life of both the party and the after-party, because everybody—and I do mean *everybody*—finds him oh, so bloody charming."

Suuzu ventured, "Are you envious?"

"Annoyed. He gets away with so much shite. Even now, Jackie's knocking elbows with the Amaranthine elite. Like … he might not be in the Council's pants, but you're all in his pocket. And you love it there." Boniface puffed out his cheeks and swore. "He's got the whole world on a string, but he's just … hell, it's just Jackie!"

"Would you like to know how I see your brother?"

14

CLAN COLORS

Boniface braced himself for another litany of all the ways his younger brother was brilliant. But Suuzu only showed him a series of photos. Jacques was in all of them, and most of the time, he was the center of attention.

Out on the lawn, saluting from the bottom of a dogpile of crossers.

At a child-sized table, knees almost to his chin, pretending to take tea with three little girls.

In an enormous bath, crowded together with half a dozen boys, all blowing soap bubbles.

Under a bower, bending to fix the knot of Argent's necktie.

Against pillows, offering a lazy smile, a sleeping baby sprawled upon his chest.

Between two Amaranthine blokes, who pressed their cheeks to his while raising champagne flutes.

"Here at Stately House, most of us call your brother *Uncle Jackie*. He insists on table manners and carrying handkerchiefs. He's famous for silk dressing gowns and croissant cravings. He takes extra turns in the naproom, even though Argent should be enough of a handful for any man. When Jacques found out that most of the children here could not swim, he founded the Fundoshi Swim Club so the beach would not pose a threat."

Boniface asked, "What's a fundoshi?"

A few snapshots served to answer *that* question. He paused at one in which a lineup of men—Jacques and Suuzu included—flexed and flashed grins over their shoulders.

"Very cheeky."

"If you were to visit in summer ...."

"Lord, no." And zooming in, Boniface exclaimed, "*Mon dieu*, is Jackie standing next to Josheb Dare?"

"Yes." Clearing his throat, Suuzu added, "His visits are not a matter of record."

"Lips sealed," he promised distractedly. "Who's the Adonis?"

Suuzu leaned over. "Ah. That is Sonnet."

"Oh. My. God." And recalling the wolf's words at the Office of Ingress, he blurted, "Jackie's gone on him, isn't he?"

"Everyone loves Sonnet."

"That's not what I meant, and you know it."

Suuzu seemed puzzled. "Wolves do not mingle freely. Traditionally, they are as monogamous as avians."

"She has a thing for him, though." Boniface pointed insistently. "I met her. And while there's no way Jackie would bother with a lady, this ...? He'd be all over this."

"Jacques is a gentleman."

"All this ...?" Boniface waved at the photo collections. "I've never seen this side of Jackie, but I know my brother. He falls in love fast. And falls into bed faster."

To Boniface's confusion, Suuzu tensed and ... sort of chirped ... and swayed.

"What? Oh, lord, you don't look well. What is it?" And at the expression of utter misery on Suuzu's face, he tensely asked, "Should I go for help?"

In a wink, another person was there, bending over them. The fellow with cascading red flowers all up in his hair. Suuzu took one look into his face and emitted a pensive little mewl.

"Do you remember me?" asked Hajime.

"Hajime!" Wrapping his arms around the tree person's waist, Suuzu clung.

Boniface fidgeted over the emotional display. "You, there. Tree-dad. Do him a favor. Know any more nippet stories?"

Suuzu turned his head and blinked damp lashes at Boniface. "How do *you* know about them?"

"I've got ears, haven't I? A star pining for a dragon. Unrequited love. Heart's call. All that."

"What?" Suuzu asked. "Lady never said all of that?"

"Nooo. Lapis did. Two hours past, more or less." Boniface angled his head toward the connecting door. "I told you. Couldn't sleep. And Lord Mossberne has a carrying sort of voice."

"A dragon's voice *is* difficult to ignore. I am not surprised he lured you closer." Hajime patted Suuzu's hair. "I was here when he told you the story of Zeriel's nippet, so you forgot. People do tend to lose track of red things in my presence."

Suuzu slowly shook his head. "I do not remember."

"Lord, who cares. You like hearing about them, don't you. Pick another color."

"Yes," agreed Hajime. "Nestle in, and I will do my part. Perhaps the coral nippet ...? To honor your clan colors."

Suuzu pulled together blankets, and Boniface snagged two fat biscuits from the tray. Pushing one into Suuzu's hand he ordered, "Eat all of that before he finishes our bedtime story, there's a good lad."

Which put a sulky expression on the illustrious spokesperson's face. But maybe he really was just a lad, because he took a largeish bite, almost like he needed to prove he could. As Hajime set up his story, he wriggled down amidst the blankets until his head rested on Boniface's shoulder. So maybe he'd been forgiven for whatever he'd said to set all this off.

"When time was young and the world was new, there were no Ephemera to be found anywhere in the Widelands. Instead, they were treasured up in celestial places. Small and varied, bright as gems, each creature playing a valued role, for such is the balance and intricacy of the Maker's design."

Boniface asked, "What's the Widelands?"

"Here," said Hajime. "In Amaranthine lore, those who inhabit the skies call our earthbound realm the Widelands."

"Has a nice ring to it." And he nudged Suuzu before pointedly taking a bite of biscuit.

Suuzu followed suit.

"The Ephemera flourished, so that the courts of sun, moon, and sky overflowed with them. And as will sometimes happen, they stole across boundaries. A few here. A bounty there. By diverse means and for various reasons, Ephemera found their way into the Widelands, where they were strangers."

"And regular people can't see them," said Boniface.

"They existed unnoticed, lost and alone, and this did not please the Maker. So a shepherd was chosen from among the angels, and the smallest of flocks was given into Mondriel's care, for he has a special affection for minutia."

"Details *are* important. And often expensive." Boniface poked Suuzu again, and they both took another bite.

"Mondriel sought good places for the Ephemera, for he knew

their needs. He wanted them to be appreciated, so he guided them into places where the Amaranthine would discover them … and treasure them." Hajime's lips quirked. "Ephemera are harmless, but they *do* get up to mischief. They offer amusement, and they are said to be harbingers of heaven."

"You like them?"

"I do. Very much."

"What about you, Suuzu?"

The phoenix stirred enough to admit, "I can see them, but perhaps I do not appreciate them enough."

"Is that what they mean in courting lore, then? New appreciation?" Looking between Hajime and Suuzu, he added, "The whole friends-to-lovers trope."

Suuzu blinked up at him, and his expression slowly shifted. "You cannot see Ephemera."

"I'm half convinced they're a Betweener hoax."

"You don't believe in them?"

"I *do*. Silly not to. Here's proof." Boniface nodded at Suuzu's pin. "I can't see nippets, but I can see their eggs just fine."

"Akira is an ordinary human, but he can see nippets now." Suuzu shyly shared, "When he left the pin with me, he told me that seeing nippets was a small thing, but it was *something*. A good beginning."

"How'd you get your boyo to see the unseen?"

"Sigils." Suuzu frowned in obvious consternation. "That is also a secret."

"You'll forget you told me, and I'll remember not to say."

Suuzu's eyes widened. "That … had not occurred to me. Why *do* you remember?"

"Haven't the foggiest. And it's dead useless as superpowers go." Averting his eyes, he admitted, "Seeing nippets sound nicer."

Suuzu gravely said, "You are a lovely person, Boniface Smythe."

"Lord. Don't be embarrassing." Clearing his throat, he said, "So … Hajime. Is that all the meanings attached to a phoenix-colored nippet?"

With a small shake of his head that scattered additional red petals, Hajime slowly and patiently relayed, "Beauty, whimsy, and showing love in small ways. It can also mean 'you are a bright spot in my day.' But coral nippets are *especially* treasured by avians who agree to a bonding that will take them far from home. Those who are joining another village or enclave like the reminder that it is possible to flourish in new places."

Boniface said, "But I'll remind you later. It's the friends-to-lovers bird. New appreciation. That's the ticket."

15

CAT TOY

Suuzu *liked* Boniface, which surprised him. It had also surprised him to come out of a dozy haze and find the man slumped across his lap, hand tucked under his chin, snoring lightly.

Based entirely on his postures and inflections, Suuzu was sure that Boniface liked him, too. They'd forged a bond of trust with unusual speed. And to Suuzu's increasing consternation, he couldn't recall *why* they'd become friends.

Today, they were making a second attempt at introducing Boniface to Stately House's felines. And they'd started small. Kyrie said, "This one is Magnifique. And here is Meilleur, and this is Douceur."

"All French names?"

"Yes. Cat and Canary and Uncle Jackie helped us choose." Kyrie fit his hand into Boniface's and asked, "Did you know Kith names nearly always have four letters?"

Boniface frowned. "In which language?"

"That is a very good question! Some of it depends on country of origin and the quirks of their language. Wordplay is often a factor. So are terms that hold significance to the family. However, Aunt Sansa says that many Kith actually have two names. One is a secret, known only to their parents. The other is a four-letter name in English, which is registered with the In-between, since they keep extensive records of Kith pedigrees."

"Aha. You like the idea of having a secret name?"

"I *do* think it would be interesting to have two names."

"You have three, hyphen notwithstanding. Or did you mean you want a middle name. They're nothing special. I'd swear they're tacked on just to embarrass children."

"Middle names?"

"Don't you have them hereabouts?" The man blandly confessed, "My full name is Boniface Percival Christobel Yves Smythe."

Kyrie's eyes widened. "Truly?"

"Alas, 'tis true. And it's difficult to say that any of them are truly mine, since my names belong to rich relatives. Dear Maman undoubtedly hoped they would show appreciation for each homage by leaving me a bequest."

"So there is a Boniface in your lineage?"

"My maternal grandfather's eldest brother. Heir to a vineyard and modest estates on assorted islands. And a savvy investor."

"Did he leave you a fortune?"

"Maman lobbied hard for my inclusion in his will. But once his wealth was divided between the children and grandchildren of four different wives …? Table scraps, really."

"Do you like your name?"

"I'm used to it." With a small pout, he added, "I like it better than every effort to shorten it."

"Uncle Jackie calls you Bon-Bon."

"Little brothers are lamentable brats." Brightening, the man asked, "Has dear Jackie never admitted to *his* full name?"

"Oh," Kyrie gasped. "No, he has not."

"Revenge is mine! Write this down. Better yet, have it mono-grammed onto a set of handkerchiefs." Boniface cheerfully announced, "Jacques Auberon Laurent Beaufoy Smythe. Although he did threaten to have it legally changed. Could be anything, now."

To Suuzu's amusement, Kyrie *did* go for pen and paper. And had Boniface check the spelling.

Names.

His child would need a name. Something traditional to his clan? Or would a Japanese name be better? It would be their first language. Maybe Akira would like to choose?

"Wolves give pack names," Kyrie announced. "It is another way to gain a new one."

"And what might that be?" Boniface inquired, actually sounding curious.

"A nickname that captures the essence of who you are."

Just then, Nonny arrived with five enormous felines padding in his wake. "Right, then! This lot agreed to give you another go. Deece helped persuade them."

The cat clansman slipped into the room and leaned against the wall beside the door. It was probably good he was going to oversee things. His boys could be mischievous. Suuzu offered a grateful gesture.

Deece responded in kind.

A moment later, five furry rumps hit the floor.

Proof they respected their papa.

Suuzu wasn't surprised when Nonny took charge—Deece was a bashful person—and Nonny was ostensibly stepping into Jacques' usual role. But without his mentor's aplomb.

"You've heard of Kith, yeah?" asked Nonny.

Boniface stifled a sigh. "I have."

"Stately House has plenty on account of Minx having two litters. She's from a jaguar clan. The father's a hearthcat."

"What's that?"

"*Who's* that," Nonny corrected. "First thing you gotta remember is that Kith are people, and you don't want any of them taking a disliking."

"Right. Fine. How do I win them over?" Boniface had a vague idea of treats and petting. He couldn't quite picture twitching a cat toy for them to pounce.

Nonny rolled his eyes. "For starters, you don't talk about people who're right in front of you. It's rude."

"Did I?"

"You totally did."

"Well, I'm not used to addressing pets as people."

"They're not pets, Bon-Bon. They're people, the same as you and me, and you're pissing them off."

"*There!*" Boniface pointed an accusing finger. "You're doing it, too."

"Wha'd I do?"

Turning to the row of felines, he declared, "Nonny just referred to you lot as if you weren't right here. Much as I did. *Is* it rude? I'd like a second opinion."

Nonny swore softly.

Five black felines looked from Nonny to Boniface and back

again, like spectators at a tennis tournament.

Boniface played to his audience. Being catty? *Well* within his capabilities. "I was expecting introductions involving four-letter names, not four-letter words."

"You utter arse. And here I thought you might be more comfortable with animals."

Suuzu tentatively interjected, "Maybe this was a bad idea ...?"

But Boniface cut across him, swift as a blade. "You just told me they're *not* animals. Ah, *pardonnez-moi*. I've gone and done it again. With deepest apologies to the clowder."

Nonny swore volubly, which Boniface took to mean he'd won. Really, it wasn't fair to toy with him. Goat boy never would have survived in Uppington's social circles. Or amidst Maman's set in Paris.

Suuzu firmly asked, "Deece, would you take over?"

A tall Amaranthine with hair the color of fine mahogany filled Boniface's view. "Hi."

"How do you do?" Boniface returned.

"I'm Deece."

"Suuzu did mention."

He nodded toward the felines. "The boys are curious."

"About me? Whatever for?"

"There's a kindred scent. And they know Jacques pretty well. They're his training partners."

Boniface sized up the strapping fellow. "You're Jackie's personal trainer?"

"Yes."

Nonny butted in again. "Deece is part of Stately House's security team."

Boniface ignored him. "You and Jacques are ... involved?"

"We're ... friendly? I guess ...?"

"Friendly *how*?"

"They're friends, you idiot!" exploded Nonny.

"I was only *wondering*."

Nonny exclaimed, "You can't just go around asking everyone you meet if they've had sex with your brother!"

"*Non*?" he asked innocently. "Why? Have you?"

Flushing bright red, Nonny hissed, "I hate you so much right now!"

It was so childish, Boniface hesitated. And took a longer look at the mortified crosser. "Lord. Are you perhaps ... as young as you seem?"

Goat boy froze.

Deece stepped between them. And nodded.

Boniface knew regret.

Turning to Suuzu, he muttered, "I *told* you I'm pants with kids."

16

HANDLING ARSES

Boniface wasn't one to back down, and he certainly never apologized. But that was in very different circles than this. Words were his weapons, the only ones he possessed, given the tight rein Maman kept on both him and his assorted inheritances.

Between her and Jackie, salvaging any dignity had always been a nightmare. But a careful combination of feigned ignorance and aloof propriety had been holding him in good stead for years. If Boniface was completely honest, he'd learned the trick from Argent.

Reviewing his part in the verbal sparring, he gathered that Nonny was uncomfortable with Jackie's promiscuity. Or this insinuation of it. Or perhaps about his own inclinations. The idiot boy was half goat, for pity's sake. That had to be *at least* as limiting as the constant chaperonage of one's mother.

Boniface was about to call on Hajime to see if the tree could make the lot of them forget his uncouth behavior when someone new strolled into the room.

Deece looked relieved.

Nonny looked embarrassed.

Suuzu looked worried.

Going to stand behind Nonny, the newcomer slipped both arms around the young man's waist, scanned the group, and naturally singled him out. With a dangerous light in stunning green eyes, he inquired, "Who did this?"

"Shove off, Cat," grumbled Nonny.

"You're in a temper, and Jacques *did* ask me to look after you."

Goat boy shot the guy an injured look.

Nuzzling his hair, he crooned, "*Do* let Uncle Catalan dote, for he loves his feisty satyr."

"I'm not yours."

"Oh, I know whose you are." Cheek pressed to Nonny's, Cat lightly inquired, "Who is the gentleman with Parisian tastes and ... oh, my. Say it's so."

"Yeah, yeah," Nonny grumped. "He's Jacques' brother."

"Lord. I *do* have a name."

Deece spoke up then. "Thank you for coming, Catalan. I'm useless in a battle of wits. You and Canarian are better with words."

"Alas, Canary is otherwise embroiled. But I have nothing else pressing at the moment." His gaze locked with Boniface's. "That means I shall be your new opponent. Shall we ... *chat*?"

Boniface looked to Suuzu for guidance.

The phoenix explained, "Catalan Evernhold is Deece's older brother. He and Canarian are both part of Hisoka Twineshaft's cortege, but they make their home at Stately House. Perhaps you noticed the theater? The railroad?"

"Ours." And with a sultry smile, Catalan inquired, "Shall we exchange names in the manner of friends? I am quite sure there's room in my heart for you."

Nonny muttered, "Bon-Bon's an arse."

"I have considerable experience handling arses."

Goat boy elbowed his self-proclaimed uncle. "Don't you dare seduce Jacques' brother. That would be weird."

"No promises. I have a thing for brothers."

"No you don't. Canarian *showed* me your family tree. You and he aren't even related."

Catalan asked, "How much farther off topic do we need to drift? I want to know which of you beautiful boys I should be taking to task."

Nonny grimaced. "I messed up. Let him get to me."

Stepping forward, Boniface said, "The fault is entirely mine. While it's not really any kind of excuse, I didn't realize I was dealing with someone half my age."

"Oi, I'm an adult!"

"You're easy prey." And bracing himself, he offered his hand to Catalan. "Are you Nonny's ... guardian? Boniface Smythe."

"Are you prepared to make reparations, Monsieur Smythe?"

"What sort?" Again, he looked to Suuzu.

The phoenix said, "He knows you are contrite, and that *should* suffice. What are you after, Catalan?"

"Him! I'm overflowing with curiosity about him."

Boniface applied to the felines, loudly whispering, "*He's* doing it now. But does anyone take him to task?"

Nonny snorted. "Arse."

But this time, he mostly sounded amused.

Cat slipped from behind Nonny and collected Boniface's hand. "You enjoy verbal sparring? Your brother is adept. Did he learn from you?"

"I *am* the older brother."

"And could you set him back as you've done our Nonny?"

"Jackie and I are evenly matched. Which is to say we argued incessantly. Uncle Percy used to say it was a shame we never chose the same side in a debate. In another time and place, we would have conquered the world," he quoted bitterly.

"You and I, we'll have a conversation, yes? Walk with me a while. I can show you our theater, and we can quibble like old friends." Catalan was suddenly very close. "Why needle when you can slash and parry and riposte. Spar with me in English. Or do you prefer French? How is your Spanish?"

Suuzu warbled a worried note.

Deece added a cautioning, "Brother …?"

"Oi! I'm telling Jacques if you bugger Bon-Bon," snapped Nonny.

"This is not *that* kind of conversation." Catalan took a dramatic tone. "Do you know how rare a man of Jacques' talents is? But the elder brother of such a man? Oh, my heart. I must know what Boniface can do. And then …!"

Then *what*? Boniface would have liked to know.

All eyes turned to Suuzu.

He slowly inclined his head. "The possibility is worth exploring. If Boniface agrees."

"Now, now. We've already established that it's rude to speak about a person when they're standing right in front of you." Boniface searched Suuzu's face, then turned to Catalan. "I can tell you have your hopes up, but I'm *not* my brother."

"Jacques is inimitable." Cat waved a hand. "And he is devotedly Argent's. But you could be my gift to Canarian. We would bring out your potential, and … ah, I will be so proud. Because if you go along with my little scheme, perhaps you could make it happen. You and your brother on the same side, challenging the world. Jacques in Argent's keeping. You in Hisoka's."

17

THREE BEST FRIENDS

few hours later, Suuzu reclaimed Boniface from aboard the *Cat's Canary*, the antique locomotive that pulled a series of similarly historic train cars, including the berth that the Evernhold brothers called home.

Boniface was quieter than usual, his smile tight-lipped, his gaze turned inward.

Suuzu hadn't even considered the possibility that Boniface might be an asset to the Amaranthine Council, but he could see it now. A man from Jacques' same household, exposed to the same social circle, with the same polish and poise. Capable of steering a conversation and verbally outmaneuvering an opponent. Different from Jacques, possibly in a similar way that Juuyu was different from Suuzu. Swift and sharp and sure.

Still, the first thing out of Suuzu's mouth was, "Did he make you uncomfortable?"

"*Non.*" Boniface glanced around, as if surprised to find they were on a woodland path. "If you really thought him capable of something illicit, why on earth did you let me go off alone with him?"

Suuzu ducked his head. "Catalan would not … ah. Not without consent …?"

"So don't insult him by asking if he succumbed to a fiendishly carnal impulse and dragged me off to some tawdry boudoir." And with a twinkle in his eye, he added, "You're probably at that age when it seems like it, but not everything is about sex."

A flustered chirp escaped Suuzu.

Boniface huffed a short laugh. "I'll bet Jackie loves to tease you."

"He does. I think he always knew how I felt. And sympathized."

"Jackie has done his fair share of pining. Maybe he's finally at that age when *he* realizes that not everything is about sex."

Suuzu must have looked doubtful, because Boniface laughed again.

"Did Catalan offer you a place?"

"*Non*. But he offered to introduce me to Canarian, should I choose to extend my trip."

"Do you like the idea?"

Boniface hesitated. "I like the idea of escaping Maman. I told Catalan as much, and he was surprisingly sympathetic. Did you know feline clans are matriarchal?"

"I did."

"Those two also fled their mother's plans for them. I'd fit right in."

Suuzu ventured, "You would *belong*."

Boniface edged closer when a group of wolves strolled past. Their tails were at an easy sway, and they raised hands in silent greeting.

"Rather a lot of wolves hereabouts."

The man sounded nervous, but the stress scent was gone. Progress. "Yes. They're Elderboughs."

"As in Adoona-soh Elderbough?"

"She sent two allotments when Argent decided to expand

our boundaries and establish this enclave. The pack adds to our protections."

"*Our* boundaries. *Our* protections." Boniface eyed him sharply. "How many other members of the Amaranthine Council consider this home? Or home away from home?"

"I ... probably shouldn't say. Argent would consider that a private matter."

"I could ask your tree. He probably knows."

Suuzu frowned. "My ... tree?"

Boniface drew up short. "You know, it's eerie whenever you do that."

"What have I done?"

"Forgotten the bloke who keeps scattering flower petals in the vicinity." He pointed to the ground. Turning to the side, he asked, "Does it get lonely, being forgotten?"

"You are a pleasant surprise, Boniface Smythe. Be sure to tell your fine cats that we have become acquainted. And why."

"Hajime," Suuzu murmured. "I apologize for my rudeness."

The tree pulled him down into a hug and kissed his cheek. "I will remind you as often as necessary that I am here ... and that you are one of mine ... and that I love you. *Almost* as much as Akira does."

Gathering hazy thoughts, Suuzu asked, "Why did Boniface notice you before I did?"

"Who can say?"

Boniface's smile was really more of a smirk. "He's been walking with us ever since we left the train. So ... should I be concerned that you're leading me into a murky wood where none can hear my cries for help? Or did you have a destination in mind?"

"The gateway." Suuzu pointed. "We are meeting Kyrie, who wants to introduce you to his two best friends."

Kyrie and Lilya were already there. The girl waved with her whole arm, and Kyrie hurried forward, first touching Hajime's hand, then Boniface's, before presenting himself to Suuzu. "You have not yet met Rifflet." Raising a finger, he added, "Rifflet is a secret, Uncle Boniface."

"You may rely upon my discretion."

Next Kyrie asked, "Did you know about wind dragons, Grandfather?"

"Yes. Yours has a sweet nature."

"Oh, Rifflet is adamantly Lilya's. But he has been polite to everyone he meets." Touching Boniface's arm, he added, "Lilya and I were born on the same day, and we have always been together. She is my best friend. Ever is not here yet, but we are his best friends, too."

"Can two people have the same best friend?" Boniface posed amiably.

"Oh, yes. We are three, and that is best for us."

While they discussed the nuances of a three-way bond, Suuzu presented his hands to Lilya and admitted, "I am amazed."

"Most people are. Even Sinder thought wind dragons were extinct." And to the little creature, "Rifflet, this is Uncle Suuzu. He's here a lot, since he belongs to Uncle Akira."

Suuzu liked hearing it said ... and smiled.

However, the wind dragon cheeped worriedly.

"I am a phoenix. He may not trust me."

So Lilya launched into a lengthy explanation as to why Suuzu was a tame phoenix and an acknowledged ambassador for peace.

"Does he understand?" Suuzu asked.

"He does. Sinder and Lapis can both hear Rifflet's voice." She shyly added, "So can I. I'm a fellow."

"Welcome news. All of it."

She went up on tiptoe and kissed his cheek. "Welcome home."

He lightly touched her hair, which she wore in two snug braids, and turned to make his own introduction. "Boniface came to visit, not realizing his brother was away."

"Oh, that *is* bad luck," Lilya said sympathetically. "But here, maybe Rifflet can cheer you up. His name means 'ribbon' in Old Amaranthine."

Suuzu was amazed all over again when the little dragon flew through the air and draped himself around Boniface's shoulders, nuzzling at his jawline in a bid for attention.

Once again, no trace of fear marked the man. Eyes sparkling, he murmured, "Elegant little thing, aren't you? Come where I can admire you better."

Moments later, Boniface sat on one of the nearby benches, Rifflet coiled upon his knees, making pleased peeps as he was petted. The man was wholly absorbed, despite the long howl that signaled an arrival, which was soon answered by a deep bark.

Ever Starmark passed through the barrier at a trot and immediately veered into a group hug with Kyrie and Lilya. Tail wagging, he next marched up to Boniface and announced, "You're new, so I need to sniffen you."

"If you must," the man answered distractedly.

"So it's okay to touch?"

Boniface finally met Ever's gaze, and his brows lifted. "What sort of crosser are you?"

"Dog!"

"Right. Carry on. This side, though. Mind the tree."

"Which tree?"

Boniface scooted a little more firmly into Hajime's side, for the tree had joined him on the bench. But Ever hadn't noticed. Probably couldn't. Not unless Hajime called attention to himself.

Suuzu had to wonder if Boniface's scent would forever be mingled with the tree's scent in the boy's mind.

When Ever's father strode through the barrier, he took the time to greet and thank the Elderboughs on guard duty, but his eyes were already on Boniface. The man hadn't noticed yet, and Suuzu found himself watching closely for the inevitable moment of recognition.

Introductions came in a quick staccato. "I'm Ever. He's Da. Who're you?"

Rather spare by Amaranthine standards, but really ... Harmonious Starmark didn't require an introduction. Anywhere.

18

IMPORTANT.ISH

What's this? Could it be? Maker bless, you must be a Smythe."

Boniface glanced up and gaped at the Amaranthine towering over him. Then shot to his feet, unspooling the little wind dragon from his lap and wavering in place.

A big hand caught his elbow. "No need to be alarmed. I'm Harmonious."

"*Lord.*"

With an easy smile, he inquired, "And you would be ...?"

"Harmonious. Starmark."

"Nooo, that's my name. What's yours? *Are* you perhaps a Smythe? Of the Uppington Smythes?"

"You know my brother." Shaking his head, he muttered, "Of course you do. Everyone does."

Harmonious Starmark's smile had significantly more impact in person than on the telly. "Jacques is a man of unparalleled loyalty." Patiently offering his palms, he said, "I can't very well go around calling you *Jacques' brother*. Everyone has their own path. And their own name …?"

"Boniface." He couldn't believe Jackie had never mentioned an acquaintance of this caliber, but—come to think of it—there were a lot of things Boniface wouldn't be mentioning to anyone either. Perhaps being trusted with secrets was part of what made a man loyal. "But my brother … he's just … Jackie."

"That's part of his appeal."

"I don't see it. I don't understand."

Bending so near that the coppery sheen of his eyes was devastating, Harmonious asked, "Do you want to?"

Boniface fidgeted.

Harmonious beamed. "If you want to know the man your brother has become since leaving home, you'll have many rivals for his time and attention." With a gentle pat to Boniface's back, he rumbled, "Don't lose heart, lad. Few people are as perceptive as Jacques. If you tell him what's in your heart, he'll understand."

Could it be that simple? He doubted it, but he murmured, "Thank you, sir."

"Now … hmm. What's that scent?" Harmonious' nose was twitching. "I know it, but I can't … quite … recall. Hmm. Does Argent know he has a … ah … new scent?"

Baffled glances were traded. Boniface wasn't sure it was his place to speak up.

Kyrie promised, "It's all right, Da. Dad knows."

Boniface was still marveling over the closeness of family ties that meant Kyrie called Ever's father *Da* when a very familiar wolf skipped into view, very obviously trying to keep to a ladylike pace.

"Sonnet!" Harmonious boomed, opening his arms to catch her. "I came as soon as I could. Rampant has been boasting, and Sentinel struts. Their only complaint is that you didn't come by us."

She mumbled something against his shoulder.

Gaze soft, Harmonious assured, "You've chosen a good place. Ah, and *here* is the reason for my visit. *Someone* let me know that the pack has been graced by another crosser! Might you be she, little lass?"

Popping out from behind Sonnet to present her palms, the mouse-child declared, "I'm Linnea, and I'm almost six."

Sonnet announced, "My granddaughter. Hazel's little one."

Harmonious knelt to gather up tiny hands. "I've met your parents. You look a bit like Florent."

"Rimesteads are frost-kissed," she declared proudly. "Also, my name is a kind of flower. Papa says in some places, it's called a twin flower. Mother couldn't give me a twin, but she could give me a twin name."

"Very appropriate for the child of a grove. Ever, come meet your ... well now. In human terms Ever is Sonnet's uncle, making Linnea a great, great niece, but *cousin* might be cozier. What do you think, Sonnet?"

While they sorted through endearments, Boniface saw another person step through the gate, two sizeable cases bumping along behind her. She was tall, slender, sophisticated, and exuding a very familiar variety of perturbation. The thwarted traveler. Or worse, a thwarted woman.

Glancing at a dainty wristwatch, she inquired, "Does anyone know if Sensei has returned? Nobody will tell me *anything*!"

Boniface was honestly relieved that he had no answer to offer.

She looked like the type who expected men like him to come to heel.

Suuzu hurried to her, and she asked him something, all concern and confusion. Her hand caressed his cheek, and he said something in a low voice, quite solemn. The woman's expression transformed to surprise, then awe, then … lord, if she didn't squeal like a schoolgirl and fling her arms around him.

So … family. Or close friend of the family.

Then Lapis Mossberne arrived in a dignified swirl of cloak and midnight blue hair. "Isla, my dear. Allow me?"

"Oh, but Timur was supposed to …!"

"Your brother was summoned, much as you have been. Come along. You, too, Suuzu. Argent awaits."

The phoenix startled to attention, then sought Boniface's gaze.

"I'll be fine," Boniface assured, waving vaguely in his nephew's direction. "Kyrie can show me the way back …?"

Kyrie promised, "I will."

Boniface let the boy tow him to where Ever and Lilya had claimed a bench. Guessing they'd know, he ventured, "Who was that woman who's just arrived?"

Lilya said, "That's Isla. My sister."

"She mentioned Timur."

"Our brother," she confirmed with a smile. "There's a lot of us. And more coming. Mum's expecting *twins*. Won't that be lovely?"

Boniface thought it sounded terrifying, but something else was worrying him more just now. "Your brother is Timur, the chauffer's son?"

Lilya's brow furrowed, and she looked to Kyrie for help.

"Uncle Boniface means Papka." Kyrie gently explained, "Lilya's father is Michael Ward. He is both First of Wards—the most powerful reaver in his classification—and the founder of a reaver dynasty. And Isla is Hisoka-sensei's former apprentice and right hand."

"Which all translates to … important …?"

"And famous," said Lilya. "But at home, we're just us. I sometimes forget that most of my favorite people are important-ish."

"So are you," reminded Ever.

Lilya wrinkled her nose. "If I never leave home, I'll always be just me."

"It's a good plan," Kyrie assured.

Boniface decided to have it out. "If I were to … oh, say … take a position in Hisoka Twineshaft's cortege, would that Isla person be bossing me around?"

Lilya rolled her eyes. "You don't have to join any cortege to get bossed. Isla bosses *everyone*."

"Papka says she's a force for good on an international level," Kyrie helpfully added.

Boniface guessed that made Isla Ward the first downside in a future that had oh, so briefly been nothing but bright. Jamming his hands into his trouser pockets, he muttered, "Bloody hell."

Across the way, Sonnet, whose ears were too sharp by far, growled.

19

FESTIVAL PREPARATIONS

Boniface could see the house now, which is why he knew they were on a slightly different trajectory. "Where are you taking me?"

"I will keep my promise to Uncle Suuzu. But first we are taking Ever to Randolla's to be fit for his festival coat." Kyrie smiled. "Mother says you must have one, too."

"We'll all match," said Lilya.

"I've only ever been here in springtime, which invariably involved flower-viewing festivals. What's the done thing in autumn?"

"A frost festival," said Kyrie. "It is an Amaranthine tradition, celebrated by the cozy clans. But we are also borrowing a little bit from Mother's memories. She grew up with the annual Star Festival in Keishi."

"So Stately House's festival is also a crosser?" Boniface posed.

"Yes! Exactly so. We shall bring two worlds together."

"What will you have? Paper lanterns and ices?"

"There will be bonfires on the beach and fireworks. And the

parents of some of our students will come early to set up booths, so there will be food and games.”

“When is this all meant to happen?”

“It depends. Another week. Possibly two. There is much to prepare.” And searching his face, Kyrie asked, “Will you stay?”

“Not sure Argent will put up with me for that long.”

“Maybe if you help with the arrangements ... and have a matching coat ... he will see how much you want to stay.”

Boniface quietly reminded, “I’m only visiting.”

“You *could* stay,” Kyrie countered. “You have family here, too.”

“Mmm,” he replied vaguely. He couldn’t picture Jackie welcoming him with open arms.

“Mother began plans for the festival to give us something to do while we wait.”

Boniface thought back. Had anyone mentioned waiting for something? “What are you waiting on?”

Kyrie hesitated. “Well, for one thing, we are waiting for Uncle Jackie to come home.”

“Lord. You’re throwing an entire festival just for him?”

Lilya glanced back from where she was walking with Ever. Her brown eyes were laughing in a friendly sort of way. He suspected that a girl who had a sister like Isla would understand something about the injustice of siblings.

“No,” Kyrie said, patient as ever. “He is not the only one who has been away. Uncle Akira went with him. And there is Boon. And Sensei. And Inti. And when they come home, they will probably bring many others, as well. It is exciting to think about, and waiting is hard. So ... we are keeping busy.”

“So you’re expecting guests?”

“We are expecting to add to the family.”

“They’ll be crossers?”

"Yes. But for me it is more. I could tell you, but maybe ... could I show you? Later?"

"I think I shall get very good at secrets. People keep heaping them on me."

Kyrie warbled in a prettyish sort of way. He sounded happy, and that lightened Boniface's mood. Then, the lad beckoned for him to bend closer.

"I have a new little sister." And with an achingly sweet smile, Kyrie shared, "I named her Mercy."

Randolla took Boniface into a side room where several bolts of cloth had been artfully draped across a large worktable. "Lady Tsumiko helped with the selection of several traditional patterns. You may choose from among these, or if none are to your taste, I have a few others in the back."

Boniface drew up short when he realized who else was in the room. "Nonny," he greeted.

Goat boy's eyebrows shot up. "Relax, Bon-Bon. I'm not angry anymore. Well, I *am*. But not about you. Unless Cat actually seduced you. Then, I'll be furious. But at him. Not that it ever does any good."

"Your ... uncle ...?"

"Kind of an honorary uncle. He and Canarian are such dads. They've been watching out for me for a while now. Anyhow ... you good?"

"I am unscathed. Catalan and I talked, and I'm to meet

Canarian ... sometime soon." But Boniface was more interested in something else. "Why are you angry?"

"Argent tossed me out of the house. They're doing secret things, and I have a reputation for accidentally overhearing stuff."

"Like what?"

"Hey. The stuff I overhear is for personal enrichment, *not* for spreading rumors." Glancing between him and Randolla, Nonny asked, "Lady decided you need festival togs?"

Boniface turned to the worktable. The patterned cloth was all in clear, bright colors. "This will be very different from the last garment you measured me for."

"By design." Randolla brought out a pattern, then showed him a few finished examples. The short coats were quilted, trimmed in contrasting colors, and fastened with frogs.

They weren't complicated, but Boniface hesitated over having the tailor go to the trouble. "I may not even be here. I don't actually belong."

"You seem to be fitting in well enough," countered the avian.

Boniface cast a sidelong look at Nonny, who was unabashedly listening in. "People tolerate me because they miss my brother."

"You have nothing to offer on your own?"

Boniface thought back over his meeting with Catalan, which had been more informational than anything. There were only vague terms that depended a lot on Canarian's impression of him and Boniface's willingness to learn as he went. He was woefully ignorant, yet ... Jackie had been, too. And Cat thought he had skill sets that would serve well in the diplomatic arena. Boniface wondered if he'd really only be helping Hisoka Twineshaft fill some minority quota. There couldn't be many non-reaver humans in Amaranthine employ.

Finally, he told the truth. "I can't imagine what I have to offer."

"If you cannot see for yourself, perhaps you should rely on the wisdom of those who know you best." Randolla busied himself with a tape measure before amiably adding, "Which is another way of saying you should allow someone to know you well enough that they can guide you onto a good path."

"Randolla? Blue as usual for me," said Nonny. "What about you, Bon-Bon? Got a favorite color?"

"I ... couldn't say. Maman usually has a plan, and it's my filial duty to go along with it. No questions asked. No complaints filed."

"Well, let's see. I'm nowhere near as good at this as Jacques, but you have the same coloring. And he likes to wear green. Says it's flattering."

"Then I shan't wear green."

Nonny snorted. "Guess you'll have to go with your gut ...? Or trust Randolla. He's a pro. What's it Jacques is always saying? The best tailors are tutors."

Boniface considered his options. None of these patterns were going to become the foundation for a new look. This was party frippery, and he really didn't care which he wore. "Hajime, which of these do *you* like?"

And just like that, he had a tree by the hand.

"You *called* me." Hajime sounded impressed.

"Help me pick a color for my festival coat." And since he was certain nobody had known to ask, he checked, "Do you want one, too?"

"Do you think it will help me wait?"

Boniface sighed. "Lord. Are you waiting for Jackie, too?"

"We have met, but no ... he is not the one I want more than anyone. Akira went to find him. To bring him to me."

"Your significant other is a bloke?"

"Tsumiko's and Akira's parent. My Naoki."

Just then, Nonny sidled up and thrust an accusing elbow into

Boniface's ribs. "Oi, Bon-Bon. Who's your friend? And … how come I feel like I know him?"

20

DISCRETION FOR DISCRETION

Suuzu sat quietly while Argent updated everyone on the latest news from the rescue operation, including communication from Boon, Hallow, and Sinder ... along with details from a brief connection via fox dream with Jacques. Suuzu wished Argent had asked Jacques about Akira. *Any* word would have been welcome.

All that mattered to the fox was that the pieces of his plan were moving. However, not everything was in place yet. And the two Suuzu considered most vulnerable were unable to communicate with them. The suspense was painful, but all they could do was wait.

"Which brings me to a matter of less urgency. This isn't Council business, but I'd like to consult with the four of you. I want your opinions."

Isla sat a little straighter in her chair, hands folded, posture pointedly attentive.

Lapis settled back and beckoned for more, regal as a liege lord.

Harmonious simply raised his brows inquiringly.

For his part, Suuzu managed a tight smile, letting Argent know that he was listening.

Satisfied, Argent began. "With regards to this spring's Scattering and the resulting grove, security measures are well in hand, Michael and I, Juuyu and Sinder, and even Jiminy contributed both suggestions and sigilcraft. Our former weak point, the seaside approach, has been made fast, in large part due to Sinder's placement of an underwater array. And the addition of Hajime to the household has only strengthened our position."

Isla piped up. "Who is that, please?"

Argent said, "I would rather not take the time to explain everything now. You haven't had enough exposure to his pollen to be inured to its effects. You'll simply forget everything I say."

Impossible though it might seem, Isla sat straighter. "Excuse me?"

With patience borne of actual fondness, Argent said, "There is a certain variety of Amaranthine tree whose pollen causes those who encounter them to forget them."

Isla blinked. "But that's *fascinating*!"

"Agreed."

"Are they native to any particular area? How long have you known about this variety?"

Argent sighed. "It is difficult to say for certain how long I have been aware since I keep forgetting. Lapis and I have been spending as much time with Hajime as possible in order to build up the necessary resistance. But it takes *time*. My own recall is imperfect. So far, Tsumiko is the only one who can be relied upon to remember him. Presumably the same will be true for Akira. Because Hajime is their parent."

Isla leaned forward. "But that's ... ohhh! Oh, that's brilliant!"

"Agreed," Argent blandly repeated. "Hajime assures me that over time, everyone at Stately House will grow accustomed to the pollen. Until then, I can only assure you that he is here, he is safe, and we are being kept safe because of it. Now … to the subject at hand."

Isla raised her hand again. "Is there any point to this meeting if we're going to forget it as soon as it's over."

Argent sighed even more deeply. "The tree's pollen does not wipe a person's entire memory. Only the parts that have to do with the tree itself. You will recall every part of our discussion *except* anything to do with Hajime. Making further discussion of him irrelevant. You really will forget it all, so I would like to move on."

"Sorry. Yes. Of course."

"Juuyu Farroost has been both helpful and thorough in delineating the rights due to members of an Amaranthine grove—meaning both the trees and their twins—and the responsibilities of those who embark upon plans for their protection. I have already brought in a handful of preservationists. Also, a member of our household has practical experience with the establishment of a grove. Were any of you aware?"

Suuzu, Isla, and Lapis exchanged glances and small headshakes.

Harmonious beamed. "Been there myself. Lovely place. Lovely people."

"I speak with permission," Argent assured. "Sonnet has lived among young trees and tree-kin for the past several decades. Merritt House's grove is relatively young and began quite small, with only three trees. But in recent years, they have expanded, giving shelter to several more varieties. I visited the grove and spoke with Lord Alderny about the more practical aspects of supporting a multi-clan community.

"However, one thing is lacking, and Juuyu Farroost insists it is essential. With the founding of Stately House's grove, we are duty-bound to provide a chronicler."

Suuzu nodded. His brother had spoken true.

"This is a tradition I plan to observe. Bringing in an appropriately qualified scribe is one of my next priorities."

Isla raised her hand.

Argent waved for her to speak.

"Discretion for discretion?" she asked, waiting for them to signal agreement. "As you may know, I work closely with the moths in Sensei's mailroom. Their duties fall directly under my oversight, and they are as flawless as they are tireless in maintaining *so* many records. Have any of you ever met Revic Nightbide?"

Suuzu's hand gesture to the negative matched everyone else's.

"He came to us from eastern Asia, and he's knowledgeable in several languages that were outside Yulwen Dimityblest's pervue. Anyway! For what I suspect is a *very* long time, Revic was the chronicler for a hidden grove."

Harmonious frowned. "And he left?"

Isla nodded. "He offered his services to Sensei shortly before the Emergence became official. He was invaluable in setting up our current mail sorting system, and all of the earliest New Saga records are written in his own hand." She leaned forward. "Because of the foundation he and the other three moth clansmen laid, the mailroom and the records room run smoothly. I think we *could* let him go ... if there was more important work for him to do."

Harmonious fidgeted. "What of the grove he left?"

Isla's expression softened, and her gaze sought Suuzu's. "Revic sometimes speaks of how proud he is that his own daughter—whom he both carried and mentored—took over the work."

Argent's brows lifted. "Promising. Arrange a meeting?"

"Noted!" Isla sang out.

"But ... hear me out?" Argent took a leading tone. "While a

moth is traditional, I believe our ultimate goal at Stately House is to embrace new possibilities."

Harmonious chuckled. "You already know who you want."

"I do, but before I send a message ... *tsk*. The ones I have in mind are not the sort to stay put, and yet I believe they would be a good fit. Perhaps with them *and* a moth ...?" Argent looked uncomfortable. "Do not laugh."

"Ohmigod!" Isla suddenly squealed. "Ohmigod, they would be perfect!"

Suuzu smiled crookedly and asked, "Miss Ward, did you have something to share with the class?"

"Am I right?" Isla begged.

Argent slouched in his chair and drawled, "If we do not have the same people in mind, then our list of candidates has doubled. Go on, child. Show us how clever you are."

Hands clasped, she exclaimed, "The Dare brothers!"

Harmonious barked a laugh that quickly took to rolling. Wiping tears from his eyes, he said, "If you can actually get them to settle, this would be the perfect place. You have my blessing. And support. And ideas for bribery. Lead off with a case of canned ravioli, a cask of star wine, and a puppy. Preferably a blood hound."

"Discretion for discretion ...?" Argent murmured.

All hands again formed the sign for secrecy.

"We already have considerable leverage for my proposal." With a faint smile, Argent confessed, "In the beginning, all I wanted was to secure a steady supply of star wine for Jacques, so we can thank him or blame him. Because ... as it happens, Caleb Dare already visits with considerable regularity. He shares a bond with Andor Skypact. And with Stately House's secret star."

21

WHISTLES AND BELLS

While Nonny wheedled for parts of Hajime's story, even knowing he'd forget all of it before the hour was out, Boniface made his own bid for a tale. "One of the other tailors, a son or son-in-law I think, mentioned that you're avians."

"Cranes," Randolla confirmed.

"Does that mean you know about courtship … things?"

"Certainly. I learned from my father, and I courted my bondmate. And I passed along the traditions to my sons in their turn." With a teasing smile, he asked, "Did you wish to learn a courting dance? Ours aren't as energetic as, say, those of the sparrow clans. Nor as perilous as the mating flights of raptors. But a basic crane step? Yes, I think you could manage."

Boniface admitted, "Those sound interesting, but …."

"But …?"

"Do you know any stories about nippets?"

"A strange request from a man who cannot possibly have

ever seen one."

"It's for Suuzu." Boniface clarified, "I'd like you to tell me a nippet story that Suuzu hasn't learned yet."

"You want to be the one to teach him his lore?"

"Maybe I like gossip."

"Or maybe you like Suuzu."

"The lad's been good to me. I thought I could return the favor."

"Kindness for kindness. Trust for trust. You understand us so well already." And with a friendly little laugh, Randolla asked, "Which colors has he already collected."

"I overheard the story of the red nippets already. And those orange ones. Coral nippets."

"And I've already told him about honey nippets, but that leaves several options. Hmm. How about azure nippets?"

"Blue? *Oui* and *merci!*"

"*Have* you ever seen a nippet? There are books by noted preservationists and ephemerologists, many of which include detailed drawings. The little things are notoriously difficult to photograph, so the old ways are best." So saying, Randolla pulled a tablet of paper close, turned to a fresh page, and began to sketch. "Nippets are known as the world's smallest avians. Tinier even than hummingbirds."

The line of birds that took shape under his pencil were chubby, almost perfectly round, with large eyes, teensy bills, stubby tails, and a wee crest atop their heads.

"Are those life size?" asked Boniface.

"Yes." Randolla asked, "You've seen Suuzu's pin? You know what it means for him?"

Soon, Boniface was up to speed and ready to add to his knowledge. "So … the blue ones?"

"Azure nippets are as blue as the open sky, which is the

realm of winds. The avian clans knew the winds best, having learned to loft themselves along their many paths, but young winds are full of mischief. Fitful. Flighty. Forgetful. And so the Maker chose Bethiel from among the angels to shepherd the winds in their courses, lest they go astray and make trouble for the other sky clans.

"Weather heeded Bethiel, and the winds even vied for his attention. But the expanse of the sky is wide and cold and empty, and he was often lonely. So as he went from place to place, doing his good work, Bethiel would befriend passing avians. Whole flocks of birds danced with the winds he herded, following in his wake. And rather than being bothered by these noisy tagalongs, Bethiel encouraged them with his songs."

"Probably liked the company," Boniface remarked.

"I think so, too." Randolla added to his sketches as he spoke. Suuzu's circlet of nippet eggs. Then a dainty bell with an egg-shaped clapper. "Amaranthine from the avian clans were drawn to Bethiel's songs because they were so sweet, and sometimes, he would sing on behalf of a friend."

"Sing in place of a bird?"

"All avians have voices, but many of us—cranes included—are no songbirds. According to tradition, Bethiel would lend his voice, which can make plain the truth of any matter. In this way, he blessed many courting couples."

Boniface hummed. "So there's the context, but what about the language of it for courtship. All the other nippets had messages to carry, secret meanings. Those are what Suuzu's after, I think."

"'Bethiel's blessing.' Or sometimes, 'daystar's blessing,' since there is another angel and nippet associated with nighttime. Other possibilities are 'the blue sky smiles upon couples,' 'the sky will ring with my song,' and 'dance upon the willing winds.'"

Randolla held his thumb and forefinger apart, the distance as small as a nippet. "I've heard two other messages, one of which is a declaration of hope—'I hear singing.' A blue egg or feather is ... oh, let's call it bashful. A suitor is saying something along the lines of, 'When you're near, I hear singing. Is it the same for you?'"

"I like you. Do you like me back?"

"That's the way of it," Randolla agreed. "Once a suitor finds welcome, other nods to Bethiel's tale are offered. Like bells and chimes and whistles. They're said to invite Bethiel to come and sing anew."

"And the second variation?" Boniface asked. "You said there are two."

"An even simpler message, because Bethiel's songs always reveal the truth. Blue nippet eggs stand for *true love*."

22

EVERBLOOMING

Suuzu had always liked children, but perhaps being sprigged changed matters? When Tsumiko placed her newfound daughter in his arms, he embarrassed himself by going all ... broody. He clucked and warbled, and she burbled back, showing no trace of Rifflet's instinctive hesitation over encountering a phoenix.

"This is your Uncle Suuzu," Kyrie solemnly informed her.

"Your own sibling," Suuzu murmured, caressing silky hair with a purple sheen. "She's beautiful."

Tsumiko, who'd perched on the arm of his chair, said, "It's like time's turned back."

Kyrie shook his head. "Dad and Ginkgo both say I was too serious as a baby. Mercy is all sweetness and smiles."

"I didn't mean *you*," she replied. "I meant Suuzu."

The boy blinked.

"I held you the same day you were born," Suuzu explained.

"Yes, I know. Uncle Akira likes to tell that story." Kyrie studied

Suuzu's face with a quiet sort of gladness. "I am fortunate to have been loved from the start. Dad and Mother. You and Uncle Akira. Mum and Lilya. Papka and Ginkgo. Uncle Jackie and Lapis. Just … everyone."

"And now Mercy has all of us as well … and you, too." Tsumiko kissed Suuzu's brow and said, "I'll leave her to you while I check with the mares. There's so much to get ready."

After she'd gone, Suuzu nudged Kyrie and said, "I am unsure if your newness was my favorite part of that day … or if it was the sight of your father wearing my traditional clothes. Him draped in flame-colored silk, you curled over his blue blaze."

"I cannot picture Dad in orange. Uncle Jackie would never let him wear it."

"Never," agreed Suuzu. "Blue suits him better."

"Uncle Suuzu?" Kyrie rested his cheek against Suuzu's shoulder. "I heard that you want to learn stories about nippets."

"True."

"I remembered reading about one in Mother's books. Well, it was not a nippet story exactly. It was an angel story, and it took me a while to go through her collection. Most Amaranthine scriptures are handwritten and bound into thick volumes."

"But you found one for me?"

Kyrie's gaze was hopeful. "To please you. To … cheer you up?"

"Do I seem to need it?"

"You do." He softly added, "Uncle Akira has *always* loved you."

Suuzu inclined his head. "As a friend."

With the hint of a smile, Kyrie asked, "Has it ever occurred to Uncle Akira—even once—that the two of you might part ways?"

"No."

"Does that not mean that you are his favorite companion, his partner in everything, his choice?"

Suuzu fidgeted. "But … I want …."

"To kiss him?" Kyrie's expression was all innocence. "I think he would let you."

But Suuzu didn't want Akira to simply *let* him. Somehow, it felt safe to confide in Kyrie. "I want him to want me, too."

He considered that, then nodded. "That *would* be best. It is important to strike a good balance. Shall I tell you the lore I found? Stories are a good distraction from sadness."

Something in his inflection worried Suuzu. "Are *you* sad?"

Trust for trust, discretion for discretion, Kyrie opened his own heart. "I am not yet used to the idea that beautiful things can spring from ugly places." He stroked Mercy's cheek with the back of a finger. "Many have called her father and mine a monster. I do not think they are wrong, and yet … I am grateful to be alive. And I love Mercy. She is mine in a way nobody else ever was before. Not even Lilya."

"Sibling bonds can be instinctual." Resting his hand over his belly, he quietly admitted, "My perspective may be colored by my upbringing. The sibling bonds of trees are the strongest I have ever encountered, but dragon society is famously familial. Humans may be titillated by the idea of harems, but they overlook the hatcheries, where siblings and half-siblings know their parents' love."

"The fathers are strong, but the brothers are not weak," Kyrie said, sounding as if he were quoting some obscure verse from the ancient texts. "I want to be a good brother."

"Then you will be," Suuzu assured.

The boy leaned close and whispered, "And you will be a good parent."

He warbled in surprise.

"The winds tattled. I will not tell, but … may I ask for one thing?" Kyrie tentatively said, "If you can trust me enough, I would like very much to hold your baby on the same day they are born. Like you held me."

"That would please me." Suuzu blinked hard and blamed it on the broodiness. "It would be a good balance. A … a pleasing symmetry."

Kyrie sat a little straighter. "And now, I will share a story of angels."

"Please do."

"I am not certain if the Amaranthine angels are all stars or if other Impressions have also become messengers for the Maker. It would be interesting to find out, but nobody seems to know for certain. Or if they do know, they like keeping secrets." With a blink, he whispered, "*You* are a tribute. Do you know?"

"I might."

Kyrie's eyes widened. "Truly?"

"I might," Suuzu repeated. "But we are not here to talk about the tenfold duties that are handed down to a tenth child."

The boy blinked. "That is *already* more than I have read in *any* of Mother's books. Ten things?"

"Ten," he confirmed solemnly. "And you will not find them in any book. They are passed down by oral tradition, from one tribute to another. Though sometimes you will catch hints in the oldest stories, especially those carried by bards."

"I have never met a bard."

"Stately House has a song circle now. Perhaps your father will invite storytellers to future festivals."

Kyrie nodded distractedly. "Does every tribute have to do all ten of these duties, or do you share them out … like … like reaver classifications?"

Suuzu simply waited in silence.

Ducking his head, Kyrie asked, "Would you tell me more another time?"

"I might." And bending to catch his eye, Suuzu softly added, "Who can say? You might *be* a tenth child. Become a tribute for your clan. Set yourself apart for the sake of the others who share your blood."

The boy actually gasped. "Oh, I think ... yes. Those words ring true."

Suuzu cautiously inclined his head. "Then they may yet come to pass."

Kyrie tipped his head to one side, as if listening to distant voices, smiled to himself, then calmly took up his story again. "This angel's name is Veliel the Everblooming. In the beginning, the earth was lush with growing things, for the Maker delighted in filling it with forests and meadows and thickets and fields. All could see that this was good, and yet Veliel grew bored with the endless green and complained to the Maker."

"Daring."

Kyrie nodded. "Yet the Maker answered his angel's restless longing by speaking a single word. *Bloom*. And all who looked on were dazzled, for the whole earth obeyed."

This lore was new to Suuzu. Was this really how flowers came to be part of their world? He could almost see the resulting explosion of beauty. All because one angel dared to ask for more.

"Ever since, the earth has never lacked for flowers. And ever since, green nippets have carried a message between courting couples."

Suuzu protested, "Courting lore couldn't possibly have been in the ancient texts."

"No. But Randolla *likes* courting games. He told me the rest." With a coy smile, Kyrie began to list all the things that the green eggshell in Akira's gift could mean. "'Young love,' 'first love,' 'budding love,' and even 'love in bloom.' I think those are kind of predictable. But probably nice if someone is actually in love."

Suuzu appreciated simplicity, but he asked, "There are others?"

"Yes. When appropriate, vert nippet feathers and eggshells might be interpreted 'love can grow anywhere' or 'petals come in every color.' But I like the last one best, because it sounds right." Kyrie slipped into a lilting recitation. "Splendid are the gifts of the Maker, and wise are those who remember that flowers cannot be found unless stem, leaf, root, and even thorn come before."

"And seed," Suuzu whispered.

"Yes, of course. Everything begins with a seed. So your green eggshell can mean 'leaf and twig before flower and fruit.' *Or* it can be a plea to one's partner. 'Help me bloom.'"

23

CLAN ROMANTICS

Nonny brought a tray. He *always* seemed to be bringing trays. In fact, Suuzu was becoming increasingly certain that the only reason Nonny ever left his side was so he could fetch a new one. And eluding Nonny was next to impossible, thanks to Boniface. Because Suuzu's responsibility to the man kept him tethered.

"Don't think I won't bring in Lady," Nonny warned. "Kindest kick in the arse you'll ever get. And probably another spoon-feeding."

Suuzu whistled a sour note.

"Lord. Do you eat like this every day?" asked Boniface. "Not sure how you resist."

"Be my guest," Suuzu murmured, gaze averted.

Boniface hummed appreciatively. "I remember these! Whatever shop these are from, it's first rate."

Nonny snorted. "You think they make your Paris-style fancies in rural Japan?"

Pausing to lick crumbs from his fingertips, Boniface ventured, "You have them shipped?"

"Daft thing. Argent *makes* them. Usually for Jacques. Which probably means he's been ... well, you know."

Suuzu nodded pensively. Argent was worried ... and probably wishing there was more he could do. The resulting glut of chocolate croissants felt like a bad portent.

Boniface picked up another and nibbled. This time his hum was skeptical. "Argent bakes pastries for Jackie?"

"So?" countered Nonny.

"I have a hard time picturing it."

"You don't have to picture it. You just gotta drop by the kitchen at three in the morning. His lordship wears an apron and everything." With a small shrug, Nonny added, "He used to let me lick the mixing bowl."

Feeling queasy, Suuzu went back to picking threads from his lap blanket.

"What's got you in such a state this morning?" Nonny came to sit beside him and tugged him into a loose embrace. "Does anything hurt?"

"No."

"Need a distraction? Trip to the naproom? Cuddle a kitten? Bit of fresh air? Maybe a book?"

Suuzu shrugged.

"Are there any books on nippet lore?"

"Dunno." Nonny gave Suuzu a poke. "But you know who *would* know? Isla."

Boniface made a face. "I hear she's bossy."

"True that, but Isla's a good sort. And ridiculously informed on everything. She's been a cultural liaison since she was what, ten?" Nonny stood and offered Suuzu his hands. "C'mon, then. Let's see if Isla has the time to natter about nippets."

Suuzu grabbed hold and let himself be led.

Boniface hurried to keep up, though he radiated reluctance.

Unsure what was amiss, Suuzu hooked the man's arm.

He pouted. "It's hypocritical to fuss over me when you won't let anyone fuss over you."

"I know."

"You … like this Isla person?"

"I do. She is like a sister."

Boniface lapsed into a wary silence while Nonny picked up the pace.

"Found her," he called over his shoulder. "Shoulda figured they'd be in the blue parlor."

Lapis Mossberne's home-away-from-home was a cozy room dominated by a fireplace. There were thick rugs, exquisite crystals, and more books than the shelves could hold. The dragon lounged artfully, clad in filmy silks and sequins. Isla, wearing a gray sweater that looked two sizes too large over jeans, sat on the floor. She was in the process of unboxing, and stacks of paperbacks surrounded her.

"I've been on a cozy clan kick, so let me take all of those," she was saying. "Will you do these fairy tale retellings? I'm getting tired of frog princes, big bad wolves, and three bear orgies."

Lapis held out his hand for a book and scanned the summary. "Don't even pretend you didn't adore that trilogy based on the billy goats gruff."

"Goats are cozies!" she protested.

Although he'd seen them, Lapis first countered, "Two words. Bridge troll."

"What's this about goats?" Nonny asked.

Isla, whose cheeks had gone pink, waved a handful of paperbacks his way. "If you're actually interested, there's an entire sub-genre dedicated to caprine romance. And that includes crossers. The satyr trope is a modern classic. Would you like my recommendations?"

"Not bloody likely," Nonny muttered.

Suuzu angled his head, scanning what book covers he could see. Most depicted humans and Amaranthine in varying degrees of … cooperation.

Boniface bent to pick up the topmost book from a teetering stack and showed it to him. "*Mon dieu*. Are these … tentacles?"

Isla breezily said, "There's a fairly recent trend toward the incorporation of briner lore. Most of it's just repackaged merfolk stories and fifty shades of *The Little Mermaid*. But … yes. Some do explore the possibilities of sea clans and sea crossers. That one's promising. It's a meet-cute involving a bashful octopus, so I don't think it'll veer into tentacle porn."

"Lord."

She primly announced, "Kimiko and I run an online book club together—Clan Romantics. We review, recommend, and discuss Amaranthine-based literature that's been published since the Emergence. And we bring facts to bear against some of the sillier misconceptions about inter-species relationships. Lapis is one of our advance readers—his perspectives are *invaluable*—and so we're divvying up this week's book box."

Boniface very carefully returned the paperback to its stack.

"I'd let you borrow it," Isla said. "I loan books to Uncle Jackie all the time. Or … something else? What are your preferred genres?"

The man actually paled.

Suuzu took his elbow.

Locking gazes with Suuzu, Boniface rallied enough to steer the conversation onto a safer avenue. "Nippets," he said awkwardly. "We're here about nippets."

"Find seats, gentlemen," Lapis smoothly interjected. "Isla,

Suuzu is looking into avian courting traditions, especially those that revolve around the giving and interpretation of nippet eggs. Have you seen his exquisite accessory?"

Abandoning her books, Isla crawled across the rug and rose up on her knees before Suuzu. "Oh, but these are …!" She whispered, "From Akira?"

"Yes."

Her expression softened. "You must be *so* glad."

Suuzu lowered his eyes, embarrassed that he wasn't. Not when Akira was gone from his side.

Isla touched his chin, lifting his gaze. Her smile was bright and resolute and as confident as always. "You've been patient for so long. You're an inspiration!"

Which didn't seem quite right. He'd been *impatient* for so long. But Suuzu supposed Isla had noticed how deeply he cared, much as he'd noticed her own tenacious attachment. He summoned up a low warble of sympathy, even though he doubted that patience and pining would ever be enough to reach the person *she* had chosen.

24

DAWN AND DUN

Suuzu's need would be doubly met, for after a brief consultation, Isla announced that she and Lapis each had a tidbit of lore to tell. She began.

"It should come as no surprise that dawn nippets are linked to Soriel of the Dawning. He is the harbinger angel, for wherever he's sent, something new is sure to be stirring."

Boniface interrupted. "Dawn isn't a color."

Isla blinked. "Oh, of course. You wouldn't know. I apologize, Uncle Boniface."

"Since when am I *your* uncle?"

"You're Uncle Jackie's brother." With an upraised hand, she serenely cut off his next protest. "And you're still here. Which means Argent is allowing you to stay. And he wouldn't do that for just anyone. Ergo … you're family."

Nonny snickered. "She's terrible at simple, straightforward answers, ain't she?"

"Pink," offered Suuzu. "Dawn nippets are pink."

"I was getting to that," Isla grumbled.

"Sure you were," Nonny teased.

"As I was about to say, dawn nippets are pink. Like the first faint blush of pink on the eastern horizon. Like the first flush of realization, when two people finally see that what they have could be something more. Pink nippet eggs are the first choice of many hopeful suitors, especially when their feelings might come as a surprise to the one they wish to court."

Suuzu thought back to Akira's expression when he'd pressed a kiss on him.

Yes, he'd blushed. Had it only been embarrassment? Or was it that 'something more'? Maybe a little of both ...? Because Akira had come ready with a courting gift. He'd acknowledged Suuzu's hopes and promised that they'd do everything properly once he returned. Probably thanks to Quen, he'd known that Suuzu wouldn't initiate anything. A tribute couldn't court someone. But they could be courted.

"Suuzu ...?" Isla ventured. "Did you hear me?"

"He didn't," said Nonny. "Better list 'em again."

"I ... what?" Suuzu asked.

Isla held his gaze and patiently said, "Pink nippet eggs *can* mean 'new beginning,' 'new light,' 'new love,' and 'first blush.' But the number one most popular interpretation for a gift that includes a pink eggshell is ... 'choose me.'"

Suuzu warbled wistfully.

Lapis offered an answering trill, then said, "My turn. I may not be as skilled at extemporizing as Isla, but bear with me."

"Nonsense," Isla countered. "A dragon's words always have the power to move."

He only gave a small headshake and began, "Dun nippets aren't particularly showy, since their feathers are a quiet, modest brown.

These little ones are associated with Cadmiel of the Echoing Song. In the days soon after what's known as the First Emergence, when the clans of meadow, mountain, and valley were preparing to withdraw from the Widelands, Cadmiel was called upon to serve as their guide. He helped them to leave behind the mementos that have become this world's greatest treasures. Remnant stones hold echoes of power, songs of portent, whispers of wisdom, and scenes of things done or yet to come."

"What now?" asked Boniface. "Sorry, but … are you talking about your crystals?"

Lapis beckoned. "Come here, Boniface. Only for a short while. Then you can return to your favorite guardian."

The man stood and cautiously lowered himself to a perch beside the dragon, who smiled and crooked a finger. When Boniface leaned closer, Lapis whispered in his ear. The man nodded, and Lapis chose one of the many rings he wore. Placing it in Boniface's hand, he whispered something more … and this time, Suuzu was sure that he'd employed a touch of sway.

Isla drew breath to protest.

Lapis raised a finger and began to softly sing.

Immediately, the crystal in the ring resonated with a clear, sweet note.

Boniface tensed, his gaze fixed on the ring. He never saw Lapis pull a dainty sigil from thin air, nor did he notice when the dragon applied it with a light touch to his shoulder. But then Boniface's eyes went wide … and slipped out of focus … and his breath caught.

Suuzu wasn't breathing either, though he trusted Lapis. He sighed in relief when the dragon gently brought the brief song to an end.

Boniface gaped at him.

Holding out his hand for the ring, Lapis asked, "Did the echo reach you?"

"There was ... that is, I think I saw ...." Boniface carefully relinquished the remnant. "Lord, I don't even know where to begin."

"Every remnant has its own song. Can you see why they're eagerly sought by Amaranthine and reavers alike?"

Boniface nodded, recalled himself, and with mumbled thanks, he returned to Suuzu's side.

Lapis continued. "Crystal adepts can coax the echoes of songs from remnant stones, but getting your hands on one isn't easy. Much like ordinary gemstones, remnants are hidden in humble earth and stubborn stone. They require seekers. They must be mined and handled with the greatest of care. And even the finest finds require shaping, polishing, and tuning to bring out their song.

"Dun nippet eggs carry messages related to the seeking and finding of remnants. 'Seek and you shall find,' 'look closer,' 'uncover the song in my heart,' and 'bring secret love into the open.' Other possibilities include 'hidden message' and 'hidden depths.'" Lapis's expression was difficult to read when he added, "The most popular interpretation of the dun egg is a heartfelt plea—*find me*."

Nobody spoke for a moment, but then a light rap came on the doorframe.

Michael stood there. "Sorry to interrupt. Here you are, Isla. May we borrow you? Timur must go, and ... well. Help us see off your brother."

She frowned. "He's going somewhere?"

"Duty calls," Michael said with a small shrug. "He's saying goodbye to Gregor."

Suuzu wanted to ask, needed to know. And maybe Michael sensed it, because he sought Suuzu's gaze, nodded significantly, and urged, "Trust him and Fend. They're really very good."

25

ALL IN A FLUTTER

Boniface tried not to be offended when he was invited to join a work crew. He might be adjusting to life at Stately House, possibly even acclimating somewhat to having children clamoring about, but ... lord, he was a Smythe! There was no way he'd go shiver on a dreary beach, pretending to know the first thing about assembling festival booths. He'd ruin his shoes. Probably risk slivers. Catch cold. *Non.* It was impossible.

However, he *did* meander as far as the garden wall in order to peer over the brink.

Far below the cliffs, waves rushed a private beach that was probably pleasant enough in summer. He'd never been around in the appropriate season, but clearly there was swimming to be had. He cast a sidelong look at an empty clothesline. One of its posts held a sign—**FUNDOSHI SWIM CLUB**.

Leave it to Jackie to bare his backside for a good cause.

And Boniface hadn't missed the peek of tattoos in that snapshot. Maman wouldn't approve. *If* she ever found out.

With the vague idea of returning to Suuzu, Boniface headed back toward the house. The garden was blessedly quiet since all the crossers were rampaging on the beach, so he reached the kitchen door unmolested. However, he'd barely made it inside and into his house slippers when Sonnet whisked over and pulled him into her arms.

"Oh, love, you're chilled right through. Let me get you some tea."

Which didn't sound half bad. But ... the wolf wasn't letting go. So Boniface's face was mashed into her apron front while she tutted and petted. "Unhand me," he grumbled halfheartedly.

Sonnet *did* let him go. She also bent to press her warm cheek to his cold one. "I never meant to neglect you, but with this and that. It's so *good* to be home, and I've been catching up with everyone and everything, but ... mmm. Did ... did anyone mention to you where Jacques is?"

"*Non.*"

"Even the stars won't say. Is it silly to worry? I must confess, I am a little worried. Are you?"

He rolled his eyes. "My brother is always finding some new way to scandalize. But he carries on and comes through, usually to applause. And swinging shopping bags full of souvenirs."

Sonnet drew back enough to search his face. "I feel a little better. Thank you, Boniface."

To his chagrin, she brushed his forehead with her lips before turning away.

"Tea," she said briskly. "It'll do us both good."

Unsure if he needed to oblige a lady who wasn't exactly female, he nevertheless shuffled over and took a seat at the kitchen table. Only to rise again when Sonnet sailed back with a tray.

She beamed at him but pressed her hands to his shoulders, making him sit. "You are a *fine* gentleman, and your manners are perfectly lovely, but please, Brother. Rest. I'll join you in a moment. Do you like seed cake? I had a sudden craving."

Boniface slouched in his chair, feeling surly. But he couldn't quite summon up the spite to fend off this doting wolf. Not after what had happened with Nonny. Still, he mumbled, "You and I aren't brothers. Or ... how would that even work? Dash it all, *I'm* not *your* brother, at least."

Sonnet's smile didn't dim as she sat across from him and poured for them both.

So she wanted a *tête-à-tête*? Right, then. He had questions. But at the moment, they weren't about his little brother. Well, not in the spill-the-tea sense. Because he'd been watching more closely, ever since Timur's departure. And Sonnet's worries might have some basis.

The feverish activity on the beach probably counted as a bad sign.

Apparently, pastries were also an ill portent.

And Boniface was guessing that Sonnet's tucking tail was also telling.

"Look. I know what I said, but ... *is* something wrong?"

Sonnet quietly answered, "I hardly know myself, but ... yes. Something must be wrong. Has anyone confided in you? I mean, you're his brother. My claim is less ... err ... well, it isn't a claim at all, to be honest."

Boniface thought back over all the things that had been said in his vicinity. "Kyrie mentioned waiting for something to happen. Seemed quite restless over the matter. And Timur's gone off with that monster cat of his."

"He's a battler."

"So ... off to war?" Boniface accepted the piece of seed cake she offered. "That's worrisome. And then there's Jackie himself. He apparently went off with Akira, and Suuzu doesn't like it."

"They're together?"

"Jackie wouldn't ... well! He wouldn't have run off with Suuzu's chap, would he?"

Sonnet blinked. And blinked again. "Nooo. Jacques might have offered to escort him ... somewhere? To help Akira be brave. That's the kind of man Jacques is."

"Is it?"

"I'm sure."

Boniface was beginning to wonder which of them knew his brother better. And if this wolf was as naïve as she seemed.

Just then, Tsumiko pushed through the kitchen door, smiled, and swayed their way, a bundle in her arms.

He and Sonnet both stood, and the wolf hurried to bring another place setting. Then stole the baby to free the woman's hands. Tsumiko took a seat beside Boniface, murmuring thanks.

Sonnet spoke in low tones. "Please, Lady Mettlebright. I'm all in a flutter. Will you tell me? Where is Jacques?"

Tsumiko seemed surprised, but she answered calmly enough. "Argent is relying on him to help collect some people who are in a difficult situation. Friends of the family. But also ... new family members. Uncle Boniface, you haven't met Mercy, have you?"

"Ah. Err." He eyed the bundle warily. "No, we're not acquainted."

"She's the answer to both of your questions."

Boniface would have liked to point out that he hadn't asked anything. He certainly hadn't asked to be handed a baby. But Sonnet was suddenly looming and lowering and crooning and ... bloody hell. He held very still and shot a pleading look at Tsumiko. Just in time for her to snap a picture with her phone.

"See here!" he managed.

Ignoring his protest and his discomfort, Tsumiko said, "Stately House has always been—and will always be—a place where crossers will be safe and loved and taught. Mercy is a foretaste of our future. Argent found out about more dragon crossers. He and the others will bring them home."

More cursed children? Boniface was almost afraid to ask. "How ... many others ...?"

Tsumiko shook her head sadly. "This has happened too many times to too many women. If what Sinder let slip is true ... there are dozens of children scattered around the world. This group, though? Argent suggested readying enough beds for twenty. But he changed his mind at the last minute, so we've found a way to fit in thirty. And if necessary, we'll overflow into the naproom."

While Sonnet and Tsumiko discussed other ways they could get ready, Boniface took a longer look at the baby in his arms. Purple fluff and freckles. Tiny claws. Soft breathing. He slowly relaxed. Maybe he was all right with sleeping children.

Just then, the sounds of infantile misery reached his ears.

Sonnet was already on her feet when two boys walked through the door, calm as you please, despite the pitiful wailing of the baby propped against Kyrie's shoulder. Unlike Boniface, he seemed entirely used to handling small people. The brown-eyed boy at his side—telltale curls suggested he was another of the chauffer's sons—hurried to tug at Sonnet's hand.

"We brought Ella. Will *you* try?" he begged. "The mares think you might be able to calm her."

"I apologize for interrupting, Mother," said Kyrie. "With both Uncle Jackie and Uncle Akira gone, there is no one ... to ... oh! Oh, *of course*! Vanya, help me trade with Uncle Boniface? He is not a reaver."

"Perfect!" exclaimed the boy, who bent to take Mercy. Meeting Boniface's eyes, he cheerfully said, "Hiya. Thanks for this. Seriously."

With enviable poise, the kid whisked away the dragon-child, expertly tucking her under his chin. Then Kyrie was handing off their crier.

"What's wrong? What am I even meant to do?" he asked weakly.

"Prop her on your shoulder," Kyrie coached.

"How?" he exclaimed.

His nephew guided his hands into a hold similar to the one Vanya had on Mercy. "Pat her. Talk softly. Wait for her to notice your scent."

"Try French," suggested Vanya. "Jacques always talks to her in French."

Boniface was fairly certain that he couldn't pat and talk at the same time. Maybe he should break down and cry, too. "I've never held a baby!"

"Not even Ceddy?" asked Kyrie.

"Lord, no. I doubt I'm fit for this sort of thing. Highly unqualified. Take her back!"

But then … the baby stopped wailing. There was a soggy sort of snuffling in the vicinity of his throat, and she whimpered softly. But small hands grabbed at his sweater, and she took a great, shuddering breath. Almost as if she'd finally gotten the thing she'd been crying for.

With a light laugh, Tsumiko said, "Uncle Boniface, you are officially a godsend."

26

GRAY BIRD

Boniface wondered if he should be worried that everyone else stepped back, leaving him alone with the baby.

"Keep talking to her," whispered Kyrie.

"I'm *not* my brother. What happens when she notices?"

Tsumiko's gaze held sympathy, but she didn't make a move toward him. "We've seen this before. Some children are instinctually wary of threats, and for crossers, that can mean both reavers and Amaranthine. Ella doesn't fully trust us yet." She shrugged wearily.

"Uncle Jackie and Uncle Akira were the only ones who could get her to settle," said Vanya, who slid onto one of the kitchen chairs. "Hey, Mama Sonnet, is that seed cake?"

And just like that, all of Boniface's very reasonable concerns were overlooked in favor of expanding the tea party.

"She'll calm more quickly if you're calm," said Kyrie.

"*Must* you ask the impossible?"

"Do you know any French nursery rhymes or bedtime stories?"

"*Naturellement.*"

"Tell her one," Kyrie lilted persuasively.

So even though Tsumiko tried to interrupt, her tone chiding, Boniface launched into a story that had always been his favorite, even though their nanny usually gave in to Jackie's pleas and told the ones he liked instead.

Somehow, when he was finished, the table had been cleared and Sonnet had gone off somewhere with Vanya, leaving Boniface with Tsumiko, Kyrie, and two sleeping babies. Ella had gone quite limp, which was concerning in a new way.

"Is ... is she quite well?" he ventured.

"She was exhausted," said Tsumiko. "She feels safe now, so she was able to find her way into sleep."

"Many Amaranthine do have trouble sleeping." Kyrie darted a look at his mother, then solemnly said, "I apologize, Uncle Boniface. I should not have *made* you tell a story. Even though it worked."

"That's a mercy," Boniface muttered.

"No. This one's Mercy." His nephew rested his cheek atop his baby sister's head. "And I really did wrong you, though I cannot explain why."

"More secrets?"

"I am afraid so." The boy looked to his mother, then sighed. Red eyes pleaded with him as he dutifully said, "Please, forgive me? I am not always wise with my words, but I can learn from my mistakes."

Boniface was no stranger to parent-induced apologies, so he did his part. "You are forgiven, lad. And if you're looking for some form of recompense, how about a story for a story?"

Kyrie's gaze softened. "I like that idea. Mother ...?"

"Haji-oji mentioned to me that you've been collecting courting lore for Suuzu's sake. That's really very sweet."

"Lord, I'm the farthest thing from sweet. I simply … well! Suuzu forgets to ask, so I do a bit of reminding. Since I have time on my hands. Oh, do stop smiling at me."

Tsumiko tried to school her features, but her gaze held an embarrassing amount of fondness when she asked, "Did you know that some nippets are gray?"

"I hadn't the foggiest. Ah, there's a thought. Are they fog nippets?"

"In the old stories, they're called seal nippets."

"Are there Amaranthine seal clans?" he asked, suddenly curious.

"Certainly. Long ago, every variety of animal on earth had its Amaranthine counterpart. In fact, I understand that there are quite a few who remain, even though the creatures they once looked after have since become extinct."

"Like dinosaurs and things?"

"Well, yes. But also no. It's a very long story, involving the beginnings of the Amaranthine people, as told by their own scriptures." And with a small laugh, she suggested, "Nippets for now?"

"One thing first?" he ventured.

"Yes?"

"What sort of baby am I holding? She has a lot of *fuzz*. And I found a tail. Entirely by accident, I assure you. And … well … she kicked out of her little socks. It's hard to miss the …."

"Hooves," Tsumiko finished, coming around to tug booties back into place. "The wolves helped us to sort out her heritage. One of Ella's parents is from a reindeer clan. It's entirely possible that she'll have antlers when she's older."

"Reindeer. Right. No end to the variety."

"How many varieties of nippets have you collected?" inquired Kyrie.

Boniface did a quick mental tally. "He's learned seven of the nine. Well, I think he promptly forgot a couple of them, but I jotted off some notes. Seal nippets will make eight."

Mother and son traded a speaking glance.

"What?" Boniface demanded.

With a small shake of her head, Tsumiko began her story. "When time was young and Impressions could still be spotted upon these lands, some do say that the sea also had its share of clans. Today, they're referred to as briners, and most Amaranthine think they're nothing more than the invention of bards."

"Are we talking … mermaids and sea monsters?"

"Impressions are sentient embodiments of nature. For instance, the sky clans include moonbeams and rainbows and winds and … well, even fog. Tales of seafolk are about the embodiments of tides, whirlpools, kelp beds, and even sea foam."

Boniface frowned. "Why would Amaranthine believe in moonbeams but call tides into question?"

"For millennia, clans kept to themselves and kept their secrets. Only bards were welcomed in every place, and their tales were thought too fantastic to be true. So lorefolk became the stuff of stories, even though a few clans knew that the lore was true."

"Like what?"

"Like Haji-oji," Tsumiko answered. "Only those who've been protecting the old groves ever mingle with tree imps. They're lorefolk."

Kyrie quietly added, "Wolves know about moonbeams. And dragons know about winds."

"And many clans have been visited by stars." Tsumiko held up her hands, stopping herself. "But … back to *this* tale. As often happens in lore, two people from very different backgrounds chanced to meet and became fascinated with one another. The first was a sunlit wave who loved to sparkle on the surface of the sea. And the second was an avian far from home—a gray parrot who'd followed their curiosity aboard a ship and out to sea."

"Riding on a pirate's shoulder, no doubt."

"Every story has a seed of truth in it," Tsumiko said with a smile. "This bird had no place in the ocean, where waves belong. Yet the avian spent long hours dazzled by the wave's flashing dances, and the wave in its turn buoyed the boat and carried it swiftly, all while keeping it safe from running aground. They even went so far as to bring schools of fish into the sailors' nets."

"Did they … well. Could they take speaking form?"

"Not at first. For in the earliest days of the Amaranthine, they hadn't learned how. *Yet*. It's said that the first who managed it did so for love. In fact, in many of the old ballads, the Amaranthine found their way into speaking form in order to steal a kiss … and to take a lover."

Boniface hummed. "If *this* story is part of avian courting lore, I'm guessing there's a happy ending."

Tsumiko smiled. "The wave drew the attention of Jashiel of Tides, the angel sent by the Maker to shepherd the seas. He asked the Maker what might be done. With a word, stone breached the surface of the ocean. And with another, its edges softened into sand. And with a song not heard since the world began, soil deepened and trees grew and fresh water sprang up. This is how the first of the Eldermost islands rose from the sea, ready to be sought and found.

"The avian abandoned the ship and shifted upon the shore, and the smitten wave dared to join them there. They spoke together and sealed a pact with their first kiss, and they joined together with much joy and gratitude. And in the fullness of time, the Maker blessed their unique union. The gray bird and the sunlit briner nested upon hot sands and hatched a child, the First of Phoenixes, mightiest of avians."

"Oh, *that* sort of seal. Well … bravo for them!" Boniface found he was smiling. "Suuzu will like that last bit, I'm sure."

"He probably already knows the story of the first phoenix, since that would be part of his own clan's lore. But … I'm guessing he doesn't know the nippet connection." Tsumiko continued, "In avian courtships, the gray eggshell of a seal nippet has taken on a few meanings. 'Impression," in the sense of making a good first impression, although it is also a nod to imps. It can also mean 'love at first sight,' 'destined,' or 'blessed union.' But the connotation is that of impetuous lovers. 'Make haste,' 'join with me,' and 'I can wait no longer.'"

27

THE NINTH NIPPET

Suuzu was honestly amazed that Boniface had gone to the trouble of finding another nippet story for him. This kind of support was usually only offered by a close friend, the kind who might offer to gather nesting materials so a suitor could devote themselves to their beloved. Suuzu was touched, but his throat ached too much to allow any tunes to pass. Not until Akira was safe in his arms. Surely then, his song would swell.

"Ah … Suuzu? Did you get that?"

"Yes. Thank you. I am glad to know the significance of azure nippets."

Boniface eyed him curiously. "That's the second time I had to tell you."

Suuzu ventured, "Truly?"

"True as blue. And true love, apparently. But every time Hajime turns up, you … oh … bloody hell. Hajime, I wasn't calling you!"

A tree had joined them, and Suuzu's memory jogged. "I see.

Yes, I see. I apologize if I have inconvenienced you.”

“Nevermind that. You remember him?” Boniface checked. “That's the quickest yet, isn't it?”

“It is,” agreed Hajime, who caressed Suuzu's cheek with a hand, then bent to kiss him there. “How are you and your leafling?”

Boniface looked between them, a quizzical expression on his face. “What's a leafling?”

“Suuzu has been sprigged.”

The man's confusion didn't lift. “I *know* I haven't been forgetting things. Is this another secret that will imperil my life should I ever speak of it to another?”

“It *is* a secret.” Suuzu admitted, “I had forgotten that you did not know.”

“And assuming you tell me, you'll very likely forget that I *do* know.” Boniface patted his shoulder. “By any chance, do you need a spokesman of your own, Spokesperson Farroost?”

Suuzu hesitated. “I ... might?”

“Would I do?” He was smiling like it was a joke.

“Such a thing never occurred to me.” And with a growing sense of amazement, he admitted, “I trust you.”

“Lord. Can I get that in writing?” With a roll of his eyes, he grumbled, “You'll have forgotten within the hour. A shame really. I'd rather not take my chances with the chauffer's daughter. Mayhap being a gentleman's gentleman runs in the family?”

Suuzu gaped at him.

Holding up a hand, Boniface promised, “You don't even have to tell me what this leafling business is about. One less secret for me t–”

“There will be a child,” Suuzu blurted, for he wanted this man—this *friend*—to know it. “I am carrying a child. They will be tree-kin.”

"You're pregnant?"

"In the sense that there will be a child … yes." And catching his hand Suuzu begged, "We should write it down."

Boniface looked between him and Hajime. "I don't think you're likely to forget a baby."

"He will not forget," the tree assured.

"I meant *you*," Suuzu said. "I do not want to forget that you have offered to be my … my man? My staff is small. Only three people, and they use a room at Hisoka's in Keishi."

"Are any members of your staff female?"

"No."

Boniface searched his face, nodded once, and asked, "Where can I find paper?"

Suuzu was relieved when Nonny didn't try to get him to eat. Just helped him into a hooded cloak and took his arm, guiding him outside.

Suuzu whispered, "Oh."

"Surprised?" Nonny asked.

"I am. The windows were draped." He lifted his face in order to feel the brush of snowflakes against his skin.

"Kind of rude of it to storm when we were planning a *frost* festival, but Lady announced at breakfast that we can change it to a snow festival. The guv comes from snow country, and he's promised some extra games he remembers from … I dunno. Forever ago, probably."

"Hmm."

"Hajime's not following you. For once."

"Hmm?"

"He's been hanging about with me more often. Guess Argent wants me canny about the trees." Nonny confessed, "Hajime tucks me in and holds my hand while I get my nightly dose of pollen. But it turns out I had a head start on this whole acclimation thing. On account of Kusunoki."

Suuzu, too, was shaking off the haze induced by Hajime's flowers. But this was news. "The sacred tree at Kikusawa Shrine?"

"That's the guy." Nonny eyed him curiously. "Bet you could see him now, too. Not that you'll be taking any trips to Keishi anytime soon."

"Kusunoki is a tree ...?" Which was a silly question. The tree was a Keishi landmark. But Nonny understood.

"Hajime claims him as a son, too."

"Red flowers," Suuzu murmured. "Strange I had not made the connection. Or ... I forgot ...?"

"*Forgettable* runs in the family." Nonny patted his hand. "Speaking of strange kin, Boniface is at Randolla's. Did you know?"

"He has been roaming more freely."

"Breezed through the kitchen earlier, saying he was taking care of some things for you."

Suuzu blinked. "Was he?"

"I mean, it was nice, seeing him all brisk and bougie. Looked like he could give Jacques a run for his money, taking on the world."

Something about that sounded ... familiar. He admitted, "I would like to see that."

Nonny grinned. "Yeah, I'm curious, too. We'll meander that way. Easy enough to come up with an excuse. Say, how are you coming along with the nippet stories? Still missing any?"

Suuzu frowned, then admitted, "Boniface might know. He takes notes."

"Does he?" Laughing toward the sky, he said, "Jacques never had anything good to say about his brother, but ... come to think of it, he never really had anything bad to say about him either. Just funny stories. And in most of them, Jacques was the one being obnoxious."

"I like Boniface."

"Well, there you have it. Anyone who gains an avian's trust is aces."

They didn't hurry. Just sauntered slowly along, enjoying the turning of the season. But Nonny eventually steered them onto the path to Randolla's, where they found Boniface in conference with both the tailor and Catalan Evernhold.

The feline immediately rearranged chairs, and Randolla brought a fresh pot of tea. Pleasantries were passed around along with teacups, and Suuzu let it distract him. But then Boniface's gaze found his, and there seemed to be a message there.

Suuzu tipped his head to one side.

Boniface waved off his concern, expression resigned.

Then Nonny butted in. "Oi, Boniface. Suuzu says you'll know if he's missing any nippet lore. What's the tally?"

"One left," the man answered.

"Oh? Which one?" asked Randolla. "We could remedy that here and now."

Suuzu wasn't actually sure, which was vaguely worrisome. He darted a look at Boniface.

The man said, "The purple one, please."

"Oho! Dusk nippets. They're associated with an angel known as Kestriel of the Closing." Randolla cast a sidelong look in Suuzu's direction, a secretive smile on his face. "While many shrink from darkness, night is the time when stars shine brightest. Kestriel loved the night so well, he would have hastened the closing of each day if he could. And so the Maker entrusted the night and all its beauties to him."

Catalan remarked, "Felines have a special fondness for Kestriel, perhaps because so many of us are nocturnal. Our nights are … *busy*."

Boniface asked, "The others shepherded things—winds, tides, and whatnot. What part of the night did this Kestriel fellow have to look after?"

"Many imps are associated with nighttime—moonbeams and stars and comets and auroras. But they're all supposed to be well-behaved." Randolla explained, "In daylight, the blue sky is a covering, but after dark, the proverbial veil is drawn aside, and the vastness of galaxies is revealed. And those who have ears to hear know that the stars do sing. Their chorusing might be noise if not for Kestriel's leading."

"He's a music director?" Boniface checked.

"Oh, it is so much more than music," countered Catalan. "Stars sing of things to come. And they celebrate the accomplishment of promised events. And … well! They serenade lovers."

"Stars do?" Boniface stole a look out the nearest window.

"Have you never been in the throes of passion and heard music?" Cat asked innocently.

The man ruffled and babbled protests.

Cat speculated that he needed better lovers. And made himself available.

Suuzu really should have gone to his rescue, but he was similarly flustered and didn't trust his voice.

"Don't mind him," Nonny advised. "If Canarian's not here, Cat will always bring a conversation around to sex if he can. Kind of like Jacques, come to think of it."

Randolla lifted a finger. "Kestriel is also known as a bringer of lullabies and a friend to those who are seeking sleep."

Catalan purred, "And nothing helps a body unwind for sleep quite like–"

Rapping the table, Boniface crisply asked, "Do purple nippets have a message *appropriate* for courting avians?"

"Oh, my yes." Randolla was ready with a list. "The shells and feathers of the dusk nippet often hold special significance to avians who sing through the night, much as stars do."

"That'd include phoenixes," remarked Nonny.

He wasn't wrong. Suuzu felt his cheeks heat. How many times had he sung over Akira while he slept?

Randolla continued, "'The night is ours,' 'your place is ever by my side,' and yes, also 'the delights of the nest.'"

Catalan kissed his fingertips.

To Suuzu's surprise, Randolla wasn't done. "'True song,' 'portent,' 'listen,' and 'sing for me, I sing for you' Although perhaps most famous is 'midnight serenade.' Which is admittedly euphemistic."

"A gift for one's lover, yes?" posed Catalan.

"Would a nine-fold courting gift truly be complete without a nod to lovers?" Randolla asked.

Suuzu wondered what Akira would say. What Akira might want. Or ... not want?

Everyone seemed to be talking at once when Argent basically crashed through the door, his full flourish on display. "*Here* you are," he snapped.

It wasn't clear which of them he was speaking to.

Maybe it didn't matter. All of them were on their feet.

Passing a shaking hand over his eyes, Argent said, "I ... cannot go into any great detail, but ... I must leave. Now. However ... first.

Suuzu, I *will* reach them. It has been promised that the way will be made clear."

Them. Did he mean Akira? It had to be. Him and Jacques. But what had happened? Why wouldn't he say? Eyes on the fox's whipping tails, Suuzu … hissed.

With a concerned look, Nonny stepped past Suuzu and demanded, "*Who* promised it, guv?"

Gesturing vaguely upward, Argent said, "The stars."

And then he was gone.

28

FANDRIEL.S FORESIGHT

Honored sister," Suuzu began. But that's all he managed. Determinedly, he tried again, "Honored sister, do you ... know ...?"

"Come with me," she countered, taking him by the hand.

"Me, too, Lady?" asked Nonny.

She glanced back, gaze thoughtful. "Yes, I think so. Come along, Nonny. You're just as worried, aren't you?"

"Should I be?" he countered.

With a gentle smile, Tsumiko only repeated, "Come with me. Both of you."

She led them to a door Suuzu rarely passed through, but it *was* a place Argent had welcomed him before. Few realized that a conservatory dominated one entire side of Stately House, and fewer still knew that the entrance was near the kitchen. The glassed-in garden was Argent's sanctuary, a truly lovely place, filled with soft grasses, flowering trees, climbing vines, and Argent's extensive collection of Ephemera.

Nonny flopped onto the grass, arms behind his head as he peered up through the intricate network of wheeling sigilcraft and suspended crystals to where gray light filtered through panes of beveled glass. It was prettier when there was sunlight shining through all those prisms.

Tsumiko sat on a bench near Nonny and beckoned to Suuzu.

He lowered himself to a seat, even more worried than before. What had happened that Tsumiko would need this much privacy before speaking?

But instead of telling him something terrible about her brother, Tsumiko asked, "Are you familiar with the angel Fandriel?"

Averting his gaze, he risked rudeness. "I would rather hear about Akira."

She nodded. "We have to trust Argent. He'll do everything he can to bring everyone safely home."

"It's not like we don't trust the guv," Nonny said. "It's more like he doesn't trust us. Do you know anything? At all? Because this is frustrating, and that can't be good for a phoenix in his condition."

"I know that Inti has been found. And I know that Hisoka-sensei is involved." More quietly, she admitted, "Argent spoke to Jacques, and I know that after their conversation ... well, you saw him, too. He's usually so much better at hiding his feelings."

"Half frantic, fangs bared," said Nonny. "And rushing about with his tails all wild. And did you hear that crack when he left? A sonic boom is *such* a bad sign."

"Not necessarily. I think it's the *best* sign. Argent has been here this whole time because there was nothing else he could do. He was waiting, much as we are waiting now. But Jacques got a message through, and Argent was finally able to act." Tsumiko added, "You can only plan for so much. Which is why I brought up Fandriel."

Suuzu took a long, slow breath and accepted the change of

subject. "Yes. I know the stories of Fandriel. He is sometimes referred to as Fandriel the Fortunate, because circumstances always conspire in unexpected ways to bring him a favorable outcome. In bard's tales, Fandriel's good fortune is often referred to as a 'confluence of destinies.'"

"I've heard reavers use his name in a kind of … really mild oath, I guess?" said Nonny. "Timur does it. When something out-of-the-way happens, he'll say 'Fandriel's foresight.'"

"Yes! Exactly," said Tsumiko. "It's a recurring theme in his … well, really, they're misadventures. Children love stories of Fandriel because he's always in trouble. But things work out, often in ways nobody could have anticipated. Most people agree that the lesson of these stories is that good fortune comes down to proper preparation."

"Seems like the sort of motto the guv lives by," remarked Nonny.

She laughed. "Schemers might be the most exasperated with Fandriel. Because unexpected circumstances force him to improvise. He does the best he can with what he has, but his path is always strewn with coincidences. And so Fandriel's foresight can also be interpreted as the Maker's meddling. Because no matter how much you plan, sometimes, you need a miracle."

Suuzu inclined his head. "This is why Fandriel's good fortune was actually Fandriel's faith. He trusted the Maker to arrange things, to fix things, to realign things … so that a pleasing outcome would suddenly appear."

Tsumiko recited, "Maker mark, and Maker move."

With a faint smile, Suuzu murmured, "My brother says that."

"So what're you trying to say?" asked Nonny. "That we're waiting for a miracle?"

"I think … oftentimes … we need a series of small miracles. Along with many people who are willing to move, even if they don't yet see the part they're playing in a larger plan. I think that our 'confluence of destinies' is working itself out under the Maker's watchful eye. Even when our circumstances seem like misadventures or mistakes. At first."

"Guess you *would* see it that way, Lady," said Nonny. "You've got Fandriel's own faith."

"And we have Fandriel's own nippet," she cheerfully returned, her gaze seeking Suuzu's.

He warbled a question.

Her smile widened, reminding Suuzu of Akira. She said, "Argent's collection truly is complete. I wonder if we can catch a glimpse?"

Nonny sat up, peering around. "Seriously? There's another nippet? Everybody's been saying nine."

"Fandriel's nippet can hatch from an egg of any color. You never know where or when. You can't plan for one, and even if you catch a glimpse of one, you might think you were mistaken." Arching her brows, she added, "They're uncommon, but they have a common name. Ghost nippets."

"Albino!" exclaimed Nonny. "The guv's got hold of a rare albino nippet! Where, though?"

Suuzu peered around, then began to softly warble. Argent's Ephemera were amazingly, endearingly tame.

"Shoulda brought some seed or something," Nonny muttered.

"Lady is here," Suuzu reminded.

Tsumiko admitted, "When Argent is away, I *do* tend to attract more Ephemera than usual."

Before long, the little creatures stole up, eager as everyone to get closer to Stately House's lady beacon. Tsumiko lifted a hand, and a pair of midivar twined between her fingers. Then high, sweet notes piped from nearby, and nippets flocked to her and Suuzu.

He smiled to see them, the little birds who were at the heart of the avian courting game Akira had unknowingly instigated, each carrying a message Suuzu now understood.

The vivid red of Zeriel's nippet, confessing a patient and persistent love that no longer wished to remain at a distance.

The bright coral nippet, who was grateful for a love that showed itself in small ways.

The soft gold of honey nippets, the ones who told one's beloved, *my need is met in you.*

The shy brown of dun nippets, with their challenge to *find me.*

And yes, there was the blush of a dawn nippet, who sweetly begged, *choose me.*

Azure nippets for true love, and dusk nippets who promised a lover's attentions. Rich green vert nippets, who asked one's suitor, *help me bloom*, and the stalwart gray of a seal nippet, declaring, *I can wait no longer.*

Nonny had just coaxed a quisp onto his shoulder when a tiny white bird fluttered down from an overhead branch, landing upon Suuzu's upturned palm. In as gentle a voice as he could manage, he asked, "Do you have a message for me?"

Tsumiko answered on its behalf. "Though ghost nippets are rare, avians pay attention to detail, so they're usually included in records, even if it's only as a footnote. A tiny white feather can mean, 'I am astonished,' 'what a coincidence,' 'surprised by love,' and even 'turn of fortune,'" probably as a nod to Fandriel. But most agree that this little one's message is an endearment—'my miracle.'"

Suuzu had long since decided that his meeting Akira at all was akin to a miracle. Gazing at the albino bird in his hand, all he managed was a wan smile.

"This time tomorrow," Tsumiko declared.

He could only shake his head, unsure what she meant.

With a confidence worthy of Fandriel himself, Tsumiko expanded. "By this time tomorrow, Argent will have them home."

Suuzu's lips trembled, and he lifted his eyes toward the dull gray sky beyond their sanctuary. Maybe it was a prayer. It certainly was a plea. Suuzu whispered, "Maker mark, and Maker move." And he hoped for any and every miracle, no matter how small, that would bring his nestmate home.

29

IN WRITING

oniface called, "Hajime?"

The tree was at his side in an instant. Peering around, he asked, "Why are you *here*?"

"The gate is this way," Boniface said, pointing along the trail. "I'm leaving. But not without telling you goodbye."

"Why are you leaving? Your brother will be here soon. Within the hour." Hajime shyly added, "Argent sent word. My Naoki is with them."

"That's brilliant. Good for you." Boniface wasn't sure which of them had reached for the other first, but his hand was in Hajime's. "So ... ah ... will they remember me?"

"You were often in my company, but not always. You will not be forgotten."

"Probably won't be missed, either."

"What of Suuzu?" the tree imp challenged.

"He's probably forgotten this." From an inner pocket, Boniface withdrew an envelope Suuzu had borrowed from Tsumiko, one embossed with Argent bloody lord Mettlebright's own crest. Take that, Jackie.

"He only needs reminding. Your offer pleased him." Hajime gave his hand a small squeeze. "It pleased me, as well, since it will bring you back. Naoki will want to meet you."

"Because I'm inexplicably unaffected by your pollen?"

Hajime's headshake was accompanied by the chiming of tiny bells. "Because you remember me."

Boniface frowned. "Isn't that the same thing?"

"No. You call for me, and you converse with me. You see me as a person." The tree imp rested his free hand against Boniface's cheek and warmly said, "I have so few friends."

"Same." And with a quirk of a smile, he confessed, "Maman is ridiculously jealous of her precious Bon-Bon. And about who's good enough to associate with him."

"She is unlikely to learn of this ... hmm. Am I defiance? Or perhaps an indiscretion?" Hajime's tone was light, even teasing. Friendly.

"As far as I'm concerned, you're a bloody miracle. And a nice surprise. I liked knowing something extra and keeping it to myself. Who knew that secrets could be even more satisfying than gossip." Boniface tucked the envelope safely away again. "Between you and me, you're a far better influence than Maman ever has been."

"Keeping secrets is good," came a new voice.

Boniface startled. "Lord! When did you arrive?"

"Just now." Kyrie tucked himself up against Hajime's side.

Boniface liked the lad. So what if there was dragon in the mix? Kyrie was gracious and mannerly and affectionate. And ... family. On impulse, Boniface rested a hand atop the boy's head, bumping his thumb against a horn and cautiously stroking silken hair. It was awkward and clumsy, but he meant well.

The boy went all soppy and flung his arms around his middle. "I love you, Uncle Boniface."

"Right. Well...." Really, he had no idea what to do next. He looked to Hajime, hoping for guidance, but that tree imp simply nodded. "Err ... right. Good lad."

Completely at ease, the boy announced, "I brought your things."

Boniface was taken aback. "I ... didn't tell anyone I was going. Except Catalan. And Hajime, of course."

"A little wind found out and found me."

"You're on speaking terms with other imps, are you?"

"Winds *do* like me." He slipped free and went to a paper bag he must have set down upon his arrival. Right next to Boniface's suitcase. "I brought your festival coat. And here is your phone. Mother charged it, and Ginkgo made certain the line is secure. If you like, I have permission to give you Mother's number. That way you could call us ...?"

"Yes, all right. Just a tick." Boniface turned on his phone, and alerts popped up in quick succession. He grimaced. Maman had clogged his voicemail and sent ... lord, there were *hundreds* of texts. Dismissing the alerts, he turned over his phone to Kyrie. "Add away."

The boy deftly complied. "This is Mother's number, which is *very* secret. I am allowed to use her phone, so you can ask for me. If you wanted. Or ... text me ...?"

"Very convenient. So I can pass along messages for you *and* for Hajime?"

The tree's eyes widened.

Kyrie beamed. "At least until Grandfather Naoki gets his own phone. *If* he wants one. Some people do not like them. Dad does not."

"It *is* hard to picture Argent with technology."

"He does own one, but Uncle Jackie carries it for him."

Hajime said, "Perhaps you will be the one answering Suuzu's phone?"

Kyrie tipped his head to one side. "Why is that, please?"

For an answer, Boniface brought out the envelope again. "It might come to nothing, but … go on, lad. Have a look."

Suuzu had insisted on putting their proposal to paper, just in case.

Boniface Smythe should report to my office in Keishi at his earliest convenience, to begin training as a member of my staff. He wishes to be retained as my gentleman's gentleman. Boniface will be my man. If any questions arise, Catalan Evernhold will know what is needed.

Suuzu Farroost

Kyrie gasped and reread the message. "You probably *will* answer Uncle Suuzu's phone! He does not like them either. Dragons do, though."

"Meaning … you?"

"I was thinking of Sinder. And Lord Beckonthrall. I cannot have my own yet. But both Mother and Ginkgo share theirs. Do you want my brother's number, too?"

Both Hajime and Kyrie turned slightly, signaling the arrival of the person Boniface had been waiting for.

"Are we making connections?" Catalan draped himself against Boniface's back. "Add me next."

Suuzu had coached Boniface on feline culture and the application of assorted rebuffs, but he couldn't bring himself to elbow Cat. Today was turning out to be unexpectedly difficult, and Boniface wasn't entirely ready to let go … let alone to go back into Maman's clutches.

Cat nuzzled his ear and began to purr.

Kyrie asked, "What about Canarian?"

Boniface said, "While I do hope to gain that gentleman's good opinion, I no longer *need* it."

"Don't be ridiculous. He's a connection worth having. Look there. Doesn't he cut a fine figure?" Cheeks pressed together, Cat guided Boniface's gaze toward the gateway, where someone was just arriving.

Canarian Evernhold wore his tasteful suit with effortless grace, and he carried a sizeable satchel as if it weighed nothing. Boniface picked out little family resemblances, like the dark mahogany of Deece's hair color and the world-famous lines of Hisoka Twineshaft's jawline and brow.

Spokesperson Twineshaft's righthand man walked right up to where Boniface still stood in Catalan's grasp. Kissing his cheeks in the European fashion, Canarian lowered tinted glasses and peered over them, an appreciative light in his eyes. Then he pressed a soft kiss to Boniface's lips.

He managed a weak, "Ah. Right …?"

Cat laughed softly and asked, "Didn't I tell you? Adorable, no?"

"Mmm," his partner agreed, kissing Cat next. "Put him in our rooms. Keep him happy."

"*Naturellement*! I'll dote on him until you're free to join us."

Boniface felt heat creeping into his cheeks. Really, they were as bad as Jackie. But Boniface vastly preferred these cats and their affectionate impulses to all of Maman's machinations.

Brushing his knuckles across flushed skin, Canarian said, "Forgive me? I cannot greet you properly now, but I'll make up for it later. Can you be patient?"

"R-right. As you say."

"*Merci*." His parting kiss included the barest flick of tongue.

Boniface craned his neck, watching Canarian stride along the path toward Stately House, right back to business.

"He likes you," Cat reported. "No surprise. But you like him? Better and better!"

"What? No! Don't misunderstand!" Canarian Evernhold had … charisma. That was all.

Cat applied for support. "Do you not agree, Kyrie? They both made excellent first impressions. Not everyone from the public sector is so accepting of our little ways."

His nephew considered them thoughtfully. "Do you understand about felines, Uncle Boniface?"

"Suuzu may have offered a few … ah … guidelines." They'd actually been *warnings*. But also reassurances. Because Suuzu trusted these two as much as he did Hisoka Twineshaft. And Nonny *loved* Cat and Canary, looking up to them as father figures. "We'll get on, I think."

Cat still hadn't let go.

Boniface wouldn't make him.

Kyrie finally said, "It *is* promising. As is Uncle Boniface's friendship with Grandfather."

"Who do you mean …?"

"Hajime." Boniface turned his head, trying to catch Cat's eye. "Can you really not see him?"

Which led to lengthy introductions and explanations and promises of future proximity and exposure, which Cat managed to frame in the most salacious of terms.

Boniface patted the tree imp's shoulder. "Friends and family and your fellow. You won't be lonesome any longer."

"And you?"

"That remains to be seen." He patted his pocket, murmuring, "Where did I …?"

"Here," said Kyrie. "May I suggest two additions? In case Uncle Suuzu needs a reminder."

The lad carefully tucked a scant handful of red flower petals inside the fold of paper. Then he began doing graceful things with his hands.

"Argent does that sometimes. Did he teach you?"

"Yes. I am creating sigils for protection. And I am confirming the truth of Uncle Suuzu's words. As a witness. Or … a vouchsafe." He smiled Kyoko's smile and promised, "Those who read it will know that Stately House supports your appointment. And that we're *glad*."

When he was finished, Boniface tucked the letter safely away.

"Visit again soon?" Kyrie asked.

"I'm not sure your father will let me through this gate again once I'm gone."

"Fear not." Tapping Boniface's phone, Kyrie urged, "Call me, and I will bring you across the boundary."

"That's … very good of you, I'm sure." He checked his phone. Lord, two more messages from Maman. "Time's getting on. Kyrie, you should get back."

"Yes, it is nearly time." He didn't leave, though. "Must you go? Uncle Jackie will miss meeting you."

"I need to report to Spokesperson Farroost's offices in Keishi. And you have friends and family to welcome home." He summoned up a little hauteur. "To each his own."

Kyrie solemnly replied, "I will try to take the long view, but it is not easy to let you go. You are one of mine now." And to Catalan, "Keep him safe …?"

"For your sake and for Suuzu's sake and for Jacques' sake."

With another nuzzle behind Boniface's ear, Cat coyly added, "Nonny was entirely adamant, as well. Though keeping you close will be my pleasure, entirely. Or yours, too, if you decide to throw caution to the wind."

Boniface smiled and shook his head.

Cat took to purring again.

Kyrie offered his palms and asked, "Next time you are in Uppington, will you pat Ceddy's head for me?"

"Lord, I suppose I can manage that much."

And then Kyoko's child darted into the woods, leaving him with Cat and Hajime. The latter stepped forward and tucked a sprig of red flowers into Boniface's buttonhole. He admired it for a moment, gazed into Boniface's eyes with a solemn sort of satisfaction, then winked ... and vanished.

"Holding up?" asked Cat.

"Not really."

"There's still time to change your mind."

Boniface simply shook his head.

"Have you settled on Keishi, then? Not Uppington?" Cat reminded, "I can take you wherever you want to be."

"Look at this," he complained. Cat peered over his shoulder as Boniface scrolled. He could almost hear Maman's outrage. "*Mon dieu.* I don't want to go back."

"Wait. Go back."

"I just said ...!"

"*Non.* Scroll back up." Cat reached around him, doing it himself. "Here. You have a message from Tsumiko."

"Oh, you're right. No, not a message. She sent pictures."

There were two.

Boniface well remembered the moment she'd snapped the first. He sat at the kitchen table, Mercy in his arms, a look of wide-eyed bewilderment on his face. "Lord, I'm hopeless."

"Inexperienced, certainly" Cat murmured. "But look how snug your hold is. The little miss was safe in your arms, much as you are safe in mine."

But all Boniface could see was ineptitude. Was there really any point to his trying to remake himself? Maybe he should resign himself to Maman's throttle-hold on his life. Only ... the next picture startled him.

Cat laughed. "The resemblance is striking."

"Ridiculous. Jackie and I are nothing alike."

"But that look. It's *perfect*. You are both so expressive when caught off guard."

Tsumiko had sent a picture of Jackie, who peered at the camera with an identical expression of wide-eyed bewilderment. The whole situation was much funnier when it wasn't Boniface. "Lord, everyone goes on and on about how fabulous Jackie is with children."

"He *is*. But I don't think he *was*."

Boniface felt a certain kinship for this frightened, vulnerable version of his brother. Tsumiko's picture had been taken more than a decade ago, shortly after the Emergence, back before anyone knew much of anything about the Amaranthine people. Back before Jackie had become the darling of the Amaranthine Council.

Had it been hard, leaving home?

Had it changed him, coming here?

And perhaps more importantly, could Boniface run away, too?

And away from home, could he become someone important-ish?

"I don't want to go back."

Cat still hugged him from behind. "I remember this. How it felt. Canary held me just like this when it was our turn to be bad sons."

"Do you think …? That is to say …." Boniface swallowed hard. "Did *your* mother disown you?"

"On that day, we decided that she'd never owned us in the first place. But there were people I loved, and I knew I might never be allowed to see them again. That part was terrible to me. But Canary was good to me. So good."

Boniface leaned against Cat and repeated, "I don't want to go back."

"Then don't." He promised, "Stately House will support your choice. And you. Beautifully."

Looking into Jackie's wide eyes, then at the snapshot that had captured his own, Boniface took ownership of his own life. With Catalan Evernhold for his witness, he banished hundreds of unread messages and blocked Maman.

Cat still didn't let go.

Boniface didn't make him.

Somewhere in the woods ahead, a wolf howled.

"That will be them," Cat murmured against his ear. "Do you want a look?"

"I think I've used up all my courage for today."

A handkerchief appeared before Boniface, and he tried to pull himself together. The world hadn't ended, but it was blurring slightly. He patted his cheeks, then marveled at the softness of the silver-trimmed cloth, then frowned when he noticed there were letters worked into the border. Shaking it out, he found his name— his full name—stitched along one entire side of the square.

"Who …?" he asked weakly.

"Argent."

Boniface's heart sank. "Is he making fun of me?"

"Not at all," Cat warmly reassured. "He's sly, our fox, but his schemes are good. I told you already. Stately House will support your choice. How could he not?"

Boniface tentatively traced the handkerchief's delicate edging of ginkgo leaves. They were part of Argent's crest. "He ... approves?"

"He triumphs."

That made no sense. "Over *what*?"

"If you had joined Hisoka's cortege, you would have slipped from Argent's grasp, but Suuzu is counted as a brother. He is Argent's denmate, and so you will belong to Stately House."

Boniface didn't want to be in anyone's grasp. "Have I escaped a taskmistress, only to gain a taskmaster?"

"You really don't know Argent very well, do you?" Catalan turned Boniface so they were facing. "Hmm. How to explain ...? You arrived at his door, which is meant to be unreachable. In a sense, you outwitted him. With tricksters, that sort of thing earns respect."

"It was sheer luck."

"Also, you were exactly the right sort of distraction for Suuzu. This whole time, while Akira's been gone, Suuzu needed you." Tapping Boniface's coat over his letter of reference, Cat said, "He *trusts* you, and Argent has to respect that, too."

That was a strange idea. Respect? From Argent, of all people?

But Boniface studied the handkerchief in his hands. He'd thought it was meant as a taunt, probably because he and Jackie used to twit each other about their unwieldy names. But if Argent had intended mockery, wouldn't he have used *Bon-Bon*?

According to the endlessly looping informational videos at the Office of Ingress, the giving and acknowledging of names was more than a courtesy. It was the beginning of trust. And Argent's gift proved that he'd learned—or quite possibly always known—the cumbersome whole of it. Boniface Percival Christobel Yves Smythe whispered, "How do I answer?"

"With foxes, it's less about what you say ... more about what you do."

Just then, wind rattled and clattered through overhead branches, and Boniface gaped as large winged shadows passed overhead. "Bloody hell. What ...?" he asked.

"Dragons. Michael must have lowered the barriers to let them through." Cat cocked an ear, then quietly added, "Your brother is safe."

"Time to go. Past time." Boniface gathered up his bags and began walking toward the gate.

Catalan quickly fell in step. "I *like* this confidence. Very Smythe. Very sexy."

Boniface set a brisk pace toward a future that had gone back to being oh, so bright.

Bright as the light of love in a wistful phoenix's eyes.

Bright as the bells twinkling above a tree's dark tresses.

Bright as the remnant stone that rang with a dragon's song.

Bright as the silver threads that made his name a truce.

Bright as a coral nippet, treasured by those who traveled far to join another enclave, reminding them that it was possible to flourish in new places.

Lord. There was so much to do.

The Language of Nippets

Zeriel's Nippet – "loved from afar"

Coral Nippet – "new appreciation"

Honey Nippet – "irresistible connection"

Dun Nippet – "find me"

Vert Nippet – "help me bloom"

Azure Nippet – "true love"

Dusk Nippet – "midnight serenade"

Seal Nippet – "I can wait no longer"

Dawn Nippet – "choose me"

Ghost Nippet – "my miracle"

Abundant thanks to all who lend their support by reading, rating, and reviewing my stories, wherever they may be found. ::twinkle::

ALSO BY FORTHRIGHT

AMARANTHINE SAGA

Tsumiko and the Enslaved Fox

Kimiko and the Accidental Proposal

Tamiko and the Two Janitors

Mikoto and the Reaver Village

Fumiko and the Finicky Nestmate

Pimiko and the Uncharted Island

Rhomiko and the Confirmed Bachelor

SONGS OF THE AMARANTHINE

Marked by Stars

Followed by Thunder

Dragged through Hedgerows

Governed by Whimsy

Hemmed in Silver

Captured on Film

Bathed in Moonlight

Flattered by Flowers

Scribbled in Margins

AMARANTHINE INTERLUDES

Lord Mettlebright's Man

Suuzu and the Nine Nippets of Legend

Kimiko and the Cycle of Moons

Coop and the Elderbough Trackers

PATREON EXCLUSIVES

Bard & Barbarian

Kimiko and the Cycle of Moons

Bard & Barbarian